About Event

The Wild Hun

Erotic paranormal ménage romance

There's a reason why Cherise Sinclair is on my auto-buy list: she writes fantastic erotic romances with great stories and wonderful characters.

~ The Romance Reviews

She risked her life to save a human child. Pain was her reward.

All her life, Emma longed for someone to love. Instead, disaster sees the brand-new bard banished from her people for long lonely years. Injured saving a child, the werebear has to steal food from humans, breaking shifter Law. The territory's Cosantir and his lethal grizzly warrior catch her in the act. To her surprise, she's healed and welcomed. Obviously, they don't know her past. But oh, she can't resist being around other shifters—especially the captivatingly powerful warrior. Maybe she can stay…just a little while.

As a grizzly warrior, Ben is ordered to house the pretty werebear until she heals. His littermate abandoned him, his home is empty, and he's been alone for a long time. Intelligent and sweet and lushly curved, Emma is a delight…even if she is oddly reticent about her past. Although having sworn off females, he's sorely tempted by this one. Damned if he doesn't want to keep her, secrets or not.

Females were trouble. Years past, one split Ryder from his littermate. Now the panther shifter is returning to Ben, bringing his cub with him, a four-year-old he stole from the abusive female. To Ryder's annoyance, his brother is sheltering a wounded bear. A *female*. Even worse, she's beautiful and gentle and loving—damned if he's going to fall for that act again. But when the dark of the moon arrives and death reigns supreme, he'll discover that not all females are alike.

In a world filled with hellhounds and pixies, can three lonely shifters and one silent cub create a new family together?

Whether you are interested in erotic BDSM, sci-fi or paranormal, Cherise Sinclair is always my top pick and number one suggestion.

~ You Gotta Read Reviews

Want to be notified of the next release?

Sent only on release day, Cherise's newsletters contain freebies, excerpts, and articles.
Sign up at:
www.CheriseSinclair.com/NewsletterForm

Eventide of the Bear

The Wild Hunt Legacy 3

Cherise Sinclair

VanScoy Publishing Group

EVENTIDE OF THE BEAR
Copyright © January 2016 by Cherise Sinclair
Print Edition
ISBN: 978-0-9861195-8-3
Published by VanScoy Publishing Group
Cover Artist: Hot Damn Designs

Acknowledgments

With grateful thanks to my wonderful critique partners, Monette Michaels, Fiona Archer, and Bianca Sommerland.

A huge thank you to Marian Shulman who took the time to beta read the rough version and weeded out numerous inconsistencies. *mwah!*

A big shout-out to Ekatarina Sayanova and her team at Red Quill Editing who tucked me into their tight schedule and did a marvelous job.

To my News & Discussion crew on Facebook (AKA the Shadowkittens), I'm sending big squishy hugs. The "inspiring" pictures and suggestions along with your enthusiasm and generosity have kept me returning to the keyboard day after day.

Prologue

Three years before
Pine Knoll, Mt. Hood Territory — full moon

WHAT IF NO one *wants to mate with me?* Arms wrapped around herself, Emma Cavanaugh stood on the sidewalk and watched shifters stream into the three-story house for the full moon Gathering. She'd be joining them since she was an adult now and ready for her first Gathering.

Finally. Most females went into their first heat before twenty-two, and she'd worried something was wrong with her, although bear shifters tended to be delayed. No matter. She was here now. Her need had driven her right to the door of the Gathering.

C'mon, bear. Time to move.

Feeling as if she walked on brittle ice, she made it almost to the door. Then a group of shifters passed her.

Males.

Their heady scent raised tingles across her skin. She froze. The masculine voices vibrated all the way to her core. How amazing was that? Would any of those males want her?

Worry flattened her bubbly excitement. What if they didn't? What if she stood against the wall all night, alone and unwanted like at the dance she'd sneaked out to attend when she was thirteen?

As she tried to get her feet to move, blonde CeeCee and her giggly friend, Marnie, shoved her to one side.

"Way to block the trail, big griz," Marnie said, deliberately loud.

"It's because her hips take up the entire sidewalk," CeeCee said. "Lovely clothes, Emma, just like my grandmum would wear."

Like swipes from sharp claws, their words hurt.

As her mother had taught, Emma bit back what she wanted to say. Sure, she was a bear shifter, larger than wolf and panther females, but she wasn't *that* big, and she certainly wasn't a *grizzly*.

As they walked away, she made a mental note to throw away the flowery skirt and loose blouse. She tried to shrug off the feeling of being of being hated. After the years at the Pine Knoll School, she should be accustomed to insults from her age mates. No one had wanted to be friends with Emma, even if her mother had permitted it.

Priscilla Cavanaugh had been self-centered, obsessed with power and status, and possessed no love for anyone, even her daughter. Every Daonain in the territory had hated Priscilla and had extended their dislike to her daughter, Emma. Her mother had died two months ago, but the animosity toward the Cavanaugh name seemed unending.

Maybe someone more vivacious and charming could have changed their minds. Emma'd hoped becoming a bard would lend her some confidence or persuasiveness. Even a bit of courage wouldn't have gone unappreciated. But no. Apparently, the talent to sing and entertain an audience didn't translate into day-to-day eloquence. Even worse, no one in town wanted to hear her sing. Emma's shoulders drooped. Maybe this evening would be different. Because, after mating, people regarded each other differently. Didn't they? Would a male still be mean after he'd…been…with her? It was time to shake out her fur and venture out of her cave. Maybe tonight she could make some friends.

I can do this.

Hope rising in her heart, she walked up the steps and inside. As with many shifter homes, the decor was traditional—dark hardwood floors and cream-colored walls with mahogany trim and crown molding. The downstairs rooms had been opened up, so the living room flowed into a sitting room on the left, the dining area and kitchen on the right. Since shifters mated in human form, territories maintained comfortable housing for the full moon Gatherings.

Everywhere she looked, females held court. CeeCee sat on a leather couch with five males striving to impress her. Marnie stood near the riverstone fireplace with her own cluster of males.

That the Daonain birthed more males than females had been merely an interesting fact until now. Enveloped by the overwhelming masculine scents and sounds, her body flared to life and into heat. She was panting as if she'd galloped up a mountain. And oh, Goddess, the *need*.

She took a step forward and stopped.

Near the door stood the Cosantir, the guardian and leader of the Mt. Hood Territory. As always, when Cedrick saw her, his eyes chilled. Because of her mother. As one of the God's avatars, he acted for the good of the clan. Her mother had acted only for the good of herself, so they'd hated each other. Emma gave him a wide berth and moved farther into the room.

A brown-haired male, lust reddening his normally pale face, stepped into her path. He raised his eyebrows. "Hey, it's Emma. Come to slum with the rest of the town?"

Despite his offensive tone, Emma still felt a tingle down her spine.

Another male moved closer. His broad shoulders blocked

out the light behind him. "It's Emma, isn't it? You look very pretty tonight." This voice was wonderfully deep and resonant, and the interest in it sent arousal streaming through her.

   .   As the song of need humming in her ears grew louder, she managed to focus her eyes. *Gawain.*

The male was quite a bit older. He'd made a knife for the bard master. His wonderful eyes were the clear blue of a summer sky—and he *wanted* her.

She shivered with the wonder of it.

EMMA HAD NO idea how much time had passed, but the night was well advanced. Standing at the drink table, she tried to gather her senses.

She'd been with several males and had enjoyed mating, if enjoyed could be the word for something so primal and out of control. Some of the males had been rough, and she hadn't known how to slow them down—or how to slow herself, for that matter.

She smiled. Thank the Mother Gawain had been patient. Gentle. He'd led her to the room, removed her clothes, and stroked each inch of exposed skin until her entire body shimmered with desire. Kissing, nibbling, licking.

Even now, her body started to warm again at the memory. Then he'd firmly—gently—laid her on the cushion-covered floor and put his mouth—his *mouth*—between her legs. *By the Mother's Grace.* Everything in her had spun out of control. By the time he'd settled himself over her, she needed him so desperately that when he'd thrust through her maidenhead, the sharp pain disappeared under the marvelous sensation of being filled.

Afterward, Gawain had held her as she shook. The room had held the scent of sex, of musky males, of her need—and her blood.

Blood. She'd *bled*.

As she'd started to panic, he'd quickly explained, although he'd been surprised her mother hadn't taught her about such a basic fact of life.

Priscilla Cavanaugh hadn't been much of a mother. Emma had grieved when her mother passed on to the Goddess, but her sense of loss had been even greater. All the chances to change their relationship had disappeared. She would never know a mother's love or care.

Even as she pulled in a shuddering breath, she felt her body starting to arouse again. A full moon heat didn't care about mourning or lost chances. Tonight, the physical ruled the mental, and her body was all about trying to mate, to become pregnant.

Why had no one ever told her about how overwhelming a Gathering could be? She gave a huff of a laugh. Who would have talked with her? The same mother who hadn't explained what a first mating would entail? Hardly.

Her bard instructor hadn't discussed Gatherings other than as a basis for songs. He was very old; maybe he'd forgotten the effect of a full moon on a shifter.

Sipping apple cider, she directed her mind to happier thoughts. After all, she now knew all about Gatherings, right? And she hadn't been ignored, as she'd feared. A lot of the males had been interested in her. One werewolf had even complimented her on her size and wasn't making fun of her or anything. She bit her lip. Of course, his appreciation might not extend past Gathering night when hormones ruled.

But, oh, it was exhilarating to be touched and treated like everyone else.

"Hey, Emma, you're looking fine tonight." The male's tenor had a pretty resonance.

She turned.

Oh my Goddess, it was *Gary*. Two years older than Emma, the Cosantir's son had been the most popular boy in high school. He wore the finest clothes, had the best car, and was now an officer in his father's bank. He'd never looked at her, not even when he'd once tripped over her feet in school.

The air disappeared from her lungs as need flared inside her like a newly kindled fire. "Um…hi, Gary."

"I hadn't realized how pretty you've become." When he stroked her loose, wavy hair, the contrast between his tanned fingers and the golden strands was striking. "I think we should find a room."

He wanted to mate…with her? *Oh my Goddess.* "I-I…sure."

Gripping her hand, he tugged her after him.

"Hey, you're too little for her." A male rudely stepped in front of them. "She needs someone her size. Another bear."

Andre. Tall and tough and dark. He was Gary's age and had been the "bad boy" in her school. He'd never noticed her before, either.

"Get lost, asshole." Gary scowled. "Lucky for you Gatherings are free, or you wouldn't have been able to get in. Loser."

Emma shivered at the animosity in his voice.

"Hey, pretty bear."

At Andre's gruff words, every cell in her body sat up and preened. He was so big and beautiful, and totally bedazzled her eyes. She swallowed, unable to speak.

"Back *off*, fleabag. You got away with poaching once; don't fucking try it again." As Gary pulled her closer, his tone turned as scornful as her mother's when she felt someone was beneath her notice. "This one's mine. And a Cavanaugh wouldn't want someone who collects garbage for a living. No female would."

"You got a short memory, wimp. Phoebe preferred me to daddy's boy, didn't she?" Andre smiled slowly and rubbed his chest. "Quite the vixen. Clawed the shit out of me when she got off."

"She'd agreed to go with *me*, garbage-guts," Gary snarled. "You're a fucking thief." He stepped around Andre, dragging Emma after him.

Her body protested—it wanted Andre. Nevertheless, Gary was right; she'd started with him first. Her mother would have insisted she be polite.

The stuffiness of the crowded main room gave way to the cooler, quieter back area, which held several tiny mating rooms on the main floor with more on the second and third levels.

Gary walked past the stairs, down the hallway past several rooms, and stopped to open a door. "Here's an empty one."

The scent of previous matings spilled out of the room, setting Emma's hormones rioting in her veins. Dizzy, she leaned against the wall.

"Oh, female, we're gonna have fun." Gary ran a hand up and down her arm to set off a new release of lust.

Her core throbbed, demanding to be satisfied, and Emma leaned against him, making him laugh.

"Flabby feline, you think you can handle mating a bear?" Andre's voice came from behind them. "You sure your dick is big enough?"

His rough baritone seeped into Emma's bones and made her tremble.

As Andre loomed over her, his heady, dark scent swept over her. Despite being only in his twenties, he had the size of a mature male. His chest stretched his tight body shirt to display hard, contoured muscles. At the surging want, her muscles and tendons felt unconnected, as if her body belonged to someone else.

Realizing she'd leaned toward him, she pulled back.

When Gary glared at her, Andre laughed.

"Get the fuck out of here, Andre," Gary snapped. "Go find

a dumpster to raid or something."

"Quit with the yowling. Go count your daddy's money and leave mating for the real males."

Emma blinked as their hatred cut through the fog of desire. "Guys. Please, don't—"

"This one's *mine.*" Gary's grip on her arm turned painful. "She agreed to come with me."

Ignoring him, Andre fixed his intense gaze on Emma. "Hey, pretty bear. Wanna mate?" He touched her cheek with a big hand. His virile, musky scent surrounded her.

Push him away. Now. She ordered her body to obey. Gary was getting more and more upset. Yet somehow, her fingers curled around Andre's hand. He leaned down. As his lips met hers, she sank into lust like a stone thrown into a warm ocean.

"You mangy dick." Gary's bellow split the air. "She's mine!" He yanked her away from Andre and shoved her toward the mating room.

Her head slammed into the doorframe with an excruciating thud, and the hallway went black.

Why am I on the floor?

She was sprawled on her side. Carpet scraped her cheek. Her vision blurred, focused, blurred. Her head felt as if it would crack open with each pulse beat—if she didn't throw up first. Groaning, she struggled to her knees. Was the floor swaying?

Sounds surfaced through the hum of pain. The smack of flesh on flesh. A grunt. Another slapping sound. Snarls, growls, and cursing. With dawning terror, she realized Andre and Gary were fighting.

No, oh no. Emma tried to stand, failed, tried again, and finally succeeded with the help of the wall. Shaking her head to try to clear it, she stared. And cringed. This—this was horrible. "No." Her voice cracked. Not even heard. "Don't. No."

They were enraged. Crazy. Grappling and biting. Growling,

Gary punched Andre's face. With a furious roar, Andre seized Gary by the throat. Choking him.

"Stop!" She sprang forward, grabbed Andre's arm, and yanked his hand away.

A fist hit her forehead, splitting the skin. Blood filled her eyes even as another blow landed on her cheek. She staggered back into other bodies. Other shifters. Watching the battle.

"Stop them!" Blinded by the blood pouring down her face, she clutched one female's arm and was pushed away.

The growls increased. Clothing tore as both males *transfurred* into animals. Panther and bear.

Savage snarls. Bellows. Shrieks. Thuds. A ghastly sound of wheezing. The bear's jaws tore into the cat's throat. Even as blood sprayed the air, the panther's hind legs clawed through the bear's fur-covered stomach and groin, shredding skin and muscles and arteries.

Bellowing in agony, Andre flung Gary away. Blood was everywhere, splattering the floor and walls.

And then there was silence.

Still dazed, Emma could only whimper in denial as, in death, the bodies shifted back to human. Bits of blood-soaked fabric still clung to them. Gary's throat had been torn out. Andre's whole abdomen was sliced open.

Her bloody hands covered her mouth as tears filled her eyes.

"In the God's name, *what* is going on?" Still unclothed from mating, the Cosantir leaped down the stairs. He shoved through the cluster of shifters blocking the halls and saw the bodies. His face turned white.

"Gary?" He sank to his knees beside his son. Touched the lifeless body.

Oh, no. The anguish in his face battered Emma, hurting her heart, bringing tears to her eyes. The shifters in the hall were silent as he turned his head, taking in the carnage.

Like a crippled elder, he struggled to his feet. "What happened?" His voice was hoarse.

"Rich bitch Cavanaugh made them fight over her." Standing next to Marnie, CeeCee pointed directly at Emma.

"Yeah. The bear teased them into it," Marnie confirmed.

The Cosantir's gaze turned cold, seeping into her, freezing her bones.

Emma shook her head. "No. I-I didn't want—"

"Wait a minute," said someone behind her. "She didn't—"

"She's as bad as her mother," a female said. "*Cavanaughs.*" She made the word into a curse.

"Getting a thrill from goading males into fights that leave them crippled. Scarred." Cedrick's fingers traced a bite scar on his shoulder before his gaze dropped to Gary's body.

She hadn't caused the fight, had she? But they'd killed each other…because of her. Emma shook her head again. *No.*

The movement made the Cosantir look at her. Grief and fury rolled from him in icy waves. "I had no choice but to tolerate your mother." His voice harshened. "You, though… I should have dealt with you before you cost us so much."

A few protests came from the shifters in the hallway—too few, too soft. The Cosantir ignored them, his gaze never leaving her. "Emma Cavanaugh, you are cast out from the Daonain, banished from us. Forever."

As despair filled her, she simply stood as he *trawsfurred* into his cat form. His paw rose. Claws slashed across her face.

And she made no sound at all.

Chapter One

North Cascades Territory — dark of the moon

BRIGHT STARS FILLED the black sky, unchallenged by any rival light, because tonight was dark of the moon.

The dank forest air was pungent with the fir and pine needles underfoot. The rain-slick mud on the trail clogged irritatingly in Emma's paws. Her fur was matted, her nose wet. She gave a grumbling cough, and her ears flickered when a rabbit darted away. Too fast for her, unfortunately. Besides, her stomach was fairly full. The stream was full of trout, and fishing was one of her finer skills.

Still… She clouted a rotting log and nosed out the scuttling inhabitants beneath. Mostly grubs. A few crunchy beetles. Only a fool turned down a light dessert. And she was no fool.

Well, not about food.

She stopped to listen to the humans in a wilderness campground. Their laughter and chatter rang through the trees, filling her heart with delight. Not her people, but oh, the sound of them was so wonderful. They, too, had been successful at the stream, and the chill mountain air carried the scent of fried fish.

Her mouth watered. Cooked food. Her bear form preferred raw, but she remembered how good prepared food had tasted. These days, she rarely bothered.

Reluctantly leaving behind the campground, Emma ambled toward her den in an uprooted tree hollow and thought wistfully of the cave in which she'd holed up last winter. Very few bear shifters ever hibernated, but she'd needed to escape the loneliness of the long, long nights. When spring finally arrived, she'd resumed wandering through the mountain range.

Daonain often died after being banished. Now, she understood why. If she hadn't been used to being lonely all her life, she'd have given up her first winter.

How many times had she despaired over the last three years?

She missed voices the most... Children's giggles. The gardener's low grumble at finding a weed. The maid's humming as she dusted. Emma could survive without hot showers and cooked food, and books. She could sing to the pixies and tell stories to the undines in the streams, but she longed for voices the way a flower fairy craved rose blooms.

Human campgrounds lured her close far too often.

A foul stench on the wind made her paw at her affronted nose. By the Hunter, it smelled like a rotting carcass covered in moldering oranges. The fur on her back rose.

Overhead, a pixie chittered and disappeared into its hole.

Emma increased her gait to put distance between herself and...whatever that was.

A scream came from behind her. Another. Then shrieks of pain and shouting filled the air. An animal snarled. A man bellowed. Something was attacking the campground. The humans.

Emma hesitated and kept going. A bear couldn't help them. And Daonain Law forbade any action that might reveal the shifters' existence to humankind.

"Mommy! Daddeeee!"

The high-pitched shriek of a child turned Emma as if a leash was around her neck. Abandoning the path, she galloped straight through the underbrush and broke into a forest clearing.

A fire in a stone pit cast flickering, red light across a nightmare. Two human men lay on the ground, one gutted. The stench of blood and bowels hung in the air, recalling the hideous night from three years past. Her stomach twisted.

Three women and two children huddled on the far side, their men trying to protect them from a...a creature.

Grizzly-sized, but rendered almost prehistoric with bony, spiked plates. Its head was shark-shaped with terrifyingly huge, pointed fangs.

Oh my Goddess, a hellhound.

As terror iced her blood, her courage shattered. She froze. Even the God's enormous cahirs couldn't win against a demon-dog. She was just a small bear.

The monster darted forward and seized a man's shoulder in massive jaws.

"Fuck. No!" Shouting, the human hammered it with his fist.

The blows rained off the creature's back like snowflakes. After tossing the man aside, it stalked toward the women. The children.

No, not the cubs.

The humans were losing. Couldn't protect them. *Move, bear.* She had nothing to lose. Not really. She could save the children.

Jolted out of paralysis, Emma charged the hellhound. She swung her paw, wide and heavy, expecting her thick claws to rip hunks from its flesh.

Her paw impacted—the creature barely swayed—and she felt a hideous snapping as the toes of her forepaw broke.

As her claws scraped uselessly across its ridged armor plates, the hellhound whipped around. Its mammoth jaws closed on her hind leg. Razor-teeth sliced through her fur and into her flesh.

Pain.

Roaring, Emma slashed her undamaged forepaw across the

thing's head. Its *armored* head. She didn't even scratch it.

The hellhound bit down viciously, and her bones shattered.

At the blast of agony, she panicked. Her paws battered at its head, but her claws were worthless against its armor. The armor covered its whole body—nothing was vulnerable. *Except...*

Instinctively, she twisted her foreleg and shoved her claws directly at the recessed left eye. One penetrated.

The creature shrieked horrifically and scrambled backward.

Freed, Emma tore away across the clearing, her savaged leg dragging behind her. At the forest's edge, she hesitated. Turned.

Shaking its head, the hellhound splattered blood everywhere. With another shriek, it fled into the forest.

Victory. But at what cost? Head sagging, Emma moaned as the pain increased, a red fire encompassing her leg.

The humans stared at her. One lifted his branch—his weapon—threateningly. As if she could be a threat. On three legs. But she was a bear. Of course they were frightened.

As she forced herself to move away, the enormity of the disaster struck her. Her leg was past merely broken. Shattered bones wouldn't heal.

She was crippled. Alone. But if a slow death was the price she had to pay, she was content. Because, with the Goddess's help, she had saved the little ones.

Chapter Two

Farway, Deschutes Territory

"**Y**OU HAVE A *cub. Just don't tell that screaming shrew I was the one who ratted her out. I still have to live in the Deschutes Territory.*"

Standing on the sidewalk in the town where he'd once lived, Ryder Llwyd remembered the pity and worry in Harold's expression. The male had good reason for his anxiety; Genevieve held vicious grudges. Sliding his hand under his jacket, Ryder touched the rough bite and scratch scars on his left shoulder. Those weren't the worst of the wounds she'd given him in their months together.

Apparently, she'd given him something else as well.

A cub. What the fuck would he do with a child? He wasn't a female or good at nurturing. He was an unmated male who didn't even have a littermate to help, because he'd chosen a malicious, self-centered female over his brother.

By the God, he was as stupid as a garbage-addicted gnome.

Deep in his soul, the frayed littermate bond ached far worse than any bite. Over the years, the link had grown more painful until he'd known he had to try to make amends. Only a week ago, he'd left the Garibaldi Territory in Canada, heading toward the Pacific Northwest.

Toward Ben.

His only hope was that his brother would be able to forgive him.

And then he'd run into Harold and ended up detouring to Farway.

"Your little girl is around four. And hate to say this, cat, but your cub isn't loved. Isn't taken care of. Looks worse each month."

By Herne's hairy balls.

Ryder scrubbed his hands over his face, feeling the rasp of unshaven skin. Genevieve with a cub? Tough to imagine. She loathed children.

He studied her house. It was a shit piece of construction. Even without a level, he could see the doorframe wasn't square. Gaps showed around the windows, and the cracked roof shingles were going bald. The house color had probably been blue before fading to a mottled gray. The thought of a child of his living here under Genevieve's care was…not to be borne.

After crossing the weed-filled lawn, he stood on a sagging step and listened. From inside came the distinctive mating sounds of slapping flesh and grunting. Obviously, the occupants were anticipating the full moon tomorrow.

Wait until she finishes? No. Ryder pounded on the door.

"Who the fuck is here?" a male snapped from inside.

Ryder knocked again.

Thumps and swearing. Footsteps. The door swung open, releasing the pungent scent of sex…and filth and rotting food. Genevieve was still a crap housekeeper, it seemed.

Buttoning her blouse, she stood in the doorway, impeccably made up…of course. The world might fall apart around her, but her appearance would never suffer. "Ryder! Well…" Her eyes narrowed.

Just the sight of her made his guts twist. He pushed past her and into the house.

Stinking of whiskey, a skinny young male on the living room couch grabbed for his jeans. "By the God, what's the rush?" The male tried unsuccessfully to stand.

Ryder turned to Genevieve. "Where's my cub?"

"Who? What cub?" She widened her eyes.

Ryder knew the *I'm-so-confused* trick. Knew most of her tricks.

Glare fading, the male offered Ryder a slack-faced grin. "You're Minette's sire? Should have seen it. She looks just like you."

Minette. Now the cub had a name. "Where is she?"

"She's around. Probably…" The male's mouth shut, and he looked away.

The cub was here when adults were fucking in the living room? Sure, the Daonain were fairly open about mating. Not *that* open.

Ryder stalked to the doors at the back of the house. One was obviously Genevieve's. Jewelry and clothing lay in piles on the dresser and nightstands. The king-size bed stank of mating and her nose-clogging perfume.

He opened the other bedroom door. The scent of mildew and dirt mingled with little girl sweetness. The room held no bed, no dresser—no furniture at all. The wood floor was gouged and rough, and the puke-green walls displayed fist-sized holes. Small, battered shoes lay in the center of the room. A pile of blankets filled one corner.

No child.

He returned to the living room. Genevieve and the male hadn't moved.

The young fuck-buddy would be easier to intimidate. "Where. Is. She?" he growled at the male.

The male paled. "Uh, sometimes she runs out back if—" He edged away from Genevieve.

If her mother had one of her screaming fits?

When he'd lived with Genevieve, he'd done the same. Ryder went out the back door and across the barren yard. A straggly wire fence. No toys. One aged oak tree. No good hiding places. However, as he crossed the weedy excuse for a lawn, he spotted a tree pixie hiding on the lowest branch. It was dividing its attention between him and something in the hollow dug out between the oak's roots.

Ryder approached the tree slowly and looked down.

A tiny child huddled in the damp and dark burrow. So thin. Big, hazel eyes stared up at him. Bruises showed on her chin and one cheekbone, with more scattered on her bare arms and legs.

The Goddess would weep.

Slowly, he went down on one knee. What did one say to a cub? Hell, he didn't even enjoy talking to adults.

"Hey." He swallowed, feeling huge as he stared at the miniature person. "You must be Minette."

She cringed away, breaking his heart.

Her shirt and shorts were torn. Her brown hair was matted. And her scent said she hadn't been washed in a long time. How could anyone—even Genevieve—treat a cub so poorly? Rage boiled in his veins—but he shut it down. And tried to smile.

The bone structure of her face was a feminine version of his own, as was the dent above her upper lip. The straight nose and high cheekbones were not only his, but reminded him of how Ben looked at five. Minette was his, all right. It wouldn't matter if she weren't. He wouldn't leave a badger cub in this place, let alone a shifter child.

"I'm your daddy, Minette." Only a hint of a growl crept into the words. "I'm going to take you to a place where you'll have a soft bed and all the food you want to eat."

No reaction. Not even tears.

Herne help him, what would he do if she cried?

Feeling like crying himself, he leaned forward. She didn't

fight as he lifted her and cradled her against his chest. She couldn't weigh more than a feather. Too fucking light.

He walked into the house. "She's going with me."

"Oh, no. No, she's not. That's my cub." Genevieve blocked the front door, hands on her hips.

His anger increased to a roaring fire. *No. Don't scare the baby.* "She's mine, as well, and you obviously aren't capable of caring for a child."

Calculation flickered in her gaze before her lower lip quivered, and she held her hands out. "You don't understand, my love. Since you abandoned me, I've had a dreadful time. Look at where I'm—Minette and I are—living. Such a dump. We need you, Ryder."

"Right. I can see how undernourished you are. The rags you're forced to wear." He ran his gaze over her well-fleshed body clothed in a perfectly fitted silk skirt and blouse. "I'm taking my child. I wouldn't take you on a bet."

"Oh, Ryder. Darling…"

"Move, or I'll move you, and you won't like it."

"Damon," she yelled. Her voice held the viciousness he'd grown familiar with before he left. "Stop him! Don't let him take my baby."

In Ryder's arms, Minette had started to shake. She still hadn't said a word. "Sorry, kitten," he said under his breath.

Having managed to don his pants, Damon almost tripped on his shoes. He stood, swaying slightly. "But, Gen, you said she was a worthless brat. Why don't you let him—"

With a scream, Genevieve launched herself at Ryder. She might be a wolf, but he'd learned the hard way she used her fingernails as effectively as any werecat.

Sidestepping, he caught her arm with his free hand and propelled her into the male. As they went down in a tangle of limbs and curses, Ryder looked back at the female who had destroyed his life.

He opened his mouth, then shook his head. There really was nothing to say. With luck, she'd forget her offspring and continue fucking her way through the males of Deschutes Territory.

Silently, he walked out of the house with his newfound cub.

Herne help them both.

Chapter Three

Cold Creek, North Cascades Territory — full moon

BENJAMIN LLWYD INHALED slowly. The firelight in the small room above the Wild Hunt Tavern glowed off the female's dusky skin. The scents of musk, sex, and wood smoke hung in the air. Ben drove his cock deeper, pumping quickly. Sarah had already climaxed twice, but had come into arousal again before he'd gotten her moving and out of the room.

She wasn't a particularly likable female. He'd only brought her to the mating room because it was easier to mate with her than to keep brushing her off. Nonetheless, a decent male didn't leave a female in need. He'd get her off one more time.

As his balls drew tightly against his groin, his teeth ground together as he fought for control.

One more minute.

The brunette's mouth twisted as she shoved her hips up. "Harder, dammit."

No soft words and sweetness from this one—just demands. This was the first and last time he'd bring her upstairs.

He easily pinned her in place and angled his cock to rub against her G-spot. *Right. There.*

Under his palms, her muscles went rigid. Her back arched. Her cries broke forth, sharp and high, as her cunt spasmed around his shaft.

And as she came, he slipped out of her and shot his seed into the furs covering the floor.

Far, far back in his mind, he felt the Mother's displeasure that he'd waste his essence this way. He had for years. After learning how his mother died, he wouldn't impregnate a female, no matter the wishes of the Goddess or clan. Didn't mean he couldn't satisfy a female, though.

Beside Sarah, he propped his head on his hand and idly caressed her lush breasts as she recovered. He could feel the thudding of her heart under his hand.

She turned her head. "You're as big as my sister said."

He grunted a response. The God endowed his warriors with added size and strength. Ben's size wasn't anything of his doing—he'd rather be admired for his character.

Pushing his hand away, Sarah sat up and stretched, obviously not needing tenderness after mating.

Truth be told, he preferred the ones who wanted his attention after sex.

After a shower, Ben walked downstairs with Sarah clinging like a burr to his arm. Other shifters were on the way up. One female had a littermate on each side; another had three brothers.

An ache filled his chest as he remembered how he and Ryder would mate females on Gathering nights. Ben would direct, and Ryder'd add his own inventive ideas. Afterward, they'd cuddle the female between them. Once upon a time, he'd planned to share a mate and children with his littermate.

Life had cut that trail short.

In the main room of the tavern, females were scattered here and there, each surrounded by a group of males vying for attention.

Ben tried to pull away. "It was—"

"You were *wonderful.*" Sarah rubbed her breasts against his arm and clung tighter. "Now that I'm living in Cold Creek, I hope to see more of you."

Did he act as if his brain was located in his dick? She didn't like him any more than he did her. "I'm afraid I'm pretty busy."

"Oh. Fine." Pouting, she looked around. "Can you take me over to the healer?"

Of course, Ben thought cynically. The god-touched—cahirs, healers, Cosantirs, and blade-mages—were popular with the females. Vicki, a werecat who'd been born human, labeled status-hunting females as *guppies*. No, *groupies*. "Sure thing."

Nodding at friends, he escorted her across the room to Donal who, as usual, had several females vying for his attention, all of whom had males trying for theirs.

Gathering nights were a type of sexual war.

"Donal, this is Sarah."

She gave the healer a blinding smile. Her cheeks were reddening as her arousal rose again.

Donal nodded to her, then glanced at Ben, expecting more.

Ben shrugged. By Herne's antlers, he had nothing more to say. The female took, didn't give, the mating had been empty. Her only interest was in taking down a high-status male.

Donal's head tilted slightly before he nodded, getting all that Ben hadn't said. The healer was no fool. He motioned to the bar. "The Cosantir's looking for you, Ben."

"Donal, it's good to meet you." Sarah moved closer.

"And you." With a smile, the healer put his arm around another female's waist. "Excuse us, please." He moved toward the stairs with his choice.

Hissing under her breath, Sarah latched onto Ben's arm again.

Demon-guts, now who could he dump her on? He scanned for prospects. Good thing he was taller than everyone in the room. He spotted Wesley, a good-looking cat shifter—and a coveted cahir—and escorted her to him.

"Hey, Wesley, this is Sarah. Sarah, Wesley is a cahir from Canada. He's here to study killing hellhounds with Shay and Zeb."

"Oooo, hellhounds. You're so brave," she cooed and ran her hand up the young cahir's arm.

Wesley's chest expanded. He tossed Ben a superior look as if he'd won a fight for the brunette rather than having her dumped in his lap.

Cubs. Perhaps in a few more years, the young, overly-testosteroned male wouldn't see everything as a competition.

Feeling more weary than amorous, Ben threaded his way through the crowd to the bar. The sexual dance was all fine and well, but he'd already had three females, and face it, as a male grew older, the obsessive lusts of a full moon diminished.

Calum was behind his bar, as usual. Although lifemated, the guardian of the North Cascades Territory still monitored the Gatherings. This male was more protective and conscientious than any Cosantir Ben'd met in his extensive early travels.

"A beer?" Calum was already drawing a glass.

"Thank you." Ben settled himself on a bar stool, content to wait. Building a Guinness couldn't be hurried. "Have you need of me, Cosantir?"

"Aye." Calum set the beer in front of Ben. Almost as tall as a cahir, leanly muscled, black haired, the Cosantir had level gray eyes that would flash to black with the power of the God. "A bear is raiding the human campgrounds located just inside the territory border."

"Is it our concern? The humans have their police—forest rangers or such—to deal with animals."

"They do. Apparently, this bear breaks into bear-proof containers and opens car doors."

"Interesting." Ben watched the dark beer's foam dissolve.

Many bear-proof containers required manipulating a key-like device. No matter how clever, a bear didn't have fingers. But Calum wouldn't bother him if a human vagrant was the culprit. "You think we have a feral shifter?"

Calum shook his head. "I can tell there is a shifter in the area, but a feral would eat the humans, not their food. It'll take some time to get there. Can you accompany me after moonset?"

"You?" Ben straightened. Herne provided cahirs to handle anything requiring warriors. A Cosantir shouldn't be at risk. Ever. "I can handle a bear, whether a shifter or not, whether feral or not."

"I do not doubt your abilities. However, a Judgment might be required."

The power of life and death rested in a Cosantir's hands. Ben was grateful the power wasn't his...and that the God had gifted this territory with a guardian both canny and strong.

"Your will, Cosantir."

Chapter Four

North Cascades Territory – night after full moon

THE SCENT OF cooking meat drew Emma back to the human campground. With every step, her broken leg caught on brush and downed logs. Pain stabbed into her over and over, and the agony was getting worse.

The knowledge she wouldn't survive much longer was actually a relief.

Since her injury half a moon ago, she'd been unable to hunt. Even going to a stream for water was almost impossible. Under brittle, dull fur, her muscles sagged from dehydration and weight loss. She was finding it harder and harder to move. But in bear form, her animal nature wouldn't quit, no matter the inevitable conclusion.

Regret for a life cut short curled through her like wood smoke from a fire. Once, she'd had dreams—how she'd find loving mates, cherish her cublings, please her clan with songs and stories. Instead, she had caused the deaths of two shifters.

If the Goddess found the rescue of the human children to be an adequate balance, Emma would call herself content...for she had no remaining time left to her.

Under cover of the forest, she surveyed the clearing. Two large men sat at a campfire. A hint of a familiar, wild scent caught her attention. She sniffed, but the elusive smell disappeared under the heavy odors of wood smoke and grilling meat.

Meat.

Despite the driving hunger, caution lent her patience. She was too weak to fight, too weak to run. Yes, patience would gain her all.

Unhurriedly, the two men smothered the fire, cleaned up, and stored their food in a bear-vault. Rather than erecting a tent, they simply stripped and climbed into sleeping bags.

Long and long, she waited. An owl hooted nearby. She caught the scent of a skunk, probably a scavenger like her. A weasel passed by, probably after the tiny shrew in the leaf litter.

The men's breathing slowed. They were asleep.

Slowly, Emma entered the clearing, holding her injured rear leg up to eliminate any noise. It hurt so badly, she barely felt the stabbing pains from her broken front toes. Step by step, she advanced.

The bear-proof container lay on its side under a tree. She hesitated, fighting the fiery throbbing in her leg and ache in her left forepaw. Where was the coin or key to open the metal-sided canister?

A pile of copper pennies caught her eye. Now she needed fingers. All she had to do was be human.

As she visualized turning in a circle, a door glowed—so very dim—in the rear of her mind. The magic was dying. She was dying. She opened the door and stepped through. Magic ran over her skin in a glorious tingling that, for one wonderful second, wiped out her pain.

A breath later, she stared at her fingers splayed on the sparse grass. Dirt and pine needles ground into her bare knees. Unable not to look, she checked her lower leg and flinched. The oozing, gaping wounds exposed the muscle and the jagged ends of bones in a ghastly, agonizing mess.

As she reached for the food container, her shattered leg grated as if blunt nails were being hammered into the bones. She clenched her teeth as tears flooded her eyes and dripped onto the dead leaves and into the dirt.

"Child." The low voice came from behind her.

No, no, no. The men were *awake.*

She jerked around. Her broken leg caught, twisted. *Oh, Goddess.* As agony overwhelmed her, she lost her grip on her shape and fell through the door to the wild. Her flesh blurred, transformed. Fur. Fangs. Claws.

As the pain ebbed, horror filled her. She'd *trawsfurred* in front of *humans.* She spun around.

A man stood in front of her. Olive skin. Dark hair. No weapon. His dark eyes were turning black and—

Bear instincts took over. She rose, trying to balance on one leg, and let out a roar of anger.

Run, human. Please, run.

Instead, an answering growl came from the side. Another bear.

She dropped to all fours and tried to flee, but her bad leg hit the container. The flare of pain shot red-tinged lightning through her. Her eyesight fuzzed and—

Slam.

The bear hit her shoulder and knocked her off her paws. Before she could move, the massive grizzly flopped across her, driving the air from her lungs.

Caught. Trapped.

Panicking, she struggled, grunting and growling.

Fearlessly, the human went down on one knee beside her head. He caught her muzzle in an unbreakable grip and forced her to meet his gaze. His eyes had turned black as a winter's night.

"*Trawsfur.*" His voice held the power of the God.

A force in her head pushed her through the door to human and locked it behind her. Her fur, her claws, her size melted into a human frame. He'd forced her to shift. How could he…?

New fear struck. She couldn't *breathe*.

The man shook his head. "Remove yourself, Benjamin, before you suffocate her.

With a growling snort of amusement, the grizzly rose, shook out its fur, and changed to human.

They weren't humans; they were shifters. The familiar wild scent she'd caught was theirs. As Emma's leg throbbed with pain, she stared at them through tear-blurred eyes.

The werebear's cheekbone held a blue knife-shaped scar. He was a cahir, sworn to protect the clan.

And the other male? Only one type of Daonain held the power of transformation. He was Cosantir of a territory and Herne's representative on earth.

Her doom had found her. She closed her eyes and inhaled, knowing her breaths could now be counted on one hand. And despite her pain and sorrow, the air was sweet, fragrant with evergreen and wood smoke, and the scent of other shifters.

Nonetheless, truly, she was blessed. Her death would be quick at the hand of the Cosantir, and…she wouldn't be alone.

She met the Cosantir's gaze. Black for the God's presence. "Send me back to the Mother," she whispered. "I'm ready."

To her surprise, he shook his head. Silver-gray was breaking into the darkness of his eyes. "I fear I am not."

He glanced at the terrifying bear shifter who was pulling on a pair of jeans. "Benjamin, get some information. I'll bring the first aid kit from my pack."

She struggled to sit up as the werebear approached. The male—Benjamin—was enormous. Over six-five. His straight, brown hair was cut to ear-length and shorter than most shifters preferred. Curly chest hair made a triangle over his thick pectoral muscles. His angular features were big-boned, his jaw square and strong. Not handsome, but far too compelling.

"I'm Ben." His deep voice held a Texas drawl. "Got a name, girl?" *"Got a nayum, gurl?"*

"Emma. Why didn't he kill me?" she whispered. "I broke the Law."

"Pretty name, darlin'." He took a knee beside her. "The Cosantir takes his time before dispensing judgment."

Should she…could she…run?

She glanced at Ben's jeans. Clothes would be a handicap if he shifted back to bear. He'd have to remove the jeans first or be tangled up until he could rip them away. She was naked, so she could *trawsfur* to bear and try to escape. Without thinking, she edged slightly away.

Ben's laugh was the rumble of rocks avalanching down a cliff. "You can't move fast enough to get away, li'l bear. Not from me and not from Calum. He's a cat."

A panther? The chill came from more than the frosted grass under her body. On three legs, she couldn't escape a panther. Or the grizzly, either. So she'd die. Please, let her at least maintain some dignity.

But fear and pain were tearing at her resolve. Averting her face, she blinked back tears.

With a grunt, Ben settled next to her, his body near enough to impart warmth to her bare body. One big hand curved over her ankle below her wound. His brows drew together as he took in the extent of the damage. "Those are bite marks. What in the Hunter's lands happened to your leg?"

"Indeed, I have the same question." The Cosantir's resonant voice held a faintly clipped British accent, a marked contrast to the bear's slow drawl. He carried two straight pieces of wood, each covered with a ripped-up T-shirt.

He set one on each side of her broken leg.

"You call that first aid?" Ben protested, although he held the braces in place as Calum secured them with more strips of cloth.

Her whole leg felt submerged in fiery lava. As the bindings tightened, her agony grew. Hands fisted, she fought back scream after scream. Finally, the pain receded enough she could hear the Cosantir.

"I am disinclined to attempt anything other than conveying her to our healer. This"—he indicated her leg—"is as bad a fracture as I've ever seen. Anything we do here is liable to make it worse or restart the bleeding."

"But…" She'd been banished and was to be shunned by all Daonain.

Why were they even speaking to her? She touched the raised parallel scars along her jawline. Didn't they see the marks? Know what black scars meant? This Cosantir had surely banished people before.

She struggled to sit up.

"Stay put, li'l bear." Ben set his huge hand on her shoulder, and the warmth of his palm seared her frozen skin.

"Aren't you going to kill me? I don't understand."

The Cosantir rose, his face unreadable. "You broke the Law by raiding human campgrounds. However, I've heard no rumors of a shifter, merely speculation about clever bears or vagrant humans." He paused for a long moment. "There will be consequences, but death will not be one of them."

Not die? Her breath caught on the influx of hope.

The Cosantir glanced at Ben.

The grizzly shifter's square jaw went tight. "Brace yourself, darlin'. This is going to hurt." His hands slid under her body, and he lifted her into the air.

The pain rose to intolerable, and she screamed before blackness took her away.

Chapter Five

Cold Creek, North Cascades Territory
Human "Easter Day"

PLANTED IN A folding chair out of the healer's way, Ben studied his inadequate guest room. He'd done well enough with the preliminary decor. The queen-sized bed was adequate. The Oriental rug over the hardwood floor was a diamond pattern in the same gray-blue as the walls. The cream trim and moldings were crisp and clean. The curtains were a traditional Victorian style in a brown, cream, and blue floral.

However, he'd only provided the minimum necessities. To his eye, the room looked stark and unwelcoming, not nearly good enough for the honey-colored female in the bed. Maybe he could ask Angie to pick up a few things. Making a mental list, Ben watched the healer silently start to examine the female.

About time.

Before the healer's arrival, Angie, owner of the diner, had shown up. The Cosantir had asked her to give Emma a quick bed bath. When done, the pretty bear had been white and shaking, but had thanked Angie with a heartfelt graciousness.

"Uh-huh." The healer made an unhappy sound, drawing Ben's attention to the bed. "You, bear, are about as hydrated as the Sahara at high noon."

Emma blinked.

Ben regarded her. Why did she seem surprised each time someone spoke to her?

"Malnourished and underweight."

Ben enjoyed Donal's blunt commentaries. Inscrutable healers were a pain in the tail. Whatever Donal learned, he shared with his patient, and in Emma's case, per the Cosantir's orders, also with Ben.

Donal pulled the sheet to one side and ran his fingers down the bear's right arm to where two of her fingers were swollen and dark red-purple. "Two fingers busted."

Her pretty lips curved up. "Is *busted* proper medical terminology?"

Donal smiled for the first time. Light from the delicate, wrought-iron chandelier illuminated the crescent-shaped scar over his right cheekbone—the Mother's mark designating a healer. Good thing, since Donal preferred jeans, boots, and flannel shirts to the more conservative healer's attire. "Why confuse my patients with gobbledygook? I bet you knew the diagnosis the first time you tried to move your fingers."

Her mouth twisted ruefully. "Oh, I did."

Ben watched the various expressions cross her face—pain, amusement, gratitude. Amazing. He'd seen young females when they were in pain. They'd demand attention and snap at anyone trying to help. Not this one. By the Hunter, she was a mess, underweight and pale, yet the sweetness of her character came through so clearly that all he could see was beauty.

As Donal continued his examination, grumbling over the various scars and scrapes, Ben averted his gaze. Most shifters weren't body-shy, but the pretty female hadn't had a choice about Ben's presence. Since shifters occasionally lost control and *trawsfurred* when hurt, the Cosantir'd ordered him to stay during the exam.

At a gasp of pain, Ben turned back.

The sheet covered the female's torso, but not her legs. With the dirt removed, the wound looked even worse. Red lines streaked upward toward her thigh. White bone poked out of the gashed area—and Angie hadn't attempted to clean away the embedded dirt and leaf debris.

"Happened how long ago?" Donal's fingers hovered above the wound as he assessed the damage.

"I-I've lost track of the days." She bit her lower lip. "It was the last dark of the moon, whenever that was."

Donal's expression turned grim.

Dark of the moon? As a chill crawled up his spine and tensed his muscles, Ben rose.

Startled, Emma stared up at him.

"Darlin'…" Ben gentled his voice. "You never did tell me what bit you."

"A hellhound." She shivered visibly. "I know all the old legends, yet somehow, I thought they were a myth. But they're not. The…creature…was just as bad as the stories say."

Donal grunted. "No wonder there's so much damage."

"By Herne's Holy Antlers, how are you alive?" This li'l female survived a hellhound? Death would have been the least of what the creature would have done, given the chance. Torture, rape…

Donal cast him a warning glance before saying to Emma, "I need to clean this out before I can heal it. The cream I used will numb some of the pain, but it'll still hurt like hell."

She tensed. "Okay."

Having been on the receiving end of a healer's digging, Ben knew even this courageous little bear would have trouble holding still. He pulled his chair to the opposite side of the bed from the healer, braced his forearm on Emma's left leg, and gripped her right knee above the wound. His left hand was free to secure the rest of her.

She took in his preparations and swallowed hard.

"Easy now." Ben patted her hip. "While Donal pokes at you, why don't you tell us the whole story?"

Donal filled a massive syringe with sterile saline and padded the bed with a heap of towels. Then he started squirting the fluid into the gaping flesh to flush out the grit.

Ben winced. Against the torn tissues, the forceful stream probably felt like an assault with a fire hose of boiling water.

Emma's hands fisted. She flinched and unclenched her broken fingers.

"Talk to me, li'l bear." Ben held her gaze with his. "What happened that night?"

"I-I heard screams from a human campground. There were children there, and I…" She whimpered in pain as Donal used tweezers to extract stubborn debris.

"A human campground? You went to save humans?" Not something most shifters would do unless the humans were friends.

"There were *children* there. I might have run otherwise. But the hellhound went after the cubs, so I attacked."

"In bear form?" Donal asked, not looking up.

She nodded. "My claws didn't even penetrate. It had…"

"Armor." Ben sure had scraped his claws against enough of the fucking demon plating to know how she must have felt. "Bullet-proof, knife-proof, fang-proof."

"Yes. Very. I hit it hard enough to get its attention away from the children, but it…bit me." She motioned to her leg.

"Most shifters facing a hellhound are dead within seconds."

Ben's comment got a disgusted glare from Donal. *Fine.* He wasn't a damned diplomat.

The pretty bear actually huffed a bit of a laugh—and then gasped as Donal's tweezers dug deeper.

Ben pressed down to keep her leg immobile and took her uninjured hand with his free one. "Squeeze, female." She had a nice strong grip. "How'd you get away?"

"I tried to get free, but nothing worked. Not until I poked it in the eye with a claw."

"By the God, you did well. I'm impressed." One-on-one, even a cahir rarely survived against a hellhound. "It ran?"

She nodded. "But the damage was done."

"I'm going to fix this mess," Donal said briskly. "But you'll have a scar. And although I can put the bones in place and start the healing, you'll need time to recover strength. It'll be a while before your leg will take weight."

"What?"

Donal ignored her and kept going. "I'll give you a brace to wear. Eventually—when I tell you it's all right—you can walk with a cane. And once the healing is complete, you won't have even a limp."

Her face went even paler. "But, I don't have any… I mean, I can't stay here."

"Don't even think about arguing." He glanced at Ben. "I want you to hold her knee with one hand and pull on her ankle. Slow and straight until I say stop."

At the foot of the bed, Ben wrapped his left hand around her thigh and curled his right around her ankle. Slowly, he pulled, grateful for the extra strength given to cahirs.

As Donal placed his hands on each side of her wound, using his power to loosen her knotted muscles, Ben continued the traction. The protruding bone slid beneath the skin.

Donal muttered, "Hold there, Ben." His fingers worked the outside of her leg, lining up the bones, before he delved inside the wound.

Emma let out a sharp scream and jerked, but Ben didn't let the leg move. After a second, she regained control and held completely still. Tears streamed down her white face. Brave female.

"Ease up, slowly," Donal ordered, and Ben complied.

Donal set one hand over the area, eyes closed. "Yes, the pieces are in the right places." He bent his head, hands on each side of the wound, and the flesh started filling in. Closing.

After several minutes, Donal lifted his head. Sweat moistened his face, and his silvery eyes had lost their glow. "You can let go now, cahir."

With obvious dissatisfaction, the healer studied the fragile, pink tissue covering the area. There would be scarring, Ben knew. Donal muttered, "I could have done better if I'd seen you right away."

Emma eyed him and looked away.

Why hadn't she had anyone to help her? "Ignore Donal, Emma. He can be grumpier than a winter-starved badger." Ben winked. He pushed the healer down into the empty chair. "Sit. I'll fetch the leg brace you brought."

When Donal dropped into the chair, Ben gratefully left the room, needing to settle his nerves. Seeing a female in pain made him want to go on a grizzly rampage.

She'd handled herself better than he had. By the God, she was brave.

She was also a mystery. Why had she been alone in the forest? Why had no one reported her missing? Where were her people?

He rubbed his neck as he trotted down the stairs. Good thing she'd be laid up for a while; he'd have time to find out all about her.

Chapter Six

HALFWAY TO THE bathroom—and the mirror there— Emma steadied herself on the back of the sturdy wooden chair, pushed it forward again, and hopped to it on one leg. Every thump seemed to echo through the house.

She stopped and listened. Only silence met her ears.

Half an hour ago, Ben had checked that she had food and water, and made sure the disgusting commode was close to the bed. He'd left to get groceries, but would be home all too soon. This was her only chance.

Oh, Goddess, she hurt. Every jump jarred her leg so badly her clenched teeth were probably going to fracture.

It was better though. Really. Today her leg only throbbed as if a dwarf was thumping the wound with a giant hammer. Uncomfortable, yes, but far more tolerable than when her imaginary torturer had used a *knife*.

She sighed. Couldn't the pain stop? Just for a little bit so she could have a break?

Break. Cute, Emma.

She rolled her eyes toward the ceiling. At one time, she'd loved playing with words. Only when alone though. Her mother believed a child should be silent. Very, very silent. Moreover, when allowed to speak, her manners had better be impeccable.

She half-smiled. Her mother's training had been effective enough that the master bard had teased Emma for being too shy and reserved. Those weren't common songster traits. Now, she was so unused to being around people that speaking aloud at all was difficult.

But she certainly hadn't forgotten how Daonain were supposed to treat a banished shifter. No one should even acknowledge her presence, let alone speak to her, yet they had.

And, oh, it was wondrous to hear other shifters, to smell their scents, to be spoken to. She'd found herself singing little tunes under her breath. Still…no one had commented on her scarred face or even looked at her strangely. She hadn't said anything, either.

What if they suddenly comprehended she'd been banished? What if they kicked her out before she could walk again? Why hadn't they noticed the banishment scars? The long, black scars along her jaw could hardly be invisible, could they? She could feel them, after all.

She needed to see them.

She eyed the distance to the bathroom. Maybe seven gut-wrenchingly painful hops. She could do it; she had to know.

One hop. Her teeth gritted together.

Ben would growl if he found her out of bed. He'd been so concerned. No one had ever treated her as he did, as if she was important. When she'd been hurting, he'd read to her to take her mind off the pain. He brought her treats to tempt her appetite. By the Mother, he'd brought her chocolate ice cream. Just the memory made her smile.

Although he'd looked frustrated at the way she'd evaded his questions about her past, he hadn't growled. However, she had a feeling he hadn't given up.

Another hop.

The Cosantir hadn't returned to question her. Ben said he'd

gone into the mountains to the territory's Elder Village and wouldn't be back for a couple more days. *Reprieve.*

Another hop.

Another.

A few minutes later, she leaned on the sink, gulping, and trying not to vomit. Agony roared through her body. Cold sweat ran down her back.

Eventually, she wiped the tears from her face and pulled in a slow breath. Anticipation and dread filled her as she leaned forward to peer into the mirror.

She blinked.

It had been three years since she'd looked at her reflection in…anything. How gaunt she'd grown. Her wavy, light hair was longer and almost reached her butt. Her face was awfully pale.

Enough stalling. Her fingernails dug into the sink enamel as she turned her head and angled her chin. The light shone on her lower cheek and jaw, and on the thin, white scars from a werecat's claws.

White. She felt as if she'd run into a tree and knocked the air out of herself.

The scars weren't black. But marks of banishment were always black…unless…the Mother forgave a shifter and erased the darkness.

Emma ran her fingers over the healed wounds. When had the thin scars changed from black to white? They'd never felt different from one day to the next. It could have been any time, since she'd never looked, not even in the lake when bathing. To see the black of a Cosantir's Judgment staining her skin would have sent her into a depression from which she'd not have recovered.

For all she knew, she might have been forgiven a year ago. Two.

Her fingers traced over the thin scars as she stared in the

mirror. She was forgiven. No longer banished or shunned.

Slowly, then faster, exhilaration filled her like a spring flood, washing everything clean before it. She couldn't stop touching the scars. The beautifully white, white scars.

Had she ever seen any shifter who'd returned from banishment? She couldn't recall. Did healed scars from a banishment look different? Maybe no one would know she'd been banished.

Maybe she could live with her own people again.

Hope swelled in her heart, so painfully she had to wrap her arms around herself to hold it in.

Could she stay here in Cold Creek? Find something to do? Maybe…maybe even sing?

"What the hell are you doing out of bed?" Ben's deep bass filled the bathroom as he stopped in the doorway.

Hopping away from the mirror, Emma tripped and fell backward.

He closed strong hands around her waist and caught her easily. His chuckle was a low rumble as he said, "Sorry, li'l bear. I didn't mean to scare you." With no evidence of exertion, he scooped her up and carried her to her bed.

"Um, thank you."

"Not a problem. Just don't do it again, or Donal will bite my head off."

"Right." As he swept the covers over her, she looked around. "Did I ever mention how beautiful your room is?"

His gaze took in the furnishings. "I'm sorry I didn't have time to do better. But you're lucky. Aside from my bedroom and this one, the rest of the upstairs is still being restored. Two weeks ago, you'd have been bunked down on the floor."

"I'd have been fine." She laughed. "Floors are softer than caves."

He stilled, surprise in his expression, and she realized she'd never laughed. She'd been so worried about people's reactions, expecting someone to tell her to leave, that she hadn't been able to relax.

But her scars were white. No one knew her here, so far from the Mt. Hood territory. No one knew she'd been banished.

Mother's forgiveness or not, she didn't deserve to live among the clan, and she shouldn't, but how could she not savor this boon for a little while? Hearing the rumble of Ben's voice, smelling his faintly wild shifter scent, seeing the warmth in his eyes…she felt like a parched desert plant greedily embracing the first drops of rain.

Her mind was made up. She'd stay as long as they'd let her.

Chapter Seven

N ESTLED IN THE white-capped North Cascade Mountains, the tiny town of Cold Creek looked as if it hadn't changed since the early 1900s. Past the two-block-long Main Street, Ryder drove to the edge of town, down a smaller road, and parked at the end. The road had a rural feel with oversized lots and older two- and three-story homes. He could see why Ben had chosen it.

"We're here, Minette." *May the Mother be with us.* He lifted his daughter from the kiddie seat on the passenger side of the SUV.

Settling her on his hip, he ruffled her silky brown hair. "Gonna need you to sit on the step for a few minutes, kitten." *While I see if we have a welcome here or not.* Anticipation, hope, and worry welled inside him in an unsettling brew.

She blinked up at him, thumb firmly in her mouth, green-brown eyes wide. No answers forthcoming. Considering he hadn't heard her speak at all in the last six days, he wasn't surprised, but he still hoped. By the Mother, he'd never hoped so hard in his life. If only he'd known Genevieve had born a child. Or not fallen for her in the first place. His jaw clenched. Fuck, he was an idiot. Nevertheless, that trail was in the past, he had a new one to follow now.

And amends to make.

He stared up at the three-story Victorian house. The dark green siding contrasted pleasantly with the white trim and a dark brown, shingled roof. The covered front porch butted up against an octagonal tower on the left. Although the grounds looked as if no one had tended them in a decade or more, the house had been recently restored. Lumber off to one side indicated Ben wasn't finished.

Ryder's shoulders relaxed. His littermate hadn't changed beyond all recognition. Building was one of the loves they'd shared. Ben preferred to work on a large scale by building and remodeling houses. Ryder favored customized finish work and handcrafting furniture.

"Let's see how loud the bear will roar." His gut was tight as he carried his cub up the sidewalk. When she was settled on the porch steps, he handed her a picture book to look at.

With a small smile—her only kind—she opened the book. Minette never moved much. Never got in trouble. Never had a tantrum or disobeyed. He hoped, prayed to the Mother for her to grow confident enough to be a normal, feisty cub.

She needed a stable home and family. Worry gnawed at his guts as he moved past her to the front door.

What if his brother had a mate? What if he was still angry with Ryder for leaving? Every second of the last five years weighed down his shoulders.

His rap on the door was answered by Ben himself.

Pleasure surged through Ryder at the sight of his littermate. The world hadn't felt right without his brother at his side.

"Griz." Fuck, it was good to catch his brother's scent—bear and male, along with hints of sawdust and pine.

"Ryder?" Ben's voice was hoarse, as if he didn't believe whom he was seeing.

Ryder hadn't changed that much. Sure, he'd put on the heft and weight of a mature male, but not much else. He wanted to laugh—whoever heard of Ben being silent—but he had to struggle to get air into his lungs. It felt as if the bear had pinned him with a heavy paw. "I—fuck, Ben. I'm…"

The broad, strong face closed up.

Ryder's words shriveled into dust. His brother should have yelled. As small cubs, they'd tussled and argued; as adults, they'd shouted and fought, yet united together against all comers. His littermate had never shut him out before.

People who saw Ben as easygoing hadn't seen his steel backbone. Injustice and cruelty brought out the bear's fury. Apparently, so did being hurt.

Ryder's hopes sank faster than a rock in the lake.

"What the fuck do you want here?" Ben's voice was a low growl, deeper than it had been before.

"I came to—"

"No." The growl grew to a shout. "No word from you for five fucking years. Bad enough you chose a female over me, but then you walked away as if I was old scat. You made your choice, *bro.*"

The emphasis was ugly—and showed the damage he'd done to his littermate.

My fault. My obsession with a female. Fuck.

Ryder let out a breath. Nothing left to say, was there? "Right. I'm sorry, Ben."

Ryder's footsteps thudded hollowly on the wood as he crossed the porch. "Let's go, kitten."

She gave him a worried look, her thumb in her mouth.

His heart twisted. By the God, he'd give his left arm, both arms, if it meant she'd be safe. Never have to worry again. Carefully, he picked her up.

Behind him came a sound as if Ben had gotten a fist in the gut.

Ryder glanced back.

Ben stared at Minette. His voice shook as he asked, "You have a cub?"

AN HOUR LATER, in the kitchen, Ben watched his littermate at the sink. By Herne's heavy balls, Ryder had grown even better looking over the years. Maybe four of so inches short of Ben's God-given six feet six, his brother had the lean musculature and grace of a panther shifter. Classically handsome, he'd drawn the females like bees to spilled honey.

Although he and Ben shared the angular cheekbones, straight nose, and thick hair of their mother, Ben's broad features and frame showed his Scottish/Welsh heritage. His light skin held a tan only because of hours in the sun.

From his sire's side, Ryder's heritage was French and, oddly enough, African American. Either the Fae's Wild Hunt had ventured farther afield than commonly believed, or a dying Daonain had Death Gifted one of Ryder's ancestors with shifter blood. Whatever the original cause, Ryder was dark-eyed with light, saddle-brown skin.

Even their personalities were different. Ben preferred things neat—kept his hair short. Was clean-shaven. His littermate didn't give a fuck about his appearance; he'd tie his shoulder-length black hair back if it got in his way. His jaw was dark with stubble.

Ben had a slow Texas drawl—and he enjoyed talking.

Ryder's speech showed his years in Idaho, and the cat would sooner claw a person than talk to him. But when Ryder did speak, people listened. He was damn smart.

Although brothers, they were as different as mountain and valley. Yet at one time, they'd run the trails as a pair. He flinched at the painful thought. Like a rose bush, even the loveliest memories could hide thorns.

Silently—no surprise there—Ryder gave his daughter a drink from the covered glass he'd called a *sippy* cup.

Such a tiny cub. They'd had to place a box on the chair to give her a seat high enough for the table. She couldn't be older than about four.

Ben took a sip of beer. "She got a name?"

Ryder nodded. "This is Minette." When Ben lifted his eyebrows at the French name, he nodded again. "Yes, Genevieve's one and only. Apparently, Minette's womb-mates were still-born."

"Ah, hell, I'm sorry." Ryder's cub. If he and Ben had mated the same female—as did most littermates—Minette would've been Ben's daughter, no matter whose sperm had done the deed. Anger and grief roiled inside him, eroding his delight at her existence. "Did Genevieve come to Cold Creek with you?"

"No. Genevieve and I weren't together even a year." Ryder stared at the table for a moment. "It's just me and Minette.

Ben relaxed. He'd despised Genevieve, hadn't been able to see what had drawn Ryder. Well, okay, he understood her appeal. Pure, slinky sex. Her personality, however, was as irritating as fangs scraping on concrete. The female was lazy, wanted to be provided with a life of ease, and demanded attention stay on her. She was more self-centered than any female he'd ever met, even the one he'd mated last Gathering.

As Minette tilted her drink, and a sucking noise broke the silence. With a flinch, she set it down, shoulders curving inward.

Why?

When her timid eyes met Ben's, he smiled slightly. "Drink, lass. Apple juice is my favorite, too."

After a second, she timidly reached for the glass again.

She was scared.

As his protective instincts fired up, he worked to keep the anger from his face, because he was probably the one scaring her. Because she didn't know him.

Ryder's fault.

She would have been an adorable baby. A cute toddler. He'd have loved watching her grow. His anger flared to life again.

Moving to the counter where the cub couldn't hear them, he motioned Ryder over. "So, the reason you left me was because Genevieve was pregnant?"

His brother looked as if he'd bitten into a rabbit's bitter gall bladder. "I left because I was obsessed. Didn't think I'd survive life without her. And you'd said you'd never lifemate."

Ben winced. He did carry some responsibility for their breach.

Five years past, he'd returned to Texas and, with crap luck, bumped into his father—well, the male who'd raised him. Although Ben had known his mother had died in childbirth, this time his sire bluntly said Ben's large size had killed her. Torn her apart. Moreover, he'd predicted Ben's offspring would do the same.

By the God, to hear that he'd killed his mother? To think a cub of his would kill a female carrying it? He'd resolved his seed would spill on unfertile ground, and he'd live without taking a female as a mate. He would never cause another female's death.

Being a complete idiot, he hadn't considered what effect his declaration would have on his littermate.

When Ryder pulled a knife from his belt sheath to cut up an apple, Ben's heart tugged. They'd been separated at five—and when they'd reunited at twenty, it seemed a miracle their brother-bond was still strong and whole. He'd given Ryder the knife after their first barroom brawl when they'd fought side-by-side as if they'd never been apart.

The bond hadn't seemed such a miracle when Ryder had walked away. Ben rubbed his chest as if he could ease the pain of the damaged bond embedded in his soul.

After Ryder handed Minette a couple of apple pieces and returned, Ben cleared his throat. "But your obsession with Genevieve faded?"

"All too soon. She didn't want me. Any male who would support and worship her would have done as well. When the newness wore off, she started playing jealousy games and hooking up with different males, even—" Ryder broke off, then continued after a pause. "I left after a Gathering where she goaded a bunch of males into a fight. I'd guess she became pregnant then."

"How'd you find out about the cub?"

Ryder handed his child another apple slice to keep her occupied. "A friend living in Deschutes Territory visited Farway, saw Minette, and told me to have a look."

One look would be all it would take. Minette's big eyes and fair skin were Genevieve's, but the nose, high cheekbones, curved upper lip and plump lower lip, and pointed chin created a delicate caricature of Ryder. No doubt of her parentage existed. "Hard to imagine Genevieve watching over a newborn."

"She lived with a couple of rich wolves when Minette was a baby, but apparently, last year, she got bored." He glanced at Minette to make sure she wasn't paying attention and added, "Sampled every male in the area, and not just during Gatherings. They booted her out."

Ben wasn't surprised. Actually, it was remarkable the promiscuous female had remained with the two wolves so long. They must have been damned wealthy. "Genevieve let you take her cub?"

Genevieve wasn't the type to surrender anything she had her paw on—even an unwanted child.

"I didn't ask permission." Ryder's jaw tightened. "Without the wolves to rein her in, Genevieve... She lacks mothering skills," Ryder said lightly, although his face was stony, and one hand fisted. He pointed to a small scar over the child's cheek-bone. "Harold said Minette stopped talking when she was alone with her mother."

A growl escaped Ben. How could anyone hurt a cub, let alone one with the biggest, most vulnerable eyes in the world?

"When I showed up, Genevieve was fucking a male in the living room. The cub's bedroom had no furniture, just a pile of blankets. Minette was hiding out in the backyard in a tiny burrow."

Ryder's anger had always been slow to rise, Ben remembered, and often would loosen his tongue...as it did now.

"So, I picked Minette up and carried her out, and I started looking for you. I hoped you'd..." Ryder's voice trailed off.

Forgive him. Ben closed his eyes for a moment. His anger wasn't gone, but it was manageable. He didn't have it in his heart to turn away a child, especially his littermate's. "I've got a big house. There's room for you and the cub."

The tightness in Ryder's face lessened. "Thanks."

"Got to say, the upstairs is a mess, so we'll have to get the rooms finished and some furniture."

"Can do." The cat's slow smile appeared. "I'm good with wood."

Understatement of the year. Ryder was the finest wood-worker Ben had ever met.

"So..." Ben leaned against the table and attempted another smile. "Want a sandwich to go with the apple slices, Minette?"

She stared at him for a second and popped her thumb into her mouth.

Ryder said, "Appreciate it."

From the cub's scrawny appearance, she'd missed more than a few meals with her shrew of a mother. Ben assembled hearty beef and cheddar sandwiches, checking with Ryder for preferences on mayonnaise and mustard. "Here you go."

Then he made some for himself and Emma, setting her sandwich, potato chips, and a glass of milk onto a tray. At Ryder's curious glance, he explained. "Got a werebear in the bedroom next to mine. The Cosantir requested I keep her until she's healthy."

"Wounded? Does she pose a threat?" Ryder glanced at his cub.

"Not at all. Emma's a nice female; she'd never hurt a cub." Another understatement there. "She..." He broke off. Ryder might be relieved to know she'd attacked a hellhound to save a human child, but the Cosantir might not want Emma's history shared, since he hadn't rendered his judgment about her. "Having someone around to run food up and assist her when I'm at work would be a relief."

"You got it."

"Thanks. I'm going to take this upstairs and then join you."

As Ben climbed the stairs, he felt his tension ease. Just thinking of Emma had a calming effect. Sure she was a lovely bear with those lush curves and big, brown eyes, but she was also quietly intelligent, fun to talk with, and simply...peaceful.

THAT EVENING, EMMA decided she'd go insane—maybe feral—if she was trapped in the bedroom another day. Now, how could she tell Ben she felt caged in his pretty room?

He'd been so good to her.

The bedside table held an empty plate and glass from the lunch that Ben had apparently left when she was sleeping earlier.

Her excessive exhaustion should ease soon. The healer had warned her the extensive healing would knock her off her paws for a few days. Tomorrow she could put some weight on her leg.

Partial weight, Donal'd said, and he'd given her permission to leave her room, as well.

Thank the Mother.

As she gazed at the dark windows, her healing leg throbbed in counterpoint to her unhappy thoughts. In the wilderness, she'd hated the long, dark evenings. Those were the times she'd felt most alone, when everything she'd lost would come back to haunt her. Knowing she deserved to be miserable had made the loneliness even worse.

The murmur of voices came from the hallway, startling her. She stared at the closed bedroom door. Although most male Daonain shared a house with their littermates and eventually a mate, she'd gotten the impression Ben lived alone, but the male speaking had a deep voice with a resonant timbre similar to Ben's.

Footsteps, light enough to be a child's, came from the shared bathroom.

Why hadn't Ben mentioned his brother, mate, and cubs when they'd talked over the past days? She'd thought they were starting to be friends. Emma tried to shrug off the feeling of hurt.

It would be nice to meet more people. Surely, Ben would have a wonderful mate and littermates.

Don't descend into feeling envious, bear. But it was difficult not to.

Her mother had been her only family. Being Gather-bred, Emma didn't know her father, and her mother had handed off Emma's two male littermates to an infertile shifter family passing through town. She'd only kept Emma because a female cub increased the status of a family. But her mother hadn't loved her.

Now, Emma had to accept she'd never have a family.

It hurt to give up those dreams, but she had to be honest with herself. She was a big, ungainly bear, and the only time males had wanted her had been because of the hormonal influence of a full moon Gathering. Now…no male would want a female who'd been banished—a punishment saved for only the most heinous of crimes.

Even if the Goddess had forgiven her, she doubted Cedrick or anyone in the Mt. Hood area would forget. As her mother had said, just because a person "didn't mean to" fixed nothing. A person was responsible for the results of her actions.

Emma hadn't meant any harm, but harm she'd done. How could she whine that she wouldn't get a family? Two males were dead because she'd looked at one with longing and had let him kiss her.

No, she'd be grateful for what she had now—for being alive, for a chance to return to the clan again.

The door to Emma's room from the bathroom opened a crack.

A little girl, possibly three or four years old, peeked in. Her loose brown hair brushed her shoulders. Her curious eyes held the colors of a late summer forest, dark green and brown.

Absolutely adorable.

The girl spotted Emma and stiffened.

Emma smiled at her. Children were open and straightforward, and wonderful. "Hi there."

Eyes wide, the girl stared and slid her thumb into her mouth.

The habit was familiar. Emma'd also sucked her thumb as a cub...until her mother noticed. When she hadn't stopped quickly enough, her mother had clawed her thumb so mercilessly that any touch hurt. By the time the gashes healed, she no longer had the habit—just the scars.

Hopefully this cubling would be allowed the harmless comfort.

"Minette?"

The child disappeared back into the shared bathroom.

"Minette?" The lean, muscled man in a black leather jacket and boots who appeared in the doorway took Emma's breath away. She'd never seen any male so striking. His features said he was Ben's brother, although he was a few inches shorter and not as big-boned. Midnight-black, wavy hair reached his shoulders; black stubble outlined a chiseled jaw. His expression was cool...and cynical.

His eyes were so dark brown they were almost black and lacked any warmth at all. When his icy gaze ran over her, she felt as if she'd stepped into a snowbank. "You must be Emma."

"Yes." Her attempt at a smile fell flat. "Do you live here?"

"We're moving in, yes." His answer was terse. "I'm Ryder, Ben's littermate. My cub and I just arrived."

"Oh, how nice you..." Her voice trailed off. Oh, this was bad. Ben'd said the only prepared bedrooms were hers and his. At least two rooms would be needed for this male and the cub. And what about the cub's mother?

Emma was occupying a room they'd need.

And really, if they knew what kind of a person she was, they wouldn't want her here. Certainly not anywhere near such a sweet little girl.

Dismay swept through her. Somehow, Ben had made her feel welcome, but under this male's cold assessment, her feeling of belonging had changed. It wasn't right to be around other people. Not when she was...tarnished.

THE FEMALE HAD stopped herself before finishing her sentence, Ryder realized. Obviously, she didn't think it was nice he and his cub had arrived. On the contrary, from the way her brows were drawing into a frown, she didn't want them here. Why?

Because she was all settled in and enjoying a good deal?

Ryder studied her for a minute, feeling an unwelcome punch of attraction.

Although obviously half-starved, this female possessed ample curves that would attract a celibate troll, let alone a male as virile as his brother.

Ryder's mouth tightened. He'd abandoned Ben because of a conniving female who'd wanted him only for what he could give her. She wasn't the first mercenary female he'd met; wouldn't be the last.

And here was this female tucked neatly into Ben's house. She obviously didn't welcome intruders. No surprise there. What female would give up a cahir with a great house and a good income?

By the God, Ryder felt twenty years older than Ben. His littermate had no idea how greedy females could be. Cahirs were protectors right to the marrow of their bones. And if a child or female needed him, Ben'd give his life to help. The bear had the biggest heart in the territory.

And he could be played. Any male could. Fuck, Ben wouldn't be able to resist this beautiful female who claimed to be ill.

But was she? She looked healthy enough. Her eyes were clear, her complexion a clear ivory, her color flushed—probably with annoyance at having her plans ruined.

Yeah, she was looking at him as if he'd stolen her breakfast bunny. He decided against attempting to be sociable—the politeness skill sure as hell had never been in his toolbox anyway.

Instead, he tipped his head and backed out of the room.

BEN NOTICED RYDER leaving Emma's room. Had she called for help? "Problems?"

"Nah. Minette popped in there, but had already left before I could retrieve her."

Ben considered him, surprised Emma hadn't tried to keep Ryder in there to talk. She'd been increasingly bored. "She okay?"

Ryder gave him a puzzled look. "I suppose." He noticed

Minette peeking out of her room. "Kitten, let's go downstairs and see what's in your bag."

Ben walked into Emma's bedroom and stopped.

Sitting on the bed with her back to him, Emma was trying to pull on a pair of jeans Angie had provided. Before he could stop her, the harsh material scraped over her wound. The pain-filled sound she made twisted his gut.

"What the hell?" He strode across the room and sat on the bed beside her. "Emma, what are you doing?"

She ignored him and managed to get the jeans to her knees. Carefully, she rose from the bed, balanced on one leg, and pulled the waist up and over her round ass.

"What happened? Was Ryder rude?" Difficult to imagine. His taciturn brother might not sweet-talk a female, but he'd never been rude to one.

"No. He didn't say anything."

Then what the fuck?

"Sit down and talk to me, li'l female." He curled his fingers in the waistband and tugged her back onto the bed.

The tears in her eyes defeated the effectiveness of her frustrated glare. "I know you have more people here now. They'll need this room, so I'll be out of your fur in a few minutes."

"Not going to happen. You're not healed up enough to leave."

"I am. Now let go of me!" She tried to make him release her jeans and failed. Tears spilled down her cheeks, and a sob escaped her. "You stupid male!"

He saw the moment she lost her hold on her control, but rather than changing to a bear and doing some real damage, she merely thumped his shoulder with her tiny fists. Even when furious, she wouldn't hurt him.

A snowdrift of pity piled up within him. This was about more than the housing accommodations, wasn't it?

He lifted her up and yanked her jeans down. Her blows landed on his back like the slight sting of hail. As carefully as he could, he slid her pants off her legs. By the God, she'd torn the fragile tissue covering the hellhound bite. Blood trickled down her leg.

"Fuck, darlin'." He grabbed gauze pads the healer had left on the nightstand.

As he bandaged her wound, she abandoned the struggle. Tears seeped from beneath her closed lids to run down her cheeks.

Fuming, he took a seat beside her. Didn't she know what would happen to her out there, injured and helpless?

He sighed. Of course she did. She'd been nearly dead when they found her. And she still hadn't told him why she'd been living in the forest. He'd let her evade his questions, figuring it was Calum's job to quiz her, but if this continued, he'd pin her down and not let her up until she answered, no matter how much she cried. Or how badly he'd feel.

Probably much like he felt right now.

Normally, words came fairly easy to him, although often enough, he'd speak without thinking and make a hash of it. He didn't want to fuck up now. Dammit.

Stroking his thumb over her soft cheek, he calmed his anger so he could talk without growling. "I don't think the Mother approves of shifters throwing away her gift of life."

"I've already destroyed lives," she whispered, eyes still closed.

He frowned. She wasn't very old. Mid-twenties, maybe. At the most. Perhaps a couple of males had asked her to lifemate, and she'd broken their hearts with her refusal? "I doubt you've done anything that awful, li'l bear."

"Ben." When she looked at him, her beautiful golden-brown eyes held more misery than anyone should endure. "I don't deserve to live among the clan. Let me go."

"No. You wouldn't live a week, even in bear form." Taking her unbandaged hand, he saw purpling bruises on her knuckles. She must have given him some pretty determined thumps.

Noticing, she turned white. "I'm sorry." She pulled in a shuddering breath. "I can't do anything right. Let me leave. Please."

"Sweetie, that's not going to happen."

Her face crumpled, and her lower lip trembled. By the God, she was breaking his heart. Few Daonain survived clanless, so why did she want to retreat back into the wilderness?

She didn't. He'd seen her light up when he walked in her room or when Angie and the healer visited. This pretty bear loved company, even though her awkwardness spoke of an unknowable amount of time alone.

"I don't deserve to live among the clan." Sounded like guilt. Mistakes in the past.

How could he get her off this trail? If ever there was a blundering bear when it came to talking through emotions, that would be him. Perhaps, so was she. *Start there.* "I don't know why you feel so guilty, but we'll talk about it later."

From the way her lips closed together, he could see that discussion would happen right about…never. Where the fuck was Calum when he needed him?

"But, darlin', we're bears," he said. "We don't hurt others because we want to play with our prey like cats. We're not wolves to be pushed into idiocy by the pack. We stumble into stuff because sometimes we're just clumsy. Yeah?"

Her eyes were still filled with tears, but she nodded.

There. He had a scent to follow, to lead her up and out of this fucking chasm. "Can't go through life without screwing up. The Mother didn't make us perfect. All a bear can do after busting something is to try to make amends, much as he can.

Even if you can't fix the damage"—like broken hearts—"you move on, living best as possible."

She dropped her gaze, staring at where his big hand engulfed hers.

THE GIGANTIC BEAR had gigantic hands. His fingers were callused to the roughness of tree bark yet, despite their strength, held hers gently. The muscles on his forearms were thick, even his wrist bones were huge. He made her feel…little.

Cared for.

He'd stopped talking, letting her turn his words over the way she'd turn over logs to see what rewards were beneath. Was he right?

He said everyone screwed up. *Truth.*

Bears blundered. Everyone knew that. And she hadn't deliberately hurt anyone. She'd never had the heart to be cruel. *Truth.*

"I don't think the Mother approves of shifters throwing away her gift of life." She flinched internally at his accuracy. She wouldn't deliberately harm herself, but trying to survive when each movement still hurt and her bones weren't melded together would achieve nearly the same thing.

She hadn't been thinking, just reacting.

With each *trawsfur*, the Mother's love would fill her, letting her know she was cherished. To be careless with this gift of life would be wrong. Hurtful to the Goddess. *I'm sorry, Mother of All.*

Ben said to make amends. If only she could. Gladly, she would have made apologies and stayed, and tried to be daughter to the grieving families, but the Cosantir had banished her. To return now would…would accomplish nothing except resurrect the pain of the bereaved.

Perhaps, she could give of herself here, instead?

As for the rest of Ben's advice: …*you move on, living best as possible.* What if people found out what she'd done? "They won't want me here," she whispered to herself. "I..."

A snort reminded her someone else was in the room—a pissed-off bear. She looked up.

At the campground, he'd calmly shifted to a grizzly—the most terrifying of animals. Now, in the same way, his easygoing expression had transformed to unyielding strength.

"You gonna let others dictate what you do with your life?" His Texas drawl had thickened with his annoyance.

"I—"

"Are these others your mates? Your Cosantir?"

He obviously thought she'd meant someone specific, not an entire town. But she shook her head.

"A bear doesn't answer to anyone else. We're not wolves who need someone handing us orders." He paused before prompting, "Yeah?"

He had no understanding of the reaction of his clan, and yet... Again, he had a point. She was being a coward, running rather than sticking it out. Could she manage to show this territory she had something to offer?

"You're stuck here for a while, li'l bear. Don't worry about the bedroom situation. We got it covered," Ben said. "But while you're here, you can work this—whatever it is—out and move past it." He aimed an uncompromising look at her.

As she nodded, a different kind of guilt washed over her. She'd caused trouble, had hit him, had taken his time. What a sad repayment of his generosity. "I'm sorry, Ben," she said softly. "I won't try to run again, at least not until I can do it on four legs."

His face softened. "That's a good bear."

A good bear. The same words master bard had used.

When she smiled at the memory, the look in Ben's eyes changed to...to something she didn't quite recognize. And then she did. It was a male's lazy appreciation of a female.

He ran his knuckles down her cheek.

With his controlled caress and his heated gaze, she was suddenly far too aware of her unclothed state. Of the way the sheet curved over her breasts. Of his strength when he had yanked her back onto the bed despite her pounding fists. Of the warmth of his fingers on her face and the stern line of his jaw.

His head tilted, and in a very deliberate move, he pressed a kiss to her wrist. His firm lips were warm.

She shivered.

A crease appeared in his cheek with his slow smile. "Since the healer said you can escape this room tomorrow, I'll fetch you for breakfast in the morning.

As he left the room, she sniffed her wrist, knowing what he must have scented—the fragrance of a female's interest.

Oh, this was bad. Very bad.

DOWNSTAIRS IN THE great room, Ryder sat on the upholstered chair and dug through Minette's bag. "Here, kitten. Do you want to play with these?" He scattered several blocks in front of her.

Ben would come down soon. That would be the time to raise the possibility the guest was healthier than she was letting on.

Of course, he could be wrong.

But, by the God, if all she wanted was Ben's status and money, she'd better rethink. Ryder knew too well the pain of being used, and he wouldn't let Ben be hurt.

On the dark red area rug, Minette set her favorite stuffed cat to one side and picked up the sanded chunks of wood...with one hand. Her thumb was in her mouth.

His heart ached. She'd made progress over the past week, had almost stopped flinching with his every movement, and started to play, even if quietly. But being faced with new people and places set her back. Poor little cub.

Damn Genevieve for not sending him word about Minette. Damn him for avoiding the Deschutes Territory. For not finding his daughter sooner. For not having a stable family to bring her into.

"I'm sorry, sweetheart," he whispered.

"You talking to me?" Ben said from the door.

Ryder jumped. "Fucking grizzly. How do you walk without making any noise?"

"Talent. Training." Ben dropped onto the L-shaped sectional with a sigh.

"Problems?"

"I'd told Emma I only had two bedrooms, so she was worried about occupying one with y'all here. She tried to leave, even though she can barely stand."

Did Ben believe her? One of Genevieve's most effective tricks was to dissolve into tears and look helpless. "She cried? And, being too weak to walk, she waited for you...so you could tell her not to leave, right?"

"Not exactly. You've turned cynical, cat." Ben showed his bloodstained hands. "She was so determined to get dressed, she tore open her wound."

Oh. Fuck. The scent was definitely hers. She had a wound, not an illness. Why had he assumed she was pretending to be sick? Why hadn't he asked?

Because Genevieve had taken him in whenever she played the ill card.

He snorted in self-disgust. "I got caught up in chasing my own tail. Sorry. What injury does she have?"

Ben hesitated. "Got her leg busted and sliced up in the mountains. But, ah...she was alone and didn't get found for a couple of weeks. The healer repaired what he could, but full healing will take longer."

Ben went into the kitchen. The faucet came on as he washed his hands.

A female? Hurt and alone? And she hadn't seen a healer for two weeks? He imagined the pretty female upstairs. Trying to get dressed. Hurting herself. And he'd been pretty fucking cold to her. Fuck, Griz should smack him upside the head.

Ben returned with two glasses of iced tea and set one in front of Ryder. He smiled at Minette's construction of a balanced Roman arch-type bridge. "You got a budding mechanical engineer there."

"She reminds me of you with her constant building projects. But she seems to be more into design than construction."

"How about you?" Ben's gaze stayed on the cub. "What have you been doing all these years?"

"I…" The question slashed claws across his heart. Littermates stayed together. The bond between brothers reached deep into their souls. One shouldn't have to ask the other about jobs and mates.

But life was what it was.

Thorny undergrowth or not, the direct route was often the best trail to take back home. He'd simply lay out the intervening years. "When Genevieve and I lived together, I started selling my woodworking at craft fairs and festivals. After we split, I moved to the Garibaldi Territory in Canada. Worked winters, did the fair circuit during the summers."

"Do you need to go get your tools?"

Ryder hesitated before baring his hopes. "I wanted to mend things between us. Emptied my shop and was already on my way here when I heard about Minette. I left the trailer in Bellingham, so I didn't look…presumptuous."

Ben actually grinned. "Presumptuous."

"Yeah, well, if you have a place for my stuff, Minette and I'll go get the trailer tomorrow."

"Got a building out back. It'd be perfect for you." Ben smiled slowly. "I might have known you'd not give up your wood. Bet you do well."

Ryder's shoulders eased. "Aye. In between the craft fair tidbits, I make custom furniture, which pays really well. Heather, a wolf in Rainier Territory, taught me to invest the profits in the stock market. I've got money, bro."

"Yeah? You've always been canny with finances."

"I don't lack for dollars." The next words emerged with more difficulty. "It's family I'm short on."

For an eternity, his brother didn't speak. Finally came the acknowledgment and agreement. "Yeah."

Maybe the way home would be filled with obstacles, but they'd found the right trail.

Chapter Eight

T HE NEXT EVENING, Emma stood at the top of the stairs
and tried to calculate how to get down. She was allowed
only partial weight bearing on her injured leg, the healer had
said. A cane would be useful, but she didn't have one.

And, by the Goddess, she wouldn't let Ben continue carrying her to the kitchen, as he had for both breakfast and lunch.
She'd get herself to supper. The scent of fried chicken drifting
up the stairs was a lovely incentive.

Putting both hands on the railing, she jumped down one
step. It jarred her leg but worked. She set her teeth and moved
her hands lower on the railing.

"If you jump down one more step, I'll paddle your ass and
tell the healer." Ben's growl carried clearly from the dining room.

Emma stiffened.

He stalked up the stairs, glowering fiercely enough she'd
have retreated if both her legs had been working.

"Ben, I need to—"

"You need to obey the healer's orders, li'l female, or you'll
get yourself in a peck of trouble." The rumble of his rough voice
was oddly soothing. Effortlessly, he scooped her up, his strength
reassuring. His massive size was always surprising, like viewing a
mountain after being raised in the foothills.

He carried her into the center of the house, through the dining area where an old-fashioned brass chandelier hung over the gleaming oak dining table, under the wide archway into the kitchen. The wood flooring and trim work in the modernized Victorian was a beautiful russet color. Off-white kitchen cupboards hung over cream-colored granite countertops. Golden, hand-painted wall tiles brightened the backsplash behind the sink and oven. Despite being enormous, the kitchen was cheerful and comfortable.

Of course, bears were known for making their dens comfortable.

Ben seated her on a stool at the square center island and arranged her injured leg on another leather-topped stool. "Now, say thank you and stay put." He gripped her shoulder firmly and waited for her answer.

"Thank you, Ben," she said obediently.

"Much better."

When his dark blue eyes crinkled at the corners with his easy smile, the stool somehow disappeared from under her, leaving her floating in the air.

With a satisfied glint in his eyes, he patted her.

Taking a calming breath, she looked around.

Ben's littermate stood at the counter, mashing potatoes with an unreadable expression. If he was less gorgeous, she'd be more comfortable. Even worse, his darkly menacing attitude reminded her of Andre.

On the other side of the island, the little girl she'd seen the previous night was staring at her. Emma winked and saw the child's eyes widen.

The male and his cub had been gone for breakfast and lunch, and she'd been disappointed at the child's absence. During her apprenticeship as a bard, she'd instructed cubs in the clan, teaching stories and songs. Children were the most beautiful gift of the Mother.

"Emma, you've met my littermate, Ryder, aye?" When she nodded, Ben started to put his hand on the girl's shoulder and stopped. "This is Minette."

The cub was shy. Very, very shy. Oh, Emma knew the feeling. Rather than forcing the cubling to engage in conversation, Emma simply smiled.

After an uncertain look, first at Ben, then Emma, the girl returned her attention to the pile of freshly picked peas in front of her. With remarkable concentration, she pried open a pod and picked out the peas one by one.

Emma smothered a laugh. She'd done the same as a child during her frequent escapes to the gardens. No food tasted as fine as garden peas. In the same way, the time spent with the elderly, wizened gardener had nourished her soul.

"We're having chicken, mashed potatoes, and salad for supper," Ben said. "Sound all right?"

Her mouth was watering from the smells emitting from the oven. Aside from what she'd scavenged, she hadn't enjoyed cooked food in three years. No matches, no pots, no salt. "Wonderful. What can I do to help?"

"Nothing." When she narrowed her eyes at him, he held up a hand. "Sorry, should have known. How about you cut up the vegetables for the salad?"

"I'd love to." Her whole day brightened. Her mother had never let her in the kitchen.

The cook can handle it. A Cavanaugh doesn't do menial labor.

This Cavanaugh was happy to do anything she could to help. "Just give me a knife and whatever you need chopped."

The other male eyed her with an awfully cynical gaze. What was he thinking—that she'd sneak extra bites when no one was looking? Or maybe he didn't trust her with his cubling.

Despite being the most stunning male she'd ever seen, he

apparently had the sociability of a wolverine.

Ben placed a knife, cutting board, and a mass of cleaned carrots in front of her and returned to preparing the rest of the salad at the counter.

After emptying the last pea pod, Minette started watching Emma, obviously wanting a carrot. As soon as Ryder looked away, Emma rolled over a cut-up piece.

The girl popped the carrot in her mouth.

At the crunching sound, Ryder turned. By the Mother, what a worried stare. He really didn't trust Emma, did he?

She glanced at his brother.

Ben winked.

Bouncing slightly, Minette inched her fingers forward on the table, seemingly unwilling to ask for more.

Emma waited until Ryder returned to his potatoes. She teasingly waggled a carrot piece over the tiny fingers before setting it in the child's hand.

Minette's mouth opened, but no laugh emerged. No sound at all. In fact, had Emma ever heard her speak?

"Um." Emma frowned at Ben. "She doesn't…"

The other male answered. "Hasn't for about a year, apparently."

"Oh." Although Minette was obviously related to the brothers, the *apparently* implied she was a recent addition to the household. "She hasn't lived with you long? Where is her mother—your mate?"

"Minette has been with me about a week." Ryder's mouth compressed into a straight line. "Her mother isn't here."

Emma couldn't read him. Was that grief? Had the mother died?

When he gave his daughter a worried look, Emma saw the child was sucking her thumb, her gaze down. Yes, the mother must have died, or Minette would be with her. Males didn't raise cubs otherwise.

No wonder the two males appeared at a loss with the cub.

"Hey, Minette," Emma whispered.

After a second, the cubling lifted her head.

"I'll give you a carrot for how many years old you are." Thank the Goddess that children diverted easily.

Interest dawned in the big hazel eyes.

"Are you two years old?" Emma held up two fingers and got a headshake no. "Or three years old?" Three fingers.

No.

Emma added another finger.

A flicker of a smile appeared. A tiny nod. Using her other hand, Minette arranged four small fingers in return.

"Very good, sweetie. You're a big girl, aren't you?" Emma grinned when the thin shoulders straightened proudly. "Four years old means four carrot pieces." Counting one by one, she set each slice in front of the girl.

Ryder made a grumbling noise deep in his throat—no, he didn't trust Emma at all—but his expression also revealed pride and worry. Maybe her opinion of him had been hasty. What would she have given as a child to have a father so involved in her care?

Laughing, Ben tugged on her braid. "I'd better remove those carrots before you give them all away." He swiped the pieces into the salad bowl, leaving a couple behind.

Emma immediately shared them...with her new cubling friend.

Chapter Nine

THAT WEEKEND, BEN walked into his office in the octagonal tower. His feet dragged as if his father—Arnold—had sent him to cut a switch to be punished. Damned if he wouldn't rather be whipped than have to fill out invoices.

Ignoring the piles of paperwork, he stood in the center of the octagonal room and took in the view. The tall windows on the four front-facing sides looked out toward the white-topped western mountains. The descending sun had silhouetted the peaks in gold.

By the God, what he'd give to be roaming the forest now. The cool evening wind would sweep off the glaciers and carry a brisk hint of snow. Birds would be chirping sleepily, and pixies would retire to their hollows…before the owls came out to hunt. Before bedding down for the night, deer and elk would visit their favorite watering holes.

Ben agreed. An hour sipping an icy brew and shooting the bull with friends at the tavern made the day's labors worthwhile.

Eventide was a special time.

Unfortunately, rather than a wilderness run or a trip to the tavern, he'd be doing paperwork. *Fuck*.

He heard the thud of Ryder's boots in the great room and heading closer. The thumps stopped, and from the doorway, his brother regarded the room silently.

Paperwork buried the heavy walnut desk, drafting table, and bookshelves. Piles of bills were mixed with invoices, forms, requisitions, and payroll statements. "There's a mess."

"You got a talent for stating the obvious," Ben countered sourly. He leafed through the papers on the desk, hoping to find the school addition specs.

"You used to have a talent for staying on top of things."

Yeah, well, back then, Ryder'd been around to help out.

But blaming his brother for the mess wasn't...completely...fair. "The business doubled over the past couple of years. You know those customizations I'd started putting into shifters' houses?"

Ryder nodded.

"Got real popular. The local shifters alone keep me swamped with jobs." Ben found a bill he'd forgotten to send out and set it on another pile. "The number of hellhounds has increased in the territory, which means more patrolling for cahirs. In addition, out-of-territory cahirs are coming here to learn from Shay and Zeb how to kill hellhounds. I help with the training."

"And now the Cosantir's dumped an injured female in your house."

"Yep. I don't have enough hours in the day. Paperwork is low priority."

"Got it." Ryder leaned against the doorframe. "Want help?"

"From you?" The memory of long-held pain edged Ben's voice. "Seriously? Haven't we wandered this trail before?" The rancor in his kneejerk response was a surprise.

Ryder stiffened as if he'd been knifed, then his expression changed to resignation. And guilt.

Ben opened and closed his hands as if the gesture would release the bitterness accrued over the years. Dammit, he'd missed his brother. What was he doing?

It'd been bad when they were separated at five. Reuniting at twenty, they'd traveled the country, brawling, mating the females, and learning about each other.

In Siskiyou Territory, Ben turned contractor and started a construction business. Building and remodeling houses fulfilled his dreams.

Ryder preferred smaller projects—the woodworking inside a home, building furniture, fireplace mantels, railings. He'd apprenticed with a master craftsman—and added on accounting classes for fun. *By the God, fun?*

But they'd both been happy...or so Ben had thought.

However, the discovery he'd killed his mother in childbirth knocked him sideways. And then Ryder'd abandoned everything and left with Genevieve. Hurting and alone, Ben'd torn up roots and wandered north to start over in Cold Creek.

He'd been more resentful than he'd realized.

Ben shook his head. By Herne's hide and hooves, he was an idiot, clinging to old pain like a child. "Sorry, bro." He scratched his shoulders on the rough doormat he'd nailed to one wall. "I'll take you up on your offer. Thank you."

Ryder closed his eyes for a second, pulling in a breath. His cave-deep voice emerged uneven. "I'm sorry, too. When you said you wouldn't lifemate, I couldn't see how a male could live without a female. But leaving—I hurt you in a way I never intended."

Yeah, he had. But the lines on Ryder's face exposed an equal amount of pain. And Ben's decision about never lifemating affected them both. Should have been discussed. "We both fucked up."

A corner of Ryder's mouth tipped up. "I missed working with you."

"Me, too." Ben asked the question they'd been dancing

around. "Is this temporary or are you going to stay?"

Ryder met his eyes. "I want to stay. I want Minette to have a family."

Well. Family was a good word. A fine word. "I want that, too." He paused. "And Genevieve?"

Ryder hesitated. "She obviously didn't care for the cub. But...she kept Minette. I don't know why or what she'll do now."

Ben wasn't surprised Genevieve was a crappy mother. Caring for a cub would take time from herself. Hopefully, she'd count Minette's loss as a win, because he found the thought of losing the cub intolerable. "With the Mother's grace, she'll stay away."

"Aye." Ryder rubbed his jaw with his knuckles—a typical feline quirk. Did all cats groom themselves when discomfited?

Ben smothered a smile. Felt like old times.

After studying the room, Ryder straightened. "There's not enough space for both of us in here. Got anywhere else? You also need a hell of a lot bigger filing cabinet." His gaze lingered on the ancient computer, the very one he'd bought for Ben six years before. He gave a snort of disbelief. "And equipment upgrades."

"I can see you're going to be a pain in the tail." Ben didn't even try to conceal his grin.

Chapter Ten

EMMA HAD REACHED the great room all by herself. *Success.* Unfortunately, she hurt so badly now she might throw up. Pain and nausea certainly shattered a sense of victory into splinters. What a way to enjoy a Sunday.

As she sat unmoving on the couch, the throbbing in her leg started to subside. Finally.

After the males spent the day setting up Ryder's equipment in a shop out back, Ben had taken Minette to the town park, and Ryder'd left to visit the tavern.

How could she resist the opportunity to see how mobile she could be? It was time. She'd been in Ben's house a week now, doing nothing productive and taking up his time, although he'd never indicated he resented her presence.

Ryder, however… Although he was polite, she sure didn't get the impression he liked her. Or trusted her.

She couldn't stay helpless.

As the aching in her leg decreased, she started to settle into the peace of the house.

The werebear had created a wonder of a "cave" for himself. The great room's oak flooring was covered with a mahogany rug. A painting of a mountain sunset hung over the creamy marble fireplace. Tall umbrella plants in hip-high, bronze planters stood next to filled, built-in bookshelves.

Bracketed by two armchairs, a dark leather, L-shaped sectional with a leather ottoman dominated the room's center. On each side of the room, small forests of plants basked in the sunlight from tall, leaded glass windows.

Truly, he had made himself a wilderness den.

Rattling at the front door made her jump—and hiss with renewed pain. Ben's rumbling laugh announced his arrival. A minute later, he entered, bending over to hold hands with Minette. Looked like he'd finally succeeded in winning her trust.

Emma smiled. Watching the two big males courting the cub was heartwarming.

Ben started across the room, saw Emma, and his brows drew together.

She stiffened, feeling a chill run through her veins. Maybe she shouldn't have come downstairs. What if he didn't want her in his living space when he wasn't home?

"The healer told you to stay off your leg," he growled.

Her leg? He was upset because…he cared enough to worry about her? As the realization melted something hard inside her, she smiled at him.

His frown disappeared. As his eyes warmed, she couldn't help seeing him as…male. So very, very male.

"I-I'm fine," she said hastily. "I used the railing on the stairs." Nevertheless, each hop to a lower step had jarred painfully. She nodded at the nearby wooden chair. "Down here, I used the chair as a crutch. I didn't put any weight on my leg."

His thickly muscled arms folded over his brawny chest. "Hopping on one leg isn't exactly safe, li'l bear."

Oh, he was a stubborn bear. "Maybe. But, I—" She broke off when Minette approached the sectional. "Hi, sweetheart."

The cubling sucked her thumb and watched Emma with her big, wary eyes.

Emma dared to reach out and touch her cheek. Children. Their joy and laughter, and even squabbles, were a delight to the heart.

Minette edged forward far enough to touch Emma's braid, stroking it with her little fingers. After a minute, she rubbed it against her cheek and leaned against Emma's uninjured leg, still sucking her thumb.

Emma's lips twitched. As a cub, she'd hidden her security blankie in her bed so her mother wouldn't destroy it. How wonderful that Minette considered anything of Emma's to be comforting.

Looking up, Emma saw Ben's tanned face had softened with a smile.

After taking a minute to savor the simple pleasure of companions, Emma asked, "What's in your bag, Minette?"

The child crossed the room to get her green bag from the bookcase.

"She trusted you faster than she did me," Ben grumbled before grinning. "Good job."

"Children like me." Her teacher had said a bard usually possessed a charisma that drew people in. Emma rather thought her "charisma" only worked on children. The master had said he'd never met a shy bard before, either. Then again, perhaps no bards had ever had mothers as cruel as Emma's.

Returning, Minette opened her bag to show off the brightly colored Legos and small plastic animals.

As the cubling leaned against her again, Emma pulled in a contented breath. Daonain weren't meant to live alone, and she had been so very lonely. "Can you make something for me?"

Minette plopped down on the thick rug and dumped the contents of the bag.

"She's an amazing builder." Ben sat down right beside Emma. To her consternation, his weight sagged the cushions and tilted her against his rock-hard chest. Rather than moving away, he extended his arm along the back of the sectional.

She frowned up at him.

He only smiled. "I take it you got tired of being in bed?"

Every breath brought her the scents of masculine sweat and musk, faint traces of sap from the wood he'd been cutting, the clean smell of laundry soap…and a whiff of his interest.

Under his appreciative gaze, she felt small and feminine. Deep inside her, the female stirrings flickered to life.

No. No, no, no. She'd given herself a lecture after the last time this happened. No interest. The Gathering had proven she couldn't be trusted. Disaster had followed in the wake of her vanity. Never, never again.

She shoved herself up off the sectional. Too fast, she realized, as her weight came down on her injured leg. A burning pain knifed through her leg, and she whimpered.

"Dammit, female."

Mother's blessing, but it hurt. Like someone was stabbing the mended bones over and over with a long sword. Tears filling her eyes, she sank down, steadied by strong hands. "How stupid." Her voice came out humiliatingly shaky.

"Shhh." He pulled her against his big chest and held her quietly as the searing agony lessened.

With a low sigh, she sagged against him.

"It's all right, Minette," he said quietly. "Emma hurt her leg. When she moves fast, it hurts."

Oh, no. She'd scared the cub. She blinked away the tears and saw the cubling studying her, little brow furrowed. When Emma managed a smile, Minette moved her toys closer and settled on the rug next to the couch.

"There, now, you worried us both." Cupping her cheek with one hand, Ben used his thumb to stroke the wetness from her skin. "You don't need to run from me, Emma. Am I that unlikable? Frightening?"

She'd hurt his feelings. Oh, my Goddess, she'd never meant to make him feel bad. "No. No. But I'm not… I don't do male-female stuff. Ever." If the Daonain had nuns, she'd enter a convent. But shifters didn't practice celibacy—quite the reverse. Female shifters went into heat once a month, and with every full moon, the Daonain gathered and mated, and ensured their survival.

"A tad difficult to avoid male-female stuff, isn't it?" The amusement had returned to his captivating voice. He not only had the rough, deep bass common to male werebears, but the bright descant of laughter in it was like moonlight on a dark lake.

"Well…" What could she say?

Not waiting for her answer, he stroked his knuckles along her cheek, and this time, his touch wasn't for comfort.

The long, slow caress set desire simmering in her veins and shook her with the long-forgotten feel of a male's hands on her body. But more than this would not—could not—be. Her mouth firmed. "Avoidance is difficult, but not impossible. Hibernation helps."

"Hibernation?" His intent eyes deepened to the intense hue of a mountain bluebird. "You're not pulling my tail? You don't attend Gatherings? How long were you in the forest alone?"

She took his questions one-by-one. "Yes. I'm not. I don't. And it's none of your business." He was right, though. All too soon, she'd have to think about what she'd do for the next full moon.

"But"—he obviously forced himself to stop—"all right." After a second, he shook his head. "You're safe with me, li'l bear. I have no interest in mating or in looking for a lifemate." As a mountain wind would reveal the granite beneath the snow, she watched his jaw harden. "I enjoy touching, but I mate only because it's required."

Why did disappointment mingle with her relief? "I thought all males wanted to mate. Why don't you?"

"I reckon my reasons are none of your business, darlin'." An easy smile took the sting from the words.

"I suppose that's fair."

"It is." He curled his warm fingers over her shoulder.

Why did he keep touching her? Stroking her skin? The sensuous pleasure sent captivating tingles up her center.

"Minette and I swung by to pick you up," he said. "We're going to the Wild Hunt Tavern to join Ryder. Are you ready to get out of the house?"

"Really?" She bounced in delight—and winced as the movement jarred her leg. "Ouch."

She forgave him his roaring laugh since at least he hadn't called her an idiot. And, if he'd spoken truth about not wanting to mate—and she'd heard no lie in his voice—she could stay for a while longer.

He'd take her to the Wild Hunt. From what Ben had said, the tavern was the life-spring of this territory.

Only…there would be people there. Anxiety sent cold fingers up her spine. After not speaking to anyone for three years, the thought of a whole bar filled with people was intimidating.

She lifted her chin. She could manage. She *would*.

She was no longer banished. They didn't know her history. And it was time to stop hiding in a cave. "Let's go."

IN THE WILD Hunt Tavern, the warmth from the crackling fire slowly loosened Ryder's tight muscles. The leather couch was comfortable, especially with his boots up on the battered coffee table. Foam tickled his lips as he enjoyed a malty Guinness. His back and shoulders ached from unloading his belongings earlier this week and setting up the shop behind the house today.

It had felt damned good to unpack. Fuck, he'd missed feeling settled. Missed having a real home. Missed Ben. And now, the parts of his life, scattered years ago, were slotting back into place like well-crafted tongue-and-groove flooring.

He'd never missed Genevieve or Farway, either. Because of her glee in goading males—including him—to fight, he'd never felt at home in the shifter community there.

If his obsession with Genevieve hadn't damaged the littermate bond, he and Ben would have been well settled into the stable life they'd both craved. Neither of them had grown up feeling secure. Ryder grimaced. His father had moved from territory to territory, female to female. Ben's father had been mentally unsound—paranoid. As young males, he and Ben had shared the dream of a permanent home, but Ben had gone after it.

He took another drink of his beer. By the God, he'd been a stupid young male, and his lesson had been a hard one. Now he knew that living with the wrong female was far more ruinous than having none at all. Staring into the fire, he lifted his drink and spoke softly, "To you, Genevieve, for the worst year of my life and the greatest gift a male can receive."

"Sounds like a contradiction, don't you think, Zeb?" The green-eyed man who settled down on the opposing couch was about six-five with collar-length, light brown hair. Thin scars, apparently from werecat fights, covered his hands and arms. As with Ben, a blue, blade-shaped scar over one cheekbone marked him as a cahir.

The other male grunted an affirmative and took the adjacent leather chair. Also a cahir, Zeb had hair and eyes as black as Ryder's, but his complexion held the reddish tint of mixed Native American ancestry. The warrior was not only scarred to hell and gone, but somehow gave the impression he'd rather kill than converse.

"Cahirs." Ryder felt dumb as a gnome. Accustomed to living with humans, he'd forgotten how keen shifters' ears were.

"Welcome to Cold Creek." The first male leaned forward and held out a hand. "Alec McGregor." The firelight glinted off the small badge on his shoulder.

"Police officer?" Both a cahir and cop? He shook the man's hand, feeling the strength and the calluses of a fighter.

"Sheriff," Alec corrected easily. He grinned. "The male there is Zeb Damron. He and his brother run the Wildwood Lodge. Be warned—Zeb chatters worse than a blue jay. He'll talk your tail right off."

Zeb's glare should have sliced the cop in two.

Ryder smothered a laugh at the familiar werecat humor. Ben'd predicted he'd like the local cahirs. "Ryder Llwyd. Ben's brother."

"He mentioned you'd moved in." Alec glanced over his shoulder, caught the attention of the female waitress, and held up two fingers.

Not interrupting her conversation with a battered older shifter, the barmaid nodded. Short and pleasantly full-breasted with rich, walnut colored hair, she was almost as pretty as Ben's lushly curved female.

Emma's eyes were stunning though—the exact color of golden oak. He frowned. Fuck it all, he would *not* become attracted to her. One of them needed to keep his head. Forcing her from his thoughts, he asked the cahirs, "Ben said hellhounds have increased in this territory and pretty much everywhere. How come?"

"The demon-dogs have always hidden in cities and preyed on the humans." Alec scowled. "But now "developments" are springing up in our mountains. Trouble is, once a hellhound catches the scent of a shifter, they're never satisfied with human prey again."

A splinter of ice formed in Ryder's belly. When he'd been in Rainier Territory, a hellhound had broken into a shifter's home and slaughtered everyone inside so savagely the bodies were unrecognizable.

How could he risk Minette getting hurt? And yet... "Seems no place is safe any longer."

"No. Hellhounds are in every territory now." Zeb had a voice like a badly maintained gravel truck.

"Ben said you're teaching cahirs how to fight the demon-dogs?" Ryder asked.

"Aye. Zeb and Shay have three students." Alec's jaw turned hard. "A hellhound was scented in the area, so chances are good they'll get hands-on experience with the coming dark of the moon."

Ryder eyed the scars on Zeb's neck and face. "When Ben was chosen by the God to become a cahir, he got extra height and muscles. Females flocked to him—and I envied him."

"Past tense?" Alec asked.

"I've seen the cost." The pain, the scarring, the deaths. Yet he knew Ben and these males didn't begrudge the price. By the God, his brother made him proud.

Zeb's gaze sharpened on something behind Ryder, and amusement lit his dark eyes. "That your cub?"

Ryder turned. His shy daughter was edging around the clus-ters of people, heading straight for him. He couldn't suppress his grin. "Oh, yeah."

"Aren't you just a cutie!" A gray-haired female at the next table held her hand out.

Eyes wide, Minette scurried away from the female, then launched herself at Ryder like a tiny missile, thumping against his knees.

"My Minette." Heart full, he picked her up and nuzzled her cheek. "You're safe, kitten." Frightened, she'd come to him.

Trusted him to protect her. Had he ever received a greater compliment? When her arms wrapped around his neck, he discovered that love was more than a feeling—it could swell inside a male's chest until he couldn't speak.

Settling her on his lap, he looked around for his brother.

Approaching more slowly, Ben carried Emma in his arms. The sight sent a pang of worry through Ryder.

Why did the female have to be so pretty? Everything about her—from the silky hair to the smooth skin, to the soft curves— enticed a male. He wasn't even sure he liked her, and he wanted to touch. Ben didn't stand a chance.

"Ben. Good to see you." Alec rose, emptying the couch. "Put her here."

"Thanks." Ben set Emma down so she leaned against the couch arm. He propped her right leg up on cushions.

"I don't need the entire couch." She struggled to swing her leg down. "I can sit like a normal person."

He set a hand on her good leg, easily pinning her in place. "No, darlin'. You just stay put right there."

"But—"

Grinning, Ben ruffled her hair as if she were a cub.

Her glare made her appear Minette's age, and Ryder chuckled. But when she turned her big amber eyes on him—those damned appealing eyes—his amusement faded. He nodded. "Emma."

"Hello, Ryder," she said with a careful politeness. The cautiousness in her voice reminded him of when he'd hurt his back and how carefully he moved to avoid a painful muscle spasm.

The thought of a female being wary around him was...distressing.

Yet when she surveyed the room, her tense posture didn't ease. Her scent held a trace of fear, like that of a cub venturing from its den for the first time.

Ryder's protective instincts roused. What was here to alarm her? The people?

Kneeling up in his lap, Minette put her hands on his cheeks and turned his head. A glowing lizard twisted within the flames in the fireplace. There hadn't been a fireplace in Genevieve's house, had there? And Ben hadn't lit a fire in the great room. "That's a salamander, Minette. A young one."

As his cub bounced on his knees, he noticed Emma was watching Minette's delight with a sweet expression the kitten's own mother had never shown. In the tangle of worries in his chest, one strand unknotted. Unlike his father's females, this one apparently had a soft spot for cubs.

With a werecat's silent gait, the brunette barmaid arrived with the drinks. "Zeb, here you go." She handed him a beer and gave the other to the sheriff. "One for you, although I doubt you deserve it. I still can't believe you told Jamie she could stay overnight with her friend."

"She'll be fine. And the house will be empty so Calum and I can do evil things to you tonight." With his free arm, Alec pulled her against him for a no-holds-barred kiss more typical of full moon lust.

Spotting the matching silvery bracelets, Ryder realized the two were lifemated. He exchanged an amused glance with Ben.

"Bad cat." With a skillful twist and a powerful punch, the barmaid freed herself.

"Assault and battery," Alec mock-wheezed, holding his gut. "I just happen to have an empty jail cell for such a violent offender."

"Isn't it a shame you gave me a key to the cells when you made me a deputy?"

"Well, damn."

Grinning, she stepped out of his reach and smiled at Emma. "Ignore the barbarian. I'm Vicki. I've wanted to meet you—but first, what can I get you to drink?"

"Emma." Her return smile was tentative. "Didn't you just say you're a deputy?"

"I am. But when off duty, I play barmaid if the Wild Hunt needs extra help."

"How wonderful to stay so busy," Emma said. "As soon as my leg heals up, I'll be job hunting. I hope I can find something."

"Don't worry. We'll figure something out," Vicki said with calm assurance.

Leaning on the couch, Ben said under his breath to Ryder, "Vicki used to be a Marine sergeant."

That explained the confidence and military bearing.

Ryder studied Emma's hopeful expression. Apparently, the female didn't object to working for a living and didn't plan to impose on Ben forever. Another knot of worry unwound.

Vicki turned toward the men. "Calum wanted to talk with you all in the portal room." She smiled at Ryder. "The room is one of our entries to the forest for when you want to run in animal form. He'll give you an orientation."

"Good plan." Ben gave Ryder a hand up.

"I'm afraid the cub will have to stay here," Alec said.

Ryder shook his head, "I can't leave her. Maybe—"

"I'd be happy to watch her," Emma said hesitantly.

Entrust her with his cub? He'd rather chew off his left paw. But…did he have a reason to distrust this female who'd already befriended his daughter? "All right." He set his daughter down by the couch.

Without any hesitation, Minette crawled onto Emma's lap and snuggled close with her head pillowed on the soft breasts. After wrapping her fingers around the female's honey-colored braid, she tucked her thumb in her mouth and fell asleep within a breath.

Ryder doubted the cub trusted her own mother that completely. "Thank you, Emma."

"Be at ease, father of Minette," she said softly. "I will guard your cub with my life."

SEEING RYDER'S SURPRISE, Emma regretted her impulsive statement, but she'd meant every word. His unreasonable aversion to her didn't matter. No one would harm this little one while she was here.

After a second, he nodded.

Ben bent and ran his hand down her hair in an unspoken leave-taking. As he straightened, a sense of warmth lingered along with his masculine scent.

"Let's go." Vicki led the cahirs and Ryder away.

As the minutes passed, Emma cuddled Minette close, brushed her lips over the cub's silky hair, and inhaled the scent of little girl sweetness. Like well-banked coals, contentment was a steady warmth. She had a child in her arms, the pleasure of being useful, laughter and conversation around her—everything she'd lost three years ago. She'd be happy to sit here forever.

"You nailed it!" The yell came from an alcove holding two pool tables.

At the loud cheers and clapping, Minette roused. Her tiny face pulled in a worried scrunch as she pushed up and looked around for her father.

Ben and Ryder never spoke about their mate, but if they were caring for this cub, the mother must be dead. How horrible for Minette.

"Your father will be back soon, sweetheart," Emma told her. But now what? The child was too anxious to sleep again, and a tavern wouldn't have toys available.

Lacking blocks and dolls, Emma knew only one way to divert a bored child. "Let me tell you a story, my small cub." She'd spent three years entertaining easily bored pixies; one sleepy child would be a joy. Her voice slid right into the traditional story-telling rhythm.

Without any hesitation, Minette laid her head down. Sucking her thumb slowly, she rubbed Emma's braid against her cheek.

"Long and long ago, in the very dawn of the days of the Daonain, wolf-shifters found a baby girl lying in a burrow in the wide, green forest. The pack named her Rhonwen, for her hair was the shining silver of a mid-winter moon."

Emma's miserable years of loneliness disappeared as she recounted her favorite story of all time—the early days of the legendary bear-shifter. By the Goddess, how she'd missed using all her skill to entertain her clan, to draw her audience with her into the heart of a story.

As she brought the story to a glorious finish, she noticed Vicki near the fireplace, probably checking to see if aught was needed.

Emma smiled. *We are fine, thank you.*

With a token salute, the barmaid-deputy moved away.

Emma looked down at her audience of one. "Do you want a song this time? Maybe one about a kitten like you?"

Minette gave an enthusiastic nod.

The teaching tune about the perils of heedless exploration—and the blessings of an understanding clan—was one Emma had always loved. Enjoying herself as much as Minette, Emma used tone and tempo to texture in emotions, much as artists layered color into paintings. Her surroundings disappeared as she submerged herself in the music.

One verse and another. Danger and courage. With joy and an aching heart, she sang the final verse about the little cat's return to her family. She trailed off with a few hummed notes.

A contented sigh came from her little-girl audience—the best, *best* reward a bard could receive.

Deep inside her bloomed a sharp joy that was almost pain.

After a second, she realized sighs and murmurs were sounding throughout the unnaturally quiet tavern. Her head jerked up. *Oh my Goddess…*

People all around the room were looking at her. Had been *listening.* Ryder, Ben, the two strange cahirs, and the *Cosantir* stood near the fireplace.

Anxiety crawled up Emma's spine like a wave of ants, waiting to all bite her at once. "I'm sorry," she said to the group of males.

"For what?" Ben sauntered forward. "Great song, darlin'." He tugged her hair lightly.

"I-I didn't mean to disturb the—"

"You disturbed no one, Emma." The Cosantir walked around the couch and sat facing her on the heavy oak coffee table. His gray eyes held hers. "How much training have you had, bard?"

She felt the blood leave her face. He knew what she was. Had he heard of the bard who'd caused the deaths of two males? Would he kick her out of his territory?

"Emma?" the Cosantir prompted. He didn't look angry. "Did you start at the usual age…as a teen?"

"Fourteen." It'd been the only time she fought her mother. She'd never have obtained permission if the master bard hadn't spoken up. Her mother hadn't been able to refuse someone so respected. "I finished my seven years of apprenticeship. And then…" And then her life had been destroyed. "I haven't entertained anyone"—besides tree fairies and forest animals— "for a long time. I'm no longer a bard." Renouncing her dream pierced her like a knife to the soul.

Wry humor lightened his lean face. "A tail does not disappear, even if not wagged. You are yet a bard." He regarded her thoughtfully. "We postponed your judgment, aye?"

When her body tensed, she felt Minette stir. *Breathe, Emma.*
"Yes." *Please, don't send me back to the forest. Please.*

"Why were you in the forest with no one to aid you?"

He didn't know she'd been banished. The knowledge loosened the constriction around her throat. She chose her words carefully. "After my mother died, I had no family left. And I was...unhappy. No one cared when I left for the forest." *Truth.* The town of Pine Knoll would only have cared if she'd returned. "So I was alone when I got hurt."

He studied her for a long, uncomfortable moment. Plainly, he knew she wasn't telling everything.

What would he decide to do with her? As guardians of Herne's territories, the Cosantirs followed their own unique logic, making decisions to benefit the Daonain as a whole, not one lonely shifter.

She looked away. Ben stood with arms folded over his chest. Beside him, Ryder leaned one shoulder on the fireplace mantel. Both were listening.

She swallowed and returned her attention to the Cosantir.

"I will accept your explanation for now." Calum's measured gaze held her. "So...for risking discovery by humans, I impose this penalty: You'll work as a bard twice a week until Lughnasadh."

She gaped at him as if he'd awoken her early from hibernation. Sing? For others? Until the harvest festival in August? "Um, where?"

"Oh, here." His gesture took in the whole room. His lips curved. "Did I forget to mention I own the bar?"

"You?" A Cosantir was a lowly tavern owner?

He didn't...quite...snort. "Your singing will draw in customers during the quiet periods, which will be good for the bar. As Cosantir, I want our people to hear their history in song and story again."

She would have an audience? A raging river of emotion surged over her banks, stealing her voice. She could only nod.

Laughter lit his eyes. "I silenced a bard. Delightful." He tapped his fingers together. "Let's plan for Thursdays from seven to nine. Do whatever suits you. On Sundays, I'd prefer traditional teaching songs and stories. We'll encourage families to attend with their cubs and set the time to be from five to seven. Are we in agreement?"

"Yes." Surely, she could do better than such a weak response. She firmed her voice. "Yes, I'd enjoy that very much."

"Then we have an accord." He rose, nodded at the others, and moved toward the bar with the characteristic stalk of a werecat.

Oh my Goddess. She turned to Ben and Ryder, and from the amused look on Ryder's dark face, she knew she was grinning wider than a tipsy flower fairy. She ignored him and told Ben as if he hadn't already heard, "I'm going to get to sing again."

Ben grinned. "And so you are. Congratulations, li'l bear."

Chapter Eleven

"**D**O I HAVE this right?" Emma asked the empty kitchen as she studied the peeled potatoes and hunk of beef in the pan. Had she rightly remembered how her mother's cook made pot roast? Questionable. Since the Cavanaughs didn't associate with hired help, Emma'd never been allowed in the kitchen for longer than it took to eat her afternoon snack.

Unfortunately, she hadn't located any cookbooks in Ben's home, which meant she was on her own in the kitchen. Scary thought. But she so, so wanted to do something nice for him.

He'd been past kind and openly pleased when the Cosantir "sentenced" her to sing as her penalty.

Wonder filled her again. The Cosantir *wanted* her to sing, to be a bard. If she proved herself useful, if people came to like her, maybe she could stay in Cold Creek. She'd run her paws off to be worthy of the chance.

First, she needed to show Ben and Ryder she understood the *Law of Reciprocity*. Ben had given her a place to stay, fed her, cared for her. Ryder had made her a beautiful hardwood cane, dark and smooth and glossy. With her brace and the cane, she didn't have to be carted everywhere.

Although, being carried by Ben was more enthralling than anything she'd fantasized about as a young female. Cared for and helpless—a very heady mixture. And Ben himself… *Well.* His easy-going nature concealed a formidable strength of will and an intimidating self-confidence. When he focused on her, she felt like tasty prey—and very, *very* female.

She gave herself a shake. *Stop daydreaming.*

The potatoes and roast beef lay like corpses in the pan, and she bit her lip. She'd managed to scour the kitchen, despite frequent breaks to let the pain ease. The countertops and table sparkled; however, cleaning wasn't enough to balance the scales.

Surely, something as basic as roast beef couldn't be easily ruined. Right?

After some puzzling, she turned on the oven. Now, what was the correct temperature?

Ryder had made a frozen pizza one night and set the oven to 425 degrees. The pizza was very thin, the roast very thick, so surely the temperature needed to be higher? She turned the dial to 450 degrees.

She did know that a roast should bake for a long time. Their cook had put the meat into the oven when Emma had been snacking, so the beef must have cooked for around three to four hours. She'd check it in three…to be on the safe side.

There. Done. Biting her lip, she hesitated. Maybe she should watch it?

Staring at the oven door would be silly. She looked around, wishing for someone to talk with. The house was so empty even the dust motes seemed to echo.

If she went outside, the flower fairies would keep her company while she planned what to sing at the tavern. The food didn't need her help to cook, after all. And when the males and Minette returned from the construction site, she'd treat them all to a tasty hot meal. Wouldn't they be surprised?

THREE HOURS LATER, Emma limped into the kitchen and gasped in horror at the black clouds of smoke pouring from the oven.

"Oh, no. No, no, no." Leaving the back door open, she turned off the oven.

With true dismay, she heard the front door open and the stomping sound of boots.

Ben and Ryder had returned.

"Fuck. Did Emma set the place on fire?" she heard Ryder ask. "I told you not to tease her about her reading. Females get all gooey over those lovesick stories."

"I smell burnt meat," Ben answered mildly. All too quickly, he entered the kitchen with Minette and Ryder.

Gritting her teeth, Emma opened the oven door, already knowing she wouldn't see the perfect, juicy, tasty meal she'd planned.

Far from it.

The smoking, shriveled carcass was surrounded by black lumps of potatoes. By the Mother, how could she have messed this up so badly? Been so stupid? She was every inch as worthless as her mother had always said.

She'd spoiled good food and wasted Ben's money.

"Well, there's a…" Ryder glanced at her and didn't finish. Instead, he moved her to one side, grabbed a potholder, and pulled out the disgusting mess. After setting the pan in the sink, he turned the water on. Steam rose with an angry hiss.

Ruined. She tried to blink back the tears. "I'm sorry," she whispered.

"It's not worth worrying about, darlin'." Ben gave her loose hair a teasing tug. "We appreciate the effort, even if it didn't turn out."

His kindness ruined her attempt at composure, and her eyes filled completely, blurring her vision.

"Sit, Emma." With strong hands, he pushed her into a kitchen chair. Crouching in front of her, he took her hands.

"I wasted your money. I shouldn't have tried to prepare a meal." She hung her head, her mother's voice in her ears. *Worthless. Stupid. Awkward. Ungrateful.* "I don't know how to cook."

Ryder frowned. "I thought all females were taught to cook and clean."

Did he think her not only incompetent, but a liar as well? Her spine straightened. "We had a cook." Her gaze dropped back to her lap, where Ben's rugged hands still held hers. "I wasn't allowed in the kitchen."

When her breathing hitched in a prelude to tears, she controlled herself. No crying. She was a grown female.

"A cook. Interesting." Ryder's black eyes were unreadable. He walked over to the doorway and scooped up Minette. "C'mon, kitten, you can work on your puzzle while I get cleaned up."

After a second, she pulled her gaze from the empty doorway and realized Ben hadn't let go of her hands. A tug not only didn't gain her freedom, but also tightened his grip.

After a second, he stroked his thumbs over the backs of her hands, sending a thrill of awareness through her. "Look at me, honey bear."

Honey bear? The tone of his voice was as affectionate as when Ryder called Minette "kitten." It sounded as if...as if he really did like her.

His level gaze was as open and easy to read as Ryder's was impenetrable. He wasn't upset. "This isn't a world-ending event; you simply burnt dinner. We've all messed up and more than once." His lips twitched. "Now, I'm an okay cook, but Ryder's damn good, yet he's concocted some real disasters."

"Really?"

Ben considered for a moment. "I think the worst stink was when he forgot he'd put potatoes on to boil. The water evaporated and burned the shit out of the potatoes. By Herne's hairy balls, the whole house stank for days."

The tightness in her chest loosened. "But I ruined dinner. Now there's nothing to eat."

"That's why the Mother gifted us with restaurants and diners. Let me take a quick shower and we'll all go out to eat."

He released her and curved his hands around her waist, rising and pulling her to her feet. Rather than stepping away, he moved close enough she felt the warmth of his body from her thighs to her shoulders. "By the God, you smell good."

His lips brushed her hair.

He was so tall, her eyes were level with his chest. She couldn't help but see how his blue work shirt strained over his thick pectoral muscles. The opened top buttons revealed springy brown hair, and she wanted to unbutton more, to run her hands over him.

How would the hair feel against her skin? Against her breasts? She blinked. By the Goddess, how inappropriate was that thought?

Tilting her head back, she tried to ignore the strong line of his throat, the square jaw, the dent in his chin. *No, Emma.* She mustn't allow herself to be so drawn to him.

Too late. His slow smile informed her she'd revealed her desire. *Oh, humiliation.* Where was a deep, dark cave to hide in when a bear needed one?

"Um. I'll just…" Her words dried up under the hunger in his eyes.

His voice came out a low rumble. "Since it's a bit soon to ask you to join me in the shower, you'd best take yourself off, darlin'."

Shower. With him?

Heat flamed up her spine, seared her face with a flush, and sizzled right to her core. "Ah, right." She eased away and moved toward the stairs. With luck, her limp would conceal the way her knees were wobbling.

He chuckled.

Guess not.

AT ANGIE'S DINER in downtown Cold Creek, Ryder sat with his "family" as he enjoyed a massive slice of cherry pie. With scuffed, wooden floors and blue-checked tablecloths over square tables, the old-fashioned restaurant served home-style food and pies that would do any chef proud.

He thought back to the shriveled mess of a roast Emma had pulled out of the oven. The poor bear'd been so upset, she'd nearly burst into tears. For a second, he'd thought she was putting on a Genevieve-style act, but Emma didn't wear perfume, and he had smelled her distress. She hadn't been playacting.

Discomfort inched up his spine. Since Genevieve, he'd only interacted with females at the straightforward, all-about-mating Gatherings. But his avoidance might have gone on a bit long. Possibly Genevieve had a more adverse effect on his life than he'd acknowledged. Possibly he'd become a bit cynical. Or maybe just smarter. Difficult to say.

He was coming to realize that Emma was easily hurt. Vulnerable. Hell, at least she'd tried to cook for them, which was more than Genevieve had ever done. He should've seen her embarrassment about not knowing how to cook and been gentler. Ben had figured it out quickly enough.

His brother wasn't smooth with words—not like, say, the sheriff—but Ben had a bluntly honest kind of charm. It was good his littermate had been there to soothe the little bear.

Ryder took another bite of pie and listened to Ben filling Emma in on some of the local "celebrities." The drunk who danced on Calum's bartop sounded intriguing, although foolhardy, considering the Cosantir could fry him with a touch.

As Ben told the tale of a female-hating cahir chasing an overly forward female out of his rental—both of them sans clothing—Emma laughed. A beautiful, throaty laugh.

Ryder leaned back in his chair and studied her without cynicism, which took an appalling amount of effort.

She was a lovely female. Under Ben's care and the quiet evening, she'd relaxed. Her happiness gave her a glow like a late summer moon. She'd shone as brightly when singing at the tavern last night.

Her singing…

By the God, her exquisite contralto could seize a male by the balls and tow him after her. When she'd sung to Minette, the entire bar had quieted to hear her, and she hadn't noticed. All her attention had been focused on Minette, and she'd kept the cub's attention with a very skilled bard's talents. He could still hear her.

The two of them had looked…heartwarming…cuddling on the couch. His daughter had looked more content than he'd seen her in a long time. Emma was good for the cub. Hell, better than he was. The mite made him feel too big, too rough, and totally at a loss. Males didn't raise cubs—especially female ones.

Emma's song had been about the courage it took to try something new. Well, a ready-made family was one "new" he'd never anticipated, but damned if he wouldn't do a better job raising his cub than either his father or Ben's had done with them.

From what she'd told Calum, the bard had even less family than he and Ben did. He'd noticed that when singing about the kitten's homecoming, Emma's voice had turned wistful. Now he knew—she had no family to return to.

Why had she been reluctant to share she was a bard? The Daonain valued bards highly. Never plentiful, the story masters had grown even scarcer over the last century. Shifters distrusted change, and bards were even more conservative, as if learning the ancient songs engraved tradition into their bones. The human encroachment drove many bards to the isolated Elder villages or to death. Few remained to teach the new generations.

Calum's opinion had been clear enough. He'd pounced on the little bard like a tasty mouse and had her obligated to sing before she could even think. Yeah, the Cosantir was canny, and Emma's past was a puzzle he might enjoy piecing together.

Smiling, Ryder returned his attention to the table.

Finishing off his apple pie with a gigantic bite, Ben leaned back with a groan. "The third piece was a mistake." He grinned at Minette. "I think only a crane will get me out of this chair. What do you think?"

Minette's eyes danced. Earlier, Ben had shown her his company's construction equipment. Now she knew what a crane was used for.

Ryder listened, longing to hear a little girl giggle from her, but it never came. Her smile was a delight though.

So was Emma's smile. Unfortunately for him, however, it was far too appealing. She made him feel as if he was standing on a rain-sodden cliff, the soil shifting beneath his paws as he watched rocks fall, knowing he'd be next. Well, he was an older and wiser cat now. Hopefully.

As Ben scarfed down the last bite of pie, he raised his eyebrows at Ryder. "Your dessert didn't last long, either."

"Says the grizzly who devoured three pieces to my one." Ryder grinned. "It's a wonder you aren't even bigger than you are now."

From the corner of his eye, he saw Emma nudge away her

half-finished cheesecake—the same dessert she'd been enthusi-astically eating a second ago.

Ben frowned and pushed the plate back to Emma. "Eat, honey bear. You need the calories to heal."

"I'm not hungry any longer." Her eyes didn't meet Ben's.

Genevieve had done the same to get attention. Was always fishing for compliments. However, Emma didn't display the posture of a female seeking admiration, but rather one trying not to be noticed.

By the Hunter, he hadn't been trying to hurt her feelings; he'd merely been teasing his littermate about being a big bear. But…Emma was also a bear. *Fuck.*

Although Genevieve never doubted her own appeal, he'd known females who worried over their attractiveness. He'd also noticed that, whereas males fought their rivals physically, females often battled with words. Had Emma taken a few verbal slashes? Perhaps she hadn't lived enough years to understand how alluring she was.

Compassion slid tender fingers between his ribs. He'd in-flicted the blow; he needed to fix the damage.

"Little bear." He waited until her eyes lifted. "Ben's right. You need extra calories to heal your wound and to keep those lovely curves." He ran his gaze over her, letting his appreciation show. "And you're still underweight."

The flush pinkening her cheeks was damned pretty. When she glanced at his littermate, as if for support, Ryder couldn't help but think of the many carnal ways he could unsettle her and have her clinging to Ben.

"I like curvy females, too," Ben stated. "Ones I can enjoy without feeling as if I'll break them. Your size is perfect."

"Aye," Ryder agreed, smothering a laugh at her wide eyes.

As she started to eat again, his smile faded. Rather than pos-sessing Genevieve's arrogance, this one wasn't at all sure of her charms. Hadn't anyone told her how beautiful she was?

Why was she out in the wilderness, anyway? He stopped himself before asking a question that would only disconcert her more. Belatedly, he realized she was as uncomfortable in public as Minette was. She'd chosen the chair facing the room, not something a female usually did. Like Minette, she'd needed a while to relax and join in the conversation. A loud laugh would still make her stiffen, which didn't make sense. Bards liked people; they weren't afraid of them.

He glanced across the table and saw Ben regarding the little bear thoughtfully. He didn't seem to have any more answers than Ryder did. Well, they'd work on the Emma puzzle together. The decision gave him a sense of satisfaction.

Having finished her chocolate cake, Minette used her finger to get the very last of the frosting, although a fair amount ended up on her face. Fucking cute. Grinning, Ryder wiped her face off. "Gotta say, the people here know how to put a meal together." He'd also noticed that the diner was almost full, which was impressive considering it was a Monday night.

"The desserts are made by Zeb and Shay's mate, Bree, who used to be a pastry chef in Seattle," Ben said. "The meals are cooked by Angie herself, and are the ones she made when her cubs were young."

Ryder exchanged a rueful glance with Ben. With their mother dying at their birth, they'd never enjoyed family dining. "You always hear a mother's cooking is special."

"Not my mother's cooking," Emma murmured as she swirled the water in her glass. "She never set foot in a kitchen except to order around the cook."

"Yeah, you said you had a cook," Ryder said.

Her head shot up in surprise. Hadn't realized she'd spoken aloud, had she? Had she lived in the forests by herself so long she talked to herself?

"I…uh, yes, we did." Emma looked past him. "I think the cahir over there is looking for one of you."

Ryder turned to see Zeb crossing the room.

Zeb nodded at Ryder and Emma. Minette got an almost-smile, which—to Ryder's surprise—she returned. Then Zeb launched into what brought him. "Ben, we could use your help." His voice was low enough to be heard only by their table. "Got a pack shifter, Tullia. Older than dirt. Her house is falling down around her."

"Sure. What can't you handle?"

"Electrical. The kitchen is a house fire waiting to happen. Some oversight for the volunteers. If you have extra time, we'll take it."

"Not a problem." Ben's gaze became unfocused as he considered. "My electrician is finishing a job tomorrow. How about the day after? And I'll pop in whenever I have a moment."

"Appreciate it." Without another word, the cahir stalked away.

"Friendly, isn't he?" Ryder commented, getting a low chuckle from Emma.

"Reminds me of you." Ben grinned. "You should have met him when he and Shay first arrived. First month, we could have counted his sentences on one hand. Cold Creek's good for him—and he's paid back the place a thousandfold."

Several more people came into the diner and greeted Ben. He responded with nods.

"Do you know everyone in Cold Creek?" Emma asked.

"Pretty much," Ben pushed Minette's milk closer to her. "Between being a cahir and doing construction, I get around." He shrugged.

"Zeb didn't ask for an estimate," Ryder noted.

"Won't be a charge." Ben sipped his beer. "The previous alpha of the wolf pack didn't do squat for the members, and a lot of the older wolves' homes are ready to fall down. Now that Shay is Alpha and Zeb is Beta, the two are stuck playing catch-up. I help out where I can."

Ryder studied his brother, looking past the surface changes, adding up his observations. The nonchalant way Ben had answered was…eye opening, as if everyone "gave" something, and his only decisions were who to help and when.

While doing Ben's paperwork, Ryder'd noticed Ben's construction workers had generous benefit packages. Several files had been marked *gratis* with the invoice totals crossed off.

Ben had always taken care of his friends. Apparently, his service had expanded to encompass the entire town.

Turning his gaze away, Ryder traced a finger over the squares on the tablecloth. Aside from becoming more cynical about females, had he changed since he and Ben split apart? Had he grown at all?

He'd worked to be successful. To be recognized for his skills. To have enough money, but everything he'd accomplished had been to benefit himself.

His success now felt…hollow, lonely.

When Genevieve had spread rumors he was abusive, Ryder'd been shaken when no one had spoken up for him. The Cosantir's lack of action hadn't been surprising since the guardian lived in a different town and remained aloof from "petty" problems. Nevertheless, in Farway, no one had stood up for Ryder.

Yet had he ever given anything to the town? He'd lived there, but never helped make it better for anyone, never participated in anything except the Gatherings—which Genevieve had turned into nightmares—and never tried to be a part of the community.

He and Ben had always wanted to belong somewhere. How had he missed learning that belonging required effort on his part?

Ryder looked around the room, observing the people. Good folks, both humans and shifters. Flannel shirts, jeans, and boots. Hardworking, independent, solid citizens. Ones he'd be proud to call friends. It was time he did some work to earn their respect.

As Ben had.

Ryder rubbed his jaw. He'd given nothing to Genevieve's territory, but here—this would be his town and his territory.

It was time he started to nail down his own place here.

LATER, IN THE great room, Emma rested with her back against the couch arm. Minette was tucked in the small space against her side. The feeling of the small body next to her was sweet enough she had a lump in her throat. A month ago, she'd never imagined she'd be so happy.

Well…mostly happy. The stench of burnt roast still lingered in the air. However, her embarrassment had diminished, leaving only resolve. She was going to learn to function like a normal person, including learning to cook.

Ben had been astonishingly nonchalant about her fiasco.

Ryder had been, as well, despite his initially cynical questions. He'd been fun at supper, teasing Ben and Minette—and even her. It seemed his brusque personality hid a wicked feline sense of humor.

Across the room, he was building a fire in the wide marble fireplace. As the kindling caught fire, a salamander poked its pointed nose out from the ashes and wiggled happily.

Minette went to watch, standing beside her sire.

Ryder tugged her down beside him. Every day, he grew more comfortable with his cub. He pointed at the fire elemental. "When the fire starts to roar, the salamander will dance for us."

When Minette gave the same squirm of delight as the salamander, Ryder laughed, and Emma could only stare in wonder. His magnificent, resonant laugh sent shivers up her spine. Why didn't he do that more often?

"Who fancies some music?" Ben thumped down the stairs and into the room. He held two classical guitars.

Guitars. Emma's fingers curled with longing. She'd missed music even more than people. *Don't touch, bear. Not yours.* "Do you and Ryder play the guitar? I thought you said you grew up in the wilderness, owning nothing more than a few books."

"Ben did—in Texas." Ryder's jaw flexed. "When we were five, my father dragged me to Montana."

Leaving Ben behind? The thought of their separation made her heart ache. She'd thought it was sad to have no siblings. How shattering would it feel to be separated after being together?

Ben ran his fingers over the guitar strings. "When we met up again as young males, we spent a winter with our mother's grandmother in an Elder Village with no electricity. She taught us to play guitars."

Ryder's chiseled face softened at the memory. "Naini was Welsh, and nothing made her happier than an evening of music. Everyone had to participate or suffer her displeasure."

Envy filled Emma at the thought of singing with others. She and the master bard had played music together. A couple of times, another bard had visited him. To share songs within a family group must be marvelous.

"Here you go, honey bear," Ben said gently. He bent and brushed his lips across hers in a kiss.

His lips were warm. Firm. His cheek brushed against hers with the slight scratchiness, and rather than pulling away, he lifted his head a couple of inches and looked straight into her stunned eyes. The line beside his mouth deepened, although he wasn't…quite…smiling. He held her eyes for a second, then another, before he straightened.

He'd *kissed* her. She could feel the blood surging in her veins and the increasing hum of interest. Everything in her wanted another kiss.

Shaking her head, she looked down. He'd put the guitar in her lap. She was holding a guitar for the first time in three years.

"Oh," she breathed. The scent, the feel of the glossy finish, the sound when she plucked the first string... *Wonderful.*

"By the God, look at her." Ryder's chuckle held the same amused enjoyment as when Minette had squirmed. "You got your prey cornered, Griz. A kiss to get her all flushed, a guitar to light up her eyes."

Ben grinned. "I hope you still have your instrument, bro. I don't think she's going to share my spare."

"Yep, I brought it." As Ryder took a log from the pile, he asked Minette, "Can you show Ben where it is, kitten?"

Minette ran across the room, took Ben's hand, and pulled him after her.

As Ryder set bigger logs in the fireplace, the scent of fir and pine filled the room with smoky sweetness.

Emma did a tentative strum over the strings, and the guitar bumped into the back couch cushions. The position wouldn't work. She struggled to sit up.

"Hold on, little bear." Ryder took the guitar from her and set it to one side. With a hand behind her back and the other under her knees, he turned her, placing her legs on the leather ottoman. His lean fingers were longer than Ben's, just as callused, and to her surprise, just as gentle. His scent held the wildness of a cat shifter and a hint of the woodsy soap he used.

Tingling sensations traced over her skin, teasing her with the knowledge she was female and he was male. *No. No, no, no.* It was bad enough to be attracted to Ben, but this male? This very cynical male who was far too handsome? *Impossible.*

She bowed her head to study her hands. "Thank you." Her voice came out a whisper.

"Emma?" When she looked up, she met night-dark eyes gleaming with laughter. "You are very welcome." He ran a single finger down her cheek.

Pulling back, he shook his head in the same way she shook out her fur when she first *trawsfurred*, getting rid of the last, lingering traces of human. "Ben and I both spent a lot of time in the wilderness. The one time I did a whole summer, I was still talking to myself a month later. How long were you away from civilization?"

The unexpected question shocked her. His dark eyes were intent and slightly frightening. "No evasions, please, little bard," he said softly. "Give me a number."

Lie? She couldn't, never could. "Three."

"Three what?"

Stubborn male. Her whisper was almost inaudible. "Years."

His staggered expression pleased her, until he followed it with another question. "Why?"

She lifted her chin. "I explained to the Cosantir." And she wasn't going to explain further.

When Ben and Minette walked into the room, she almost cheered.

"Here's your guitar, bro." Ben handed it to Ryder.

With a frown, Ryder sat in a chair, but his gaze kept returning to her.

It didn't matter, she told herself. She didn't have to answer any more questions. She shouldn't have answered him at all. Stupid male.

Stupid Emma.

"Problems?" Ben's regard warmed her skin.

"No? I have a guitar. Nothing can be a problem." Music could heal almost anything.

The minute the males started singing together, she knew she was right.

So *beautiful.* In a sonorous baritone, Ryder carried the melody. Ben added the harmony in his deep, rumbly bass.

More than beautiful. Like one of those fabled aphrodisiacs, the sound of their beautiful male voices danced across her skin, trailing desire behind it. Nothing, not even the Gathering, had ever affected her so deeply, in every sense.

When she looked at Ben, all she could see was how broad his shoulders were, how his biceps strained the fabric of his white shirt, and how the collar framed his corded neck. She wanted to press her lips right there, to the tanned skin exposed by the two open buttons.

When she looked at Ryder, she couldn't look away from the beauty of his wrists and his powerful fingers on the strings. What would those hands feel like on her body?

Stop.

She switched her attention to Minette. In front of the fire, the cub swayed in time with the music and watched the salamanders dance amidst the flames.

Lovely.

Unable to stop smiling, Emma curled her hand around the guitar neck and added some fancy fingering to the music. Happiness welled up and overflowed inside her as she lifted her voice in a descant, above and around the melody.

Minette bounced as the music became richer.

The males turned to look at her. Ben's gaze filled with pleasure; Ryder's softened to a liquid darkness.

Maybe this sunlit time wouldn't last, but for now...for this glorious moment in time...she'd wrap herself in the warmth.

Chapter Twelve

I N THE WILD Hunt Tavern, Ben leaned on the fireplace mantel and enjoyed himself.

Seated in a nearby chair, Emma sang to the crowd, accompanying herself with the guitar Ben had given her.

Ben grinned at the Cosantir's disgruntled expression. Hosting the bard had been a brilliant idea, but he'd obviously considered only the benefits to the Daonain, not how the local residents would flock to the tavern for the new entertainment. A typical cat shifter, Calum hated crowds.

Too bad for him. Word had gone out, and although this was the bard's first Thursday performance, every table was full. People lined the walls. Even the pool players had stopped to listen.

The shifters and the spattering of humans were enthralled. He smiled as she slid smoothly into another song—a more ribald one that set the tavern to rocking.

Ben understood. Her songs drilled deep enough to draw tears, before bathing the ache clean, and closing it with comfort. Her tenderness and enthusiasm touched everyone who listened.

Emma had a lot of love to give. It wouldn't be long before she was lifemated. Hell, any male would be proud to care for her, protect her, and cherish her.

However, Ben wouldn't be that male. He couldn't be, mustn't be.

Emma was only a small black bear, not a grizzly, and his cubs would still be too large for her to birth safely. His sadness cast a pall over his surroundings. Over the past few weeks, she and Minette had shown him what his life lacked. He wanted a mate. Wanted to share her with his brother and watch her swell with their offspring. Wanted to be surrounded by love and the infectious laughter of cubs.

With a shake of his head, he pushed the regrets aside and concentrated on the music.

Emma brought one song to an end and segued into a hymn to the Mother. Around the tavern, people seemed to barely breathe as the spirit of the goddess shimmered in the air.

When the song finished, Emma sat back, easing people down with slow fingerings on the guitar and soft humming. Finally, she spoke.

"Thank you for your attention. May the Mother's love forever light your trail until you return safely home."

When applause swept the room, her solemn expression sweetened with her smile—and her surprise was clear in her voice. "Thank you."

A couple of people moved forward to speak with her. More gathered. Emma's eyes widened, and she recoiled back into the chair.

Ryder had said the bear lived in the wilderness for three years. Three fucking years. A tavern filled with people must be overwhelming.

Ben stepped behind her. Over the noise, he said softly, "Fine job, bard." Setting his hands on her shoulders, he growled loud enough to make the closest people—even the humans— take a step back.

Better.

"Ben," she chided, glancing over her shoulder.

He squeezed her shoulders and felt her tension ease, then pleased himself by stroking the newly solid muscles. She was recovering nicely, gaining weight and muscle. The weather last winter had been colder than normal—and she'd mentioned she had hibernated during the worst months. *Hibernated.* By the God. Even his paranoid father had never hibernated. Shifters rarely did. The females never.

Emma's isolation—for whatever reason—was in the past. She looked happy, which satisfied his protective instincts, and her curves were filling out, which enticed other parts of his nature. She had a beautiful body he was craving to touch. Every day, the need grew to explore her softness, her curves, her scent.

She was letting him touch her more often.

He really shouldn't have put his hands on her in a way that would claim her in front of the clan—the little innocent probably thought he was just being friendly—but the males in the audience had taken notice.

Good.

As she answered questions, Calum strolled through the crowd, carrying a glass of red wine. After handing her the glass, he went down on his haunches, an unexpected courtesy from the Cosantir.

"Excellent evening, bard," Calum said quietly. "I enjoyed your selection. 'The Wolf's Revenge' has always been one of my favorites."

As Emma smiled with pleasure, Ben said, "Yeah, the tune was good. I favor the Rhonwen stories, too."

"The stories of Rhonwen were my favorites as a cub." She frowned at the dark wine in her glass. "But the tales are perhaps too optimistic. Teaching our cubs the world is fair might be faulty judgment."

Clearly, she'd learned the world wasn't fair, and from the

sorrow in her voice, the lesson had been a painful one. What the fuck had happened to her? Obviously, the Cosantir wasn't going to quiz her further. Ben could push, as Ryder had, but by the Hunter's bow, he wanted her to trust him. To share her past willingly.

"Optimistic? If you only view one moment in time, pessimism might be warranted—depending on that moment," Calum said. "However, I don't view events as being balanced on a set of scales at one given instant. Our lives run like a river through a mountain range, rushing noisily, then flowing quietly. Spilling over its banks one season, barely a trickle during a drought. And eventually, every drop of water returns to the ocean that gave it life."

He patted her uninjured leg. "There is a balance. However, during a raging spring flood, it's difficult to remember how tranquilly leaves will float on a leisurely current."

Her smile was rueful. "This is true."

Calum rose. "I'll have someone take you home when you're ready."

"I—"

"I'm taking her home," Ben said.

"No, Ben," she countered. "I can manage."

Ignoring her protest, Calum inclined his head to Ben in acknowledgment and strode back to his bar.

For another half hour, Emma answered questions about the history of the songs and stories.

When Ben saw her shoulders sag, he interrupted. "Time's up. I'm taking Emma home." As people moved away, he plucked the glass from her hand, set it on a table, and lifted her to her feet. Fuck, she felt good in his hands.

He looked down into startled eyes.

"What?" he asked. Had he hurt her?

"I'm always surprised at how strong you are," she said. "I'm so big. And heavy."

"Hardly. You need to eat more. You're still too thin and—" He stopped. By the God, he was being rude. Yet her expression showed only delight—not upset.

"You did a good job tonight," he murmured and pulled her into a hug. Even as he tightened his hold, half-expecting to get slugged, he savored how her full, soft breasts flattened against his chest—not his belly, as with the shorter females. She was the perfect height.

She didn't say a word, but the color in her cheeks deepened. Her scent changed, not into a moon-driven need, but to an even more appealing fragrance holding the first hint of arousal.

Well then. He lowered his head, giving her time to retreat, and took her lips. Soft and receptive.

Her hands closed on his biceps, and a tremor shook her. Her mouth opened under his, giving him access.

Center of the tavern or not, he didn't give a damn. He pulled her closer and explored, teasing her tongue with his, plunging deep, retreating to nibble the fullness of her lower lip.

But before lust pushed him too far, he stepped back. His cock throbbed a protest; his blood roared for him to complete the mating.

She shook her head as if to cast away the same arousal he felt and frowned at him. "That can't happen again. I'm not doing this."

"You're here; I'm here." He chuckled and ran his thumb across the wetness on her lips. "And, darlin', we're already on the path." Although he couldn't take her to the end of the trail— a lifemating—they could, at least, enjoy each other for a while.

Her hands tightened on his arms. "No. You need a female who will stay here in this town, not one who—"

His eyebrows went up. "What the hell? You're fucking *not* going back to the forest."

"No. I just will…move on…eventually." Her gaze evaded his.

"Why, Emma?"

She shook her head and pulled out of his grip. "Let's go." With cane in hand, she limped toward the door.

He crossed his arms on his chest. *Oh hell, no.* He'd let her go this time, but sooner or later, he was going to find out what had driven her into the forest and kept her there.

Chapter Thirteen

BEN HAD KISSED her last night before they'd left the tavern. Emma finished towel drying her butt-length hair and stared at herself in the bathroom mirror. He'd not only kissed her, but she'd let him. What had she been thinking?

Ah, but she knew. Despite her mind's determination to avoid mating, her body longed to be touched. Held. Kissed.

Ben would be the shining star in any female's dreams. The most stirring tales in a bard's repertoire were of the cahirs, huge and muscled, brave and strong. Yet the songs never mentioned that a cahir could be so…gentle…with a female.

These days, merely catching Ben's scent in the air sent weakness through her. Hearing his voice made her insides melt. And when he looked at her with a heated glint in his blue eyes, she wanted nothing more than to press up against him and let him have his way.

Mating with Ben. No, no, no.

As she pulled on a pair of jeans and a soft blue shirt Angie had dropped off, she scowled. Sex wasn't going to happen. Ever. In fact, she should move out of his house. But to where?

After strapping on her leg brace, she sat on the edge of the bed, staring out the window at the ruins of his backyard. He'd said his efforts had been dedicated to restoring the rundown interior, and the outside had to wait. Her fingers itched to go out and make order of what had probably been spectacular gardens. As a child, she'd escape the repressive atmosphere of her house and trail after the old gardener.

Seoirse had been a bear, big and burly and, as with many bears, easy to be with. He'd chafed against her mother's regimented order, and defiantly tucked herbs among the flashy flowers. Ignoring Emma's shyness, he'd talked to himself. *"Appears I need to dig up these iris and divide them."* He'd stick a finger in the earth. *"Not too wet, good. Bulbs don't fancy wet, now do they?"*

When he caught her singing to the flowers, he'd called in a master bard to speak to her.

She'd had two years left of her apprenticeship when Seoirse had gone ahead to the Mother. Had he ever known how much he meant to her? She smiled slowly. Yes, the male who could read a plant's health by the slightest droop of its leaves would have understood a child.

Right now, he'd tell her to stop moping around and get her tail out to clean up those flowerbeds.

"All right, Seoirse. I will."

After she'd done her duty to the gardens, she'd find herself a place to live. For now, while she was here, she'd simply enjoy every moment of being in Ben's presence. Like a parched lilac, she'd drink in the sound of his laugh, the amused gleam in his gaze, the way the sunlight glinted off the light brown hair on his arms, the shadowy valleys created by his heavy muscles. She would allow herself to delight in the way he'd lift Minette over his head, not caring if the little girl made no sound, but openly reveling in the light in her face and her soundless laughter.

If Emma stayed in town—while she stayed in town—she'd be able to see him. Her heart lightened. She wouldn't lose him completely.

Oh, she knew her respite in Cold Creek wouldn't last forever. Eventually, the truth would come out about her banishment. Every tale about a person holding a secret made that ever so clear.

And, although the Mother had forgiven her and erased the darkness of the scars, if the town learned of her banishment? Well, few shifters held an overabundance of understanding and forgiveness in their hearts. Just look at how Pine Knoll had treated her.

If…when…people turned on her, she'd be forced to move on. Maybe she'd travel far away to the eastern forest communities or the northern ones.

She had no reason to return to the forest.

Well. Her mouth tightened. No reason except for the upcoming Gathering. What should she do about the full moon? Just the thought of being around all those shifters while she was drowning in hormones made her stomach clench with nausea. If she attended, a male—or more—might want to mate with her.

What if she caused another fight? She still didn't know how she'd started the last fight. How could she prevent herself from causing another?

If only she could avoid the whole thing. But the Daonain had traditions—laws, even. By the mingling of the genes during the times of increased fertility, the Gatherings ensured the survival of the people. Attendance was mandatory.

With a low sound, she straightened her spine. Other females managed to attend and even anticipated the monthly Gatherings. If she wanted to stay in a town, she must conquer her fear. To find her courage and start living her life, this would be the first step.

She could do it.

She would.

Carefully, she cleaned up her bedroom and the bathroom,

pleased she'd exceeded her mother's maid's spotless efforts. A shame she wasn't as good at cooking.

Good job, Mother. You raised a child incompetent in the very basics of living.

Using her cane, she left the bedroom. The sound of crying drifted down the hall. Emma followed the pitiful noises to Ryder's bedroom.

"Just let me get this Band-Aid on your leg. It'll be okay, kitten." Unhappiness had deepened Ryder's voice to a low growl.

Emma almost laughed. The terrifyingly tough male turned helpless as a bunny when his daughter gave him those big sad eyes.

He made another frustrated sound.

Ryder hadn't been a father long...and he really was trying. Would he let her help? She knocked on the door.

"Yeah. We're in the back."

She crossed the bedroom and walked through an open door into a wide, unfinished room. From the location and the faint petroleum scent, it must be above the two-car garage. A large filing cabinet stood against the right wall. Boxes and empty shelves lined the left. In the center of the room, a computer, monitor, and printer occupied a massive desk.

She grimaced.

Ryder was kneeling on the other side of the desk, his gaze dark. "If you have a problem with computers, leave. I don't have time for it." The lash of anger in his voice made her jump.

"I...I don't." She pulled in a slow breath. Many shifters weren't fans of modern living, especially computers and televisions. "My mother liked human technology. More than she did me."

"By the God." Ryder rubbed his shadowed jaw. "Sorry, Emma. I'm frustrated and taking it out on you. What can I do for you?"

Emma limped around the desk to see him better.

And there was Minette. Clad in a T-shirt and pink shorts, the little girl sat on the floor, legs outstretched before her. Tears rolled down her cheeks as Ryder fumbled with a Band-Aid. His hands dwarfed the tiny bandage—already partially torn.

"Need help?" Reading his glower, she knew he would say no.

"I…" He scowled at the Band-Aid. "Fuck, yeah."

"All right." She took the Band-Aid from his hand. The adhesive was stuck to itself and partially torn. Worthless. "Do you have another one?"

He handed her the box sitting beside him.

Boring tan adhesive. "You might consider getting some decorated ones. If she has to choose which cartoon character she wants, she won't be thinking about owies."

His eyes lit with humor. "You're almost sneaky enough for a feline."

Was that a compliment? He'd actually complimented her? "With children, diversions are wonderfully effective. Meantime, might I borrow a pen?"

As Ryder rose to find one, Emma smiled at Minette, leaned her cane against the desk, and painfully lowered herself to the floor. The stupid brace on her leg destroyed any semblance of grace.

"Let's see what's going on, kitten." She checked the wound on the girl's shin. The inch-long gash was too small to require a healer, and the lighter patch of skin showed Ryder had managed to wash the area. "What happened?"

"She was playing near those metal window guards in the garage and fell. Could've been worse."

Emma knew the tightness of his voice was an attempt to conceal fear. The accident had scared him badly. "Construction materials and children are not an auspicious combination."

"Got that." He handed her a fine point marker and watched as she made a happy kitty-face on each side strip of the Band-Aid. When Minette saw the faces, she smiled…and he relaxed.

Emma carefully placed the bandage over the cut. "I thought you and Ben were working on the new three-story."

Ryder set his hip on the desk. "Ben's there. His order for a bunch of window guards came in late yesterday, and since dark of the moon is tomorrow, people are in a hurry to pick them up. I came back to hand out a few more."

Ryder was donating his time. Emma's heart softened further. She knew Ben cared for other people in the clan, but hadn't realized Ryder would as well.

He shoved his fingers through his hair with a grunt of exasperation. "Minette was *supposed* to be playing in a corner away from the bars. I didn't watch her close enough."

Emma grinned. "Even when you think cubs are somewhere safe, if there's anything dangerous, you can be sure one will find it, play with it, trip over it, or fall into it." Apprentice bards spent a fair amount of time with the young of the clan.

She'd loved teaching.

"Minette is one fast little kitten." Ryder's wry smile carved his face into appealing lines as he stroked Minette's hair. "Damned if I know what to do with her at construction sites."

"Um…" Emma's stomach quaked. A rejection would…hurt. Her gaze fell on Minette. She didn't have a choice. The child's safety was more important.

"What?" Ryder asked.

Needing to be able to retreat quickly, Emma tried to struggle to her feet.

To her surprise, he gripped her waist and set her on her feet. Easily.

As he resumed his seat on the desk, she gaped at him, still feeling his strong hands on her skin.

Pull it together, bear. "Well"—she cleared her throat—"if you need to return to work with Ben, Minette can spend the afternoon with me."

"No." Ryder leaned away from her. "Thanks, but—"

Minette scrambled to her feet and curled her tiny fingers around Emma's thumb.

Ryder stilled before shaking his head in refusal. "She'll stay with me." He glanced at the door, at Minette, at Emma, at the door.

"Are you sure?"

His scowl grew. "By the fucking God of the fucking forest. Fine."

She fought to suppress a grin. He really was rather adorable—all helpless father. "We'll stay right here in the house. We won't go anywhere else."

After a pause, he muttered, "Thanks."

Emma led Minette through the door and waited until they were almost...*almost* out of earshot. "So, Minette, how good are you with chopping up carrots with a butcher knife?"

A roar of protest came from behind them.

Emma burst into laughter, ruffled Minette's hair, and managed to choke out, "Kidding. Just kidding."

Chapter Fourteen

Cold Creek, North Cascades Territory – dark of the moon

IN THE RUSTIC Wildwood Lodge, Ben drank a cup of Breanna's excellent coffee in preparation for the lengthy night ahead. Against the glass in the iron-barred windows, the red-tinged sun hovered over the mountaintops. It would set soon.

Standing on one side of the room, Shay and Zeb ran through the patrol patterns the cahirs would follow. A year ago, the brothers had moved to Cold Creek to teach the local cahirs how to survive fighting hellhounds. More recently, they'd extended the training to out-territory cahirs.

Watching the two work together, Ben felt a stab of pain. At one time, he and Ryder had been so close, sometimes they'd almost read each other's minds. Zeb and Shay weren't even littermates; both cahirs had lost their littermates to hellhounds, had been alone. Nevertheless—Ben shook his head—for them to become brothers-in-blood had to have been a gift of the softhearted Mother.

Tonight was dark of the moon, the only night of the month when a hellhound could shift from human to its armored demon form. Since only the ridged eyes and a narrow strip down its belly were unarmored, a hellhound was almost impossible to kill.

Cahirs often died protecting their people from a hellhound.

At least Emma and Minette were safe at home with Ryder to guard them. Unlike some of the crap construction in town, the old Victorian was solid. Ben had added iron window guards and reinforced doors. His…family…would be fine.

And it looked good for the cahirs, as well; tonight, they had a surplus of help.

Ben glanced at the males sitting in the big room. Shay, Zeb, Alec, and Owen, the North Cascade Territory cahirs, all experienced hellhound fighters, were relaxed. Thanks to Zeb and Shay's training, Ben had two hellhound kills and had assisted in three more.

The three other cahirs were from out-territory. The two older males from northern California worked as a pair.

The third, the panther shifter from Canada, was in his thirties. His blonde hair had been chopped into a buzz cut. Against Zeb's advice, Wesley wore a skintight body shirt and jeans rather than the leathers worn by the rest. Well, he'd undoubtedly learn the pain of abraded flesh soon enough. If flesh met a hellhound's spiked and scaled armor, the armor always won.

Imitating Zeb, Wesley preferred to fight in human form so he could carry his weapons—a knife on the left hip, a serrated dagger and revolver on the right. Amused, Ben shook his head. It was surprising the cub didn't stagger under the load of weaponry and ego.

The ego was a problem. Taking on a hellhound alone was basically suicide; Zeb and Shay's strategy required the cahirs to work together in a fight. Unfortunately, cat shifters—especially young males—had a difficult time with teamwork.

Huh. Ben shook his head. Wesley seemed damned young, which implied years were passing. Fuck, Ben was…he was on his way toward fifty. Then again, he wasn't ancient yet. Those descended from the Fae lived twice as long as humans did and matured late. Females didn't reach their first heat until their twenties; males were stupid until well into their thirties.

Shay tapped the map of Cold Creek. "As usual, Alec, Owen, and Ben, you're assigned the east side of town. Wesley joins you tonight." He glanced at Ben. "You get the killing blow. Try for the gut so Wesley can watch."

Ben nodded. Standard teamwork. One cahir would divert the hellhound while the other rolled beneath the demon-dog to gut it.

"Alec and Owen, you take backup," Shay said, "since no strategy goes as planned."

Yeah, Ben had learned fuck-ups happened all too often.

Shay turned his attention to the younger male. "Wesley, if contact is made, you pretend to be prey. As we've practiced, your job is to lure the hellhound into chasing you."

"That's bullshit. I'm no fucking rabbit." Wesley jumped to his feet. Although well muscled, at only six feet, he was shorter than the average cahir. Maybe insecurity explained some of his bluster. "I want the kill."

"No, you're not a rabbit," Shay agreed, showing admirable control. As alpha of the local wolf pack, he was probably accustomed to swaggering young males. "But this is our protocol. Cahirs who haven't fought hellhounds are assigned as decoy first. This gives you a chance to experience a hellhound's speed before you go hands-on."

"But—"

"We ready to go?" Zeb interrupted, his irritation obvious. Wesley had been playing dominance games since arriving, and Zeb wasn't known for his patience.

Wesley shut up.

Honed to a fighting edge and scarred from years of fighting hellhounds, Zeb exuded danger. No smart shifter fucked with him—and Wesley wasn't stupid. He was just a typical young male, more mouth than brains, who'd mature into a decent cahir with time. The God hadn't chosen badly; the cub had a good heart and ample courage—if perhaps a tad too much testosterone.

He'd learn. And after seeing his first hellhound, he'd be far more willing to be part of a team.

"Let's go," Shay said. "The sun is almost down."

RYDER PACED THROUGH the house, checking the heavy, iron window guards and the door locks...again. All good. Unfortunately, the activity didn't relieve the worry wafting up his spine like an icy breeze off the glacier-covered mountains. His littermate was out in the night, hunting hellhounds.

He'd never worried about a dark of the moon night before. Then again, when a youth, hellhounds had been more of a legend than a reality.

Not any longer.

The past few years on dark of the moon, he'd taken panther form and gone deep into the mountains where hellhounds hadn't penetrated. But he couldn't run the trails with a cub. Instead, he was stuck in town, worrying about...fuck...about everything. Not only Ben, but also whether the last shifter who'd picked up a window guard had managed to install it. And whether Tullia, the old wolf shifter of Zeb's, was safe in her ramshackle home.

Even though Ben had assured him the Cold Creek shifters would remain inside their well-fortified homes, he still worried about them. And about Ben.

Half of him wanted to be beside his brother, shoulder-to-shoulder, facing down danger as littermates should. The other half needed to be here, guarding their cub.

And guarding Emma, as well. Anything trying to hurt the little bear would have to go through him first. Of course, protecting her was merely a…natural…instinct, nothing more. So why did guarding her give him such a bone-deep satisfaction?

He kept moving through the silent house.

Undoubtedly picking up on the adults' anxiety, Minette had been nervous. After an extra two stories from her favorite picture book, she was still awake.

But Emma had shown up to sing her lullabies while Ryder patrolled the house.

He'd heard her singing softly in Minette's room. Her presence in this house felt as right as when he *trawsfurred* and breathed in the scents of the wild, knowing he was in exactly the perfect place and shape for him.

He shouldn't feel this way about the little bear. Females were purely trouble. Didn't he ever learn?

Growling under his breath, Ryder built up the fire in the great room until the resident salamander spiraled in joy. At least Emma had stayed upstairs, leaving him to his silence.

Damned if he'd think about how comforting it would be to have her gentle company right now.

IN BEAR FORM, Ben ambled through the dark town, sniffing the moist, clean air. A storm had passed earlier. Stray rumbles of thunder and lightning streaks tracked its passage toward the eastern side of the mountain range.

The brisk wind ruffled his shaggy fur pleasantly. Not so pleasant was the cold mud packing between his paw pads.

Tonight, he'd have to resume human form if a hellhound was detected, but until it was time to fight, he wanted his animal-enhanced senses. On his right foreleg, he wore a sheathed knife that a blade-mage had magicked for him. Akin to a lifemating bracelet, the band changed sizes when he *trawsfurred*.

He lifted his nose into the wind, scenting Owen and Alec.

As usual, Owen had remained in werecat form, while Alec had stayed human. Both cahirs hung back, letting Ben and Wesley take the lead.

Ben snorted. After Zeb and Shay had split off, Wesley'd argued again to be allowed to fight. He didn't want to be prey. Owen and Alec had ignored him, forcing Ben as Wesley's token "partner" to give a firm no—which he had.

Results? One sulky young male filled with attitude. A hefty paw upside the head might knock some sense into the lad.

Hearing a door open, Ben edged farther into the shadows. Although humans in Cold Creek were used to wild animals venturing into town, grizzlies were damn rare in Washington, and Ben tried to keep a low profile. Besides, getting shot would suck. Discharging a firearm inside town limits carried a fucking huge fine, but terrified humans weren't always rational.

As a small poodle pranced out to piss on a bush, Doug Banner, the school's principal, stood in the doorway.

By Herne's deadly horns, get your ass inside, Banner. Sure, hellhounds didn't attack humans if they could scent shifters, but still… No one should be in the open on a dark of the moon night.

As the poodle trotted back into the house, and the door closed, Ben huffed a relieved breath and resumed the patrol.

The night was only half over, and they'd found no hellhound tracks or scent. From the silence, the cahirs on the other side of town hadn't had better luck.

A hellhound in human form had been scented last week. Chances were good the monster would show up here. Ben wasn't sure he'd call it luck, since any meeting with a hellhound might be a cahir's one-way ticket to the Mother. But death was simply the underbrush on a cahir's path—always present.

Normally, the thought of dying didn't bother him, but he had more to lose now. Ryder and little Minette…and Emma. It felt damned good to have people of his own to guard.

The wind shifted and carried a stink like weeks-old carrion sprinkled with orange rinds. A hellhound was close.

Possessing the most sensitive nose on his team, Ben usually scented problems first. With a quiet huff, he alerted the others.

Still out of sight, the cougar—Owen—snarled softly in acknowledgement.

Wesley lifted his head, sniffing, and caught the stink. He nodded.

Wind in his face, Ben headed toward the scent, using the shadows as he led them down Bonnyrigg Street. If he'd been tracking a shifter, he'd have gone slower, but not with a hellhound.

Descended from an unholy crossbreeding of human, demon, and fae, the arrogant hellhounds rarely utilized their senses. Demons were lazy—and hellhounds were nearly indestructible, after all.

His nose lifted. The scent came from the back of the line of houses.

He slowed and cut across a front lawn. Sensing the other three following, he motioned with his head to the left to direct Wesley.

As Ben veered to the right of the small, one-story house, the smell of garbage assaulted his nose. In the blackness between the houses, he paused. The back yard was unfenced and butted up against a rising, forested slope.

The creature crossing the patchy lawn had the heft of a grizzly, but the light from the windows glinted off the dinosaur-like, spiked—bulletproof—plating.

Yay, team. We got us a hellhound.

The night was going to get bloody.

The shifting breeze carried the scent of Sarah, a female shifter Ben had once mated.

The hellhound prowled along the back of the house, obviously displeased with the iron guards on the windows. It stopped at the backdoor, raking the wood with grizzly-bear-long claws.

Time to move.

Ben stepped farther into the darkness and *trawsfurred* to human. He stood for a second, adjusting to his diminished size, strength, and senses. At least the garbage didn't stink so bad. But he couldn't hear shit, and he felt as if he'd shrunk to the size of a fucking dwarf. Great feeling when planning to take on an armored demon tank.

He glanced around the corner.

The hellhound was still trying to claw through the door, and chunks of wood hit the stoop with each swipe. Sarah needed a thicker door.

Inside the house came the tap-tap-tap of shoes. A female's face appeared at a back window followed by a high, piercing screech of fear.

The sound of a frightened female flooded Ben's system with adrenaline. Even knowing Sarah wasn't in danger, he realized he'd drawn his knife.

Undoubtedly driven by the same protective instincts, Wesley showed up on the other side of the backyard. Only the paleness of his complexion made him visible.

Fighting the need to act, Ben evaluated the terrain. The open backyard had two old maples. *Good.* Wesley could dodge behind one if needed. Hellhounds were fast, but less agile than humans.

The yard merged into the edge of the forest, creating an escape route, which the hellhound would want to block.

He scowled as he studied the hellhound. Bigger than average, thus older, which often meant smarter. Smart was not good.

Fabric rustled behind Ben, and he caught Alec's scent. The sheriff checked out the field of battle with a quick, assessing gaze.

Owen wasn't with him; the cougar would have followed Wesley.

Ben edged out far enough to signal Wesley without success.

The younger cahir's attention was all on the hellhound. He charged around the house, knife in one hand, pistol in the other, and skidded to a stop in the center of the backyard. His eyes were brilliant with excitement. "Demon-dog! Try someone your own size."

"Hell," Alec muttered.

Ben silently agreed.

The hellhound spun around to face its opponent.

Inside the house, Sarah burst into loud, relieved weeping...and Wesley's chest puffed up.

Behind the hellhound's back, Ben stepped out and waved his arms over his head. *Look here, dumbass.*

Wesley startled and stilled, and regained control. As taught, he waved his weapons conspicuously and retreated a few steps to trigger the demon-dog's predatory instincts.

As was typical, the creature padded toward Wesley. It wouldn't charge. Not yet. Hellhounds fed on emotions as well as flesh and would delay the kill to increase the prey's fear.

A shriek came from the house. "Hurt it!"

"What the hell?" Alec said under his breath.

Visible in the window, Sarah pressed her hands against the glass. Fear gone, her expression held only bloodlust. "Hurt it. Kill it! Shoot. Shoot. Shoot!"

Ben gritted his teeth. *Shut up, female.*

As Wesley continued to retreat, luring the hellhound after him, Ben sprinted down a course directly behind the creature to stay out of its field of vision. The female's goading screams disappeared under the roaring of his pulse.

He dove, twisted in midair, and hit the ground on his back. The ground scraped Ben's bare shoulders as he skidded directly under the hellhound. Perfectly aligned to gut it.

Wesley's pistol barked.

Pain slammed into Ben's right shoulder like the kick of a bull moose. His arm went numb. The knife dropped from his hand. *Fuck!*

"No!" The desperate cry came from Wesley.

Ben's arm was limp. No way to recover the knife. Heart hammering, Ben rolled out from under the hellhound, knowing he was dead meat.

"Eat this, hellhound!" Wesley yelled. Two more bullets whined off the hellhound's armor.

Rather than turning to savage Ben, the demon-dog charged the younger cahir.

"Run, Wes!" Ben yelled and *trawsfurred* to bear while still on the ground.

Swearing loudly, Alec tore past.

Two more cracks of the pistol sounded. A snarl. A scream from human lungs—one of mortal agony.

By the God, no.

Ben lurched forward—and fell. Pain raged through his shoulder. Right foreleg useless, he struggled to rise.

The demon-dog was tearing at a body on the ground. Owen attacked from the rear. The cougar bit into the hellhound's left hind leg, dug in his fangs, and darted away before the hellhound could nail him.

Silently, Alec eased forward from behind, zigzagging to stay in the monster's blind spot. Fury seared the air around him.

Owen attacked again, and this time, the creature caught him, huge jaws clamping onto his shoulder.

On three legs, Ben charged, unable to suppress the animal moans as his limp leg dragged at his shattered shoulder. He hit the hellhound from behind, knocking Owen loose from its jaws, losing his own footing, and rolling over.

The hellhound was on him instantly. Its teeth clamped into his side. Caught, Ben struggled, roaring in his ears. His claws scraped uselessly over the bony armor.

Boots stepped up right beside his head.

While the hellhound's jaws were still clamped in Ben's flesh, Alec stabbed his stiletto directly into its recessed eye.

The death-shriek was satisfying.

As the hellhound transformed back into an oversized, naked human, Alec dropped down beside Wesley.

Owen shifted and knelt beside Ben. Blood poured from ugly bite marks far too close to his neck. "Thanks for the save, cahir."

Ignoring him, Ben struggled to look at Alec.

His stillness and sagging shoulders confirmed the outcome. The young cahir was dead.

The sense of failure swept over Ben.

"Hang on, Griz. Gonna hurt." As Owen pressed his hands directly over the gushing gunshot wound, fiery agony engulfed Ben, and only a huffing moan escaped.

IN HER NIGHTGOWN and fuzzy robe, Emma watched Ryder pace around the great room. In the flickering firelight, his carved features resembled those of the Greek god of war.

Somewhere in the night, Ben was patrolling Cold Creek, looking for hellhounds. If he found one, he'd die. Hellhounds were impossible to kill.

Although the red-tinged salamander was dancing in the blazing flames, Emma felt as if ice had taken up residence in her bones. She pulled her robe tighter for the hundredth time.

Making another circuit of the room, Ryder shot her an annoyed stare. "Why don't you go back to bed? Nothing's happening down here."

Nothing was happening upstairs either, since Minette had

fallen asleep hours ago. Emma had tried to stay in her room, but the walls had inched closer with each passing minute until she hadn't been able to breathe. "I want to be down here." She knotted the fuzzy belt, unknotted it. "He's out there. With a hellhound."

"Yep."

Ryder's reply was so even and calm she wanted to slap him. Didn't he understand his littermate's danger?

"He's going to die, you gnome-brained idiot." Too loud. She couldn't help herself. "No one can kill a hellhound. It'll rip him to pieces and—"

A snort interrupted her. "You've listened to too many stories, bard. Try talking to someone who's seen a hellhound."

His sarcastic voice slapped against her nerves like icy sleet. "I've seen one, you-you *stupid* male. What do you think slashed my leg to pieces?"

He halted so suddenly he almost tripped. Then he laughed. "By the God, you almost had me. You busted your leg while you were in the forest—Ben told me. Hellhounds don't range wilderness areas, and no female would survive a hellhound attack. At least offer me a story I can believe."

The insult was deep. Nasty.

She pointed to the far end of the room. "Just you stay over there and don't talk to me."

He blinked, and his eyes narrowed as if she hadn't reacted as he expected. But he did as she asked.

The jerk. She'd never lied.

As he returned to pacing the room—stewing about Ben, she knew—her anger started to fade. She had to admit she hadn't been...exactly...forthcoming about her past. And if he knew what she'd done, of the Gathering, her banishment, he really would hate her.

The thought hurt, because she'd come to like him. He was

all stone-faced and terse with her—and most people, really—but his icy exterior dropped when he was around Ben or Minette. Affectionate. Slyly funny. Thoughtful.

Recently, she'd gotten the impression he liked her, too…although she could tell he didn't want to.

Her brows drew together as she considered. Why wouldn't he like a perfectly nice person such as herself? Maybe there was a sad tale in his past, something dark. Maybe he'd lost someone he loved—maybe Minette's mother? Having a female around might unsettle him.

Stories of disastrous love affairs abounded in her bard's repertoire. If she could only pick out the strands making up his past, she'd know how to help him. As she studied him, seeing past the threatening-to-her handsomeness, she realized the lines fanning the corners of his eyes weren't all from laughter. Other lines beside his mouth told a tale of unhappiness. Had he been different before he'd suffered…whatever had happened?

Compassion softened her heart. "I'm sorry for whatever made you so suspicious of me," she said gently.

He looked as if she'd slapped him.

A forceful pounding on the door wrenched Emma to her feet, her pulse thrumming in her veins.

With a werecat's speed, Ryder was already in the foyer. He peered through the glass peephole and threw the door open. "What the fuck happened?"

Alec walked into the room, carrying Ben over one shoulder.

Horrified, Emma realized Ben was covered in blood. More dripped onto the floor.

"*Ben.*" She rushed toward him, stumbled, and steadied herself on the entry table.

He didn't move. Wasn't even conscious.

She tried to take another step, and her knee started to buckle. By the Mother, she had no time to be weak. Her frustration turned into a glare at Alec. "Get a healer. Right now!"

"Got it covered, Emma." Alec tilted his head toward the still open doorway.

Donal walked in, nodded to her, and pointed to the staircase. "I'm sorry, my lad. I know he's heavy, but I want him upstairs on his bed."

"You're the healer?" Ryder asked. To Emma's surprise, he put an arm around her waist to steady her. "Why is he still bleeding? Why didn't you work on him where this happened?"

"I slowed the bleeding down, but his shoulder bones are shattered," Donal said. "I'll have to make an incision to get in and align the fragments."

Cut him? Emma wanted to shake the stupid healer, to shove him back out the door.

"And, as you noted, he's bleeding," Alec said. "On the off chance there's another hellhound, the scent of blood would draw it like a fly to carrion."

She felt Ryder flinch. He pulled in a breath. "Got it. Healer, what do you require?"

"Just yourself. And Emma." Donal led the way up the stairs. "The cahir must return to patrol, so I'll need you both to help hold Ben still."

Hold him? While the healer hurt him more? Her feet stopped. Her throat tightened with tears. She couldn't. Ever. The breath she released held a sob.

"Shhh, little bear." Ryder squeezed her waist and pulled her along with him. "He'll be all right. We'll see to it."

She'd asked the Mother to watch over Ben. To bring him home safely. Now it was her turn to pull her weight. "Yes." She looked up into Ryder's dark, intense eyes and felt only gratitude. "Thank you."

AN ETERNITY LATER, Ryder's guts were so knotted that his insides threatened to come up. After healing the savage bite wounds on Ben's side, Donal had sliced into Ben's shoulder so he could push the bones in place.

Ryder was holding down his brother's injured right arm. Emma sat on the other side of the bed, leaning against Ben and holding his left hand. Neither of them were needed, because Ben had awakened even before the healer started. Although sweat covered his face with the strain of holding still, he hadn't moved an inch.

Watching his littermate suffer was the most horrible thing Ryder had ever endured.

When the healer dug his fingers into the sliced flesh and pushed a bone somewhere, Ben let out the moan a bear only gives when in agony.

Ryder's control snapped. "For the Mother's sake, healer, give him something more than a fucking local for the pain."

"You've spent too much time around humans, cat. Seen them handing out narcotics like candy." The healer didn't look away from his work, although his lips curved cynically. "Giving pain medication to a Daonain is...chancy. Some shifters do fine having their senses blurred. But if hurt badly, some will *trawsfur*. I can handle a cub or small wolf, but an enraged grizzly? Not so much."

Ryder shook his head. "He wouldn't—"

"He might," Emma interrupted. Ever since the healer had started, she'd been silently crying, and her face was wet from tears. "When the healer hurts you, it's difficult not to shift. Especially when"—she breathed out slowly—"when evil caused the injury. Pain brings the memories back."

Donal shot her a quick smile. "Your restraint was appreciated, especially if you thought I was a hellhound attacking you again."

Ryder straightened. "You really were attacked by a hell-hound?"

Scowling, she met his gaze…and then her face softened. "Yes. I really was."

"It was a wonder the bard survived," Donal said. "Demon-dogs leave behind only savaged flesh and shattered bones."

Returning to his work, the healer dug deeper into the wound, and Ben moaned again. Donal pulled out a fragment of bone. "Easy, Griz. Almost done here."

Ryder felt Ben's pain pulsing through the brother bond—and had to concentrate to keep himself from *trawsfurring*.

Instead, he turned his gaze to the little female. She'd wrapped her right hand around Ben's wrist. In turn, his fingers were wrapped around her left so tightly his knuckles were white. She made no effort to free herself from the painful grip.

Genevieve wouldn't have let herself be hurt; Emma hadn't said a word.

Savaged flesh. Emma regarded the clean hole in Ben's shoulder. "A hellhound didn't bite him. His shoulder isn't a mess like my leg."

"You're right." Alec walked in the door, his gaze on Ben.

Feeling as if he was waking from a nightmare, Ryder realized sunlight was spilling into the room. The long night was over. "If not the hellhound, what fucked up his shoulder?"

"A bullet from one of the cahirs here to be trained." The sheriff dropped into a chair off to one side. "Wesley was supposed to get the hellhound's attention—nothing else. Ben's job was to gut the demon-dog with a knife. He was under the hellhound when Wesley started shooting. I don't know if Wesley hit Ben directly or if the bullet ricocheted off the hellhound's armored plates."

Some cahir had shot his littermate? Fury rose in Ryder. "Where is the bastard? I'll—"

"He's dead." Ben's voice was hoarse with grief and pain.

"Aye. He has returned to the Mother." The sorrow on Alec's face matched Ben's. "The bullet destroyed Ben's chance to use his knife, and the hellhound charged Wesley."

"Why did he shoot if he wasn't supposed to?" Emma asked. "I didn't think cahirs got scared."

The healer snorted. "Only an idiot would face a hellhound without fear."

Ben met Ryder's gaze and half-grinned his agreement.

"We were scared, Emma," Alec said softly. "Cahirs only manage to continue because our protective instincts are stronger than our fears."

"You attacked a hellhound to save a child." Donal gave her a glance from silver-gray eyes. "Weren't you afraid?"

After a second, she nodded her understanding.

Her *understanding*? To save a child? Ryder's preconceptions were disappearing faster than shadows fleeing before the dawn.

Her nightgown and robe had worked up to above her right knee, exposing the remnants of the wound. The pink and white scars laid out an ugly pattern of torn muscles and skin. The rows of puncture marks were mute evidence of a bite from a huge jaw.

She hadn't lied. And she'd risked her life to save a child. Taken on a hellhound. By the God, no wonder Ben had assured him she'd never hurt Minette.

Fuck, he'd been as blind as a drunken dwarf at dawn.

An hour later, Ryder staggered into his bathroom. Sweat had plastered his shirt to his back. Tears burned his eyes; his throat felt raw, and his hands shook as he bent over the sink to splash cold water on his face.

"By the God, bro," he whispered. He'd far rather have his claws ripped out one by one than watch his brother put through such agony.

With a grunt of effort, he straightened. It was over. Ben would be all right, although he'd have to take it easy for a few days until the re-set bones had a chance to knit and finish healing.

Leaning on the sink, Ryder let his mind think toward the future. He wasn't as good a crew boss as his littermate, but until Ben was back to normal, Ryder would do whatever needed to be done.

Right.

Time to check on Minette. And somehow watch over Ben as well.

Two steps outside his bedroom, he ran into someone. The soft squeak and light cinnamon-and-flower scent told him who. "Emma."

"Sorry," she whispered. "I was… He might get chilled." She lifted the blanket in her hand.

"You plan to sit with him."

"Yes." Her voice was hoarse from the tears she'd smothered. "I'm afraid he won't call out, even if he needs something."

"You know him well." Ryder studied her, this little female who obviously cared for his brother. All night, with every moan Ben had made, the anguish had deepened in her face. "He'll be pleased to have you beside him."

Her blink of surprise at his compliment shamed him. *Time to man up, cat.* "Emma, I'm sorry for accusing you of lying. For the coldness I've shown you since I arrived. I hope you can forgive me."

"O-of course." She hesitated. "Can you tell me what I did to make you…um…"

"Be such an asshole?" By the God, he should be taken by the scruff and given a good shake. "You did nothing wrong," he said firmly. "Aside from being female."

"You hate me because I'm *female*?"

She sounded so appalled, he grinned. Because she deserved far better than the way he'd treated her, he tried to explain. "I've obviously met the wrong kind of females. And the last one"— the last one had totally screwed with his head—"was Minette's mother."

"Oh. I wondered." She paused, and her brows furrowed. "How did she die?"

"Die?" His bitter laugh made the little female flinch. *Hell.* Carefully, he laid his hand on her shoulder. So soft and warm. "I'm sorry I laughed. But Genevieve isn't dead."

"Oh." Her pale brows pulled together. "Then...why do you have her cub?"

"She wasn't taking care of Minette. Genevieve craves having males waiting on her. To be the center of attention, she'll scheme, tell tales, manipulate—and even set male against male. Minette was...inconvenient."

"Oh." Emma looked disgusted. Then she frowned. "So mostly because of one person, you think all females lie?"

Didn't that make him sound like an idiot?

Accepting the hit, Ryder gave her a rueful smile. "I didn't catch on until now how distrustful I've become. But, yeah, with everything a single female says, I look for hidden meanings and lies."

"That's not good." Her eyes lit with hope—for him? Damn, she was cute. "But you know now you've got a problem with your interactions with females?"

"Yeah." He tugged a lock of her hair in the way Ben would. "I'll work on it. Will you help out by walloping me if I mess up?" A wallop from the little bear would be far less painful than one from the grizzly.

"Me?" She almost squeaked.

"Please?"

In wonder, he watched her straighten her spine. "Yes, of

course. I'd be happy to assist."

The shy little bear would step out of her cave because someone needed help. He really had been a dumbass.

Regarding her, now with no preconceptions, he noticed that everything about her was appealing—her straight gaze, the way she faced her problems despite her fears, how she tried to pull her own weight no matter how much her leg hurt, how she cared for Minette, her joy when she was singing.

And more than anything, the way her kindness flowed from her like a blessed fountain.

Chapter Fifteen

BEN'S SHOULDER FELT as if a dwarf was excavating it with a pointed pickax. Pain or not, he was fucking starving. Time to raid the kitchen.

With a grunt of effort, he managed to sit up in his bed. He cursed as the sling Donal insisted he wear slipped sideways and pulled painfully.

"What are you *doing*?" Leaning on her cane, Emma stood in the doorway.

"What's up, honey bear?" His question came out jagged as hemlock bark.

Glowering, she limped into the room—and he didn't…really… notice the way her hips filled her jeans. "You're supposed to be sleeping."

Fuck, she was cute. And he inwardly cheered when her emotions swept away her shyness. "Sun's up."

"But…but you nearly died." She pointed a finger at him. "Don't you *dare* move. Donal said you were to stay in bed this morning."

He planned to ignore the idiotic restriction. Although he might have to skip work for a day or two. Thank the Mother that Ryder'd volunteered to oversee the crews—and the poor cat would hate every second of being forced to interact with others.

"I'll be good," Ben said. "If you bring me some breakfast."

"Already prepared. The Cosantir arrived and said he'd carry it upstairs." She bit her lip…her very soft, curved lip. "A Cosantir shouldn't perform such a lowly task."

Calum entered the room behind her with his customary cat-footed silence, and his dark gray eyes lit with amusement. "As the owner of a tavern, I am quite accustomed to carrying trays."

Emma spun and almost tripped.

Calum tilted his head. "You see why I carried the tray? You aren't yet up to managing without your cane."

"She isn't, so thank you, Calum."

Wearing a quite kissable pout, Emma propped pillows behind his back before pulling out a lap table from under the bed. As she set it over his thighs, he smelled freshly cut, unfinished wood. "Where'd you get this?"

"Ryder made it this morning before he headed out to check on your construction crews." She moved out of Calum's way.

Calum put the tray down, glanced at Ben's shoulder, and poured the coffee for him as well.

Ben looked down at the tray. Someone knew his preferences. The plate held a heaping mound of bacon and freshly scrambled eggs. The toast was already buttered and covered with a generous amount of honey. As the scents wafted up, his appetite turned to a raging hunger. "Thank you, Emma. I'm starving."

Her flush was delightful. "I hope it's edible. Ryder showed me how to scramble eggs and cook bacon when he made breakfast for Minette."

Good job, Ryder. Ben took a big bite and another. Excellent. The little female learned fast. And she'd shown courage in risking another culinary failure; he'd seen how the last one had devastated her. "You're a damn good cook, li'l bear. This is fantastic."

Her audible sigh of relief made him laugh.

Even Calum grinned. Just why was the Cosantir paying him a visit?

"Did anything else happen last night?" Ben asked. Surely, there hadn't been another hellhound.

"The rest of the night was quiet." When Calum settled into a chair beside the bed, Emma stood by the window like a silent guard. "A car accident down Highway 20 has Alec occupied, so he asked me to update you on our conclusions." By Calum's request, after any incident during their patrols, the cahirs reported to him. He'd have heard how and why the young cahir died.

As dark guilt flooded his veins, Ben set his fork down, appetite gone. "Wesley was my responsibility last night. His death is on my head."

"*No.*" Emma moved to stand between him and the Cosantir…who hadn't stirred. "Ben didn't cause his death. He couldn't. Don't you blame Ben."

Calum's lips twitched. "No, Benjamin didn't. But I'm glad to know he has someone to guard him until he's back on his feet."

With a suspicious stare, she settled at the foot of the bed, as if ensuring she'd be close enough to take action if need be.

Ben felt an unexpected warmth burning away some of the chill.

"The other cahirs agreed you did everything correctly," Calum said quietly. "They also said Wesley started off in the right way, playing decoy for the hellhound."

Ben shook his head. "I didn't do everything, or—"

"Stop." The word wasn't loud, but held enough of a Cosantir's power to make Ben's jaws snap shut. "I want you to think through the event—only this time, imagine Alec in your place. Tell me what he'd have done differently."

Under the level gaze, Ben replayed the night's disaster, minute by minute. Alec would have run up behind the hellhound, done the same twist onto his back...would have been shot. The sheriff possessed as much determination as Ben, but his frame was smaller. The bullet could have killed or completely incapacitated him.

Either way, the result wouldn't have changed. Wesley would still have died.

Calum leaned back in his chair, not needing to hear Ben's conclusions. "Exactly."

The knot in Ben's gut relaxed slightly. If only Wesley hadn't fired, Ben would have gutted the hellhound. "But...why? Why did Wesley shoot?"

"Ah. Alec said Sarah was screaming at Wesley to kill the hellhound. To save her. Right before he lost it, she'd started shrieking, '*Shoot. Shoot. Shoot.*'"

He must have been rolling under the hellhound right then. "I heard her. No wonder Wes lost focus." By the God, what a mess.

Emma asked, "What does her screaming have to do with anything?" She was rubbing his leg, as if trying to comfort a cub. It worked, actually.

"At a certain age, male shifters are impelled to procreate and are susceptible to emotional females," Calum said. "The drive to impress a female can overcome even the instinct for survival."

"So he wouldn't have died if..." The color faded from Emma's face, leaving her milk white. "The female caused the young male's death?"

Calum nodded. "She couldn't have anticipated the result. Nonetheless, some females revel in inciting males to violence."

Ben nodded.

Calum set one finger on the tray. "If you don't eat this breakfast, I will."

The gesture and threat set off the bear instincts. With a low growl, Ben pulled the tray closer and started to eat, rediscovering his appetite.

Emma gave a half-hearted chuckle. "We're truly ruled by animal instincts, aren't we?"

"Often more than we're willing to acknowledge," Calum said ruefully. "If Wesley had been warned about the effect of an endangered female's screams, he might have been able to throw it off."

"Aye," Ben agreed slowly. "He was a sharp lad, although hankering to be a hero. The decoy assignment annoyed him, so her goading fit right in with his own inclinations."

"Ah. I see." Calum rose.

"The rites for Wesley will be at sundown." Calum inclined his head toward Emma. "If the bard would care to sing, the gift would be valued. But it isn't mandated."

Emma nodded, not committing.

But why?

As Calum left, Ben considered her. Her golden eyelashes were a thick fringe on her cheek as she stared at her hands in her lap. Her loose hair blanketed her shoulders in a silken mass. By the God, she was a compelling female. And impossible to understand. "I thought bards liked to sing."

Her soft brown eyes were unhappy. "I didn't know Wesley. How can I do him justice in a song?"

"Do bards know everyone they sing about?"

"Well, no." A crease appeared between her brows. "They ask questions. Find out everything about the person from friends, family…and enemies. Find out what people think about the shifter's life—and death."

"Can't you do that?"

"It wouldn't be…perfect. Not in so short of a time."

And this little female needed things to be flawless. The humans on his crew often displayed the odd compulsion. Shifters tended to have a better balance, since animals weren't obsessed with perfection, just results. "The Mother doesn't hold "perfection" up as an ideal, honey bear," he said softly.

His words struck home with an almost audible plop.

Having made his point, he moved on. "Don't bards create sending-off songs on short notice? The lyrics are set to just one tune, aren't they?"

"The 'Return to the Mother' melody. Yes."

Not there yet. "You know, he shouted when he realized the bullet hit me. And he kept firing—even though he knew it would only draw the hellhound's attention."

Realization dawned in her eyes. "He drew the hellhound away from you."

"Aye."

Tears glimmered in her eyes and her jaw slowly tightened. "He deserves more from me than silence."

Ben waited, letting her work out her own destiny.

Then she narrowed her eyes at him. "All right. Since I'm asking questions of people, how do *you* feel about what happened?"

Hell. He guessed turnabout was fair, but by Herne's horns, he wished she hadn't asked. "I'm sad at the loss of life."

Her amber eyes sharpened until her gaze penetrated his defenses. "That's not all."

Fuck. He'd pushed. Now he owed her answers. But he'd far rather scoop out his guts with his own claws. "By the God, I still feel as if I fucked up. Maybe if I'd advised him better, he'd have stayed focused. Or if I'd let him make the kill as he wanted instead of staying with the procedure of him being the prey. Or if I'd moved faster, maybe I'd have killed the hellhound before he fired."

Her gaze softened.

If she told him she was sorry for him, he'd throw his tray

against the wall. "This won't help you construct a song, honey bear. What I feel isn't about him; it's all about me." And far, far too close to the guilt he felt for killing his own mother with his birth.

"I understand guilt," she said in a level tone. "However… As a polite male, Alec might moderate his judgment to spare you. But, according to local opinion, the cahir named Owen says whatever he thinks. If Owen thought there was something else you could have done, he'd have said."

Ben blinked. Apparently, Owen wasn't the only one who could be blunt.

"No one could have anticipated some female would order Wesley to shoot—or that he'd obey her."

"I should have guessed." He knew Sarah. Had mated with her last Gathering. "A male versus a hellhound would set Sarah all a-tingle. She's a great one to set the males to fighting."

Emma paled, and her hands tightened in her lap. She was probably re-living her own near-death from a hellhound.

"Best you get moving and do your interviews," Ben prompted.

"I will, if you'll eat and stop feeling guilty for something you couldn't have changed." She rose and, to his surprise, leaned forward and wrapped her arms around his waist.

And by the Mother's grace, she gave him the warmest, most comforting hug he'd ever received.

SITTING NEXT TO Ben in the second row of Ryder's SUV, Emma closed her eyes, wishing the day was over. Behind them in the third row, Minette snoozed quietly. As he drove, Ryder talked with his brother about their construction projects. His dark, smoky voice was somehow comforting, maybe because he was her friend now.

Friend had to be one of the most beautiful words in the language. And how funny was it she'd thought he hadn't liked her, and it turned out he just didn't trust her gender? Maybe she'd learn not to make assumptions.

Poor Minette, having a mother who wasn't nice. Oh, Emma understood how devastating it felt not to be wanted. As long as Emma was at Ben's, Minette would receive all the love the cub could handle.

The vehicle went over a bump, and Emma gritted her teeth as her brace scraped over her leg. Her muscles already ached with exhaustion from all the walking she'd done earlier. Even worse, she itched from the metal in the stupid vehicle. Descended from the Fae who couldn't tolerate iron, the Daonain tended to avoid cities and…hated cars.

In fact, right now, she felt grumpier than a burrowless gnome.

Ben's nearness didn't help. His shoulders were so wide, he brushed against her with every sway of the car. His arm was firm and warm, and she took a calming breath.

It didn't help. The air carried his rich masculine scent, which today lacked the usual accents of wood and leather. He hadn't been around his tools and wood, and the thought was distressing.

Reminded of his wound, she leaned forward to ensure his shoulder wasn't being jostled. No, he'd adjusted the shoulder strap to one side, and his white shirt was unstained.

As she sat back, his dark blue gaze caught hers. "Am I all right, oh, healer?" The laughter had returned to his voice.

He really was going to be all right. As her worries unknotted, her smile came unbidden. "Everything looks good."

"Did I thank you for caring for me last night?"

She shrugged. "I didn't do anything. Not like the healer. I just held your hand."

"Ah, darlin', you did far more. Having you there gave me a reason to fight the pain, to fight against dying."

The knowledge she'd helped him warmed her faster than any fire—but his terrifying words struck deep. "Don't die," she whispered.

The sun lines beside his eyes creased, and he shifted to put his arm around her shoulder and pull her against his powerful frame.

She gasped in surprise, but the sense of safety kept her from moving. He was so big, so strong.

During the Gathering, she'd been held by males. But…this…this was a different kind of being held. There was a sense of tenderness and comfort shared. Something she'd never experienced…ever. With a slow breath, she closed her eyes and snuggled closer, and he made a rumbling sound of satisfaction.

He'd come so very close to returning to the Mother. The thought of a world without this big grizzly just wasn't to be borne.

And the healer had hurt him so badly. Each time Donal had delved deeper into the wound, she could have sworn she felt each pain as if the healer was torturing her instead. Each of Ben's moans had sent a lance straight into her heart.

Yes, her heart. Because with each day in his presence, she'd fallen for him more. His big laugh, his rumbling voice, his gentleness with her and Minette, even his easy affection with his brother.

By the Mother, she loved him.

Love. How many songs had been written about the emotion? Now she knew why. The feeling was overwhelming, spilling into the hollows in her soul and filling them with a golden warmth.

At the same time, caring that much…hurt…because, by the Goddess, she had no future here. In her favorite songs and tales, love was the reward for being courageous—and the good shifter female would win her mates in the end. But Emma wasn't a good shifter female. Rather than saving others, she'd caused their deaths.

Love wouldn't be her reward in the end. Ben would turn away from her if he knew what she'd done.

No, she must simply cherish the friendship he offered and not yearn for more.

Moving a few inches away from him, she set aside regrets and turned her thoughts to what was to come.

The Return to the Mother Rites of Passage.

She was ready. Mostly. All day, despite the growing pain in her leg, she'd searched out shifters who'd known the young cahir. She'd heard what had happened during the moonless night, learned about the people involved, been instructed about young males.

If she'd known more at her own first Gathering, surely she'd have been better able to prevent problems. All day, she'd been reminded of Andre and Gary's deaths.

Beside her, Ben scratched his back against the seat and winced at the pull on his wounded shoulder.

Pulled from her moody thoughts, Emma narrowed her eyes at him. "Stop scratching."

He picked up her hand as he murmured, "You're damned cute when you get bossy."

"What?"

"Thank you for worrying about me, darlin'." He lifted her hand, kissed it, and started nibbling on her fingers, sending shivery sensations up her arm to her…surely not her heart.

"I hate cars." Ben's lips curved up, and from the front seat, Minette turned to look, and he winked at her.

Ryder, who was driving, shot him an amused glance in the rear view mirror. "This from the shifter who owns so many cranes and trucks that the cub was impressed?"

"Now you know why I keep humans on the crews. So they can drive the damn things." Ben pointed. "The turn is here on the right."

Ryder turned, drove down the small forest road past shifters walking on the side, and pulled into a grassy area carved out of the woods. He parked at the end with several other vehicles. "Looks like you two wimps aren't the only cripples."

"Bite me," Ben grumbled.

Laughing, Ryder opened Emma's door.

She stared, then slid out—and almost fell when Ryder assisted her with a hand under her arm.

"Easy, pretty bear. We're friends now, right?"

She couldn't think of anything she'd like better than to have him as a friend. "Yes," she whispered and watched his slow smile appear.

"Good."

When he touched her cheek with gentle fingertips, she realized he still made her uneasy, but in a way that made her aware of his size, his graceful strength, his dark voice. Looking up into his intense black eyes, she felt a quiver start deep in her core.

As he pulled the seat forward to get his daughter from the third row seat, Emma frowned. His apology last night had come as a surprise, but after hearing about Minette's mother, she understood his wariness. If the mother was the reason Minette was so quiet around people and flinched when someone moved too fast, well, the female must be simply vile.

Ryder had learned females were untrustworthy. As his friend, she'd do her best to teach him the opposite.

He set Minette beside her, then walked around the SUV to open Ben's door.

The bear shifter edged out of the car, carefully not bumping his oversized shoulders against the doorframe. He straightened with a sigh of relief. "I could have walked, dammit."

Emma smiled in sympathy. The grizzly didn't deal well with being an invalid. No one did, but Ben was so physical, he took being incapacitated worse than most. "Grumbly old bear."

He huffed at her.

Ryder grinned as he retrieved their food from the front seat.

With Ryder carrying their food offering, Emma held Minette's hand and walked between the two brothers toward the side of the clearing where people milled around the food. Wide boards on sawhorses had been covered with colorful tablecloths to provide tables for an enormous amount of food.

"Hey, Ryder. Ben." A grizzled shifter stood with several other males. "I saw what the hellhound did to Sarah's crappy door. We have some questions about reinforcing doors."

Ryder and Ben stopped.

"I'll take the casserole to the tables," Emma said.

"Thanks, Emma." Ryder handed it over and picked up his daughter.

With the heavy dish in one hand, using her cane with the other, she made her way over to the tables.

"Emma, what have you got there?" Obviously in charge of the food, Angie smiled and held her hand out.

"Some kind of casserole. Ryder made it this morning."

Angie blinked with obvious surprise. Males often learned to cook, but females always prepared the important meals.

"I-I don't cook," Emma said, her voice almost inaudible.

Angie snorted. "No need to act like you slaughtered a pixie. There's no law against avoiding the kitchen."

"I don't—I mean I wouldn't." It hurt to admit she was so incompetent at the basic life skills. "I just don't know how to cook."

"Oh. Hmm. I've got to say, I appreciate Calum's dictate that all shifters—male and female—should be taught to cook. But the decree is only enforced in our territory." Angie regarded her.

"Would you want to learn?"

"Oh yes! I really, really would." If she could, she'd have leaped and bounded like a spring foal. And wouldn't a bear look stupid imitating a horse?

"Easy enough. Anytime you're eager for a lesson, come to the diner. I enjoy having help, and you'll learn to make whatever is on the menu for the day." Angie removed the cover of the casserole and inhaled. "A venison and cheesy noodle casserole. Very nice. I'd think either of those brothers could teach you."

"Ryder taught me to make breakfast. But he's overseeing all the construction work while Ben recovers." She grinned. "And if I asked Ben to teach me, he'd try to do everything himself so I wouldn't get tired."

"You know him well." The soft voice behind her made Emma turn so quickly she almost lost her balance.

"Sorry, I didn't mean to startle you." The female was short and fair-skinned. Her golden hair held streaks ranging from platinum to light brown. Her blue eyes held a smile. "I'm Bree."

"Emma."

"I was with the pack and heard what you said." Bree nodded to the left at a group of females. Shifters. Of course, they'd heard her conversation with Angie. Unfortunately, Emma could hear their whispers in turn.

"Gawky bear can't even cook," a slender female with red-brown hair whispered to the other.

"Probably too busy singing instead of being a female." The brunette smirked. "After all, what male would have her?"

Emma's stomach tightened at the familiar sensation of being reviled.

To her surprise, Bree set her hands on her hips and gave the females a...*look*.

The two females went silent.

"Emma?" Just past the pack, Ben stood with several males.

He was watching her, his thick brows drawn together. Worrying about her.

Pushing her unhappiness away, she offered him an easy wave and saw his shoulders relax. His eyes crinkled and his gaze stayed on her, a long look that turned warm and warmer, and awakened slow flutters low in her belly. The world around her faded until all she could see was the intense blue of his eyes and the hunger simmering there.

"Ben, it's good to see you." The shrill voice broke their link. Three of the pack females had walked over to Ben, surrounding him and offering commiserating pats over his wounded shoulder and offers to help do…anything…he might need.

Emma turned away.

They were all smaller. Prettier. Thinner. He probably preferred fragile females. She watched him smile down at them, all big cahir male. Easy-going. Strong. Brave. Caring.

Her hands closed into fists.

What if he brought one of them home? The taste was bitter in her mouth. It wasn't her home, after all. Ryder would probably be delighted to share a female with his littermate.

As the female with red-brown hair stroked Ben's muscular arm, a worm of jealousy ate holes in Emma's heart. *Jealousy?* How in the world could she be jealous?

Was this what came with love? No…

Yet, every time she looked at the females around Ben, she wanted to…to pull their hair. Drag them away. Knock them deep into the forest. A low growl escaped her.

"Hey," Bree said softly. "It's just the typical fluttering of females around unmated cahirs. Nothing meaningful."

"It's not—he's not mine. Or interested. Or anything," Emma said hastily.

"Uh-huh." Bree's blue eyes were sympathetic. "Anyway, I heard you and Angie talking. I make all the diner's desserts, so when you want to learn to make treats for your guys, you come to me."

"Really?" Emma whispered, stunned into incoherence; Bree's words offered lessons, but her smile offered friendship. "Thank you." She turned to Angie as well. "Thank you both. I'd love any lessons you have time for."

"Awesome. Angie and I both enjoy company when we're cooking."

"Hey, Emma." Vicki, the black-haired female mated to Alec and Calum, approached.

Watching her, Emma sniffed the air.

Vicki frowned. "What? Did I forget deodorant?"

"Sorry. It's just…your posture looks like you're ready for battle, only you don't smell angry or afraid."

"The bard is pretty observant." Bree pointed her finger at Vicki and laughed. At Emma's confused stare, she added, "Vicki was in the military—a soldier."

"A Marine. Not a soldier," Vicki muttered.

"But no Daonain joins the army," Emma protested. The metal alone would make them ill.

"Not the fucking army." Vicki was interrupted by Angie's laugh.

"She was born human. She received the Death Gift and wound up being a werecat," Angie explained.

"Really." Oh…wonderful. Such a transformation would—should—be a *story*. It was a tale crying out to be told. Maybe even turned into a song. "Can I talk to you about it sometime?"

"Now there's a light I haven't seen in an eon or two." The voice was rougher than a gravel avalanche. An old shifter, face scarred from numerous fights, approached.

"Emma, this is Joe Thorson. He owns the town's bookstore." Vicki rubbed her shoulder against the male's in a friendly feline greeting. "What light, Joe?"

"The shining curiosity of a bard who's caught the scent of a new story. I've missed seeing that." The shifter gave her a respectful nod. "We're pleased to have you in Cold Creek, bard. Songs and stories are the strongest fibers in the tapestry of life—without them, the strands holding us together start to fray."

His gruff welcome made her eyes sting. Unable to speak, she bowed her head in acknowledgement.

He barked a laugh. "A shy bard. There's a marvel."

"She is…" Angie paused, her gaze following the Cosantir as he walked across the meadow toward the trees. "Time for the ritual."

Emma's stomach dropped, but she silently followed the others through the forest into a small clearing. Fresh dirt marked a new grave.

The Cosantir, clad all in black, spoke first. "Daonain, we are here to mark the passing of Wesley Tremblay, a werecat shifter. Who among us remembers this lad?"

Shay spoke up from the crowd. "He was a young cahir, still new in his powers, here to learn to kill hellhounds."

"Down from the Tongass Territory. They will mourn his loss." Zeb's rough voice came out even harsher.

"A good-hearted lad, brave and strong. Trying to prove his worth." Ben's grief and lingering guilt shadowed his deep voice.

She wished she was close enough to put an arm around him; wished they were close enough friends she'd dare to offer comfort in public.

"He had a sense of humor and loved practical jokes," Owen added.

"He picked me flowers," one female said. "He missed his family."

"He ate more like a bear than a cat," Angie said. "The boy could inhale an entire chicken without taking a breath."

Laughter rippled around the clearing before more people

spoke, telling their memories of the male, shaping a sense of the hole left by his loss.

Finally, no more spoke.

In the silence, the Cosantir said, "Our young cahir has returned to the Mother." He lifted his voice. "Wesley, may you refresh your spirit in the Summerlands. Know that you will be missed by your people until you return to us again. The clan mourns."

The chorus of voices returned like the wind in the trees, "The clan mourns."

After a slow breath, Calum looked around at the crowd. For her.

This was her moment if she chose to take it. The master bard had said she had a talent for composing, so perhaps…perhaps she could do the young cahir justice.

Yet a song of her own making would reveal her own realities, her insecurities before this community. Baring her soul had never gone well for her in the past. But Cold Creek had welcomed her. They were hurting. A song would give them closure.

The Cosantir's eyes were still dark with the presence of Herne as his gaze met hers. She felt his grief and her own need to offer something to mark this sad passing of a youth taken before his time. Under the God's silent call, she could only answer.

The first notes were ascending into the air before she realized she'd begun.

In the thrall of the song, stillness surrounded her, and she could feel each and every person in the clearing. She touched the depth of their loss, shared their sadness, and their emotions filled her voice as she sang the song of Wesley, the brave young cahir who had wanted only to protect.

All day, she'd turned the story over in her mind, swimming in the currents of the river of life, blending together what people had told her. Her duty as a bard was to look beneath the water's surface, all the way to the murky bottom, and return with treasures others might overlook.

And now, she slipped into minor chords for the dark of the moon. Note by note, word by word, Emma steered her audience into the night, the darkness, the fear. Into the drive to protect, the desire to be a heroic member of the team.

She pitched her voice higher, soaring into the scream of the female in the house and her exhortations to kill, then dropped lower for his surging instincts to prove himself worthy of a potential mate. She laid out how his nature had lured him into error and shattered his hard-won control.

Her hands slapped together with the barking pistol—her audience flinched back—and her arms dropped to her sides as she sang for young Wesley, the despairing knowledge of his failure, of his task left undone.

Her voice was pitched for mourning as the bond between the cahir's body and spirit broke apart. In notes of sadness, she mourned his shortened life, his unfinished job, tempered by the knowledge he'd someday return to take up his tasks again. That he'd do better the next life around.

Finally, she released the restraints on her voice as joy erased the past, as the young cahir moved toward his forever welcome in the arms of the Mother.

Her song whispered into silence.

No one stirred.

After a time, Emma moved to wipe the tears from her face and saw others doing the same. One person silently left the clearing, followed by another, beginning a slow exodus.

As shifters passed her, most touched her shoulder in formal respect.

Most. Not all. Not the females who'd made fun of her. As they moved past, the buxom brunette glared at her. And the brunette was on the receiving end of a multitude of frowns.

Could this be Sarah, the female who'd goaded the young cahir?

A hand closed on Emma's shoulder, tingling slightly with power. Calum stood beside her. He gave her a faint approving smile before moving on.

The last of the people left the clearing, leaving her standing with…two males and a child.

"Well done," Ryder said quietly. He stood on her left, Minette on his hip.

"Done here?" Ben asked from her right.

Their strength and support flowed into her, giving her courage.

"Yes, I'm done." She looked up, studying Ben's face.

His face resembled stone, his jaw tight with pain and grief. But his eyes were clear, no longer muddied with his guilt. His shoulders didn't hunch as if awaiting a new blow. Because he had done nothing to be ashamed of.

Not like Emma. In some way, she must be like the self-centered female who'd goaded Wesley. In her own contempt for Sarah's behavior, Emma could understand how the shifters in Pine Knoll must have felt about her own actions at the Gathering. However, Sarah hadn't been banished. And the Mother had forgiven Emma and erased the banishment blackness. Now all Emma had to do was forgive herself. It was time to move on.

"C'mon, honey bear," Ben said softly, tucking his massive hand under her arm and moving her forward.

The meadow was filled with people, sad-eyed, silent. No one seemed interested in food.

"Bard." Calum's brother, Alec, was tall and sandy-haired with eyes of a dark green. "The Cosantir requests another song—one that will help the clan move on to acceptance and life."

"As the Cosantir wishes," Emma responded with the traditional reply.

Slowly, she scanned the crowd, but her gaze returned to the ones closest at hand. To the tear-stained face of the child she'd come to love—and Emma knew the two songs she wanted to sing. First a song of gratitude to the Mother...and then the very old tune about a young kitten learning the joys—and wetness— of fishing in a tiny stream.

Because sadness should be followed by laughter.

Chapter Sixteen

MIDWEEK, BEN SAT in his office, scowling at the list of things he needed to do. By the God, broken bones were far worse than shredded muscles. Normally, after a healing, he'd be stiff and sore, and weak for only a couple of days. This time, his shoulder still fucking hurt.

Emma hadn't had a healer right away—no wonder she still walked like an old granny—although she was doing better than he was, what with caring for Minette every day. She'd even started teaching the mite the alphabet.

He pushed his To Do list away with a low growl. He needed to be at work, but Donal had said construction work—pounding, sawing, lifting—might screw up his shoulder permanently.

Being crippled wasn't on the To Do list. Nonetheless, he couldn't afford to give his recovery more than another day or so.

"What's the matter, bro?" Ryder prowled in and set down a coffee cup with a grizzly bear painted on the ceramic. The cup he sipped from was decorated with a cougar. They'd been presents from their Naini.

"I've got too much to do and only one arm to do it with," Ben said.

"You're not gonna do squat. Donal said you're off the job

this week."

"I can't." Ben pointed at the two sites where active building was happening, then the two volunteer projects. "They all need—"

"I got them covered. We're managing all right without you."

"You have your own work."

Ryder put a foot up in the chair and leaned his forearms on his thigh. "My woodworking projects can be postponed until you're back."

"You don't like supervising the crews."

"Not particularly." Ryder shoved his fingers through his hair. "But we're brothers, which means I pick up what you drop. Just get your ass back to work in a week or your crew will probably quit on you."

As the weight lifted off his shoulders, Ben laughed, remembering their first year in construction when Ryder'd taken a turn bossing the crew. Three humans had quit before the day was over. "Just treat them as if they were oversized Minettes, and you'll do fine."

Ryder snorted. "So I need to buy them Superman Band-Aids?"

"You can fire them if they start scamming you about their owies." Minette had been thrilled with her Little Mermaid Band-Aids...and had been pointing out the tiniest scrapes in hopes of scoring more. Ben's smile faded. "Seriously, thank you, bro."

"I'm enjoying it. Well, not the bossing, but working with shifters again. And doing charity stuff. Feels good to give something back for a change."

Ben smiled. Seemed his brother was starting to let go of the hardass finally. "Good to hear."

Ryder glanced around the piles of paper in the office. "Meantime, you get a chance to catch up with deskwork."

"Yeah, nothing I'd rather do. Oh, well, maybe snorting cougar piss would be more fun."

"Asshole." Ryder smacked Ben upside the head. "C'mon. Donal said you could *trawsfur* if you didn't exert your shoulder. Emma said she'd cub-sit, and I need to be a cat for a while."

Ben studied his brother. "It's been a while, hasn't it? Have you shifted since you got Minette?"

"Nope."

Hell, for the sake of his construction crews, he'd better get Ryder into fur or he'd be liable to claw out someone's guts. "Let's go."

He led the way to the garden shed, which shared a wall with the back fence. Inside, they stripped and exited through the concealed backdoor. Forest surrounded them. Salmonberry and red-stemmed salal created a dense understory below the hemlock and firs, blocking any access from possible human intruders.

Ben motioned to the right fork on a small deer trail. "I can't go too far, but that one leads to a small lake within a couple of miles."

"Perfect." With a grin showing his relief, Ryder blurred as he shifted to his animal form.

Ben pulled in a slow breath and watched, feeling the thickness in his throat. He hadn't run with his brother in five lonely years.

The cat had put on muscle and weight. His fur was a tad darker than most golden-tawny cougars before shading to almost white under his belly. With a low purr, Ryder butted his head against Ben's thigh—a nudge saying to get a move on.

Laughing, Ben *trawsfurred*, feeling the Mother's love sweep through him. He dropped onto his front left paw, keeping his weight off his right. He wasn't going to win any races today, but by Herne's hairy balls, it was good to have dirt under his paws again.

He huffed and motioned with his head for Ryder to go on

ahead. His housebound littermate would need to run for a while, feel the freedom, and catch the scents. Ben could bring up the rear.

With a low yowl, Ryder sprang forward.

Even lumbering along slowly, Ben enjoyed himself. Summer was on hand already, the wildflowers beginning to bud and bloom. Cheeps from fledglings sounded from high nests. He caught the scent of deer and a lone coyote.

The trail ran upward, through stands of towering silver fir, and then switch-backed down a steep slope. Going downhill without a healthy foreleg was a pain in the tail. Ben's grumbles came out as harsh breaths.

Ryder flashed back to him, rubbed his muzzle along Ben's head, and disappeared again. The sound of bark tearing said he was sharpening his claws on a tree trunk. A few minutes later, a sharp squeak said a mouse or shrew had met its doom.

There was nothing as tasty as fresh snacks.

The air grew moist and cool as they descended to the alder and vine maples surrounding the small glacier-fed lake.

After a protracted stretch, Ryder shifted to human and sprawled in the sun on a flat expanse of moss-covered rock.

Ben shifted and joined him. "Did you save me a snack?"

"Nope." Ryder pointed at a patch of monkey flowers and bluebells. "Smells like good hunting there though. I'll catch you something before we leave."

"A rabbit would go down good." Ben tipped his head toward the sun, enjoying the warmth contrasting with the chill of the rock under his ass. "Thanks, bro. I needed to get out."

"Yeah. You've been…off." Ryder's gaze was a little too intent. "Must be tough to lose a cahir partner that way."

"Goes with the territory." The lazy relaxation slid out of his muscles. Dammit, he didn't want to talk about the cahir's death.

Ryder waited silently, tossing blades of grass into the still mountain lake.

Ben caved in. Brothers shared, even the ugly shit. If he and Ryder were to get back to where they'd been, they had to be able to talk. "Wesley's death…brought back old shit. Fucked me up to be the reason someone died. Again."

"Again?" Frowning, Ryder held grass up to be ruffled by the snow-chilled breeze. "I'm missing something. Was another cahir killed?"

"Not a cahir." In the cloudless blue sky, a hawk circled. Hunting. "Didn't your father tell you? My birth killed our mother. I was too big. Tore her inside, and she bled to death. It's why your father took you and left town when we were five. I kept getting bigger and he couldn't stand looking at me."

Ryder sat up, a scowl on his face. "Where the fuck did you come up with this shit?"

"My sire told me when I visited Texas five years ago." And ever since, the guilt had flowed through Ben like muddy floodwaters. He'd killed their mother.

"Wait, wait, *wait*." Ryder straightened, his face darkening. "Arnold fed you that crap? And you've carried this shit around for years? You must have… By the Gods, this is why you said you wouldn't take a mate?"

"Aye. I'm a grizzly. Any female I mated would risk dying in childbirth the way our mother did. I won't take that chance."

"By the God, you are so—"

"Not something we're going to discuss," Ben said.

"Shut up, bro. You talked. Now you'll listen, as I did."

Ben blinked. His littermate rarely snapped at him. A glimmer of pride ran through Ben. Not many took on a grizzly, but Ryder was prepared to fight to be heard. "Go on. I'll listen."

" 'bout time, yeah?" Ryder said in a dry voice. "First, my father wasn't mad at you, or disgusted, or anything, bro. But he was damn well furious at your father. He had a hell of a fight with Arnold before we left."

Ryder's father hadn't hated him? Ben's brain felt as if it was being hammered with a nail-gun. He remembered Ryder's father—a lanky male with black hair and black eyes—who had never been anything but kind. "Why the anger and why the fight?"

"You were overly large for our dam," Ryder said, ignoring the question. "She was a cat; you're not only a bear, but a grizzly one."

Ben felt his shoulders hunch under the burden of the guilt.

"But, bro—wolves and cats have borne bears for all the generations of the Daonain. A healer told our mother she'd have trouble with the birthing—any birthing. Did you know she'd already lost one litter?"

"No," Ben said huskily. "And she knew she'd have trouble?"

"Yeah, she'd been warned before even getting pregnant the first time. Her pelvis was narrow. But she favored big males. Wouldn't have been a problem if a healer had been in attendance, but Arnold..."

"What did my father do?"

"Pa said Arnold was paranoid to the point of insanity."

Ben rubbed his face. No news there. Most shifters didn't live so isolated they saw no one for months at a time. "Figured out he was a bit unhinged once I met normal people."

Ryder leaned back on one elbow. "The story played out like this: Our mother met Arnold and his brother—and my sire—at a Gathering. When she ended up pregnant, Arnold and his brother talked her into living with them, although they never lifemated. When the brother got killed by a feral, Arnold turned into even more of a hermit.

"The way my father talked, I thought she was his lifemate."

"He wanted to lifemate, but, it never happened, maybe because he wasn't stable." Ryder continued, "That's why our mother had mated with several males on Gathering night, but in such a small town, my sire knew a child with black eyes and black hair was undoubtedly his. After he saw me, he moved next door to Arnold to stay close while I grew up."

"I never heard any of this."

"Eh, not something you discuss in front of a cub," Ryder said. "The split-up was my fault, by the way. Arnold caught me sneaking food from the fridge and walloped me. Pa saw the bruises and yelled at him, and Arnold went batshit and tried to kill Pa. That's why we left. Pa wanted to take you with us, but Arnold insisted you were his. Father figured he wouldn't kill his own son, or he wouldn't have left you."

"Unfortunately, Arnold found out I wasn't his when I *trans-furred* the first time." Ben smiled slightly. "We may both have blue eyes, but he's a wolf. Obviously, our mother mated with a blue-eyed bear at the Gathering." Yeah, the year he turned thirteen had been when the blame had turned into outright abuse. At least being a big grizzly meant, when he'd run away at sixteen, he'd passed for an adult.

"Oh, hell. Pa shouldn't have taken that fucking nutcase's word for anything."

"Your father couldn't have known."

"No. Guess not. But you know, he loved you. Missed you." Ryder scowled. "And I was a righteous mess. Figured it was my fault we'd lost you."

"Give me a second." Ben turned away, staring at the dark depths of the lake, trying to process the information. Seemed like the solid foundation for his life had turned to swampland. One fact remained. "But I still killed our mother."

"By the God, you're stubborn," Ryder muttered. "Yes and no. Knowing she was pregnant and Arnold was fucking unstable, Pa had been stopping by to check on her. But he came too late that day to get her into town and to a healer. Arnold said she started bleeding with my birth, your birth made it worse. But she might well have bled out anyway, just from having me."

Ben couldn't find any words.

"Ben." Ryder waited until their gazes met. "If she'd had a healer like she'd been advised, she'd have lived, but Arnold refused to move into town for the last month of her pregnancy. When her labor started, he didn't rush her to a healer although he'd had time. The only guilt I see is his."

Ben stared at him, his mind numb.

"Instead, he laid the blame on you. He couldn't admit his inaction killed the female he loved. That he'd been too much of a yellow dog to take her into town."

She'd been told to be under a healer's care. Any birth would be risky. She'd started bleeding with Ryder's birth.

It hadn't been his fault—or at least not all his fault.

As Ryder silently watched the lake, Ben examined the conversation, picking up and turning over the sentences like logs in a forest to see what lay beneath.

Finding truth.

And after a few minutes, Ben rubbed his face, considering another statement Ryder had made, ...*wolves and cats have borne bears for all the generations of the Daonain.* True enough. "A female might not die from bearing my cub," he said slowly.

"Deaths during birth don't happen often, even if the females are cats or wolves having bear cubs. I haven't ever heard of a death if there's a healer present."

Ben sat for a while longer, unwilling to leap right into hope. But the fact remained—having his cubs wasn't an automatic death sentence for a female.

Ryder scowled. "You went to Texas right before we met Genevieve—and Arnold lied to you. That's why you came back and told me you'd never take a mate."

"Aye."

"And because I was young and stupid, and couldn't imagine never mating or having cubs, I left with Genevieve."

"Sounds about right." Ben half-grinned. "At least, the young and stupid part."

"Asshole." Laughing, Ryder flicked a twig at him. His smiled died. "I don't suppose we can look up your sire and beat the scat out of him?"

"No need. My friends in Texas let me know that he'd gone feral and died. Couple of years past."

"Not surprising, actually. He had no one left to care about." Ryder tilted his head, listening to a bird sing.

It was nesting and birthing season. The trilling melodies reminded Ben of how Emma sang to Minette in the kitchen. As if they were in a real home.

In the uncanny way of brothers, Ryder followed his thoughts. "I don't think I've ever met anyone as simply…sweet…as Emma." He shook his head. "At one time, I thought pretty outweighed personality. It's amazing what you learn as you get older, isn't it?"

Ben grinned, knowing exactly what his littermate meant. Young, hormone-driven males went after superficially attractive females. It was a status thing. Once a bit older, the male might mate pretty, but would spend his time with smart and nice. A few more years, and unless pushed into it—as Sarah had done—a male had no time for mere prettiness. There had to be more. "Sweet. Smart. Generous. And damned lovely, too."

Ryder rose and gripped Ben's undamaged shoulder. "Agreed. And in case you haven't noticed, bro, I thought I might mention—she isn't a tiny female."

She wasn't small. No. She was a bear. A *bear*. Before Ben could shake off the stunning revelation, his littermate shifted and pounced on a rabbit in the boggy area.

Ben watched, rubbing his foot against the rock. Looked like

he might have a bunny for a snack. Smiling, he realized the bond between him and Ryder no longer hurt, and was intact. Progress.

And his past? Well, he needed to think all this over. Ponder for a while.

As he watched Ryder, he realized it'd been a while since he'd hunted with his brother. What would Ryder say if Ben told him he wanted to hunt something far more appetizing than a bunny.

Maybe they'd start with a pretty little bear…

SCOWLING, RYDER TRIED to read the notes on what needed to be done for Albert Baty's kitchen remodel. By Herne's hairy balls, Ben's handwriting sure hadn't improved any in the last few years. Was the word there *undine* or *under*? Undine counter lighting didn't make sense; water elementals wouldn't be caught dead in a kitchen. So, *under* it was.

He looked up to check on Minette. Emma had dropped her off while she popped into the Wild Hunt to clear her song list with Calum. For a while, the cub had made what Emma called "mud pies," although the bard had assured him the cub wouldn't eat them. Now Minette was kicking a soccer ball against the fence.

"Ryder." Kenner wandered up. "I have downtime while things dry. Where do you want me?"

The burly drywall finisher could have had his own business, but the bear was an easy-going, sociable sort. He preferred working on Ben's crew even when doing tasks other than drywalling.

"You have a choice of installing the new stove or working on the bathroom remodel," Ryder said.

"I hate ba—"

From the corner of his eye, Ryder saw Minette trip over a stick and fall. "Minette!"

He charged across the lawn, dropped to the ground, and scooped her into his lap. Fuck, she was *crying*. Panic threatened.

Breathe, cat. "Let's see the damage," he managed to say…almost calmly.

Her hands and knees were dirty, but not scraped, not bleeding. Still, big tears ran down her face.

"Oh, kitten." The helpless feeling was like a current dragging him underwater. How could he fix her world? She was *crying*. As she clung to him, he held her against his chest.

Her crying slowed.

"Whoops, did someone take a bounce on the ground?" Kenner went down on one knee and brushed the dirt from her hands and legs. "There go. All better. Just like magic."

Sniffling, she solemnly inspected her palms and her knees before looking up at Ryder for his opinion.

The bands loosened around his chest. "Yep, all fixed. Guess you're good."

One red mark got a dubious frown before she agreed and wiggled to get down. Trauma forgotten, she picked up her ball and gave it a kick. A glance over her shoulder established that he was watching.

"Excellent kick, kitten. You have a good eye."

For the compliment, he received a far better reward—one of her tiny smiles.

As she resumed her solitary game, Ryder scrubbed his hands over his face. He'd far rather fall straight off a cliff than to see his cub in tears. "By the God, I'm not good at this."

"Bullshit." With a booming laugh rivaling Ben's, Kenner smacked his shoulder. "You can't keep a cub perfectly safe, cat. But if a hug from you makes things better, then you're doing it right."

A hug was considered helping? But…her crying had slowed when he held her. The knowledge was gratifying. He stood and bumped his shoulder against Kenner's. "Thanks."

"No problem, boss."

An hour later, Emma had Minette by the hand as Ryder showed them through the remodeled house. He really appreciated the customizations Baty had ordered...like the glassed-in fireplace that let salamanders dance without scattering coals across the hearth. He pointed out the abundance of natural materials. "The previous owners—humans—had put in stainless steel appliances in the kitchen. Albert could hardly stand to come in the room."

"Ew, I bet." Emma looked up as a stray sunbeam danced across the wall. "Skylights. What a great idea." She turned in a circle and stopped, frowning toward where the baseboards had been. "If you're planning to repaint the walls, what happened there?"

"The humans had installed plastic baseboard." He half smiled. "The molding didn't look bad, but Ben had a fit. Said it'd make brownies ill if they tried to burrow through it."

"Amazing. I've never considered the OtherFolk and what they need to live or be happy. Then again, we didn't have brownies when I was growing up."

Because her mother sounded as if she'd been a real shrew. Brownies only lived with stable families. "Us, either." The unexpected jolt of longing made him shake his head. He wanted Minette to grow up in a happy home where brownies would industriously clean the kitchen and wait for the little daughter of the house to set out their treats of cake and cream.

"Oh." Emma's eyes held remorse. "I forget you and Ben were separated. That must have been terrible."

"A bit." He'd been five and hadn't spoken for nearly a year. Cats didn't lose people well. Didn't make friends easily.

"Smith, you moron, what the fuck did you do?" The yell came from the bathroom.

Great. Wishing Ben was back, Ryder strode through the living room and into the bath, and stared.

The young human male had fucked up the granite tiles. Badly. He opened his mouth…and remembered Minette's reaction to shouting.

Two days ago, when Ben had been swearing and bellowing into the phone about a missed shipment, Minette had disappeared. They'd found her hiding outside in the bushes.

Sheathe the claws, cat. Ryder sucked air in through his nose. As his anger dimmed, he realized the young male looked like a pup expecting to get kicked. His eyes were almost as vulnerable as Minette's.

Hell. Now what? Ben had given him advice, right? *"Just treat them as if they were oversized Minettes, and you'll do fine."*

"I'm sorry, Ryder." The pup ran a finger over the gap between the granite and the wall. "I messed up the measurements."

"Yep, you did." Ryder considered. "Hang on to the granite pieces. They might look good as part of the fireplace hearth. And have Kenner double-check your measurements today, until you know you have it down."

The lad nodded. "Yes, sir. I'm really sorry."

"You'll learn." Remembering Minette's smile when he'd noticed her kicking skill, Ryder added, "We all make mistakes. And you've got a talent for laying tile. Ben's lucky to have you."

The glow in the youngster's eyes was…yeah…worth breaking a fang trying not to yell. Ryder glanced at Kenner and got the male's confirming nod that he'd pup-sit.

Emma was waiting outside the door, and the smile she gave him was wide and open, and filled his heart as if she'd installed golden lighting in a dark room.

Chapter Seventeen

IT'D BEEN A week since Ben had been hurt, and after okaying him to work, Donal also stated Ben would know if he was overdoing. *No fucking shit.*

Since it was Saturday, Ben and Ryder had been fixing up the house for Zeb's pack member. Ben finally gave into the throbbing pain and called it quits.

Damn healer.

Leaving his littermate to finish framing in the windows, he walked out of the decrepit house. The sagging porch groaned beneath his weight.

He hadn't seen a building in such poor condition since his younger days when he lived among humans. Damn place should be torn down, but Tullia had lived here since she was first mated. She was in about the same shape as the house. At her age, she wouldn't do well with change, so they'd do their best to get her home into livable shape. Considering the crap job the original builders had done, the structure would end up more solid than when it was new.

On the steps, Ben halted. *Now there is a sight.*

Emma was kneeling in the neglected flower garden bordering the street.

Drawing on a small tablet, Minette sat cross-legged beside

her. Satisfaction welled within Ben. The cub's cheeks had filled out, and her small arms no longer looked like skin stretched over bones. Her smile came far more often now.

Donal had checked her over, saying her silence wasn't caused by anything physical. With time and love, she should recover.

Well, they had the time. As Ben watched the two females, he knew love wouldn't be a problem either. The mite had taken up residence in his heart as if she'd been born from one of his own matings. She was a bundle of sweetness…and was beginning to show hints of the mischievousness her sire had possessed when a cub. When she was healed, she'd probably run them all ragged.

His gaze turned to Emma. Also recovering. No longer underweight, she was beautifully rounded. She'd left her hair loose to spill down her back in a golden sheet that begged to be tousled by a male. Her cheeks were the color of ripening peaches, her mouth a kissable pink.

And she was fucking kissable, wasn't she?

He realized he was smiling. Yeah, well, he'd been doing that more, first when the three additional people filled his home, then three days ago when Ryder had laid out the facts of their birth.

His guilt was gone, and he felt lighter, as if he'd removed a heavy tool belt.

Even more… Ben inhaled slowly, catching the scent of the golden female in the garden. He now had a future, something he'd lacked since his trip to Texas. For five long years, when he'd heard cubs laughing, he'd known he would never have any offspring to raise, to protect, to love. And now, suddenly, the narrow, dark valley was filled with sunlight.

He could take a mate. Share one with his brother. Have cubs. Have a future that held love. Females were trouble—just ask Ryder—but they were also the glory and brightness in a male's life. Feeling he couldn't take a lifemate had dimmed his world.

When Ryder had walked away, the darkness had been complete.

Now, change had come again. His littermate was back. With a cub. And they had a female living with them. The sweetest, bravest female he'd ever known.

Ben's house was filled with people, with laughter and song, and even bickering. Fuck, he loved coming home now.

He watched as Minette poked at a bug in the dirt, and Emma laughed. She didn't laugh enough—but, like Min, her smiles came more often. It would be an honor, a delight, to be the one who helped her lose her shyness. To be the one who won her trust.

Her love.

Yeah, he wanted that female right there.

She was…amazing, constantly surprising him with her intelligence, her unexpected flashes of humor, her sheer kindness.

She was big enough to fill a man's arms and wonderfully soft. Her scent held her sweet female musk with traces of flowers and cinnamon.

And even when speaking, she sounded as if she was singing.

The tavern had been packed again two days ago with shifters in to listen to the bard. Ben had taken himself another kiss before walking her home. Kissing Emma was more satisfying—and intoxicating—than actual sex with any other female.

What would mating her be like?

Even better would be sharing her with his brother. It'd been too long since they'd enjoyed a female together. But those teamwork skills didn't go away, and no female had ever complained about their favors in the past. On the contrary.

But he wanted to stand shoulder-to-shoulder with his littermate as they slid lifemating bracelets on their chosen female's wrist.

He wanted to see their female swell with their young. The mere thought sent hormones dancing in his veins.

Could Emma learn to love them?

Winning her wouldn't be an easy trail. Something in her past had derailed her from the normal enjoyment a female felt toward sex. She certainly wasn't going to jump right into his bed. It was time to get to the bottom of those secrets.

At least his brother had started to realize not every female was like Genevieve, although her memory was still a splinter in Ryder's paw, prickling him every time he paced forward.

With the Mother's grace, there would be enough time and love to get them to the trail's end.

Leaning a hip against the railing, Ben watched his two females…until he noticed a brown-haired male coming up the sidewalk.

The wolf shifter detoured across the yard to join Emma.

Ben scowled as possessiveness welled within him. *Mine.* He jumped off the porch and stalked toward where the brash male was trying to make conversation with her.

When Emma saw him, she smiled in welcome. "Ben. I thought I scented you."

After setting his hand on her shoulder—*mine*—he smiled down at her, then studied the interloper. The wolf was young. Closer to Emma's age. Would she prefer youth?

Trying to keep from shoving the male away, Ben told him, "Work is inside."

The young male stiffened as if he'd been poked in the side with a stick. "And just who are you to tell me what I should do?"

Catching the scent of fear from Emma, Ben glanced at her. Her color had paled. Her scent held no sexual interest for the wolf—just fear. The bastard had scared her somehow.

"I'm supervising the work on this house." Ben's voice dropped to a low growl. "Get moving."

When the wolf drew himself up, Ben followed suit—and towered over the puppy by almost a foot.

The young male took an involuntary step back and muttered, "Fucking bear." And he caved. "Fine. I need to get to work anyway."

Spineless, Ben thought with annoyance. What kind of cubs were they raising in Shay's pack?

Emma pulled Minette into her arms, and both females stared up at Ben as if he'd gone on a feral rampage. "Wh-why are you upset?" Emma asked shakily. "He wasn't doing any harm."

By the God, the puppy hadn't scared her; Ben had. *Hell.* "Sorry, honey bear, it's habit. I forgot not everyone on a work site is one of my crew." A growl escaped him. "When my employees are at a site to work, they actually work...not flirt with females."

Perhaps he should follow his own advice and get his ass back to work. The south side construction site needed to be checked.

But...first... Slowly he bent, cupped Emma's soft chin in his hand, and held her for a carefully controlled, persuasive kiss. When her lips softened and opened, he plunged his tongue into the dark recesses of her mouth, savoring her taste, her willingness to participate.

A shaking sensation recalled him, and he opened his eyes.

Minette was silently laughing her little ass off.

"You liked watching, cub?" he asked, tapping his finger on her adorable nose.

She wrinkled it up, still grinning.

"Well at least *she* appreciates the way I kiss," he told Emma and surprised an amused snort out of her.

He leaned down, nuzzling the little bear's temple, feeling the brush of silky hair...and inhaling the interest in her scent. "And so do you, darlin','' he whispered. "So do you."

AFTER ASSIGNING THE newly arrived male wolf to attaching iron bars to the reframed window, Ryder paused to drink the tea Tullia had brought him.

Tea. Complete with a pot and cup. Whoever heard of drinking tea on a job site? But she was so pitifully grateful and eager to repay their work that Ryder hadn't been able to refuse.

She'd told him her three mates had built the house an eon ago. Ryder scowled. Given the crookedness of...fucking everything...they shouldn't have been allowed anywhere near a hammer.

He and Ben hadn't planned on messing around with the windows. But when Ryder'd attached an iron window guard, he'd realized a child could yank the screws right out of the dry rot. So he'd spent most of today removing windows and reframing them with solid wood.

All of the construction work was going well. Ben's two crews accepted direction well, and although he didn't enjoy being crew boss, he could manage. Just as Ben managed handling the finances and payroll when needed.

He smiled as he finished the last window and repacked his tools. Being partnered with his littermate was like pulling on a worn pair of jeans—nothing fancy, simply a good fit. Comfortable and right.

Ryder walked out of the shabby house to see Ben kiss Emma. By the God, seemed Ben hadn't hesitated to act on Ryder's advice.

His brother definitely wanted to mate with her.

They were littermates; they'd share. Ryder felt...unsettled. He should have thought this all through before pointing Ben in her direction.

Then again, maybe it was only his brain falling behind. Everything else in him—his body and his spirit—said the little bear was fucking appealing. Soft. Lush. The breeze carried her wildflower scent, and the sun lit her hair until she seemed to shimmer with gold.

Ben nuzzled Emma's cheek, gave a tug on Minette's hair, and sauntered down the sidewalk, heading toward home.

Ryder stayed in the doorway, watching as Emma tried to regain her composure. She looked a little dazed.

He damn well knew the feeling. What did he want to do?

Minette adored her—and no wonder. Even when Ryder'd been acting as if he had ice up his ass, Emma had remained sweet. And she was damned smart, the bard.

And wary.

Well, so was he, for that matter. He could see taking Emma to bed, but hopefully, Ben wasn't thinking about lifemating her. Hooking their lives—their very souls—to a female? Maybe. Maybe not.

"Hey, Ryder." The call came from the south where Bonnie was coming up the sidewalk from town. The female was one of Zeb and Shay's wolf pack, and she often took time to bring Tullia some food. Wolf packs took care of their own.

Ben was teaching him how other shifters took care of the whole clan.

"What's up, Bonnie?" Ryder walked out to meet her.

"I found those papers you wanted." Bonnie handed him a manila envelope. "You really think you can get Tullia some assistance?"

"Probably." Partly as a result of their isolation, the Daonain tended to see "help" as being physical, not financial, and often forgot they were part of the United States. But they were shortsighted. He'd learned a lot in his years hanging out with humans. "We pay taxes to the government. A percentage of those taxes fund programs to care for the elderly and indigent. Tullia worked all her life. She deserves a break now."

"I totally agree." Bonnie noticed Emma and walked closer. "I see she's going to have flowers, too. Those will be beautiful."

Budding with gold flowers, small plants filled the bard's market basket. Softhearted female. She knew Tullia didn't get out any longer, only went as far as her porch.

"Hi, Bonnie." Emma fingered a tiny bud. "Another week and Tullia will be able to sit on her porch and see the blooms."

Ryder made a mental note to fix the porch swing.

Ignoring Bonnie and Ryder, Minette patted Emma's thigh and held up the tablet. She'd written a wobbly 6 under Emma's drawing of six golden flowers.

"Wonderful counting, kitten," Emma said. "And you made a perfect six."

Minette beamed and set the tablet in Emma's lap for her next task.

"All right. People next." Emma sketched a curvy female with braided hair, a male with jaw-length hair and a dark beard shadow, a bigger, clean-shaven male, and a child. "How many are in this picture?"

Minette held up four fingers.

"Exactly right. Four. Can you write the number?"

Minette took the tablet. Her tiny mouth was a determined line, her thumb-sucking hand fully employed to hold the paper steady. He recognized that focus—his focus.

He had a cub. The wonder of it still stopped him in his tracks several times a day. How had he and Genevieve created something—someone—so very special?

"She's a bright little sprite." Bonnie said. "How old is she?"

"Four." Ryder's throat was so tight the word came out hoarse. So many years where he hadn't been there for her.

"Only four?" Bonnie turned a speculative look at the girl.

"How long has she been counting and writing?"

"A week," Emma and Ryder replied.

Smiling at the pretty bard, Ryder continued. "Emma's been working with Minette. Teaching her. Before last week, she could only color. Printing and counting past four is new."

"Amazing." Bonnie studied Emma. "Why aren't you a teacher?"

"Part of my bard training was about education," Emma said, "but the human law requires formal credentials for anything other than preschool or tutoring. I didn't go to college."

Many Daonain didn't attend college since being surrounded by humans and held to their rigid schedules was uncomfortable. But from the wistful look in Emma's eyes, she would have gone. What had prevented her?

He frowned. She'd had a rich mother who hired and fired cooks. If she hadn't been caught singing—and questioned by the Cosantir himself—would anyone even know she was a bard?

And she'd spent three years in the wilderness. She'd have barely been an adult, for fuck's sake. Why would a talented shifter—a bard—isolate herself in such a way?

Damned if he wasn't going to get some answers from her. For now, he said, "You might consider taking classes, Emma. See how you do."

"I-I never thought about it." Her confusion was adorable. Sometimes she was fully as cute as Minette.

With a worried frown, Minette patted her thigh and received a kiss on the top of her head.

Bonnie smiled down at the cub before glancing at Ryder. "I'm envious. My little terrors are about the same age and sure aren't learning their numbers. It's a problem, actually."

"Illiterate toddlers are a problem?" Ryder grinned, thinking she was joking.

"I'm serious. Pack cubs are tended by single females. Other

Daonain children stay home. There isn't any consistent or proficient instruction. The lack wasn't a concern in the past since human cubs were treated much the same."

"And now?" Emma asked.

"Now, most human children attend preschool, or have TV or computer preschool programs. Our cubs are behind when they start elementary school."

Ryder frowned, realizing Bonnie's concerns would apply to his daughter. Damned if he'd let his child be behind anyone. "Guess I need to get Minette on the computer. I'll check out some of those preschool programs."

"Relying on technology isn't the answer." Bonnie scowled at him. "Our children aren't mindless trolls needing to be spoon-fed. They're—"

"They're losing the race to the humans," Ryder snapped, then winced. "Sorry."

Bonnie drew herself up straight. "I didn't mean we should—"

"Actually," Emma interrupted, "I can see where a…judicious…use of computers might serve our people well."

Ryder stared at her. She agreed with him? A tradition-driven bard?

Catching his astonishment, she flushed. "We live in a world filled with humans. With technology. If we're not going to get destroyed, we need to be at least knowledgeable of their tools. There's no reason we can't employ the best of both worlds." Emma's golden-brown eyes were alight and her body seemed to hum with energy.

As she and Bonnie discussed possibilities, Ryder studied the little bard. She was so fucking sincere. So open and easy to read, as if her years in the forest had driven any pretense out of her.

She had a past where something not good had happened. Although he wanted to know, it didn't really matter, did it? They were friends, and he damned well stood by his friends. If someone had caused her grief in the past, well, he'd shred them to little pieces for her.

As Bonnie headed into the house, Ryder crouched down beside Emma, pleased with how she cradled Minette in her lap. Happy little kitten.

"Tonight, we can look for some good software programs for Minette," he said. "You'd know better than me what we should be looking for."

She tilted her head. "All right."

As he inhaled her soft floral scent, he lost the hold on his control and took her hand. Kissing her fingers, he felt the beginning calluses from the guitar and saw the small red spots from where she'd been spattered with grease while learning to cook. "Thank you for your care of my cub."

"I love looking after her," Emma said.

"I'd better get moving; I have another house to check on today." He bent and kissed Minette's soft cheek, then dared more and kissed Emma's as well.

When she stared up at him, speechless, he gave her a smile that promised next time he'd take her lips. "Later, bard."

"I…um, later."

As he headed away, he figured even when he was as old as Tullia, he'd still enjoy teasing the little bear…and winning her wide-eyed responses.

Chapter Eighteen

O N TUESDAY, THE construction site reminded Emma of the bustle of an ant colony, each worker tending his job, almost oblivious to what his fellows were doing. The screech of a saw came from under a carport. Thudding noises came from inside the house's new addition.

Ben and Ryder stood at a table near their vehicles, examining an oversized paper. Architectural drawings, she decided as she crossed the lawn toward them.

Ben spotted her first. "You going to join my crew, li'l bear?" He held out his hand.

"Um…no. I…" It would be rude to ignore his hand. So she set her hand in his. The way Ben had kissed her outside Tullia's home two days ago had been unsettling. Different from his lighter kisses. She sure wasn't experienced, but his grip had been tighter and more…possessive. And he'd taken his time, surrounding her with his strength, his clean masculine scent, until everything inside her had gone all gooey.

His fingers closed, trapping her in warmth. Over the past two days, he'd been going out of his way to touch her.

"Want to see the house drawings?" he murmured, pulling her up to the table…and trapping her there with her bottom pressed against the edge, her pelvis against his.

"I…" Under the hunger in his gaze, she felt as if the chill spring day had turned to the hottest day of summer. And he knew it, the beast. "Why do you keep doing this to me?"

"Doing what?" he asked innocently. Too innocently.

"Touching me. Making me…flustered. Uncomfortable."

"You know why. We told you last night…after I kissed you goodnight."

Oh, she remembered. He'd done it right in front of Ryder and she blushed. Laughing, Ryder had decided she wasn't comfortable being handled by males…and the two decided to help her get past her fears. She'd thought they were joking.

"We worry about you." Ryder stood beside her, and the sharp lines of his face smoothed out when he smiled at her. He took her free hand, opened her fingers, and put a kiss in the center of her palm.

How could she feel a kiss travel from her hand all the way to her center?

He was doing it, too. Were they trying to drive her crazy? "Why would you worry? I'm fine," she said faintly.

"You said you don't do male-female stuff or attend Gatherings," Ben said. He ran his hand under her braid and closed his grip around her nape.

"We've noticed you look nervous…and your scent changes when the subject of Gatherings comes up." Ryder took her hand, placing her palm over his jaw, scraping her palm over his light stubble. The sensation seemed to travel over her body in a wave until all of her skin zinged.

"Like we said, we're going get you used to being touched." Ben leaned in and kissed her lightly.

Her pulse was hammering. "Oh, so this is all for me?" she managed to say.

Ben moved back, and then Ryder had her pinned against the table, his hand on her nape. "Oh, little bear, you know we're enjoying the hell out of doing this to you." His voice, so low and smooth, slid along the nerve endings he'd awakened.

And he kissed her, his lips teasing hers, nipping lightly at her bottom lip until it softened. Holding her firmly, he deepened the kiss, taking her under.

Oh my Goddess.

He pulled her closer, one hand curving under her ass. He lifted his head a millimeter, his breath on her lips. "Yeah. I wouldn't mind touching you all day long."

The thought sparked a fire in her center. And the feeling was terrifying. "No. I don't want you to."

Ben rumbled a laugh and lifted her wrist, blatantly sniffing. Oh, yes, her interest in them was evident to anyone with a nose, as was theirs for her.

When she inhaled their intoxicating scents, she wanted to put her hands all over them. Only being aroused by males hadn't gone so well for her three years ago.

"Hey, Ben. Got a minute—when you're through there?" The call came from the house.

"Guess we're setting a bad example," Ryder said. He looked down at her with a slight smile. "You're definitely worth corrupting the lads though."

Oh, they made her feel so good. So…wanted.

Nevertheless, they did have work to do. "I just came by to tell you Minette's playing with Bonnie's children at her house. I'm going to Angie's Diner for a while."

"Got it. I'll pick the cub up on my way home," Ryder said. He brushed his lips over hers and released her.

She had one second of freedom before Ben's arms enclosed her. "Have fun, honey bear." And he kissed her until every thought in her head drained out into the ground.

ANGIE'S KITCHEN WAS fragrant with mouth-watering scents. A roast beef and trimmings baked in one oven. Cupcakes were in another. As Emma stirred a thick, smoked ham and bean soup, she daydreamed a little about providing a wonderful meal for Ben, Ryder, and Minette. They'd all sit down at the oak dining table, and she could pretend they were her family.

Of course, she certainly wouldn't travel that path, but there was no law about daydreaming.

When the swinging door sent the steam swirling over the pot, Emma looked up.

Angie and Bree had been restocking the glass cabinets with Bree's newly cooked desserts. Bree walked through first, followed by Angie.

"You doing all right there?" Angie asked Emma.

"I'm getting hungry. This smells incredible."

"It does, doesn't it?" Angie nodded toward the wall of ovens. "But I'm in the mood for dessert first."

Bree pulled a pan of cupcakes out to assess for doneness. The perfectly puffed cupcakes looked delicious. "See how the cake springs back, Emma? And how the tops are light golden-brown?"

Emma watched, memorizing her words, the color. "Got it." Since she'd gotten to lick the bowl after she and Bree had made them, she knew they'd taste fantastic.

"After we whip up some frosting, you'll be ready to practice making them at home," Bree said.

The males adored sweets—Ben, especially. Bears were sweet-o-holics.

The thought of feeding her…family…something she'd made herself was thrilling. "I can't thank you enough for helping me learn to manage in a kitchen. You're sure I can keep coming?"

"Honey, you've been a big help. Come anytime you're free." Angie's forthright invitation made Emma's eyes sting.

She was useful. Liked. Wanted. "I will. I have Bonnie's children and Minette in the mornings, but Bonnie wants to pay me back by taking Minette in the late afternoons after she gets off dispatch duty."

"Excellent. I can put you to good use," Angie said.

"Hey, Angie, I'm here. Want me to start taking orders?" A young brunette adolescent stuck her head into the kitchen.

"Yes, Lacey. Get to work and let me know if you get behind." After the girl grabbed an apron and popped back out, Angie said to Bree. "I'm glad you sent her to me. All her bouncy energy keeps the dining room lively."

"Actually, we appreciate you taking her on," Bree said softly. "Shay's been worried about her. It was bad enough that Klaus taught her to fear males, but now Chad and a couple of the Gerhard-influenced wolves are harassing her after school lets out."

"Bet they don't pull any crap around Zeb or Shay," Angie said in a dry voice.

Emma remembered the two cahirs. The dark one had been seriously scary-looking.

"Hardly. Last year when Zeb caught Chad manhandling her, he showed the little snot how it feels to be shoved around." Bree half-grinned. "Their behavior mostly happens at school where they're unlikely to get caught. Damn Klaus and Gerhard for giving the youngsters a taste for abuse."

Poor Lacey. Emma understood how she must feel. She had plenty of memories of being picked on, shoved, poked, and derided.

"Such behavior is difficult to break." Angie checked on her roast in the oven.

"Shay is working with the males. We hope having Jody as a mentor and working with you will show Lacey how tough females really are, and that they don't take crap from anyone."

Emma smiled. Angie's expression would give any young male second thoughts.

But who was Klaus? And Gerhard? "Um…" With a puff of frustration, Emma bit back her questions. Curiosity was rude, her mother had said. Emma'd begun to think anything interesting was rude.

Bree burst out laughing. "Look at you. You're just dying to ask what happened."

A flush heated Emma's cheeks. "I'm sorry."

"So, why don't you ask?" Bree's brows drew together.

"I… Because it's rude to be nosy." At their questioning expressions, she added, "Isn't it?"

"Not among friends. Especially if we're discussing it in front of you," Angie said gently. "Why don't you know that, Emma?"

A question. A nosy question. But it didn't feel rude because Angie…cared.

"Well…" Should she actually answer? But friends told each other things—or so the stories implied. "My mother was a…heartless person and only interested in her status. She didn't have friends and didn't let me have friends. So I know how to behave with strangers, but not with people I like." She stirred the pot more vigorously as anger at her mother welled up. "Sometimes, I can't tell if it's impolite to ask questions or ruder to act as if I wasn't interested."

"Your mama didn't teach you to cook. Didn't teach you about friends." Angie scowled. "How short-sighted. I wish I'd had the upbringing of the both of you."

Angie's grown daughter lived upstairs—and the love she had for her mother was beautiful. Lucky female. But why had Angie said "the both of you"? Emma turned to Bree, "Did you have a bad mother, too?"

"I had none at all. I'm an orphan and was raised in foster care homes. Human ones." Bree offered her a half-smile. "Some were good, some not so good."

"Oh." An orphan. Raised by humans. How dreadful. "Just when I start to feel properly sorry for myself, the goddess smacks me silly with a ruthless paw."

Angie laughed. "Oh, I do like you, bear."

Her declaration silenced Emma completely. A friend. Two friends. Wealth beyond imagining.

"Shay said you're still at Ben's house," Bree commented. "I'm so glad. I bet you've brightened up his lonely life."

Lonely? Ben? "He's so friendly. How could he be lonely?"

Bree squirted frosting onto the cupcakes in elaborate whirls. "He has lots of friends, but no family. Bears don't do packs, and until Ryder arrived, he didn't have a littermate."

"After a drink at the tavern, he'd go home to his big empty house." Angie added, "I'm not sure why, but Ben's never…socialized…with females between Gatherings."

They were actually *gossiping* with her. Emma shivered in delight. "He did say he enjoys having people in his house."

"I'm glad you're there. He looks happier now," Bree said softly. "And, as for the questions you were too polite to ask: Our wolf pack's previous alpha and his littermates damaged the pack. Now Shay's the alpha, and things are improving, but…as you heard, we still have problems. I'll explain sometime over a beer."

"A beer? You mean at the tavern? Just females?" Her mother would've been appalled. But, Emma had seen females sitting together at tables. Without male escorts.

Both females stared at her. "By the Mother's tits, you really were isolated," Angie said. She frowned at Bree. "Take this bear out—get Vicki on it—and show her what females do. Better yet, have Calum set her to waiting on tables. He's been complaining about the lack of barmaids."

"I'd love to help," Emma said. "I'm allowed to walk without a cane for two hours at a time now." Although Donal hadn't permitted her to remove the stupid brace.

"Great." Bree grinned. "After you're through singing on Thursday, we'll both help out with the barmaiding. Then when the crowd thins out, we'll have a beer and chat."

"Really?" Emma bounced on her heels with anticipation.

"Never seen anyone so delighted to work in a bar." Angie shook her head, her face soft.

Lacey stuck her head into the kitchen. "Hey, Angie, I have orders. Is the food ready?"

"Coming right up," Angie answered. "Emma, are you going right to your house now?"

"Yes. Ben and Ryder were going to pick Minette up, so I can just head home."

"Perfect." Angie pulled a deep basket from under the counter. "You can take your cub and males some supper."

"Oh, but—"

Angie gave her a stern look. "I've seen how much time they're putting in at Tullia's. They're doing what we couldn't for our pack member; they deserve a reward."

"Don't even try to argue with her." Bree dropped six cupcakes into the basket. "Or me."

Chapter Nineteen

DURING EMMA'S THURSDAY performance, people had packed the tavern, as squished together as grubs under a rotting log.

Afterward, the numbers had diminished until the country-western music could be heard under the hum of conversation, and Emma—Calum's newest barmaid—could walk between tables without being tripped. Considering she was still a bit clumsy without her cane, the decrease in crowding was a relief.

She stopped at a table of four older male shifters. "What can I get for you?"

At their welcoming smiles, she realized she was growing accustomed to being treated politely. Cold Creek was truly a wonderful place.

"Fine music, bard." Joe Thorson, the scarred-up male she'd met at Wesley's rites, nodded to the short, pudgy shifter beside him. "Albert Baty runs the grocery. Quentin and Walter own the hardware store."

"It's a pleasure to meet you." If nothing else, her mother had had taught her how to greet people—although three years of isolation had rusted her manners.

"An honor, bard," Albert said with the other two chorusing in.

"Refills on anything?" she asked.

"Another round, please," Joe said. "Tell Calum it goes on my tab."

"Yes, sir."

At the bar, she waited and admired Calum in action. Leanly muscular, he had all of a werecat's grace as he moved up and down the bar, opening bottles, pouring glasses. Every now and then, his smile would flash, lightening his tanned face.

He was amazing…although she was still scandalized a Co-santir would own a tavern—let alone work in one.

"Here you are." He handed over her tray with the drinks on it. "After you deliver those, you are off duty."

"But"—she looked around the room—"most of the tables are still full."

"Rosie and her daughter can handle the crowd at this point." His grin came quick and fast. "Although I appreciate your help, I *have* noted that your music is the reason the place is so full."

"Um…" What could she say?

He chuckled. "Lass, don't apologize for being an excellent bard."

The compliment hummed warm and soft inside her. "I can work longer."

"You cannot." He tilted his head toward the fireplace. "My mate and Breanne are waiting for you."

"Really?" Despite the ache in her leg, she bounced on her toes in delight. *Friends.*

"Aye. They already have a beer for you."

"Thank you."

After delivering drinks to Joe Thorson and friends, she crossed the room, stopping frequently. Would she ever lose her wonder when people actually smiled at her, greeted her, asked her about music, or requested a song for a future night?

In the U-shaped sitting area in front of the brick fireplace,

Vicki and Bree occupied the two facing couches. A leather chair formed the bottom of the semi-circle.

"Look at you," Bree said, grinning. "When I waitressed, I'd finish feeling as if my tail was dragging on the ground. You're glowing."

"I had fun." Uncaring of grace, Emma plopped down into the chair in a way that would have made her mother send her to her room. "I met more people in this one night than in my entire time here. I didn't know taverns were like this. I thought they were mostly filled with males hunting for females to pick up—and vice versa."

"They usually are, especially human ones." Vicki smiled. "But Calum spent time in Ireland where the bars are almost community centers. Everyone goes there, from youngsters to seniors. He wanted Cold Creek to have something similar."

Bree grinned. "But we never see this many people. Your singing filled the place."

Emma hugged the words to her like a warm blanket. "Thank you." She wiggled slightly to get more comfortable, enjoying the hum of conversation around her. Calum had created a wonderful atmosphere. Although she still had trouble believing the Cosantir owned a bar.

She couldn't imagine having a Cosantir for a mate. She studied Vicki, wondering if—

"Did I forget to put on a shirt or something?" Vicki asked.

Oops. "Uh, no. I was just"—*just being really rude*—"Um…"

Vicki grinned. "Just ask. We already know you're insatiably curious about everything. Calum says it's because you're a bard."

She hadn't realized she was so obvious. Oops, again. "Right. Well, speaking of Calum, uh…what's it like to live with the Cosantir and all his power?"

"You mean does he fry me with it in bed?"

When Emma's eyes widened, Vicki laughed so hard her eyes

started to water. "Okay, I'm sorry." She pulled in a breath. "It's just your expression was…" Still giggling, she said, "The power doesn't come into the bedroom. And really isn't very…present…in just daily stuff. Calum says his connection to the God is normally like a light switch. He can flick it on to check where the shifters are in his territory."

The sense of disappointment was keen. "Oh. Here I thought it was so much bigger. I guess the tales were exaggerated."

Bree frowned. "When the Cosantir confronted Klaus, he was humming with power."

"He does, sometimes." Vicki considered. "If he actually *invites* the God in by opening his soul—rather than drawing a little juice—the connection is more like a massive power line. But he said when the God takes over, he has very little control over the outcome. I get the impression he doesn't always agree with how expeditiously Herne will execute the Laws."

"Well," Bree said diplomatically, "your mate *was* a lawyer."

A lawyer? Calum? Oh, so many tales here in Cold Creek needed to be written. "So he doesn't…call…on the God if he can avoid it?"

"Fuck, no." Vicki sent a fond look toward the bar. "It's why Herne has Cosantirs rather than just handling everything Himself. The Cosantirs might be human and imperfect, but they'll listen to everyone and take their time in deciding what's best for the clan. Far better than the *Bad Daonain; Dead Daonain* style of judgment the God is known for."

"This is true," Emma muttered, feeling a shiver seize her as she remembered the alternate, *Bad Daonain, Banished Daonain*. "So if Calum calls on the God's power—say to compel someone to tell the truth—the God might just take over completely."

"Exactly—which is why Calum invokes the least amount of power needed to get the job done." Vicki moved her shoulders. "If you're being all bard-like and collecting information, Calum did say each Cosantir works out his own balances with Herne."

"Herne apparently gives the guardians more flexibility than the cahirs," Bree said. Considering she was married to two of them, she would know, Emma decided. From what she'd heard about Zeb and Shay, their history would be fascinating.

"By the way, Emma, did Angie mention the Beltane preparations?" Bree asked. "An hour before the meeting on Saturday, a lot of us will gather wood for the two bonfires. Also, people bring finger foods and drinks, and blankets."

Beltane, already? The sun festival marked the beginning of summer. Time had certainly gone by quickly. "I can manage finger foods." And if she felt adventurous, Angie'd give her some ideas. Ben and Ryder could bring the drinks. "When is the meeting?"

"Before sunset. It's the usual Daonain meeting," Vicki said. "Calum hoped you'd give the people a Beltane song. He told me you'd know one, but—"

"If you don't, it's all right," Bree said hastily.

A bard not know a sun festival song? Emma stared at the females and recalled they'd been raised as humans, and hadn't heard of the Daonain until grown. Having lost her shifter parents as a toddler, Bree had been raised in a human foster care home. Vicki'd been changed into a shifter by a young werecat's Death Gift. "Am I the first bard you've met?"

Both nodded.

"Well, a bard must memorize the songs of our heritage, as well as add to them." She smiled. "I know about a dozen Beltane songs."

Bree blinked. "I think I know about a dozen songs. Total. You know a dozen just for one holiday? Does your head hurt?" She handed Emma the still full glass of beer sitting on the coffee table.

Grinning, Emma took a sip—and a deeper one as the icy

liquid slid down her throat. "Not any more. But when I was an apprentice and memorizing a song a day? Oh, most definitely."

"A song a day. Damn, that's amazing." Vicki raised her glass. "To Emma."

Bree followed suit.

Emma had to clear the thickness from her throat before she could speak. "Right. Please inform the Cosantir I'd be honored to sing before..." Her voice faded as fear filled her center. The meeting was before sunset.

Beltane was celebrated on a full moon...which meant a Gathering would start immediately afterward. A *Gathering*.

"Jesus-fuck, what's wrong?"

At the sharp voice, Emma's head jerked up.

Vicki was leaning forward, scanning the room, her posture that of a male ready to fight.

Bree took Emma's hands. "Are you all right? What scared you?"

"S-scared me?" Emma shook her head. "I'm not..." She was. She could smell her own fear stench.

"You're as fucking terrified as fresh meat facing their first battle," Vicki said bluntly. Her determined copper-colored eyes held the same protectiveness as Ben's. "Who are you afraid of?"

"No one. Not exactly." Emma closed her eyes and breathed out in the way the Master Bard had taught her to avoid freezing up before a performance.

"Emma?" Bree prompted, her blue eyes gentle.

"It's not a person," Emma said. "My last Gathering"—*her first and only Gathering*—"was a disaster. I haven't been back since and...I'm scared."

"Oh, I know how that can happen," Bree muttered. She squeezed Emma's fingers. "My first Gathering was so bad that Calum made Donal knock me out."

"Seriously?" Her story simply cried out for a song.

Vicki half-grinned. "I don't think I was terrified. But to learn I had to go through this shit every month—and fuck all night long? I was more than pissed off."

Bree rolled her eyes at her friend. "Why am I not surprised?"

"You both had trouble?" Emma shook her head. Why had she assumed everything went perfectly for everyone else?

"Oh, definitely." Bree smiled. "Do you want to tell us what happened?"

Never. Emma shook her head. "I'd rather not talk about it. But, isn't it silly? I knew the full moon was coming." Ben and Ryder had even told her they were helping her get used to having males' hands on her. "I'm just...scared."

She stared at the orange fire, seeing the black eyes of a salamander resting in the coals. She'd already had this talk with herself. Had decided to stay.

No one here knew her, so being revealed wasn't the problem. The question was... Would she put young males in danger if she showed up? Would she somehow incite them to fight? If only she knew what she'd done to incite Gary and Andre to fight. The fear that she'd inadvertently repeat her actions was crippling.

Unfortunately, the night was a blur. Her memories had been tattered by the overwhelming nature of uncontrolled lust and then the terrifying end.

But...she was older now. Maybe she could handle herself. Keep from doing...whatever she'd done. A tiny, hopeful song wafted into her mind. Calum said it was the young males who had trouble with their own control—she could try to stay away from them.

"You know, you live with two males," Bree said. "I don't know Ryder, but Ben is awfully nice."

"He is," Emma said. "Actually, Ryder is much nicer than I

thought at first."

"If they know you're worried about the full moon rites, they'll help, you know," Vicki said. "You can start the Gathering by taking them to bed. Once the ice is broken, you'll feel more comfortable. They'll also help you find other males who will be good to you."

Start with… Vicki meant she should mate with Ben and Ryder? She could. Sex was what happened at a Gathering. They'd touch her, kiss her—and she'd be able to kiss and touch them back. *Oh. Yes.*

The tavern seemed to have grown extremely warm, and she realized she was hugging herself.

Bree and Vicki were laughing.

"I'd say she's on-board with the idea," Vicki said.

Emma bit her lip before grinning ruefully. "I guess I am." Needing time to cool down, she drained her beer and rose. "My turn to provide drinks. What can I get for you two?"

"Calum will know," Vicki said. "And when you return, we'll discuss what you're going to wear. We're talking sexy, sexy, sexy."

Clothes? Emma stared for a second, thinking about the conservative clothing she'd worn to her first Gathering. Obviously, there was more to learn than she'd thought. "Be right back."

She made it halfway across the room when a massive male stepped in front of her.

"Li'l bear, you smell like Gathering night already," Ben rumbled. He bent, sniffed her hair, and pulled her into his arms. "Fuck, you're testing my restraint."

Oh, by the Mother, he felt good. As her breasts flattened against his solid chest, she gripped his muscular biceps. They were harder than the boulders that scattered the mountainsides.

When she tipped her head back to tease him, he took her lips.

Startled, she tensed, then as his scent reached deep into her soul, her mouth softened.

His hand fisted in her hair, pulling her head back as his tongue took possession. He held her firmly...and took and took and took.

Everything inside her melted like a snowpack under a hot sun.

He lifted his head and chuckled, low and deep. "Fuck, you're gorgeous."

Her eyes opened wide. "Really?"

Ben grinned.

"Really, little bear. You're gorgeous." Ryder's voice was a resonant baritone under the noise in the bar. When he moved closer, Ben turned her and steered her right into his littermate's arms.

Ryder, shorter than Ben, still towered over her. His muscles were lean—ripped was the term—and he was far stronger than she was. When he gathered her to him, molding her against him, she felt wonderfully trapped. Powerless. Fragile.

Female.

He nibbled her lips, and when she opened her mouth under the silent pressure, he slid his tongue in. Like his voice, his kiss was smoother than Ben's, darker, and he encouraged her to kiss him back, giving a hum of satisfaction as her tongue fenced with his.

When he released her, the brothers had her penned between them, each with a hand on her upper arm. And the scent of their desire—for her—was headier than the first fragrance of spring.

They wanted her.

The corners of Ben's eyes creased with his smile, and he ran his finger down her cheek. "You've got us all het up, darlin'. Were you doing something now, or shall we take you home and to bed?"

Bed? Doing something?

She stared at him blankly. He was looking at the empties in her hands. Alcohol for her friends. "I…I have friends here." The hum of desire almost drowned out the music from the jukebox. *Friends. Right.*

"All right." Ben let her go.

She took a step forward.

Ryder laughed, and with a steady hand, he steered her around the chair in her path before letting her go—with a pat on her butt.

"By the God, I love her ass," he muttered to Ben.

"Mmmhmm," was Ben's gravely agreement.

Okay, maybe all their desire was merely anticipation of the full moon, but oh, she loved being wanted. She managed not to turn, not to hug them for making her feel absolutely sexy and beautiful, but she couldn't help walking to the bar with a wide smile on her face.

And her ass swaying.

NOT MUCH LATER, Ryder was deep in a discussion with Owen and Ben about the best way to secure isolated cabins against hellhounds when he noticed the time. "We'll need to continue later. I have a cub to pick up." Angie's second daughter was in town and her children were Min's age.

When Ryder had left, the cubs had been tumbling over each other like kittens in a basket.

"Nah, you stay put. I'll get the cub." Ben rose.

Ryder frowned. "You usually stay longer."

When Owen asked, "Are you all right? You look like hell," Ryder realized the lethal-looking cahir did have a heart.

"Just tired." Ben grimaced. "Donal said my energy will be used for healing for another week. I fucking hate it when he's right."

"No shit," Owen muttered in sympathy, despite his grin.

"I'll put the cub to bed." Ben hesitated and glanced over where Emma was laughing with the Cosantir's female and Breanne.

Reading his littermate's concern, Ryder said, "Don't worry about the little bear. I'll walk her home."

"Females," Owen muttered in disgust.

Ignoring the cahir, Ben smiled at Ryder. "Might be a fun Gathering this month."

"Yeah." Anticipation curled in Ryder's gut, and he hardened. He'd never kissed any female as sweet as the little bear. Even better, he'd get to share her with his brother. Nothing felt as right as pleasuring a female with his brother beside him. "It might at that."

Ben lifted his chin to Owen and left.

Leaning back in his chair, Ryder studied the brusque cahir for a second. "Been wondering. Do you have an aversion to Emma or bards, or…"

"Bards are all right." Owen took a drink as if he had a bad taste in his mouth. "I don't like females."

Ryder nodded. "I had the same opinion. My experience with one shrewish cat was so bad I figured all females were untrustworthy."

"My friend," Owen said, "They are. Don't get taken in."

Ryder almost grinned. And he'd thought *he* had problems. "You need to get to know the bard. She—"

"Ryder. I found you." The female's voice was one he knew too well. All silky seduction. The razor's edge that'd leave a male scarred was well hidden…for the moment.

Gut knotting, Ryder turned. As always, her scent was masked by the expensive human perfume she wore. "Genevieve."

"My darling, we need to talk." Her gaze swept over Owen, obviously noting the cahir mark over his cheekbone. She gave him a predictably flirtatious sweep of her artificially lengthened eyelashes. "I'm sorry, cahir, but I have to talk with my male."

Not gracing her comment with an answer, Owen turned to Ryder. "Want me to stay, or want me to dump her ass outside?"

The cahir *really* hated females, didn't he? As tempting as it would be to sic Owen on her, Genevieve was Minette's mother. Unfortunately. He'd try talking first.

"How dare you speak about me with such disrespect." Her voice had sharpened.

Owen ignored her.

A glance at her heightening color and flashing eyes suggested their talk had better happen outside the tavern. Ryder tossed some bills on the table and rose. "Thank you, but I think it's best if she and I go for a walk. Sorry to cut our talk short."

"No problem. I'm due at my sister's house soon anyway," Owen said.

Ryder motioned to Genevieve. "We'll take this outside." Not waiting for her answer, he walked across the tavern and into the chill night air.

Left without a target, she followed. She wasn't yelling at him yet, which meant she wanted something.

He doubted that *something* was her child.

"Ryder, I've been looking for you everywhere. I can't believe I finally found you." She put her hand on his arm, turning at an angle to showcase her curves. "I'm so happy you finally spent time with the cub we created together. Isn't she wonderful?"

What the *fuck* did she want? As if he didn't know. How had he ever been so lust-struck as to fall for her act? Disgust with himself made his gut twist. "Get to the point, Genevieve."

"Oh, Ryder, how can you be so cruel?" Her hazel eyes filled with tears, desolation in her expression.

Damn, she was good. And he wasn't even tempted. "We're done here." He tried to shake her hand off his arm.

Her grip tightened. "You don't understand. We share a child—a beautiful little cub—who needs her mother. I know that you and Ben are rattling around in his big house like two acorns in a squirrel hollow. You need a mate."

Disquiet ran an icy hand up Ryder's spine. Genevieve had seen Ben's house. "You stay away from Minette. Far, far away."

She recoiled as if he'd slapped her, and her tears spilled over. "I miss you, my darling. I want to be with you—and *my* child. We can be together." A faint smile tilted her lips. "I know you remember how very good together we were."

"Oh, you're a fairly good fuck. Considering you've probably practiced with every male in the Pacific Northwest, you should be." He peeled her hand off his arm. "I don't like you. Don't want to be anywhere near you. And you're not going to get anywhere near Minette after the way you abused her. So crawl back into whatever slimy hole you emerged from."

Anger narrowed her eyes. "You think you're going to mate with that enormous, ugly female? You think she's prettier than me?"

Enormous female? Did she mean Emma? His laugh burst out. "If you mean the beautiful blonde, yeah, mating with her is exactly what I intend." Soft and sweet, inside and outside. Generous and real. Oh, yeah, he definitely intended.

"No one takes what's mine." Her face twisted—and there was the real Genevieve. "You are mine—and so is Minette. I'll be damned if I let you get away with this."

He shook his head, disgusted with her, with her selfishness, her self-centeredness, her petty tantrums. "Right. Go away, Genevieve."

The tavern door creaked as few of the wolf pack emerged. He recognized the snippy one named Candice.

"You'll be sorry you screwed with me," Genevieve gritted out and burst into loud weeping.

The shifters stopped to look.

"I want my baby back." Genevieve clutched his arm, pulling at him.

"Stop it." He shook her off. "You know you—"

"How could you steal my cub from me?" Her voice cracked as she backed away from him. "You're evil. A *monster*." Sobbing as if her heart was breaking, she staggered to her car and got in.

"You're the monster," he gritted out. Should have yelled the words, he thought, as he saw the way the stunned group of shifters watched her drive away.

Oh. Shit. This felt far too familiar.

Chapter Twenty

Cold Creek, North Cascades Territory – Beltane's full moon

As RYDER DROVE the SUV down the road to the Wild Hunt Tavern on Saturday, he glanced over at Emma. A fiasco with a construction job had kept him on-site for most of the hours since he'd seen Genevieve. He'd welcomed the work. Welcomed not having to deal with anything emotional.

But, he'd stalled enough. Friday morning, he'd told Ben about Genevieve's presence in town, and his littermate had guarded Minette.

Emma also needed to know.

As it had every time he thought of Minette's mother, his anger rose again. She wasn't in town because of any motherly concern. No, Genevieve was hoping for a free ride. From the looks of her house, she hadn't been doing well. Perhaps, since she'd already fucked just about every single male in Deschutes Territory, she was having trouble finding a male to support her.

A shame she'd been able to find him. But cahirs were fairly well known. Tracking Ben's location wouldn't have been difficult. Undoubtedly, she'd now discovered that the cahir was doing well. With her impervious ego, she'd never realized how much Ben had despised her five years ago. She'd figure if she made a play for him, he'd let her do anything she wanted. Even worse, Genevieve might cut a male loose, but in her mind, he was still hers. He didn't get to move on to a new female.

On Thursday, she'd seen Ryder and Ben kiss Emma.

Not good. Not good at all, because Genevieve could be vicious. Her jealous tantrums had been so unpleasant that Ryder had stopped mating with other females at Gatherings because any female he'd mated at full moon suffered her virulent spite. She'd reduced several to tears.

When he'd told her he was leaving her—and hadn't been broken-hearted about it—she'd destroyed his reputation in Farway. Made it look as if he was a violent, abusive liar.

No one had come to his defense. His own fault—he hadn't tried to become part of the town. On first arriving, he'd joined a construction crew and quit after a week, too heart-sore about leaving Ben to continue. Instead, he'd made a business of his own handcrafts, planning to let the local stores sell them. Only, as his obsession with Genevieve died, he'd decided to sell at craft fairs. So when the people in town believed Genevieve and acted as if he was almost feral, he'd simply moved to a different territory.

Their opinion of him hadn't mattered.

But he cared about Cold Creek, dammit. He wanted the town for his cub. Wanted the town for himself.

After a second, he realized Emma was studying him. "What's wrong?" she asked.

Amazing. He'd always prided himself on being inscrutable. "You read me well, little bard."

"It's not difficult when you look like a boggart stepping in a pile of blessed salt."

A boggart? "Ouch." The disgusting little goblins were not only vicious, but ugly, as well. He tried to rearrange his face into more pleasant lines.

"You're still glowering," she pointed out mildly. "Has something happened?"

"Aye. Something you need to know." He pulled into a parking space, turned the vehicle off, and faced her. "Minette's mother was in the tavern Thursday."

"Oh." Emma tilted her head. "She sounds rather nasty, and I suppose it's not comfortable having a former lover here, but wouldn't Minette like to see her?"

What had he told her? Ah. He'd said Genevieve was manipulative and a liar, and how she'd found Minette to be inconvenient. He hadn't given the little bear enough information. "She wasn't a good mother. It's why Minette is afraid of people."

Emma's eyes darkened. "She hit the cubling?"

"Aye."

"And you let her?"

"I didn't know Minette even existed until right before I got to Cold Creek." Ryder half smiled. "And when I saw the bruises, I took my cub and left. Genevieve was...angry."

"Oh." Emma bit her lip. "That's not good."

Quite the understatement. Sires usually only raised cubs alone if their lifemate died. Gather-bred children rarely even knew who'd fathered them. If Minette didn't look just like Ryder, he wouldn't know he was her sire. "No, not good. So, if Genevieve shows up, please keep her away from Minette."

"Got it." Her jaw lifted with determination. "She won't get anywhere near Minette."

He could trust her to guard his cub. The knowledge was heartening—and humbling. "Thank you."

Her smile was warm as she unbuckled her seatbelt and opened the door.

"Hold on, bard." He leaned forward and curved his fingers over her nape. Her silky hair slid through his fingers.

Her eyes widened as he touched his lips to hers, and lured in by her scent, he deepened the kiss. Her mouth opened under his, and he gently teased her into responding, feeling the resistance melt out of her.

But when he tried to move closer, the seat belt stopped him. Restored to his senses—more's the pity—he chuckled and lifted his head to look into meltingly sweet brown eyes.

She stared at him, obviously bemused, and he kissed her lightly. Damn, she was cute. The way she responded to him made him exert more control than he'd needed for many a year. "I'd blame the impending Gathering for sparking my hormones, but, little bear, even if it was dark of the moon, I'd still have kissed you."

Her response was a small huff. "Oh." She shook her head, as if to settle her senses and looked at him cautiously. He might have been worried, but the open door wafted him her scent.

Interested.

Good enough. "Tonight at the Gathering, Ben and I will find you." *Will have you.* At the assurance in his voice, she flushed the prettiest peach color.

"Um…right." She bit her lower lip. As worry and fear tinged her scent, his heart almost broke.

"Emma." He ran a finger over her dented lower lip. "We'll be careful with you. If there's anything you don't like, just say no. Even if you decide you don't want us."

"JUST SAY NO." Emma stared at Ryder in surprise. "I can refuse something? At a Gathering?"

His puzzled look was…reassuring. "Of course. Or any other time. Mating is supposed to be fun for all parties—or what's the point?" His brows drew together. "How many Gatherings have you attended?"

Unable to deal with further questions, she pretended not to hear the question, shut the door, and hurried to the tavern.

Rather than pressing her, he started the SUV and drove away, lifting his hand in a quick wave.

All right then. He wasn't angry.

She didn't want him angry—because everything in her tingled at the thought of being with him and Ben.

Tonight. The Gathering would start when the moon rose and would stop when it set.

In the tavern, Calum's teenaged daughter was picking out songs on the jukebox. After greeting her, Emma walked down the back hall and through the portal room with its well-hidden door to the caves below.

The cave was cool and dark. Small cubbyholes were filled with clothing from the shifters who'd changed to their animal forms and were roaming the forests.

But she needed to stay human. Outside the cave, she paused to listen, then followed a trail toward the sound of people.

"Hey, Emma." Bree stood on the south side of the sunny clearing where a table had been formed from split logs lashed together and set on stumps. Over her head, a tree fairy swayed on a branch as it suspiciously monitored the activity.

"How can I help?" Emma asked. A half dozen people were bustling about, all looking as if they knew what they were doing. "The territory I came from didn't have official Beltane celebrations. Did you say families and children will attend this Gathering? Not just single males and females?"

"You got it. Those wanting to mate will move farther into the forest, and the families will remain here. Actually, most of those with children leave before it gets too late. And everyone comes to the breakfast feast in the morning."

"Our Cosantir is both traditional and innovative." Shay came up behind Breanne, wrapped an arm around her waist, and stole a cookie from the plate she'd just set out. "Some territories celebrate Beltane during the day, some make a slightly bigger

Gathering, some celebrate traditionally like Cold Creek. So far no Daonain community has assigned Beltane to a set calendar day. Only the humans would have such gall."

Bree grinned. "Hey, I always thought May Day had a nice ring to it." She nodded to the wood being stacked in the two fire pits. "I don't think humans know about having two bonfires though."

"Although blessings come to those leaping a Belfire," Shay said, "the less athletic types prefer the blessings found from between the two fires."

Walking between the Belfires. Emma hugged herself. This was living inside one of the ancient songs. Bless Calum for following the old ways.

Even more wonderful, she'd have friends here to help if she got scared during the Gathering. That was so, so heartening.

"We have a few hours before the meeting. Why don't you help with gathering"—Bree glanced at Emma's brace—"Hmm. Actually, could you make bouquets for the tables? We already have flowers."

"Emma, I'm glad you're here. Bree, the area for the dancing and fiddler is set up." Vicki stole one of Bree's cookies and easily dodged the baker's punitive hand-slap. She took a big bite. "Fuck, you can cook."

Breanne grinned. "And you can swear. Good thing the Daonain don't have priests, or you'd be doing penance constantly."

"Can't you see a priest here during Beltane? He'd have a heart attack." Vicki waved her hand.

Oh, do not tell the Priest our plight,
Or he would call it a sin;
But we have been out in the woods all night,
A-conjuring Summer in!

"Nice. What's the poem from?" Bree handed over another cookie in appreciation.

"Kipling, of course. The only poet a military person bothers to memorize. I'm off to fetch a load of blankets. See you two later." Vicki saluted them with her cookie and headed down the trail.

Almost two hours later, the bonfires were ready to be lit in the fire pits, with extra wood stacked to the side. Buckets of sand and water were there as well, although it had rained last night.

The banquet tables were beautified. Non-refrigerated food had been set out and covered. Tubs were ready for ice and drinks.

Most of the people had gone to the tavern where Calum was serving a lunch to the Beltane gang. Feeling too nervous to eat, Emma kept working.

In the numerous tiny clearings and niches in the underbrush, she'd hung blankets on low branches. Shifters who wanted a more comfortable mating than in the sparse grass would have blankets available.

With her last blanket dispensed, she stretched, feeling the slow ache of her leg. She'd been on her feet too much.

But this had been one of the final tasks until meeting time.

As she stepped out onto the trail, she bumped into a male.

He grabbed her arms to steady her. His scent, his size too familiar.

Emma's happy glow shattered into a million pieces. "Gawain."

His icy blue stare burned into her. "Emma Cavanaugh. What are you—"

Before he could finish the sentence, she turned.

And ran.

Despite her brace and her injured leg, she fled up the trail, away from the tavern, away from the people. Straight up the slope where the trail plunged into deep forest. Fear buzzed in her ears like a broken beehive.

"Emma. *Wait*," he called.

She slowed slightly—and her brace caught on a broken branch, holding her. Trapping her.

"Emma!"

No, no, no. Panic roared in her blood. She tore at her brace until the straps came loose, threw it aside, and her clothes, too.

In her mind, she opened the door to the wild…and stepped through. The hum of magic ran over her skin with a thousand tiny prickles, followed by the warmth of the Mother's love in her unmistakable caress. The overwhelming dread paused for a second.

What was she doing? Running? How stupid was that?

Then she saw again Gawain's blue eyes. The first male she'd ever mated with at her first Gathering that had ended in blood and death. CeeCee's yell echoed in her ears: *The rich bear-bitch made them fight over her.*

Andre and Gary had fought and died. *Because of me.*

Gawain was here, in Cold Creek. What would Ben say when he knew? Or Ryder who already thought females were suspect? She imagined the two males she loved looking at her with disgust. Cedrick's pronouncement of banishment was like acid in her ears.

Footsteps sounded behind her. Running toward her. *Chasing* her.

Bear instincts took over. *Flee.*

And she ran. Up the slope, veering onto one fork, then choosing another. Miles passed under her paws, miles between her and Cold Creek.

Hours passed.

Her panic retreated slowly. Far too slowly. The descending

sun rested on the mountain peaks when she finally regained control of her bear.

Sides heaving with her breathing, she stopped. Her head hung with exhaustion.

What had she done? As her fear disappeared, shame took its place.

Shifting to human, she stared at her back trail in dismay. How far had she come? She sniffed and caught nothing but the scent of the forest—no wood smoke, cooked food, gasoline, machinery. No stench of civilization.

She was nowhere near Cold Creek.

Looking back, she knew Gawain had been as surprised to see her as she'd been to see him. He'd probably come to Cold Creek for the full moon. To ensure a diverse gene pool, non-mated males were encouraged to visit distant Gatherings.

Her legs had turned as brittle as toothpicks. A fallen tree trunk provided her a seat.

Everyone would wonder why she ran. And Gawain would tell them how she'd incited Gary and Andre to fight. How the Cosantir of the Mt. Hood Territory had banished her. Cold Creek was small. Every shifter would know by morning.

She stared at the dirt under her bare feet, remembering the stares that night, and the hatred on Cedrick's face. The banishment and the guilt. By the God, the Gathering had happened three years ago. She hadn't done anything wrong since.

Why hadn't she been an adult and faced Gawain instead of bolting like a rabbit confronted by a coyote? She was no longer banished. The Mother had obviously forgiven her. She could have pointed that out. But nooo, she hadn't thought, hadn't talked, had simply fled.

By the God, Emma, grow up.

She should go back.

She stood.

Ben and Ryder. What would they say? What if they looked at her and...despised her? Her courage faltered.

She sat.

Okay, they might. Everyone might scorn her...and her heart would break.

Tears burned in her eyes, and then she lifted her chin. Cold Creek was her town now; she could take what they felt they needed to hand out. After all, she'd shouldered worse.

The chill wind slapped against her bare skin, making her shiver.

Ben...Ben was her friend. He might hate what she'd done, but he'd listen. He might even understand her confusion.

Ryder... Who would have thought he'd come to be her friend? And more. Would he now think she was as horrid as Minette's mother? The idea hurt her deep inside. If she shook him—smacked him as he'd told her to do—then might he listen? Maybe. Whatever happened, she really did have to shake out her fur and go back, and face her past.

With a huffing sigh, she rose and shifted back to bear. Her shivering stopped as her fur wrapped her in warmth. Turning, she started back down the trail, feeling the ache of her hind leg.

Three legs or not, she felt...good. Oh, it seemed like forever since she'd been in bear form.

Each breath brought her the lush fragrance of damp evergreens, the icy scent of the breeze off the snow-packed mountaintops, the tang of metal and rock from a nearby dwarf trail.

The last rays of the slanting sun glinted through the trees. Beautiful, but...worrisome. She could feel the hormones starting to bubble in her veins.

By law, she needed to attend the Gathering...and she was so, so far away now.

All too soon, the sun would be down, the moon would rise,

and her need to mate would begin.

HEARING THE FRONT door open, Ben said into the phone, "That's probably her now. I'll call you back." He set the phone down, strode into the foyer, and stopped at the sight of Ryder. "Shit, it's you."

"Hell of a greeting." His brother's eyes narrowed. "What's wrong?"

"Breanne called. Said Emma disappeared from the Beltane festival area around lunchtime. They found her clothes and leg brace up a trail and figured she'd probably taken animal form and gone for a run."

"Logical. Since she hasn't *trawsfurred* since being hurt, she'd be craving getting into fur again." Ryder frowned. "Did the healer clear her to *trawsfur*?"

"Nope. And she hasn't returned to help Bree. You know Emma doesn't bail on a job." Worry tightened a band around his ribs. "Where've you been? Have you seen her?"

"Uh-uh. I dropped the kitten off to join the other cubs."

Damn, he'd forgotten the cub preparations. "Is Minette comfortable with being away from us?"

Ryder's expression softened. "Yeah. Bonnie says the cub-sitters will bring the mites to the festival for an hour before bedding them down."

"Minette'll like the bonfires." She'd have more fun if the bard was there. "You haven't seen Emma at all?"

"Not since I dropped her off at the tavern. What the fuck is she thinking?"

"A while back, she said she doesn't attend Gatherings."

"Not surprising if she lived in a cave, bro," Ryder said. "But I got the impression she wanted to be with us tonight, even if she was nervous."

"Maybe." Ben scrubbed his face. "Maybe her nerve broke."

"Missing Gatherings in the wilderness is one thing. But in town? The Cosantir wouldn't permit a fertile female to remove herself from the gene pool."

Ben winced. He'd effectively done the same by never spilling his seed inside a female. The Mother couldn't have approved, but maybe She'd understood why. "What the fuck could have happened to make Emma so wary?"

"No clue, but it's fucking past time she shared with us." Ryder scowled. "She'd better not have run from the Gathering. Her leg's not very strong yet."

"No." If she was hag-ridden by her past, would she even return? And what if she got hurt? Although no hellhounds would be out during a full moon, accidents could happen any time.

By the God, Emma.

Ben opened the closet door and took out a jacket. "I'm going to the festival area to pick up her scent."

Without hesitation, Ryder pulled a coat out, too. "I'll help."

The knowledge he and his littermate were in step about Emma was heartening. "Thanks, bro. But after we find her trail, you need to stay at the Gathering in case she comes back—or if Genevieve tries to get her hands on Minette."

Warring expressions crossed Ryder's face before he nodded. "Agreed. I'll wait—no matter how long it takes you. If she goes very far…"

"Yeah." Worry settled in Ben's gut. "With her leg, she might have trouble getting back."

Chapter Twenty-One

Cold Creek, North Cascades Territory — Beltane's full moon

MOTHER'S BLESSING, BUT *why wouldn't it stop?* By the God, she'd never felt desire so strongly before. Not since her first time. Tears streamed down Emma's cheeks as she staggered down the trail toward Cold Creek. She had no choice. Every nerve in her body screamed with the need to mate. The full moon heat boiling in her veins was driving her down the mountain to where there were males.

With every step, pain stabbed deep into her right leg. Her leg brace was on the trail somewhere near the tavern, and she had no cane.

Four legs would be better than two, but with moonrise, lust had bloomed in her blood, and her body had shifted to human. She hadn't been able to *trawsfur* back to bear.

Shifters mated as humans; under the full moon, her body would stay human.

She glanced up. The night was clear. The silvery moon had lowered only an infinitesimal amount since her last look. Moonset was hours away.

Even if she even managed to reach Cold Creek, she might not have a leg left. Already she'd fallen several times, narrowly avoiding breaking her still fragile bones.

Would anyone search for her? Loneliness welled up and shattered her awareness. She stumbled and fell, catching herself on her hands and undamaged knee. At the impact, her injured leg blazed with new pain as if she'd shoved it into a meat grinder.

Ow, ow, ow.

Head hanging, she tried to rise, but after the day of fleeing from her past and hours of stumbling back toward Cold Creek, her strength was gone. Yet the full moon heat towed her along like a fast-moving current. Why was it so much worse than before?

The sound of a four-legged animal on the path brought her head up. Not good. It was big enough to rustle the brush on both sides of the trail and coming fast. She sniffed the air, but the wind was from the wrong direction—and undoubtedly had carried her scent right to the animal.

She struggled to stand and failed. Heart pounding, she closed her hand around a fallen branch.

The animal burst into sight. A massive grizzly bear, more than double the size of her bear form.

Her mouth went dry. *Don't move.*

The bear's mouth opened to display terrifying fangs.

Oh, she knew how much those would hurt. A shiver ran through her.

As the moonlight shone on the grizzly's silvered outer coat, she caught its wild scent...accompanied by a familiar, heady, masculine fragrance.

"Ben?" she whispered.

The bear rose to its hind legs, and the terrifying sound of angered grizzly filled the air and echoed from the peaks.

Her muscles turned to water, and she dug her fingers into the pine needles and dirt to keep from collapsing.

Then he shifted. Yes, it was Ben, and he was furious.

He stalked over to stand above her, as huge a male as he was a bear, his face dark with anger. "By the God, I should spank your ass the way my father thrashed mine. What kind of a stupid—"

"Thank you for coming after me." It was Ben. *Her* Ben. She blinked back tears. "I thought I'd die here."

His mouth closed. The slow, deliberate breath through his nose made his broad chest expand. After studying her for a drawn-out minute, he squatted in front of her.

"How badly are you hurt?" His Texas accent was thicker than usual, but his rumbling voice was level and controlled. Ben's temper was a fast-moving thunderstorm, one that shook the windows and moved on.

She sagged with relief. "Not bad. I'm mostly exhausted."

He made a disbelieving sound.

"Well, when the moon rose, I couldn't stay in bear form." She bit her lip and admitted, "So my leg hurts."

"I bet." He ran his hand down her right lower leg and pressed to assess the injured bone.

A mew of pain escaped her.

"Donal would be pissed if you busted the bones again. You don't want him yelling, do you?"

The silver-eyed healer was scary. She shook her head emphatically.

Ben's laugh was deep and masculine.

As she stared up at him, the ache in her leg disappeared under a new throbbing, one located right between her legs. Her breasts swelled and ached. The night air brushed cool against her suddenly sensitive skin.

Naked skin.

When Ben started to release her leg, her hand was right there, pressing on top of his, keeping his warm, callused palm on her.

He blinked, then his eyes narrowed before his fingers curled around her calf and caressed.

Everything in her melted at his measured touch. At the strength in his grip.

"Ah, like that, is it?" he said softly.

Her mouth was so dry she couldn't swallow. Her lips tingled.

His intent gaze trapped hers, immobilizing her as he lifted her hand toward his face...and inhaled.

There was no disguising the scent of an interested female. He would know how much she wanted him.

"Li'l bard." His voice lowered to a growl. "Unless you send me away right now, I'm going to take you."

By the Mother, what control he had to be able to walk away from a female in heat. A female he wanted—for the scent of his hunger tinged the air she breathed. But he was giving her the choice.

How could she not want him? She loved him, had desired him forever. Had almost lost him to a hellhound.

"Stay," she whispered. She ran her free hand over his corded forearm. He was a cahir, more powerful than other males, and his muscles were pumped from the run up the mountain. She yearned to run her hands and tongue over those ridges and valleys. To touch him everywhere. "Please."

"All right, honey bear." His eyes never left hers as he curved a hand around her nape and held her. His mouth was skilled, his lips firm, his tongue demanding, and he kissed her ruthlessly until every drop of blood in her body sparkled.

A surge of desperation made her moan.

He chuckled. "Easy, darlin', I'll get right to that...soon." To her frustration, he rose, looked around, and scooped her off the ground.

Why did he keep *carrying* her? "I'm too big. Put me down."

"You're not more than a mite." He walked off the trail and down a tree-covered slope toward the sound of water. The forest opened into a moonlit meadow of softly flattened winter grass bisected by a rushing creek.

He laid her down in the cool grass. For an eternity, he towered above her, looking down as the moon bathed her in light. Under his smoldering gaze, she felt…beautiful.

"I've wanted you for a long time, li'l bear," he said softly. Down on one knee, he cupped her face, brushed his thumb over her lower lip. "Do you have any idea how magnificent you are?"

His gentle touch and quiet words shook her, breaking through her need, and she could only stare at him, unable to breathe. Even the pain in her leg had faded to a low simmer under the roar of her need.

With care, he lowered himself and covered her body, settling between her open legs. His furnace-like warmth seeped into her, adding to the fire in her blood. Her lower half throbbed with her pulse, and the demand raged hotter when his rigid shaft pressed against her lower abdomen.

As he took her lips again, he cupped one breast, his thumb circling the nipple. He tugged lightly on the peak, and lightning sizzled right to her clitoris.

Her back arched, forcing her breast into his palm.

"That's the way, li'l bear," he murmured. Slowly, he kissed along her jaw, beneath it, and down her neck. His day's growth of beard scraped her sensitized skin, sending sparks of craving in its wake.

Breathless, she gripped his rock-hard biceps. The way his wide shoulders blocked the entire sky sent her brain into shutdown. *Ben.* Her voice didn't work—thank goodness—or she'd be blurting out protestations of love.

Nothing worked except her desperately yearning body. Her hips ground against his heavy erection.

"Nope, my female. You'll have what you need…when *I* decide." Taking her wrists in one enormous hand, he lifted them over her head. Her futile struggles made him grin before he slid down far enough to take a nipple in his mouth.

"Oooooh." His mouth was so hot, so wet. His tongue rasped in teasing flicks over one jutting nub and the other, circling each areola until her breasts swelled and throbbed.

His teeth closed over one nipple, bearing down to the very edge of pain, to an excruciating, spiking pleasure.

Her blood boiled and raged with need. "Please…"

"Soon, darlin'." Releasing her wrists, he moved down her body. Inch by inch, he tasted her skin. He teased her with scrapes of his stubbled chin, a nip to her waist, a lick up the crease between her thigh and pussy.

Purposeful. Methodical. Until her skin hummed with pleasure, anticipating every touch of his mouth. Her muscles tensed as he neared his goal.

Please, please, please.

His warm breath touched her clit—a glorious warning—and his mouth closed over the swollen nub.

The ferocious pleasure sent fireworks into the night sky. Her hips bucked wildly.

He huffed a laugh and laid his muscular forearm over her lower abdomen, forcing her to lie still.

To take what he wanted to give.

"No." She actually whined. "No, please. I need—"

His tongue went to work, driving every thought from her brain except the feeling of the heat and wet, the probing, rubbing motions, the circles. A gentle suck turned her brainless, and then he flicked the clit hood back and forth. Teasing.

All the blood in her body rushed to her core, swelling her pussy to a thrumming tightness.

He sucked harder, lashing the tip with his tongue. His callused finger slowly traced a circle around her entrance. She was slick with need, and he penetrated her easily. His blunt finger pressed deeper, stretching her in a way she hadn't felt since...since her last Gathering.

She shuddered with the memory.

Lifting his head, he studied her, eyes intent. "Does this bother you, honey bear?" He asked softly, even as he pulled back his finger and ever so slowly pressed in again.

The wonder of his controlled gentleness, of his care, melted the earth right out from under her.

"Darlin'?" His gruff voice sent more sensations consuming her.

Her only answer was a futile attempt to tilt her hips.

The laugh lines beside his eyes crinkled. "All right then." He lowered his head, and his lips closed again around her clit, pulling lightly, even as his finger slid deeper.

Her seething tension grew and grew, boiling away thoughts and words, and any sensation beyond sheer need. He slowly thrust in and out, adding another finger, even as he sucked her clit, his tongue lashing at it.

With a feeling of inevitability, everything within her drew together like the center of a tornado, then exploded outward, whirling pleasure along the terrain and through all the rivers of her body. Her cries were still ringing off the mountain heights when he moved up her body, positioned himself, and slowly, steadily filled her.

Then he stopped.

His shaft was thick, so very thick, and long, and hot... Her neck arched as another climax roared through her.

"Hang on tight, little bard." His voice was harsh. A muscle flexed in his jaw.

Her world still spinning, she gripped his shoulders. Under her fingers, his muscles bunched to granite as he pulled back and powered in again, deeper.

So much deeper.

He was enormous, filling her almost unbearably full. And yet the feeling was so thrillingly carnal she could only hang on as he increased the pace to a relentless hammering. Her own pulse sang in her ears, filling her world as she came and came again.

Finally, with a guttural roar, he thrust deep, completely to the root.

And froze.

Seconds passed. He seemed elsewhere.

"Ben?"

His gaze met hers and intensified until it penetrated deep enough to touch her mind. Her heart.

"Been a while, li'l bear." His lips curved. He slid his hand under her ass to pull her against him as his cock pulsed inside her.

Filling her.

Satisfying her demands in a way nothing else could.

Her core blossomed with delight, with the reception of his seed, and her whole body shimmered with physical joy.

His fingers slowly opened, freeing her. As he came down on her, she exulted in his heavy possessive weight. *Oh, I love you, love you, love you.*

Lifting up on one forearm, he nuzzled her neck. "Thank you for your trust, honey bear."

Who wouldn't trust this male? "Mmm." Unable to resist, she kissed his cheek, inhaling the masculine scent. So wonderful.

Needing more, she held his face between her palms and kissed him tenderly. Once he knew about her past, he might turn away, but for now? Now he was all hers.

He cooperated, then took control, driving every thought from her mind as her body recovered and demanded more.

A happy, four-more-orgasms time later, she realized the sizzle in her blood had waned. Slightly.

Raising her head, she looked over his shoulder. The moon was markedly lower.

He followed her gaze. "Time we got moving. Ryder's worried about you, as are a lot of other people. Think you can shift now?"

She breathed out a sigh. Yes, it was time to face her past. She had courage—she did—even if it occasionally got misplaced for a bit. "Yes. Let's go."

PREDAWN MIST SHROUDED the evergreen branches and swirled around the tree trunks. After getting a cup of coffee—bless Vicki for brewing it strong—Ryder staked out a spot near the trail Ben had taken.

When they'd arrived, Bree had taken them up the trail to where Emma had discarded her clothing. Fear scent had permeated the fabric. Ben had stripped and shifted to track the little bear.

What the hell made Emma run? Ryder's worry had grown with each passing hour.

The moon was nearly down, and shifters were wandering back into the clearing to warm up before breakfast. The light from the bonfires showed females with cheeks reddened from beard-stubble, swollen lips, and mussed hair. Many shirtless males had bite and scratch marks over their shoulders, backs, and chests.

Beltane was a fun time for most.

Ryder had performed dutifully—the Goddess required no less—but without enjoyment. He hadn't been able to stop worrying about Emma and had spent most of the night at the trailhead. Her female friends had joined him off and on. They'd been full of questions, wondering where she was. Why she'd left without any word.

Damned good questions.

Around midnight, Calum had stood beside him, his gaze on the trail. Ryder had started to ask if he could locate Emma. But when a Cosantir's eyes darkened to the color of night, no shifter with a love of life would interrupt.

After a minute, Calum had looked at Ryder and said he wanted to see Emma as soon as she returned.

By the God, his request had sounded ominous.

Leaning his head against the tree trunk, Ryder watched the shifters in the clearing. Getting water. Resting. Talking. A few males still clustered around accommodating females, obviously hoping for another quick mating. Vicki, Bree, and a few others were preparing the breakfast feast. Shay and Zeb were building up the Belfires again.

A shrill laugh caught Ryder's attention. He tensed and turned.

Genevieve. Still here in Cold Creek. She wouldn't stop until she got money...and probably revenge, as well. No one who dared to reject her escaped unscathed.

Dressed in a skintight leather skirt and low-cut tank top, she stood next to Sarah and a wolf named Candice, and two females Ryder didn't know. From the glances cast in his direction, Genevieve was ripping apart his reputation.

How did an honorable male combat something as elusive as gossip? If Genevieve were male, he'd use his fists or claws. But males didn't hurt females. Ever.

Frustration simmered in his gut.

A minute later, the rustle of brush on the trail caught his attention. Ben appeared. Emma walked slowly beside him, using his arm as a crutch.

The rush of relief swept Ryder's weariness aside. He set his coffee down and rose.

Seeing him, Ben lifted his chin. "Hey, bro."

The two were dressed in the clothing they'd left beside the trail. Scratches and scabs tattooed Emma's face and arms as if she'd torn headlong through blackberry tangles. And fallen. Often. Despite the brace on her leg, she limped badly.

Dammit, Emma.

But she'd returned to them and relatively unharmed, thank the Goddess. With a start, Ryder recalled the Cosantir. A warning was in order. "Emma, the Cosan—"

"Emma," Calum interrupted in a deep, icy voice. He stood between the Belfires, arms crossed over his chest.

EMMA COULD SEE the Cosantir's austere expression in the light of the flames. Even as her heart sank, fear chilled her blood. The guardian of a territory held the power of life and death, received directly from Herne's hands.

Gawain must have told him about the Gathering in Pine Knoll.

Straightening her shoulders, she started toward him before realizing Ben was beside her, still serving as her support. *Stupid Emma.* "Ben, he's angry. Stay back."

He caught her arm before she could step away. "Nope." Although worry had driven the laughter from his eyes, he set his hand over hers, trapped her fingers on his arm, and continued forward. Stubborn, stubborn bear.

To her dismay, she realized Ryder walked on her other side. He put his arm around her waist. How could she possibly risk him—both of them?

Ryder's implacable gaze said she might as well save her words.

When she tried to stop, Ben tugged her along as if she'd been Minette's size.

Bracketed between the brothers, she approached Calum.

"Did you want to speak with me, Cosantir?"

"Aye, Emma." He studied her silently. His gaze took in her scratched face, scraped hands. Her injured leg was so swollen Ben had needed to loosen the brace. "I gave you a home in this territory. In this clan."

Her mouth went dry. "I'm grateful," she whispered.

"Yet you defied our laws, running *away* from a Gathering—the tradition that has kept the Daonain alive for these many generations." The softness of his words only emphasized his wrath.

"Cosantir, I—"

"Each individual in our race must play a part to keep our people from a slow death. You know this, bard."

"I do," she whispered. Her heart pounded so violently against her ribcage she couldn't breathe. Would he banish her again? Now, when she'd just found a home? She'd be alone once more, never to speak with another shifter, to touch another.

She swallowed down the nausea and managed—barely—to meet his black, black eyes. "Please forgive me, Cosantir. I panicked. I panicked and ran. From someone—not from the Gathering." When he didn't move, she offered, "I was trying to return. I just couldn't move very fast."

The darkness receded from his gaze. "I know. Your efforts to return are why this is only a warning."

He knew? Of course he did. A Cosantir could locate any shifter in his territory. He probably knew right where she'd turned and started back toward Cold Creek.

The Cosantir inclined his head and released her from his gaze.

Her knees buckled, and only Ben's strong hand under her arm held her upright.

"Come, little bear. You need something to drink," Ryder said.

"Oh, that's a superb idea," she whispered. Her throat was so dry she might never be able to swallow again. And still, the moon's influence started to bubble in her blood, making her far too aware of the warmth of Ryder's hand in the hollow of her back. Of how tall he was beside her. Of how a night's beard growth shadowed his jaw.

And of how concern darkened his eyes.

"Ben, got a second?" Joe Thorson stopped him.

"Ah…" Ben gave her a concerned look.

"I'll get her fed, bro," Ryder said. "Don't worry."

As she continued beside Ryder toward the tables, a lanky shifter approached with a cocky swagger. "Hey, new female." He stared at her, his cheeks and lips reddening with lust. "I met you at Tullia's house, remember? I'm Chad. What's your name?"

Seriously? After the Cosantir almost put her to death, now this…idiot…wanted to flirt? What an insane night. Where was a sturdy tree on which to thump her head? "I'm rather busy right now."

"Aw, c'mon. You're really pretty. How about—"

"How about you move away?" Ryder suggested in an edged voice.

The male sniffed the air, and his lip curled up. "You got no say over what she does. She obviously didn't want to mate you."

The scent of aggression rose into the air.

"Back off, asshole," Ryder growled.

"Please," Emma whispered, putting her hand on his arm. "Don't. This isn't the place. This is never the time."

"Yeah, you dumb fuck, listen to the female," the male said. He grabbed Emma's hand, his grip hurting on her scraped palm.

She sucked in a breath from the pain and saw his eyes light. And he squeezed harder. She felt a trickle of blood.

Ryder's powerful hand closed on Chad's wrist, and as he bore down, the tendons stood out on his wrist. "Let her go."

"Fuck, asshole!" Chad dropped her hand.

Ryder pushed him. "You hurt her." Ryder gave him another shove, and Chad staggered back again. "Deliberately."

Emma started to shake. Angry males. Loud voices. Then there would be blood and—

Chad charged, ramming his head into Ryder's stomach so violently that Ryder hit a tree with his back.

Oh no. Dread seeped into her blood. Fighting. No. She ran to Ben. "Ben—stop them. Please."

Joe looked up. "Stupid dog needs a lesson. Let 'em fight."

"Please…"

With a blustering noise, Ben sauntered toward the males.

RYDER HAD CHAD on the ground, straddling him, and was enjoying the hell out of each blow he landed. By the God, he could smell Emma's blood on the wolf's hand. Heard again the soft sound of pain she'd made. The asshole had hurt her while she was under Ryder's care.

Oh, this fucker was going to pay.

Before Ryder could move, Ben grabbed his shirt and yanked him up. "Stop it. This is a Gathering, not a war."

"Fuck. You." He drove his fist into his littermate's gut—it was like hitting a rock wall—and his next followed to the jaw. "You're always butting into my fun."

After staggering back, Ben regained his footing and lunged forward. He slammed a huge fist into Ryder's belly, grabbed his shoulders, and threw him across the clearing.

People scrambled out of the way like fleeing mice. Landing painfully hard, Ryder rolled up onto hands and knees. He shook his head, feeling the hum of the full moon, revving into battle-fever, which would be followed by a good mating.

His blood churned in his veins. He needed to hit something. And nothing was as fun as pounding on the grizzly. Hell, it'd been years since they had a good brawl.

He gave a shake as if to settle his fur and shoved to his feet, charging the grizzly with a happy growl.

"No!" EMMA SCREAMED a protest as Ryder rammed his shoulder into his brother.

Ben backpedaled and punched Ryder again, knocking him away—then attacked.

Fighting. Her world was fragmenting, fracturing, tearing itself apart with loud, discordant notes. The smack of fist on flesh. Grunting. Snarling. Swearing. Tears blurred her eyes.

They loved each other. Were hurting each other. Because of her. "Stop. Stop, please, *stop!*"

Never, never again.

"No!" With a soul-stricken cry, Emma threw herself between them. Ben's mammoth body hit her like a falling oak tree and knocked her sideways into Ryder. His fist smashed into her stomach.

Pain. So much pain.

Two shouts made her ears ring as she fell to her knees, arms wrapped over the agony in her middle. Knives stabbed her leg as she dropped onto the stony earth. Everything hurt and she couldn't…couldn't *breathe.*

An arm supported her. "By the God," Ben growled. "Shhh, darlin'. Don't move."

"Herne's balls. Little bear, I didn't want…" Ryder dropped down beside her and massaged her paralyzed abdominal muscles.

Interminable seconds passed. The buzzing in her ears grew. Then her gut relaxed, and her lungs expanded. One breath. A miracle.

She gasped for more air and found her voice. "Don't fight." She grabbed Ben's shirt, Ryder's wrist. "Don't fight."

"By the God, I knew you wouldn't change your ways." The furious roar came from Emma's nightmares. Cedrick, the Cosantir from her former territory, stalked across the clearing. Gray streaked his hair now; lines were deeper in his face.

A blast of hatred came from him. Her mouth opened, and nothing came out.

"Just like your mother. Boosting your overblown ego by making males fight over you."

Cedrick was here.

Here.

"What's your problem?" Ryder paused, undoubtedly seeing the power of the God emanating from the Mt. Hood Cosantir.

A smothering wave of silence filled the clearing.

Cedrick pointed at her. "She was banished from my territory after she goaded two young males into attacking each other. Their battle was so vicious they both died."

Gasps sounded around the area.

Roaring filled Emma's ears and red seared the edges of her vision.

Not again. No, please, Mother of All, not again.

"What?" Ryder stared down at her. "No..."

His voice disappeared in the roaring in her ears. Someone took her hand...said something...but above it all, she heard Cedrick's snarls. "She..."

His tortured snarls carried her down, down, until memories were a fire of agony riding her bloodstream, burning her heart to ashes. Her sight blurred into a shroud of gray, her ears tuned to the song of tragedy where all she could hear were the sounds of two males fighting, savaging each other, growling, and roaring.

Her screams echoed down the hallway. Blood covered the walls, the floor, filling her vision with red. "I'll leave. I'll leave. Don't fight—oh, *please*, don't fight."

Tears burned her abraded cheeks as she grabbed Ryder's

arm and shook it. "I'll leave. He loves you. Don't fight."

The arm tightened around her.

Everywhere she looked was red, blood everywhere; the unspeakable stench of death filled the air. Her ears heard only the gasping last breaths—and still fighting. Fighting. Grunts and thumps, growling and roaring. Why wouldn't they *stop*?

"No more!" She tried to put her hands over her ears and couldn't move. "Stop fighting. I don't want you to fight! I'll take you both. Don't hurt each other." Her fingers curled around an arm, and she shook it. Tried to pull him away from the fight. "Don't hit him. You don't need to hit him—I'll do anything."

"What the fuck?" Voices sounded around her. The battle filled her head. Andre's swearing. Shrieks of agony. "Please…no, please, please."

Cedrick's furious voice broke through. "See how she makes the males fight? Damn you, you—" A blow—and pain burst in her cheek.

More roaring sounded. Her body shook. The world itself was falling apart. She wrapped her arms around herself, unable to look. There would be blood everywhere. Her men—dead, her heart with them.

"You got her wrong, you fucking asshole. Cosantir or not, you're an idiot."

Was that Ryder? Was he still alive? More snarls drowned out the voices. She was drowning in blood.

"Emma." The rough, deep voice filled with the power of the God sliced through the snarling and cries of pain. "Tell me who's fighting."

"Andre. Gary. Stop, stop, stop." She struggled against the arms restraining her. She had to stop them. Ice filled her center—she knew what would happen.

"Easy, little bear." A familiar, smoky voice was gentle…for her. "You don't have to—"

"I do believe she does. It is time to get to the heart of this." The clipped voice reverberated with so much power that every instinct in her cried for her to find a dark cave far, far, far from anyone. *Run. Hide.*

"Not your business, Calum. It's between me and this female." The angry voice made shivers start up inside her.

In her lap, a hand clasped hers. She stared at it, blinking as her vision cleared. Lean fingers, reddened knuckles, the wrist bones strong. Dark hair lightly furred a leanly muscled forearm. Ryder. He was pressed cat-close against her left side, his other arm around her waist.

A powerful arm crossed her thighs, and a big hand curved around her hip, holding her in place. Ben. He was on her right, his left arm behind her shoulders.

She pulled in a careful breath. She was pinned between the brothers. They weren't fighting. She'd stopped them before…before…

But they were surrounded by shifters staring down at her. At the forefront, Cedrick stood, hands fisted, radiating hatred. When his hand opened into claws, she'd be condemned again. Sent away from love and hope and home.

Banished.

But her males were alive. They mustn't fight—not with a Cosantir.

She closed her eyes. "I'll go," she whispered. "Just let me go."

A feminine growl came from her right. Vicki stood on the other side of Ben. Her tight expression held not anger, but concern. For Emma. Catching Emma's gaze, Vicki straightened her shoulders, lifted her chin. *Get a spine, bear.*

"Yes, ma'am," Emma whispered and saw the twitch of her friend's lip.

Next to Vicki, Angie gave Emma a firm nod—one a mama

bear might administer to a loved cub in danger.

Behind Cedrick was Bree. Only Shay's arm around her waist kept her from joining Emma. She was openly crying.

Crying for me? Emma blinked back her own tears and pulled in a small breath. Then a bigger one. She wasn't alone. She had…friends. The miracle edged into her heart, and the fear receded slightly.

She'd planned to return and face down Gawain, the male from Pine Knoll, before telling Ben and Ryder about her past. This was just…a bit…more than she'd anticipated. She needed more courage. *Dig deeper.* She realized the warmth seeping into her came from Ben and Ryder.

"Bard."

At the title of respect, she looked up. Calum—*her* Cosantir—stood in front of her. The shimmer of power increased as his eyes darkened to black with the presence of the God. Her judgment was at hand.

"Tell me why the males in the other territory fought," his British-accented voice demanded, brooking no refusal.

"They fought over me." Misery swept over her. "I flirted with them. My fault."

"By the God, all females flirt at a Gathering," said a gruff older male.

The arms around her didn't relax at her confession. Ryder's hand actually tightened around hers.

"Females flirt." The Cosantir repeated, "Tell me why the males fought."

Ben pulled her closer to his massive frame. His huffing growl wasn't directed at her, but at the Cosantir.

The Cosantir didn't even flinch. His black gaze burned, drawing out her memories the way she would gather the strands of a song.

"I was going to mate with Gary, but Andre followed us,"

she whispered, unable to look away from Calum's depthless eyes. "Andre was angry; he'd wanted Phoebe, but she'd chosen Gary instead. Andre said I should go with him since he was bigger."

A snort. "Young males." Alec's voice.

"And then…" She started to shake. If she could have run, she would have. Would have fled. She yearned for the safe, quiet…empty…forest. No one to judge.

Ben squeezed her shoulder, holding her in place, holding her in the present. "Darlin', did you mate with Gary?"

She pulled in a shuddering breath and felt Ryder rub his shoulder against hers in feline support. *Courage.* "No," she whispered. "At the mating-room door, Andre stopped us. Gary told him to leave, only Andre ran his hand down my face. And I…I could smell him and hear him, and…"

The hideous cry broke out of her. "Andre kissed me, and I kissed him, and Gary shoved us apart, and they started fighting, and it was all my fault!"

The first sob wrenched at her, tearing apart her ribs, clawing her heart. The ones following were even more painful.

"Hell." Ben pulled her into his lap, surrounding her with his arms, his size, his strength.

So much blood. So much death. Guilt crushed her under an implacable paw. "Let me go." She struggled against the bear's hold. "I did it. Why did I do that? I was with Gary. I shouldn't—"

"By the God." A callused hand caught her chin, forcing her to meet Ryder's harsh gaze. "You're not exactly old, so when did this happen? How many Gatherings had you been to, Emma?"

"Three years ago. It was my first Gathering. The only one I've ever been to." She wrenched away from Ben and spat at Calum, "I don't know what I did that night, but I'll never again be the reason anyone dies. Banish me again. Here…" She leaned forward and tilted her face so he could claw her. "Do it. I'll go away and—"

Ben yanked her back.

Ryder's hand closed over her mouth, muffling her. "Uh-uh, little bear."

She strained against the two males, just wanting to run, and then all the energy drained out of her. She sagged in Ben's arms.

Ryder took his hand away and stroked her hair away from her face.

After a second, she opened her eyes.

The Daonain silently stared at her, brows furrowed, shaking their heads. Yes, she'd disappointed them all. Horrified them.

"That's not how it happened," Cedrick growled. "She's—"

"That was exactly how it happened." Gawain gently moved Angie to one side as he stepped out of the crowd with Owen at his back. He scowled at the Cosantir of his territory. "I told you so then and there."

Cedrick's color heightened. "Watch it, cat, or you'll find yourself out of—"

"Ssssst." Hissing, the cahir Owen stepped in front of Gawain.

"Well," Alec interrupted, "I think my mate would call your Gathering a clusterfuck." His voice was easy. Smooth. "It seems odd the God would banish a female for merely being a battle prize."

"Odd indeed." With a frown, Calum bent and ran his fingertips over the scars on Emma's cheek. Did it again. His fingers were hotter than normal skin temperature and left tingling in their wake. "Emma, why did you say you were banished?"

"Because I-I was…." She was shaking so hard it was impossible to breathe.

"Easy, little bear," Ryder murmured. His hands closed around hers.

"I banished her. Rightfully so." When the Mt. Hood Cosantir curved his fingers into claws, Emma shuddered.

"You tried." Calum's accented voice had chilled. "It appears the God disagreed."

Ben cleared his throat. "When the Mother forgives, the black disappears, leaving only normal scars behind. So…"

So how would Calum know if her banishment had happened or not? Emma frowned.

Calum glanced at Ben and then smiled at her. "To the eyes, nothing is left. But a banishment leaves marks on the soul for those who can see." And a Cosantir could see.

"She wasn't?" Cedrick stared at her. He stepped back, looking as if he'd been punched. "She *wasn't*."

Emma touched her face, feeling the thin scars. Cedrick had pronounced her banishment, but she'd never been able to face seeing the black marks on her face.

She'd never looked.

I was never banished. "But Andre and Gary died because of me."

"You were the excuse. You didn't do anything." Gawain glanced at Calum. "Hell, Emma was so innocent she didn't even know how to flirt, let alone get two males to fight. I was the first male she'd ever had. Each time someone took her to a room, she was surprised—filled with delight—someone wanted her."

Emma shook her head. "But, I—"

"By the God," Ryder muttered and pulled her tighter against him. "Little bear, don't you see? Those males were primed to fight. If you hadn't provided an excuse, they'd have found something else."

Ben kissed her fingers. "Honey bear, did you ask them to fight for your favor?"

"No, of course not!"

"A fair number of females do." Ryder glanced toward the right, his eyes turning cold. "Genevieve always did. It's not against the law…just crappy behavior."

"But I'd chosen a male and turned to another."

"Aye," Ben agreed. "It's okay. It happens. A more experienced female might—*might*—have been able to control her response."

"But a female at her first Gathering is usually overwhelmed," Vicki said. "You're out of control. Your mind is trapped in all the sensations."

Every male's scent, the sound of a voice, a laugh…she'd kept getting lost. She turned to Gawain. "I didn't flirt? Didn't do anything wrong?"

"No, you didn't do anything at all." His lips turned up. "There's no law against being adorable."

Ben's growl rumbled through his chest and vibrated across her skin.

Gawain took a careful step back.

With a satisfied grumble, Ben stroked her hair. "You reacted like any young female, darlin'. You did nothing wrong."

Her eyes filled with tears. She'd paid, perhaps unfairly, but she was here and… "They died."

One arm around Vicki, Alec stood next to Calum. "The consequences of being stupid can be harsh. They were young, driven by testosterone, and out of control. They paid an ugly price."

"The world isn't always fair." The God still rode Calum's shoulders as he turned a black gaze upon Cedrick. "But judgments given by a Cosantir should be."

"Three years." Ryder's hand tightened painfully on hers. "You lived wild for three fucking years." With every breath, his growls grew more audible.

"Emma. By the God…" The Mt. Hood Cosantir sank to his knees as if unable to remain upright. "What have I done?"

"You drove a vulnerable, innocent female into the wilderness. Made her think she was guilty. Alone for three. Fucking.

Years. That's what you *did*." Ryder's fury reverberated from the ridges. He rose. His hands were claws at his side.

In the clearing, the shifters whispered, and Emma realized their anger was focused on the Mt. Hood Cosantir. On Emma's behalf.

She had friends. *Friends.*

Before Ryder could attack, Emma grabbed his calf with both hands and held him back. "No fighting."

"He wronged you. He—"

"Maybe. But Gary was his *son*. You know how you'd feel if Minette was hurt or…" *Died.* She couldn't even say the word. The world would stop if Minette died.

Ryder froze, and after a second, his fingers uncurled. "Fuck." He met her eyes, sharing the knowledge. A child's death would be the worst pain ever possible.

"Emma." Still on his knees, Cedrick had tears in his eyes. "I've been so…filled with hatred. Gary's death. Andre's death. Neither was your fault." His jaw tightened as his voice lowered. "In my grief, I looked for someone or something to blame."

Pain radiated from him.

"Cosantir—"

He shook his head, his lips twisting into a half-smile. "Not for much longer. I think when I return, the God will lift his hand from me and choose another. My vision has grown…narrow."

"But…" He'd no longer be the Cosantir of his territory?

He leaned forward and took her hand.

Ben tensed behind her. Ryder stepped closer.

"Emma, you are not like your mother, and you never were. I see that clearly now. The town and I treated you unfairly—as a child, as a female, as a bard. Eventually, I hope you can forgive me."

"I already have," she said gently.

She'd learned something about people. About Cedrick. And

about Ryder, as well. Both her mother and Genevieve were like stones falling into a small pond. The self-centered impact sent anger and hatred rippling outward to affect those around them.

Chuckling, Alec helped the stunned Mt. Hood Cosantir to his feet. "Emma has a soft heart. My female would've gutted you and left you for the coyotes."

"Damn straight," came from Vic.

"I don't care if she'd disembowel him or not. Got other concerns here." Ryder lifted Emma from Ben's lap and onto her feet. His dark voice took on a sharp edge. "Dammit, female, why the fuck didn't you tell us about all this before?"

"Dammit, female?"

Excuse me?

She'd survived Cedrick, banishment, hiking down a mountain. Her polite allotment was gone. All used up. "Let me think." She put her hands on her hips. "Maybe because I've only liked you for a week or so? Or maybe because you have issues with females?"

He blinked at her, as startled as a cougar bitten on the nose by a mouse.

Dammit, female. Oooh, the insult still burned. Come to think of it, hadn't he asked a favor of her? *"Will you do me a favor and wallop me when I mess up?"*

"So…*male*…be warned. Anytime you address me as *dammit, female*, you'll get this for an answer." She punched him on the arm. Hard.

Hard enough that he winced.

Ben looked shocked. "Emma?"

After a stunned moment, Ryder roared, his laughter deep and rich. "I need to be more careful about what I request."

She checked his face carefully, surreptitiously shaking her throbbing hand. The man's biceps were harder than rocks. "You're serious?"

"Oh, yeah." He hugged her and kissed her lightly. "Shows me you care, or you wouldn't have bothered. I'll try not to mess up again."

He read her well. "Okay, then."

As the anxiety trickled out of her, she started thinking about escape. She needed quiet. She wanted to hide. What must everyone think? Would they look down on her for…for causing this mess during Beltane?

Before she could take a step, the Cosantir—*her* Cosantir—stopped her. "Bard, Vicki said you knew Beltane songs. After some food and drink to revive you, might you grace us with a song or two?"

Rousing cheers filled the clearing and warmed her heart.

She looked around. The shifters of Cold Creek were smiling. Happy with her and for her. Yes, this was her town.

Angie pulled her away from Ben for a hug. Bree and Bonnie followed. Vicki grinned and said quietly, "Ice down your hand—and next time aim for a softer spot."

Next time.

Knowing Ryder, the occurrence of a next time was entirely possible. Even better, Emma would be around to chastise him and would have the courage to do so.

With a wavering giggle, Emma hugged the small, incredibly tough female. "I will. I will do that."

AFTER THE ENDLESS night, the breakfast feast, and the singing, Emma had only enough strength to pull on a robe before she collapsed on her bed.

Brow creased with concern, Ryder hovered in the doorway. Behind him, Ben was making worried sounds under his breath like an aged grandsire.

Although their concern turned her insides squishy, she

needed to be alone. Her breath hitched, and her eyes prickled with tears.

"By the God, Emma." Aghast, Ryder started forward. "Don't cry."

She motioned toward the door. "Go on, you two. I'm fine. I just need to rest for a bit." To be alone.

Ben nodded his understanding, yanked his littermate out of the room, and closed the door.

She had a moment to think how funny it was that the aloof cat was the brother most upset by her tears, and then…those tears spilled over and scalded her scratched cheeks. A sob escaped, and she buried her face in the pillow to muffle her weeping.

Oh, she wanted to scream. To hit something. To yell and mourn, and laugh and cry. And all she could do was cry.

Gary and Andre's deaths hadn't been her fault. *Not. My. Fault.*

She hadn't been banished. Not ever. The God hadn't agreed with the Cosantir's judgment. She hadn't had to spend years alone, feeling hated.

So many long, silent nights, cold and hungry, yearning for her clan. Ragged sobs tore at her throat.

And still, she couldn't hate Cedrick. He'd lost his son. Was no longer the powerful male of her youth. The years of grief…and hatred…had damaged him. Broken him.

The years had changed her, as well, for better and for worse.

Her weeping slowed. Stopped.

The pillow was wet against her cheek as she lay quietly, feeling better for the catharsis.

The years were over and done, and couldn't be reclaimed. However, the master bard had taught her to study the past, even while remembering the Mother was a goddess of balance.

A wise shifter would note her blessings as well as her trials.

Blessings. Hmm. Well, although the years in the wilderness had been lonely ones, she'd also matured. She wasn't as...flutter-brained...as many females her age.

During the time alone, she'd also grown as a bard, even if her audience had been tree fairies and birds.

Looking back on her youth, she knew her mother had left her overly...sensitive...to opinion. Emma expected other people to judge her harshly, and being alone had made the problem worse. She needed to work on those insecurities—although, like Ryder, she might mess up now and again.

Her lips curved up. It had been fun to punch him. However, considering the size and hardness of his fist, she wouldn't ask him to do the same with her.

He'd sure been unhappy she hadn't shared her past with him. She should have, but she'd been afraid. Fear had made her do quite a few stupid things, hadn't it? Starting with behaving like a pursued goose when she'd run into Gawain.

Sitting up, Emma wiped her face and grinned ruefully. She deserved points for...eventually...conquering her panic and turning around. A half-laugh escaped her. Maybe *conquer* wasn't the right word. More like *barely managed*. Still, she'd been return-ing to face him. She wasn't a coward. Not completely.

The time when her need had controlled her actions had been frightening in a whole different way. Living around other shifters—male shifters—had apparently increased her sex drive to a fearsome pitch. In her desperation to return to the Gather-ing, she could easily have gone off a cliff.

She shook her head as she stared at her dirty hands. Two fingernails had been shredded down to the quick. Her palms were abraded and sliced in places. Her whole body was scraped from branches, bruised from falls. She'd been out of her mind.

Mating with Ben under the full moon, on the other hand, had been a whole different kind of madness.

She closed her eyes and remembered the feel of his sure hands, the powerful way he'd taken her, so fierce, yet totally in control. His demands had pulled her with him until she hadn't felt anything except her need and his pleasure in satisfying it.

At her first Gathering—before everything had gone wrong—the matings had been pleasurable. With Ben, the sex had been overwhelmingly, terrifyingly intense. But, could she have let go if she hadn't felt so safe as well? In his arms, she was sheltered.

Over the weeks in his home, she'd come to trust him. To desire him. To love him.

Was this what lifemates felt?

A breath caught in her chest. Maybe now she'd have a chance to answer the question.

She could stay here in Cold Creek, where they valued her as a bard. Where she had friends who stood beside her. She snorted. And where friends instructed her on the fine art of punching a wayward male.

Above all, the most thrilling—frightening—wonderful part of staying in Cold Creek was that Ben and Ryder lived here.

Needing comfort, she gathered her pillow into her arms. For years, she hadn't needed to think about risking anything other than her physical safety. Risking her heart was—*be honest, bard*—a done deal. The two males already owned her heart.

She'd fallen for Ben a long time before, Ryder more recently, but no less powerfully. Just as well she loved them both, since they couldn't be separated.

What did they think of her, though? Could they possibly…ever…want her for more than a female friend?

She'd mated with Ben. Ryder'd kissed her. He'd wanted to mate with her at the Gathering, Would he still be interested when the moon waned?

With an irritated laugh, she buried her head in her pillow.

Actually living life was nerve-racking.

But she had time, didn't she? Perhaps that was the greatest gift Cedrick's appearance and the resolution of her worries had given her. There was time to figure all this out.

She gave a determined nod. And she would.

A tap at the door dislodged her thoughts.

Before she could answer, the door opened, and the healer stepped inside. "The Cosantir said you needed tending." His silvery gaze took her in, head to toe, and his lean face darkened with anger. "By the God's fucking balls, what have you done to yourself?"

RYDER OPENED EMMA'S bedroom door and stepped in. Sounded as if Donal was still on a rant.

"By Herne's holy prick, I better not have to come and do another healing. If you want to go running off in the forest, you fucking wait until I say you can. Am I clear?"

Her eyes, red-rimmed from recent tears, sparked with irritation. Nonetheless, she said, contritely, "Yes, Healer."

Ryder grinned, his worry receding. She'd had one fucking traumatic night, had undoubtedly had a cry fest and, despite the healer's work, still looked battered, but her spirit was alive and well.

Damn, she was something.

When Donal turned his back, she made a face. Ryder couldn't smother his snort of amusement.

Donal turned his icy glare on Ryder. "After she showers, keep her off her leg. I healed the damage she did, so tomorrow, she can go back to using the brace and cane for another couple of days." He stepped around Ryder and stalked out, slamming the door behind him.

Ryder considered following. *Nah.* By now, the healer knew

his way out.

Ryder turned his attention to Emma. Donal had reduced the swelling in her leg, but the rest of her was a mess. "Ben's taking a shower. He sent me to help you with yours. He doesn't want you to fall. Again."

The pink in her cheeks increased to a sweet red. Fuck, she was pretty. "I can stand up by myself."

"Nope." He plucked her off the bed. Had anyone ever felt so perfect in his arms?

Ben, being both grizzly and cahir, had always preferred larger females.

Once Ryder'd reached his mature weight and size, he, too, had discovered a preference for females tall enough to kiss easily and with ample flesh to fill his big hands. Although females of all sizes were appealing, he liked not worrying if he'd break a female when he was on top.

Nuzzling her hair, he held her closer, enjoying the soft, round curves against him. Reminded him of the human Goldilocks story. This pretty bear wasn't too little, wasn't too big; she was just right.

When he didn't set her on her feet, she realized he planned more than helping her out of bed. "I can walk, you know."

He headed across the room.

She started to squirm.

"Uh-uh," he warned—and was ignored.

She'd learn. Threatening to drop someone was a sneaky technique—definitely not one his straightforward brother would employ. Being an evil-minded cat, Ryder had no such scruples. Loosening his grip, he let go.

"No!" With a satisfying gasp, she grabbed his shoulders.

He caught her with nary a jolt and managed not to laugh— barely.

Her glare made him feel a hell of a lot better. He could deal with anger. But tears? Emma's tears? Seeing her cry earlier had shredded his heart into confetti.

After sneaking a quick kiss, he carefully set her on her feet in the shower. Without asking permission, he stripped off her robe and received another glare. Now she was naked and thoroughly annoyed. Under such provocation, some shifters might *trawsfur* and seriously damage the instigator, but Ryder knew right to the bottom of his soul this little female would do anything to avoid hurting a person.

He turned on the shower and handed her the shampoo. "Need help?"

"Absolutely not."

"Don't be mad, little bear. I've been worried about you." He ran a finger down her soft cheek and frowned at the scratches from bushes.

"I…" Her expression softened. "I'm sorry for being grumbly."

"Understandable." He gave her a wry smile. "I daresay I'd be worse. I hate feeling helpless."

"I bet." Her smile flickered. "But thank you for caring."

Oh, he'd gone far beyond caring and was well into much, much more.

He stepped far enough away to stay dry, but close enough to grab her if she lost her balance.

Rolling her eyes, she stepped under the water, and her sensuous sigh hardened his cock. "After three years of washing in icy streams, I'll never take hot water for granted."

Bet not. "Aye. And soft mattresses. When I spent a summer in the mountains, I missed my bed." He grinned. "Ben would probably pine for sweets—like your cookies."

Her laugh could make a dwarf smile.

As she bent to wash her hair, the overhead light revealed pink bite marks on her neck and shoulders.

His brows lifted. Her nipples were red and swollen. Faint fingermarks showed on her round hips…and she still smelled of a thorough mating.

Well, well, well. Ben had definitely found her well before the moon had set. *Good for you, my brother.*

His cock surged awake, right along with the urge to take her and leave his own handprints and bite marks alongside his littermate's.

That would feel right; the way it should be. Littermates shared.

As she washed, he leaned against the wall and kept an eye on her. So beautiful—not only on the outside, but on the inside as well, even to forgiving her previous Cosantir.

He fucking wouldn't forgive the weasel who'd banished a young, confused female. By the God, he wished he'd been there to defend her. To protect her, even if it meant living in the wilderness for three years.

He still had trouble believing she'd survived.

But she had. And he had a feeling she'd emerged stronger for the ordeal. She had a…balance…to her. Yes, she worried about what others thought, but she also had rock-steady values no one's opinion would shake.

The longer he knew her, the more he respected her. And more.

When she turned the water off, he lifted her onto the bath mat and set her hands on the grab bar just outside the shower. With a fluffy towel, he started drying her off.

"I can do it." She tried to take the towel from him.

"Little bear, you concentrate on keeping your weight off your leg." He stroked down her back, her sweetly rounded ass, and her long curvy legs. Around to the front, carefully over her sore leg, and up her thighs. He patted dry her mound and her soft abdomen and her full breasts.

Catching the scent of her interest, his desire surged. Everything in him longed to abandon the towel and fondle and lick, and—

No. She'd had enough. Although the fragrance of her awakening was sizzling through his blood, more upheaval at this time wouldn't be good for her.

He could wait. For this female, he'd find infinite amounts of patience.

After tossing the towel into the hamper, he helped her into Ben's brown robe. It swamped her smaller frame, and as he rolled up the sleeves, she looked up at him. Her lower lip quivered. "Thank you, Ryder."

Heart aching, he traced a finger under her still puffy eyes. Was something else wrong? Unable to help himself, he pulled her into his arms. "Little bear, what can I do to help?"

Without any hesitation, she leaned into him. Trust. She trusted him. Gratitude for the gift filled him to overflowing.

"I'm all right. Really." She rubbed her forehead on his shoulder as Minette did when she was exhausted. "I just needed a good cry. It's a female thing."

Genevieve never cried unless she had an audience...and needed something.

Emma...

She'd become far more than a female he wanted to mate. He cared...truly cared for her. Worried about her. Knew her better than he'd known any female, and still, still she had hidden depths he hadn't discovered. Did being friends deepen the pathways to a true mate?

"All right." He kissed the top of her head as he would his cub. "I've heard you *damned females* enjoy chocolate. I'll make you a cup."

The way she was laughing as she gave him a token punch warmed him from the inside out.

Chapter Twenty-Two

AFTER ENTERTAINING THE tavern crowd and answering questions in her after-performance chat, Emma relaxed in the tavern kitchen and savored the light Riesling wine Calum had brought her. The fragrance of popcorn hung in the air from the last batch made, and Vicki'd left a bowlful for Emma to enjoy. The jukebox had been restarted, and Tim McGraw's "One of Those Nights" drifted down the hallway. Oh, how she'd missed hearing music during her years alone.

Now she had all her heart could desire. Festivals like Beltane last Sunday and these nights at the tavern along with playing guitars with Ryder and Ben at home. She smiled. She could swear she'd heard Minette humming along once or twice.

Emma sipped her drink. Although the sounds of the packed barroom were audible, the kitchen was quiet and empty. She had time to unwind and evaluate her performance.

She did love Thursday nights. Well, actually, both her nights at the tavern were fun. On Sundays, the children listened with touching attention to the traditional ballads and teaching songs. On Thursdays, she could be more versatile, changing her song choices depending on the mood of the crowd.

Tonight, she'd planned a romantic theme, but after seeing Ben and Ryder, she'd changed to some less revealing, more historic choices. No need for everyone in the world to know how she felt.

Someday, she'd have to share her feelings, but...not yet. Maybe she was a coward, but she couldn't get past the memories of when she'd blurted out her love to her mother and received a dismissive look. Or when she'd hugged the maid and learned her affectionate behavior was *inappropriate*.

If she said she loved Ben, he wouldn't be cruel, but...what if he didn't feel the same? No, she wasn't ready to expose herself in such a way. Not yet.

Her lips curved up, because...she'd found other ways to show her love. For the last few nights—ever since the Gathering—Ben had taken her to his bed. The first night, she'd tried to object out of a sense of decorum, and he'd laughed, sniffed her wrist, and kissed her so thoroughly she'd forgotten anything other than his body, his taste, his scent.

The male was insatiable, and mating with him had been an education. Sometimes, as the target of his intense passion, she could see and feel nothing beyond desire. At other times, he was sweet and gentle. Or playfully affectionate. Sex could be...fun.

And she'd never felt as safe and loved as when he pulled her against his massive body, wrapped his arms around her, and...simply cuddled her.

Oh, she loved him so, so much. Thank the Goddess, she could show him physically even if her tongue froze on the words.

And Ryder? Slowly, surely, she was sinking under his spell. Did he care for her at all? He'd seemed interested during the full moon, but...perhaps no longer. The thought set up a slow aching, as if she'd bruised her heart.

Brothers often shared their females, but maybe...maybe Ben and Ryder didn't. She shouldn't make assumptions.

Maybe Ryder wasn't interested in her...that way.

With a sigh, she scooped up some popcorn. The buttery scent made her smile. Perhaps one of these days, she'd declare a movie night and make popcorn for Minette.

Tonight, the cub was visiting Bonnie's children and delighted with the "tradition" of visiting playmates on Thursday nights. After seeing her mother on Tuesday, she'd been subdued, clinging to Emma or Ryder or Ben, and hadn't wanted to leave the house on Wednesday. Thank goodness, she was almost back to her bright little self.

Emma scowled. The males never hurt females, but females didn't have such restrictions. Genevieve could certainly benefit from a nice wallop or two.

Of course, someone would have to point her out, since Emma'd never met her.

The thought of Minette's foul mother had destroyed the quiet of the kitchen. With an annoyed huff, Emma drank the last of her wine and rose.

A glance at her legs lifted her grumpy mood. Earlier, the healer had visited and announced she could give up the leg brace and cane. She could even go on outings into the mountains. Of course, being Donal, he'd scowled and added, "*Short outings.*"

He'd probably have had a heart attack if she'd kissed him…although she'd been sorely tempted.

Grinning, she walked into the chaotic, mesmerizing bedlam she'd only heard in this tavern. People at the tables talked over the music—and each other. Raucous laughter came from males standing two deep around the bar. Pool table balls clicked and thudded. Females giggled, others hooted with laughter. Older males added baritone notes to the raucous song.

The tavern smelled of popcorn and roasted peanuts, of wood smoke and beer, of human perfume and cologne, and the wild fragrance of shifters.

Near the pool table alcove where Rosie was assigned, Ryder

and Ben were with a group of other males. At the sound of Ben's rumbling laugh, Emma's heart did a disconcerting, syncopated drumbeat.

In the center of the room, Vicki was taking orders. The rightmost third of the room was waiting to order. Time to work. Emma grabbed a tray and signaled she'd cover the fireplace and surroundings. Grinning, Vicki gave her a half-salute. Rosie offered up a raspy cheer.

After several trips to the bar, Emma had only the section near the big windows left to serve. Without thinking, she'd left the table of young shifter females for last. Someday she'd manage to overcome her nervousness around females in her age group.

As she approached, she was blocked by a burly human male. He swaggered away from the table, zipping his leather jacket up over a stained tank top.

"Hey, babe." He held up a hand in greeting, and the lights from the wall sconces flashed off gaudy rings. His gaze dropped to her breasts, and he grinned. "Want to hook up later tonight?"

Hook up. Did he mean mate? *Ew.* She'd rather mate with a vile, ugly boggart. From his cocky stance, he thought himself attractive...and obviously couldn't smell her lack of interest. "No, thank you."

Sidestepping around him, she reached the table of females, all wolf-shifters. "Can I get drinks for anyone?"

"Well, it's about time. We've been waiting forever," Sarah snapped. She probably still resented the song delivered at Wesley's rites. "I'll take a glass of the house chardonnay if you think you can get it here before closing."

"Oh, now, don't be mean." Candice flipped her red-brown hair over her shoulder. "The way the tables are crowded together, it's difficult to get through, especially for someone who is...large."

"And slow," someone else said under her breath.

Be polite. Maybe she should be grateful for her mother's harsh training—except her mother had also made her feel large and slow. "Anyone else need a drink?"

"I've heard you're living in Ben's house." The brunette sighed. "Ben is a cahir. And Ryder is to die for."

True enough. "Did you want something to drink?" Emma asked her.

"You? *You're* living with Ben and Ryder?" The stunningly beautiful redhead gave her a top to toe scrutiny.

"Only because she was hurt, and she's a bear. Calum didn't want her savaging anyone if she lost control," Candice said.

"Oh, why you poor dear." Sympathy dripped from the red-head's sugary voice. "I'm so glad you've healed up well enough to work now."

"Huh, if you're working, you can move out of Ben's house." The curvy brunette tipped her lips up in a false smile. "When's the big day?"

Actually, they were correct. The time had come to find her own place. The thought dug a hollow next to her heart. "We haven't discussed it."

"Oh, honey, you aren't staying in hopes of attracting their attention, I hope. I know Ryder. He prefers his females…well, smaller."

The insult was sharp, sliding soundlessly between her ribs. But it reached her heart. Oh, it did. Emma tightened her fingers on her tray.

The redhead made a sympathetic tsking sound. "He's prob-ably found other uses for you around the house, but I'd hate for him to take advantage of you."

"Oh, I guess a female bard would be a good cub-sitter," Sa-rah pointed out.

"And a maid and cook. It's good you're learning to cook,"

Candice said. "Males love cheap help."

No. Ryder and Ben weren't like that. They…weren't. But the sinking feeling in her stomach said she might be wrong.

"But don't be unhappy. I'm sure other males might be interested in you." The redhead smiled at Emma. "We heard about the gory Gathering in Pine Knoll. Obviously your looks appealed to at least a couple of males."

Who fought and died.

The falsely sympathetic words raked over Emma's senses cruelly. This conversation was worse than blundering into blackberry bushes and emerging covered in blood.

"You know, when I mated with Ben at the last Gathering," Sarah said, "I had to insist he take me downstairs and let me go. He's quite possessive."

Ben had been with *her*? He'd never mentioned it when they'd been talking about how Wesley died. Emma stiffened. Had he taken Sarah to his home? Enjoyed her in his massive bed? Laughed with her? Tucked her against his side? Rumbled his enjoyment and appreciation? Feeling her lower lip start to quiver, Emma pressed her mouth into a straight line.

"Oh, Ben. He's so big and strong. I have my eye on him for next Gathering." The female sitting beside Sarah pushed her curly, blonde hair over her shoulder.

Emma looked around the table. All of the females were pretty. The redhead was spectacular. No male would refuse them.

Standing over them, Emma felt…enormous. And ugly. Realizing her shoulders had started to hunch, she straightened.

Did barmaids have to put up with this kind of sly abuse? Vicki would probably knock them on their asses.

Maybe, someday, Emma would have the courage to get physical. That day had not yet arrived.

But a refusal to be prey could be delivered courteously.

Thank you, Mother for those lessons. "I am so very sorry. You are quite right—I'm a slow bear. Since the service isn't meeting your needs, perhaps you should take your orders to the bar."

Gratifying sputters came from the females.

Emma walked away with her back straight, head held high. She still felt ugly.

AFTER PARKING HIS SUV on the street, Ryder strolled up the sidewalk to the house. A glance at the stars told him the time was around midnight. With the clearing of the sky, the temperature had plummeted. Frost glazed the grass, and the clean scent of glaciers filled the air. After the heat of the tavern, the chill wind was bracing.

He glanced at the dark windows in the main house. In the tower, Ben's downstairs office and upstairs bedroom windows showed no light. Didn't look as if anyone was still awake. His littermate had worked a twelve-hour day and would be on the job early tomorrow morning. Even grizzlies wore out eventually.

Ryder didn't feel tired. Emma's performance had included several bitterly tragic Daonain tales. Afterward, he, Ben, Quentin, Owen, and Joe had downed a few while dissecting the history behind the stories. Ben had wanted to play a new board game with Minette, so he left early to pick her up. After Quentin and Joe had gone home, Owen had challenged Ryder to a game of chess, which had turned into three.

Good music. Good conversation. Good beer. He hadn't had so much fun in a decade or more.

Hadn't had good friends, either.

Years ago, he and Ben hadn't figured a predominantly shifter village could support a construction company, so formed their construction company in a human town. Their friends there had been human.

During the time with Genevieve, Ryder hadn't made friends. She threw a screaming fit if he wasn't dancing constant attendance on her. When they were with others, all conversation revolved around Genevieve. Discussing historic battles would never have happened.

On the fair circuit, he'd enjoyed the humans—some were damned smart—but as in the human towns, he'd had to monitor his words and behavior. Drunken discussions were out.

It was fucking nice to be amongst his people again.

Smiling, he let himself into the house. The various electronics—the glow from the various kitchen devices, a ceiling smoke detector in the foyer, a clock's digital readout—lent enough light he didn't turn on the overheads.

The soft strum of a guitar from the great room surprised him. Since the Gathering, Emma had spent her nights with Ben.

Pleased his littermate had slid past her defenses, Ryder'd been content to wait. She was a shy little bear. He wasn't about to do anything to distress her—she was worth a long, slow hunt.

But why wasn't she with Ben now? In a mournful minor key, the haunting tune indicated a little bard might be unhappy.

With a feline's soundless stalk, Ryder entered the room. The only illumination came from the fireplace where a golden salamander basked in the red coals of a dying fire.

On the sectional, Emma was curled around her guitar as if she'd suffered a blow to the gut. With her face turned toward the black forest beyond the windows, she looked…sad. Lonely.

The little bear should never look so lost.

"What happened?" His voice came out gruff.

She startled. "Oh. Hi."

He removed the guitar from her lap and sat close enough his thigh rubbed against her soft hip.

Her eyes widened…but he could detect no scent of fear. *Progress.*

"Emma?" he prompted.

"Um. Nothing. Nothing happened."

He took her hands, feeling calluses on the fingertips from her playing. "Try again, little bear."

"Enough, Ryder. I'm just in a bad mood." Her laugh was bitter. "No need to sit with me or try to be nice when you undoubtedly want your bed."

"Good to know." He studied her silently. This wasn't the Emma he knew—not that he knew her well. But he'd never seen her grumpy without a reason. Something had created a storm in her sunny personality. When? During her performance, she'd glowed with delight in the music and the audience. Soon after, he'd seen her laughing and chatting as she served drinks.

But when she'd moved farther away, he'd become immersed in the discussion at his table. "What happened at the tavern?"

"Nothing." Yet the twitch of her fingers said he was on the right trail.

He considered the possibilities. Had something happened with her friends? Unlikely. With the tough old barmaid, Rosie? Be a hell of a fight, but, no, Rosie appreciated Emma's music and was grateful for her help afterward.

Maybe a customer had been rude?

A disturbing memory nagged until it came clear. On his way out of the tavern, he'd seen Genevieve. Seated with a group of females, she was in Emma's section. The trail held a disturbing scent, especially since Genevieve had already mentioned Emma once. The shrew would have gone for her. Yeah. "What did she say to you?"

"What? Who?"

"Genevieve." At the bard's confused stare, he prompted, "Redhead, pretty, at the tavern. Sitting with Candice."

Her amber eyes widened. "She was Genevieve?"

"Oh, yeah. And she's well-known for sinking her teeth into

anyone who provokes her jealousy."

Damned if the little bear didn't look even more surprised. "Why in the world would she be jealous of me?"

She didn't know. Her lack of pretension was more compelling than any flirtatiousness. "Because you're beautiful, Emma. Because I like you. Because I want you."

His direct stare let her know exactly what he meant by *want.*

Her lips formed the word *oh,* and he had to grin. By the God, she was lovable. He pulled her onto his lap, so her legs dangled off his left side and his right arm braced her back.

Her ass was a warm circle on his thighs. Perfect.

"Ryder." With her gasp, her breasts strained against her shirt in a carnal invitation. "I'm too heavy. I'll squish you."

"Mmm, I'd say you're just the right weight. Right size." He pulled her closer, until her hip rubbed his rapidly thickening cock, until he could touch his lips to hers. Then her claim caught up with him, and he frowned. "She said you're too heavy?"

The stiffness in her shoulders said yes.

"What else? She wouldn't stop at one insult."

Emma's attempted laugh sounded like a sneeze. "It's nothing." Her gaze wouldn't meet his.

He rubbed her cheek with his, marking her with his scent, inhaling hers. He nipped her earlobe. "Talk, bard."

Her fragrance changed, deepened with arousal. "Ryder."

"I can torture the information out of you," he whispered in her ear. And wouldn't he fucking enjoy that?

When her breathing actually halted, he grinned and teased her ear with his teeth.

"Oh, fine," she huffed. "She simply said you preferred smaller women, and how you and Ben were probably using me for other things around the house. A cub-sitter and maid were suggested."

He looked into her wary eyes. "Not a cook as well?"

"One of them said it was good I was learning."

At the hurt in her face, he wanted to claw something. "I'm sorry, Emma. I should have known she'd come after you."

Emma shrugged. "She didn't say anything I didn't already know about myself. I just—"

WHEN RYDER FISTED her hair, Emma forgot what she'd been saying.

He gently, but determinedly, tugged her hair, forcing her to meet his sharp, perceptive gaze.

Her heart did a slow flip-flop within her chest.

"What exactly is it that you know about yourself?"

Lovely. Force her to speak the humiliating words aloud. "That you weren't interested in me…that way. For mating."

He gave a deep, masculine laugh. "Oh, little bear, you're very wrong. Have I mentioned you're gorgeous?"

"Uh…" He had, hadn't he? She hadn't believed him.

"And I don't usually kiss females unless I want them…that way." He smiled slightly. "Do you remember that I'd been looking forward to mating with you at the Gathering?"

"Oh. Well. The kissing was you and Ben helping me get used to males. And the effect of the moon." Wasn't it? Her heart started to thud rather fast. He meant so much to her. Thinking he didn't find her attractive had…hurt. Had that female lied to her?

"I see. Little bear, the moon is waning now." His mouth closed over hers, forceful, demanding.

Her startled inhalation brought the scent of his desire for her. His thick erection pressed against her hip. He wanted her. He did.

He pulled her hair, deepening his possession of her mouth. His other hand held her hips firmly against his cock.

Like icicles under a hot sun, her bones were melting.

He lifted his head. "Genevieve was trying to make you feel bad. Ben and I can cook and clean, although it's nice you can, too. We don't need a housekeeper, Emma."

They weren't using her. Even more, they were planning a future with her in it. The knowledge was heartening. Frightening. "But…"

"I can find babysitters anywhere for Minette." Ryder kissed and nipped her jaw, then down her neck, sending shivery sensations outward. "However, a female who loves the cub like you do? Whom she loves? That's worth more than money—and can't be bought."

How had he known how much she loved his cubling?

Slowly, under his lips and teeth, her body was coming alive, even as her spirit revived like flowers in a spring rain.

"Do me a favor and ignore Genevieve and her mean-spirited females."

His beard-stubbled jaw against her neck created an exciting abrasion that sent tingles all the way to her depths.

"I'd suggest you pay attention to me and Ben, instead. Especially me, right now." He'd pinned her left arm against his side. His right arm was around her waist; his hand gripped her right elbow. The amusement in his eyes said the werecat knew he had his prey trapped.

A shiver shook her deep inside.

With his free hand, he unbuttoned her shirt until the front gaped open and bared her round belly to his gaze. His gaze smoldered, and he purred in appreciation. Slowly, he stroked from her neck to her breasts. His skillful fingers undid her bra's front clasp to free her breasts. Cool air wafted over the exposed skin. Barely breathing, she tensed in anticipation of his touch.

"Been wanting to enjoy these." He cupped his lean, callused hand over her right breast and lifted, as if weighing it. The heat from his palm sank deep, pooling like a sunlit lake in her groin.

When his thumb circled the areola, her clit began to pulse with urgency.

"Oooh…" Her breath left her on a long sigh. This desire wasn't the raging flood caused by a full moon, but a slow, inexorable tide of sensation that wakened nerve after nerve until her entire body felt sensitive. She struggled to touch him, in return.

His grip on her elbow tightened, staying her movement. He considered her, and the corner of his mouth tipped up. "All right." Releasing her breast, he grasped his T-shirt behind his head and yanked the garment up and off.

He was s*hirtless*. The feeling of his smooth, heated skin against her side and back was more tantalizing than having him entirely bare all at once. The tanned skin was taut over his muscled chest—a lure she couldn't resist. She made a needy sound.

Releasing her elbow, he kissed her fingers and pressed her palm against his sternum.

Oooh, yes. "You're so warm," she whispered.

"You make me that way." He nuzzled her temple, nibbled the top of her ear, and triggered flutters deep in her core.

She ran her fingers down his neck and frowned at ugly scars from bites and nails. When her gaze met his, she knew. That cruel female had hurt him physically as well as emotionally. Pushing the thought out of her mind, she moved her hand away. Instead, she traced the contours of his chest, the valley between his pectorals. He had satin skin over rock-hard muscles.

He mirrored her movements. When she brushed over his collarbone, he ran his fingertips over hers. She ran her hand over his washboard abdomen and felt him stroke her much softer belly.

Experimentally, she touched his button-flat nipples and gave one a light pinch.

"Good idea." His fingers tugged on one nipple and then the other.

A storm of sensation blew through her, abolishing inhibitions, leaving only desire in its wake.

"Mmmhmm." His dark voice held a buzz of satisfaction as he continued. Watching her face, he rolled her sensitive nipples between his fingers, slowly increasing the pressure, until the throbbing peaks jutted into spikes.

The tightness in her clit grew to an aching demand. Her thighs rubbed together uselessly. Despite the dying fire, the room had taken on a pulsating warmth.

Ryder moved his hand down, and her abdominal muscles quivered under his palm. When he unzipped her jeans, she caught her breath.

"Stand up, little bear," he murmured. "I need a taste of you."

Gripping her hips, he lifted her to her feet next to the couch. While she was still getting her balance, he yanked her pants down to her thighs and tugged off her shirt and bra. Before she could register that she was naked from the waist up, he rose and scooped her into his arms.

"*Ryder.*" Why did he and Ben keep carrying her around?

Laughing, he laid her on her back in front of the fireplace. Within a minute, he had her jeans completely off.

Propped up on her elbows, she felt the still-glowing coals bathe her right side in warmth. On one knee, Ryder stared down, his eyes almost black, heating her more than the fire. Silently, he took her in, making her conscious that all of her was revealed, every bulge, every scar.

She started to sit up…Then she scented his lust. It matched hers. His gaze lingered on her breasts, her stomach, the golden down of her sex. Under his hot perusal, she felt…beautiful.

"By the God, you're too fucking gorgeous. I don't know

where to start." His gaze passed over her peaked nipples and returned. "There will do."

His arm behind her back supported her as he pressed feather-light kisses over her breasts. His breath bathed her skin a moment before his mouth closed over one nipple, engulfing it in wet heat. His tongue touched her, tasted her, and a ferocious quivering set up low in her belly. When he sucked, she felt her toes curling.

Oh, by the Mother, yes.

His free hand settled on her other breast, squeezing and caressing. He nipped the peak he was working on, and she gasped at the zing of pleasure. He sucked even more fiercely. Nipped again. His mouth was hot, wet, and determined.

Her breasts swelled, the skin tight and hot. Her nipples ached and tingled, and sent urgent messages south. She ran her hands up into his hair—thick and wavy, cool against her skin.

"You're so pretty," she whispered.

He gave her an appalled look and bit her harder.

She gasped. And squirmed. Oh, she needed…more.

"Easy, little bard. We have all the time in the world." He pulled her arms forward, forcing her to lie flat on the soft Oriental carpet. Following her down, he straddled her hips.

Needing to touch, she ran her hands up his sinewy arms to his powerful shoulders. The way his muscles flexed and bunched as he moved made her breathing hitch. How could someone so graceful be so strong?

He kissed his way in a weaving pattern across her torso, licked around her belly button, and moved down.

Her fingers twitched on his shoulders with a sudden surge of anticipation.

Firmly, he parted her legs. As he settled between them, his abrasive jeans rubbed the inside of her legs. Bending, he inhaled and smiled. "Mmm."

Her whole body filled with a carnal hunger.

His warm hand on her pussy made her tense in anticipation. He lowered his head. His lips touched her…just above her clit.

Oh, oh, oh.

As he held her folds closed over her clit, his tongue licked long and slow over the top. She could feel it, but it was…too distant. Too tantalizing. "Ryder…please." Her voice came out in a distinct whine.

"Shhh, little bard." After a few licks, he opened her a tiny amount, letting more of his tongue graze over the target.

Not enough. With a frustrated sound, she lifted her hips.

"Uh-uh," he chided under his breath, setting one merciless hand on her pelvis to pin her in place. Then he opened her labia slightly, enough that his tongue could run over one side of her clit, then the other.

Like a whirlwind, urgency spiraled upward through her whole body. "Moooore." She caught his hair in an unbreakable grip.

"Fuck, you taste good." His tongue and lips were far too knowledgeable, and exquisite pleasure grew until his tongue moving over that one acutely sensitive spot filled her world.

Her grip in his hair tightened as her thighs started to tremble.

"Emma, look at me." He lifted his head.

"Don't stop." Her eyes opened. "Ry—" The air thickened in her throat.

He was watching her. His gaze was so filled with desire and appreciation that she could only stare back.

And then he lowered his head. As if the momentary break had been hours long, when his lips closed over her clit, the heat of his mouth felt scalding. His lips tightened around her and he…sucked.

Fierce urgency pulled her right under, submerging her in

sensation.

He licked and sucked again, and licked… The current turned into a whirlpool, pulling her under, the pressure expanding, widening, engulfing her body. Her pulse roared in her ears as she fell into a tsunami of pleasure, tumbling over and over with each incredible breaker of sensation. She could hear her soft cries echoing from the walls.

As the waves of pleasure diminished, she realized Ryder was stripping off his boots and jeans. He settled himself over her body. So very hard, every muscle seemed to be chiseled from stone.

Propping himself on one arm, he kissed her slowly and deeply, even as he fitted himself to her opening. And paused. One black eyebrow lifted in silent inquiry.

"Yes," she whispered. "Yes."

Holding her gaze, he pressed in, his shaft hot. Her breathing hitched as he slid deeper and deeper, startlingly long. He stretched her, filled her. The feeling of being taken was…wonderful.

When he was fully in, he waited, not moving, studying her face.

She tensed. Was he disappointed?

He slid his cock out.

With a gasp, she grabbed his hips to stop him. No success.

"You feel as good as I knew you would, little bear. Fuck, you really do."

He wasn't disappointed. She closed her eyes for a moment in relief. And, by the Mother, she liked his bluntness. Neither Ryder nor Ben held anything back. Just laid it out.

But with the happiness came other, more urgent needs. And he wasn't moving. When she bucked her hips and tried to pull him in, he chuckled.

Wicked werecat.

Then he pressed in, penetrating her deeply, before withdrawing again. In and out, three measured thrusts as if establishing that they fit.

Didn't the slick hotness convince him? "More," she breathed.

His black gaze assessed her before his lips curved. "Seems you can take me without a problem."

He was worried? "Yes."

Despite her agreement, he idly played with her breasts with one hand as he continued to thrust slowly. Far too slowly. Her clit ached and throbbed as he brushed over it with each stroke. Under his attentions, her nipples tightened.

Her urgency grew. She dug her nails into his rock-hard butt. "Faster." Her voice came out husky and desperate. "Harder."

His laugh was deep and pleased. "So be it."

Abandoning her breasts, he moved fully on top of her, and—*oh, Goddess*—he cast off his restraints. Each stoke hammered her, hard, deep, and overwhelming.

Her muscles clenched around him as the tension built, spiraling up and up, taking her mind with it. Sweat slickened their skin. Her hips met his with every thrust, and the slap of flesh on flesh echoed in the room. As his cock thickened, her body tensed and then pulsed in glorious waves as another climax rolled over her. "Oh, oh, oh."

With an approving hum, he slid a hand under her bottom to lift her up. He thrust deeper. Once. Twice. His jaw tightened, and the cords on his neck stood out. He growled as he buried himself to the root and filled her with his heat.

"Mmm." He lowered his head, rubbed his cheek against hers affectionately, and rolled, setting her on top of him without withdrawing.

Limp and sated, she sprawled, cheek against his chest, and listened to the solid *thump, thump, thump* of his heart. Cupping her ass in one hand, he rubbed her back with the other in long, slow, mesmerizing strokes. "You're amazing, little bard. And I like the music you make when you get off. Mating music."

Now *that* would be a tune to compose. She grinned. He'd probably be upset if she called it "Ryder's Ride."

With a happy sigh, she let herself drift.

Sometime in the night, she wakened to Ben's rumbly voice. "Ah, I was wondering why she hadn't joined me. Was afraid she might've run into trouble on the way home."

"Sorry, bro. I didn't think about you worrying." Ryder's hand moved up and down her back. "Genevieve made her worry she was too big to be pretty."

The grizzly gave a huff of annoyance. "I know some males prefer sleek females, but hopefully, Emma now understands that you and I think she's just fucking *right*."

Ryder's laugh came from deep within his chest. "Did my best. But she's a tad insecure. Keep it in mind."

"Aye." Ben made an amused sound. "Won't be any chore to reassure her the same way you did. Good job, bro."

As his footsteps headed up the stairs to his tower bedroom, Emma let herself fall back asleep, comforted by the slow rise and fall of Ryder's chest...and the knowledge that she was just fucking *right*.

Chapter Twenty-Three

T HE NEXT DAY, as Ben drove down the small road toward home, he counted off the blessings the Goddess had scattered into his life.

His house was no longer empty…it was a *home*.

Ryder's return had healed the soul-deep pain of the damaged littermate bond.

Minette's silent joy had changed the very air. Fuck, he'd never thought he'd have a child. Her tiny smiles filled his spirit to overflowing.

Then there was Emma. She made him feel so many things—aroused, insane, and just plain happy. Whenever he saw her, his heart glowed, as if lit by a roaring fire.

He needed to discuss her with Ryder. Although Genevieve had burned Ryder badly, Emma was healing his distrust. They'd been together last night, and he'd never seen Ryder look so content.

There was no hurry though. He could wait, rather than pushing ahead, although patience wasn't a bear's strength.

As he pulled into the driveway, he saw Emma sitting beside the flower garden that bordered the curb. At one time, the yards had boasted extravagant landscaping, but the place had stood empty for years. Concentrating on repairing the house, Ben hadn't given the grounds any attention.

After parking in the garage, he walked across the front yard and stopped beside her. "Are you taking care of that leg?" She'd actually danced across the room when Donal announced she didn't have to wear the brace any longer.

"Yes, Daddy Bear." She rolled her pretty eyes.

Not nervous with him any longer, was she? Pleased, he stood and enjoyed the view. The sunlight lingered on her as if finding a mate for its glow. Her hair rivaled its rosy shine; her golden skin held the palest of pink flushes.

She'd donned a flannel shirt he'd given her. Despite rolling up the sleeves, she still resembled a cub trying on her father's garments. With her every movement, the fabric curved around her full breasts.

He remembered the wondrous weight of those lush breasts in his palms...and the feeling of her curvy body in his arms. He'd missed her last night.

"Do you mind me cleaning up the flower beds?" she asked. "The crocus is blooming, but it's buried by so many weeds, you can't even see it. And you have daffodils coming up."

He squatted down beside her. "Have at it, darlin'. Anything would be an improvement."

"This is true," she said. "I'm surprised at the mess, actually. You look after everything else so carefully."

He was warmed by the compliment, since he did try to tend well whatever was entrusted to him. "The landscaping is on my list—but not soon. So, once you finish here, feel free to start in the back gardens."

She blinked in surprise. "I know the Cosantir pushed you to put me up until I could get around on my own and find a job. But I'm moving all right, and now the mess with Cedrick is over, I can access my bank account." She smiled slightly. "I guess it's good that Cosantirs don't control human banks. Anyway, I should find my own place."

The thought of her leaving shattered his tranquility. "No." His voice came out as a growl.

She looked up at him with big eyes, her soft, pink lips slightly parted. The skin above and between her breasts was damp with sweat.

As he caught the light feminine musk of her scent, all the blood in his body went to his cock. His growl deepened. He wanted to lay her back and feel her squirm as he licked the salty sweat away and suckled her rose-tipped nipples. He'd work his way down to every other scent on her body.

"No?" she repeated. "What do you mean?"

"I don't want you to leave."

"But…" She stared at her hands, then her shoulders straightened, and she summoned the inner courage that still made his heart skip a beat. "I would like to stay, but there are other people here than just you and me."

With a grunt of understanding, he lowered himself onto the lush grass, close enough that his shoulder rubbed hers. He took her hand and brushed the dirt from her palm before kissing the warm, soft center. "This is true," he echoed her from before. "Tell me, honey bear, after last night, how do you feel about my brother?"

An adorable flush pinkened her cheeks. "I—"

Behind them, the front door slammed. Like a woodpecker, Minette's little feet tapped across the wooden porch, down the steps, and the cub dashed across the lawn toward them.

Ben stood. The discussion of Emma's staying would have to wait.

He caught Minette up, raspberried her belly, swung her over his head, and let her pull his hair. *Cubs.* When he set her down, she hugged his leg.

Ryder came out the door and prowled across the lawn,

working his arms and shoulders. "Home early, bro? Going to help me with the payroll?"

"Right about the time the dwarves give up mining. That payroll shit's a major pain in the tail." Seeing the cub's mouth go O-shaped, Ben caught what he'd said. Swearing. *Bad bear.*

Despite a frown of disapproval, Emma laughed.

Hell of a laugh, with the low, husky notes of summer breezes through an ancient forest.

Thankfully, Minette spotted a pixie in the roses lining the side yard and trotted in that direction.

Ben grinned at his brother. "Sorry, bro. Didn't mean to corrupt your cub."

"*Our* cub. I daresay she's heard worse from me."

Emma turned her frown on him.

Ryder winced. "Guess we both need to watch our language."

"Undoubtedly," she said in a dry voice. "Unless you want her first spoken sentence to get her kicked out of kindergarten."

"That would suck." Ryder exchanged a rueful glance with Ben.

Ben laughed. Their two months of human kindergarten before Ryder had moved were not exactly a success. Raised by males, he and Ryder lacked anything close to manners.

Minette heard him laughing, ran back, and stopped beside Emma. With not nearly enough care for her wounded leg, Emma pulled the cub down onto her lap.

The child immediately appropriated a loose strand of the golden hair and snuggled closer. Just like a healthy, loving cub. Ryder's pleased gaze met Ben's.

Yes, this was a home.

"Hey, Minette, I have to pick up some hardware," Ben said. "Could be we'll find ice cream and a playground in town. Want to come?"

She bounced up to take his hand. In many ways, she was a

delightfully normal cub, which meant food and fun made excellent bribes.

"Hell, that means I have no excuse to stop doing payroll," Ryder grumbled.

Ben glanced at Emma. "The poor kitty looks like he got his tail stuck in the door."

She snickered, earning herself a quick tug of her hair from the cat—followed by a brush of his lips that really did silence her.

The wide-eyed look was a good one for her, Ben decided. He grinned at Ryder and asked Emma, "Want to come with me and Minette?"

"No, thank you." She yanked a wayward weed. "I'm going to clean this mess up and start supper. Angie gave me a recipe for meat loaf."

"Whoa, Griz. She stays *here*," Ryder said firmly. "I haven't had meat loaf since…since we spent that winter in Elder Village. Naini knew how to make a hearty meal."

Ben smiled at her. "See? Ryder agrees that you'll stay." *Forever.*

Shaking her head in exasperation, she threw a clod of dirt at him.

"Time to go, Minette. The honey bear is getting feisty." Ben swung the cub up onto his shoulders, grinning as he felt her silent, little laugh. She'd obviously inherited her father's feline sense of humor—which probably meant she'd be a cat-shifter rather than a wolf like her mother.

An hour later, kitchen fittings and door hardware bought and loaded, Ben leaned against a tree in the park behind Thorson's BOOKS and watched his brother's cub. No, Ryder was right; she was his cub as well. How could anyone not love such an adorable cub?

Her eyes were as bright as any kitten's as she led her small pride across the playground. He grinned as she jumped, caught a bar, and swung up into the climbing web with a grace that rivaled her father's. Her two buddies followed, screaming with glee as they joined her on the top.

Her silence hadn't prevented her from making friends. Even better, over the weeks, much of her timidity had disappeared, and she was exploring her expanding world with a joyful courage. She was as smart as her sire, which pleased Ben no end.

It was true that her mother wasn't stupid, but Genevieve's mind functioned with more cunning than intelligence. She sure knew how to manipulate males to get her own way. Ryder said she'd been at the Gathering, picking up males to mate, and making friends with some younger females. That was worrisome.

Absently, Ben rubbed his shoulders against the tree trunk, probably wearing another hole in his shirt.

Across the park, several humans watched over a group of pre-teens. On a nearby bench, two young shifter mothers smiled at him. He'd seen them in the park before.

"It's not often we see a male bringing his offspring to play in the park," one said.

"Now that's a shame. Watching a cub is far more fun than supervising a construction crew." He wasn't going to explain why Minette's mother wasn't available.

They laughed—exactly his intent—and went back to dissecting some poor buddy. Females sure got off on gossiping.

By the time, Minette had played on the swings, the climbing web, the two slides, collected a couple of scrapes, and made another three friends, Ben figured it was time to haul her home. After all, they had meat loaf—and hopefully mashed potatoes—for supper. "Minette."

She ran across the wood shavings-covered playground onto the grass—and stopped so abruptly she stumbled.

"Hey, kitten, be ca—"

"Look who's guarding the cub." Hips swinging like a wrecking ball, Genevieve approached from the parking lot.

He frowned. She hadn't been so…blatant…when he met her five or so years ago, had she? With jeans so tight he could see her private folds, and a tank top lowered to the edge of her nipples, her attire today seemed more desperate than provocative. "Genevieve, what are you doing here?"

"I saw you. I wanted to talk to you." She gave her cub a disinterested glance. "Go play somewhere."

Minette's thumb was in her mouth.

"Minette." Ben knelt, pleased that she came immediately, as if knowing he'd protect her. "Your mother wants to talk with me. Since grown-ups are boring, why don't you play with the dump trucks until we're done?" He pointed to the sandbox, which was safely out of earshot.

She clung for another few seconds, and he ached at the return of her timidity. Finally, she let him go and obeyed. When he noted the wide detour she made around her dam, his lips tightened.

He gave Genevieve his attention. "You have to be the worst mother I've ever seen."

"Oh, Ben. That's a mean thing to say." She donned a pitiful look in the way he'd pull on a jacket. "That's because I just don't know how; I didn't have a mother."

No, instead her three doting fathers had pampered her. From what she'd told Ryder, she'd conned them for anything she could get. Her free ride had stopped when they were killed in an avalanche around six years past.

Genevieve was looking for someone to pamper her again, but she'd give nothing in return. Her attempt at looking pitiful moved him not at all. "So, talk."

"All right then. You're getting attached to the cub, and from what I've heard, so is Ryder." Genevieve crossed her arms over her chest, pushing up her breasts to emphasize the cleavage.

Ben gave her a cynical stare, hoping her tits didn't pop out and give the human mothers a shock. "Your point?"

"She's mine, and every shifter in the world would agree that a cub should live with her mother."

Unfortunately, she was right. Daonain cubs always lived with their mothers. "They wouldn't if they'd seen what kind of shit mother you are. Minette will get nowhere near you."

"You mange-ridden, toothless—" Genevieve's lips curled back from her teeth, and he wondered if she'd lose control and bite him. She took a step back. "I'm sorry," she said, tears in her eyes. "I realize Ryder's turned you against me, but"—she pulled in a shaky breath—"I only want what's best for my baby."

Yes, she was a sneaky one. "Then you'll leave her with me and Ryder."

"You and Ryder can keep her on one condition." To his disbelief, she moved close enough to stroke his chest seductively. "If I move in with you. I can be your mate and take care of her."

"She'd be better off raised by a gnome than a *mother* like you." Ryder had been right about her scheme. Ben wanted to spit. "And I'd rather mate with a hellhound."

She slapped him hard enough for the splatting sound to ring through the park. As his cheek stung, the young mothers heard and turned.

Minette? He checked the sandbox. The cub's friends surrounded her and insulated her with their happy noise.

The shrew lowered her voice. "You'll suffer for that insult. When Minette gets handed over to me, you'll pay and pay to get her back."

"You're not gonna get money—or Minette. I'm a cahir, chosen of the God. I own a house, a company. Ryder has money and is employed. You're an abusive mother who lives off of others. Only a fool would choose you over Ryder and me." He stepped around her and headed for Minette, adding a final, "Be gone with you."

Her low growl came from behind him, and he heard her padding away. By the God, he hoped that was the last they'd see of her.

As he picked up Minette, he felt her trembling. He needed to get her home. Knowing the honey bear, she'd find some comforting, diverting activity to soothe the cub.

Genevieve wasn't the only cub to grow up without a mother. But Emma was showing not only Minette, but also Ben and Ryder, what a mother's care might have been like.

Chapter Twenty-Four

Cold Creek, North Cascades Territory — last quarter moon
Human "Mother's Day"

CLAWS SAFELY SHEATHED, Ryder slapped Emma's hind leg with a paw and launched himself into the undergrowth.

Blustering with mock annoyance, the bear spun—faster than he'd expected—but he'd already dropped, letting the salal and huckleberries hide him. Safely hidden, he watched for his next opportunity. The tip of his tail twitched.

Such a pretty bear.

Although Emma was in the "black bear" species, her thick, shaggy fur was as honey-colored as her hair—and shone with health. Darker over her head, her fur lightened to pale gold on her Roman-bear-style nose. She turned her head, back and forth, trying to locate him. Some stray berries on the bushes caught her attention, and she stopped to nibble before continuing to search.

As Ryder watched her, the sun filtered through the tall plants and bushes, warming his shoulders. He'd forgotten how much fun it was to play in animal form.

This outing was a form of rejoicing that Genevieve was gone. Yesterday, Ben'd told her that she'd get no money from them. Last night, Ryder'd visited the tavern for news. The young male Genevieve had stayed with was drinking and mourning that the pretty female had packed her bags and returned to the Deschutes Territory. Ryder had barely refrained from telling the lad what a narrow escape he'd had.

Minette's mother had given up. So, on the Sunday that the humans called Mother's Day, their small family was celebrating. Ben had decided they all needed four-legged time, so they'd packed food and clothing.

In the forest behind the house, when Emma had *trawsfurred* to bear, Ryder'd suddenly had a terrified cub clinging to his neck. *By the God.* Who would have thought Minette'd never seen shifters take animal form.

She had now.

Fuck, he had a brave little cub. As she watched, they'd taken turns shifting. Soon she was clapping her hands in delight.

He and Ben had started her off on top of Emma—and she'd been thrilled—then had taken turns being her "horse." Because of his size and long, shaggy fur, Ben became her favorite, which was why he and Emma were playing games. The Griz had a tendency to mosey.

But he was here now. Ryder's ears swiveled at the sound of Ben coming up the trail. There was still time to score one more point off of Emma.

Nose in the air, the honey bear was working her way closer to him. Bears definitely had the best sniffers in the woods.

Wait…wait…

He stilled his twitching tail to prevent the salal from any telltale swaying.

From the forest, Ben lumbered out into the marshy area. Bouncing happily on his back, Minette had her tiny fingers clenched in his fur.

Emma turned to look.

Now. Ryder's haunches tensed. He bounded forward out of the salal bed and sprang right over Emma's back.

Mouth open in a laugh, Minette bounced on Ben's back.

Not slowing, Ryder charged Ben. As he leaped over, he snatched the pack with their clothing from Minette's lap. With the bag in his jaws, he trotted toward a thick stand of trees. Although shifters didn't notice nudity, especially after they themselves started trawsfurring, the cub didn't need to be stressed further. They'd get dressed privately.

When he reappeared, wearing a thin T-shirt, jeans, and moccasins, Minette was seated on a log, watching Emma tussle with Ben. Needless to say, the massive grizzly was in no danger of losing.

Ryder picked Minette up and nuzzled her soft hair. "Pretty kitten."

When she lifted her face and kissed his chin, his heart felt as if his rib cage was too small to contain it.

At a low grumbling noise, he turned. Emma was up on her hind legs, undoubtedly wondering where he'd left their clothes.

He pointed to where heavy undergrowth concealed a small clearing. "Pack's hanging from a dead limb."

She dropped to all fours and loped away. Damn, but it was nice to see her moving without pain.

Ben watched her, waited a calculated amount of time—probably until she *trawsfurred* and was naked—and followed. Canny male.

Ryder smiled in approval as he remembered her softness and sweetness as they'd mated. Having slept alone last night, his brother undoubtedly wanted to collect a kiss or two now.

Having her alternating beds wouldn't last long. As soon as the little bear was comfortable, he and Ben would enjoy her together, and then would sleep with her between them.

AFTER STOPPING TO rub her shoulder against a cedar to

eliminate an annoying itch, Emma found the pack where Ryder had indicated. She shifted to human and pulled the small nylon bag off the branch.

As she rummaged through the clothing for her own, she realized she was…happy.

She'd never had a chance to play with other shifters in animal form. Grinning, she pulled her jeans from the pack. Cougars were definitely sneaky. And, even though he'd been in cat form, Ryder had definitely been laughing whenever he took her by surprise.

Ryder liked stealth.

Ben liked to tussle—and the grizzly made her feel positively tiny. She might mass a couple of hundred pounds, but he had to be three to four times her weight. Yet his care not to hurt her was sexy as anything.

She realized she was hugging her shirt.

"Now, there's a fine sight on a summer day." Ben's appreciative rumble had her spinning in place.

Ryder wasn't the only sneaky brother, was he?

The warmth of a blush started at her breasts and swept up into her face.

Appreciative blue eyes watched the progress. Watched her nipples tighten.

Not knowing what to do or say, she started to pull on her shirt.

"Oh, not just yet," he murmured. With a cahir's strength, he pulled her against him, bare skin against bare skin, and tossed the shirt to one side.

She felt as if she'd waited an eternity to feel his hands on her body again. His arm around her waist felt like an iron bar as he fondled her breast with skillful fingers.

Heat streaked up her center, and her toes curled into the soft pine needles beneath her feet.

"Oh yeah." He flattened a hand on her ass and pressed her pelvis against his erection. His nip on the curve of her shoulder made her gasp. "Unfortunately, with Minette here, we can't play the game I'd enjoy right now."

"Oh." Her voice was hoarse. "That's a shame."

"Yeah." He kissed her, long and slow and deep. "For teasing me, honey bear, you owe a forfeit. I expect you in my bed tonight."

Her mouth dropped open. "But—" She stopped the protest, because the forfeit of a night in Ben's bed sounded…just fine. The scent of his desire filled the air. "Uh, I'm so sorry." She smiled and used Ryder's nickname. "I'll pay up, Griz. Of course."

The sun lines fanning from the corners of his eyes deepened when he grinned. "I do so enjoy honorable bears." He kissed her lightly and stepped away.

As she pulled on her clothes, he took his jeans from the pack. But didn't put them on.

"What's wrong?" she asked as she slipped on her mocs.

He glanced down at himself ruefully. "You'd best join Ryder and the cub. I'll be out as soon as my jeans fit again."

Her gaze dropped. His cock was almost the girth of her forearm and…beautiful. She swallowed, as her core pulsed with the need to be filled. "Right. I'll just be—" She waved a vague hand toward the others, turned, and walked into a tree.

He caught her before she'd staggered back one step and gave her a guiding push between the trees with an amused snort.

As she strolled to the stream, she shook her head, still feeling her body humming with lust. By the Mother, the male was potent. And tonight… *Mmmm. Stop.* Think of glacier-topped mountains. And ice and snow.

By the time she'd crossed to where Ryder sat with Minette on a log, she'd managed to recover. Or so she thought.

Ryder lifted his head, sniffed the air, and his rare smile flashed. "I see Ben found you."

From the glint in his black eyes, she knew her face was turning red. "He did. He's getting dressed," she said stiffly and accepted the cup of water he handed her.

"Relax, little bear," Ryder said as he opened a sandwich for Minette. "So, you're joining him tonight?"

She choked on the water.

He gave a masculine chuckle. "Poor bear," he told Minette. "She needs to learn to swallow instead of breathing the water, right?"

Minette nodded solemnly.

"You did that deliberately," Emma muttered. Had she really thought the male had no sense of humor?

"Aye." Ryder took her hand and kissed her fingers before curling them around a sandwich. The heat in his midnight-dark eyes sent a frisson of awareness through her. "I'd be pleased if you…joined…me the next night."

Oh. Oooh. Her toes curled in her soft shoes. He wanted her. Wanted her after having spent another night with her. Wanted her after seeing her as a bear. "Yes," she agreed, almost breathless.

"Yes is the right answer," he said agreeably. He rubbed his shoulder against hers before turning back to Minette.

The cub was watching a scrub jay flit from branch to branch in the fir trees. At the bird's ripping-metal screech, Minette startled and spilled her water on the ground.

Scrunching her shoulders to make herself smaller, she looked anxiously from Emma to Ryder.

"Minet—" Emma started to say.

"Oops," Ryder broke in lightly. "You spilled." He grinned and swept dirt over the wet spot. "All gone. Want to go get some more from the stream? I need some, too." He rolled to his feet with a powerful grace and held out his hand.

Minette hesitated, as if waiting for him to react the way she'd expected. When he simply waited, she took his hand to be pulled to her feet.

Adoration filled her eyes.

As the two of them walked to the stream, Ryder holding his cub's hand and talking about catching fish, Emma felt a tugging warmth deep in her chest as her heart expanded to add another love.

Minette was already there. The kitten had set up residence within the first week.

Ben had been there since the night of the hellhound.

Now there was Ryder. Oh yes, she loved that terse, loner cat with his covert humor, devastating smile, and surprisingly tender side.

Ben walked out of the forest. He sat on the ground, his back against the log, his shoulder against her knees. "You're smiling like you found sweet berries in the weeds."

"Something like that." She looked him over. A half-erect cock bulged under his jeans, and exercise-pumped muscles strained against his worn T-shirt. She wanted to touch and stroke and taste. And she wanted to play with his brown hair that was the same color as his fur. Could she talk him into wearing his hair longer? Feeling quite daring, she tangled her fingers in the thick, soft strands.

Rather than objecting, he moved closer and closed his eyes in open appreciation. Someone enjoyed being petted. She could pet this male all day long.

After clearing her throat, she asked, "You keep your hair shorter than most shifters. Is there a reason?"

"Construction. Too easy to catch hair in those fancy-assed human machines." He held his hands out, fingers spread. "For the same reason, Ryder and I don't wear rings."

"Ah." His big hands had scars on the back and the knuckles.

She leaned forward and ran her fingers over the reminders of pain. He had other scars scattered over his body. From construction. From hellhounds. From fighting. Tonight, she'd find them all. Kiss them.

When a crease appeared in his cheek, she realized her scent had gone all lustful again.

The log settled in the dirt as Ryder sat down on her other side. Minette walked carefully to Ben to offer him a tin cup of water.

"That's just what I needed, kitten," he said. "I was thirsty. Thank you."

The cub smiled proudly as he drank the water down, his head tipping back, his Adam's apple moving up and down in his strong neck.

Emma wanted to fan herself—and then felt mortified. What was wrong with her? This was—

Ryder wrapped an arm around her, his dark voice a low whisper in her ear. "Little bear, no matter what your idiot mama taught you, desire is a gift from the gods. Nothing to hide or be ashamed of."

She met his serious eyes. "Right."

"If it helps, Ben and I feel exactly the same way about you." His gaze took her in, appreciation plain, his scent deepening with lust.

Now she really did need to fan herself. But… "It does help. Thank you."

When Minette yawned, Ben glanced at the early afternoon sun and pulled her down next to him. "I think it's nap time for kittens. Settle here, cub, while the old ones talk."

The cubling leaned into him, looking pixie-sized against his huge body. Before Emma had finished her sandwich, the little girl was sound asleep.

Ryder smiled at his daughter before looking at his brother and Emma. "I'm glad we had a chance for a four-legged day. Thank fuck we found out that Minette hadn't been around shifters in animal form." He scowled. "I should have anticipated it. Genevieve never shifted until she had to."

"It won't be a problem, bro. Minette has got a decade before her first *trawsfur*." Ben touched the cub's cheek gently. "We'll make sure she's comfortable with what happens long before that time."

Thinking back to her own first *trawsfur*, Emma watched the cub sleeping…until the silence registered. Both males were looking at her. "What?"

"I get the feeling your first *trawsfur* sucked." Ben pulled her clenched fingers out of his hair. He stroked her fingers over his cheek in the same way Minette played with her braid. "Now, mine started well enough. My pa took me out, and we both shifted. The door to the wild was nice and clear. Smooth as an eagle's dive."

Ryder frowned. " 'Started well enough' sounds ominous."

Sensing a story, Emma leaned forward. "Did something go wrong?"

"Yep. You see," Ben said, "my father figured he'd sired me. When I shifted into a grizzly, he knew I wasn't from his genes. And he blamed my size for my mother's death in labor. After shifting and yelling at me, he stormed off."

"The fucking insane bastard," Ryder muttered. "He left you to figure out how to get back to human by yourself, didn't he?"

"He did." Ben's voice was easy, but the fingers holding her hand tensed. "Took me a while."

Oh, sweet Mother.

Appalled, Emma could only stare at him. A new shifter could easily lose the "door" in their mind—especially if they were upset or afraid. And the longer it took, the less likely it was that they'd see it.

He could have died that day. Her fingers tightened around his. He'd been just a boy. The thought of his fear that day hurt her deep inside.

"So, little bard, did your first *trawsfur* go as badly?" Ryder took her free hand, rescuing her from the bleak thoughts.

"Not as bad as Ben's. But, like Minette, I'd not been around shifters in animal form." She lightly touched the sleeping cub's cheek. "Mother hated picnics and dirt, and trees and the mountains. I didn't go on excursions with anyone else since she didn't let me have friends. No one was good enough for a Cavanaugh." An unexpected anger filled her. How selfish her mother had been. Emma had been no more than another status-enhancing possession—and had received the same emotional care as the expensive statuary in the foyer.

"What happened?" Ben asked.

"She hired a shifter to serve as my first *trawsfur* mentor when she…eventually…realized I was the right age." After the maid had reported that Emma had soiled the bed with her menstrual blood. Thank goodness for the school's education classes that explained menses. "I was shocked when I first shifted, but…I loved it."

Ben gave her a keen glance. "Loved it almost too much?" His words held a world of understanding.

"Yes. I knew where the door back to human was. I just didn't want to use it."

"Glad you came back, little bear." Ryder squeezed her hand. "Well, compared to you two, I had a nice, normal first *trawsfur*. And a hell of a better childhood."

"Yeah, sure you did. Sorry, bro. If we're sharing traumatic childhood stories, you won't escape." Ben lifted his thick eyebrows. "Remember when we downed a bottle of Jack Daniels to see what *drunk* felt like? You babbled worse than a flooding brook."

OH FUCK. RYDER did remember. Wished he didn't. "I don't babble." Because he never consumed that much alcohol again.

"You did. You said your pa was a good male."

Ryder nodded, relieved. "Yeah. That's right."

"But he went through females faster than wildfire through the east range, and none liked his skinny, silent cub."

Ryder turned his head away. Also true. During his father's frequent absences, whoever the current female was would send him to his room. To get him out of sight. He'd learned early how shallow and unloving females were.

He realized he was holding Emma's hand and started to pull away.

Her fingers tightened to the point of pain as her soft brown eyes revealed a compassion he didn't want to accept.

"Got a grip on you, little bear," he said roughly.

She didn't let go. "I hang on to what I lo…" She broke off, leaving him staring. *To what I love?* Did she…

She finished, "…to what I want to hang on to. So, your father's females didn't like having another's cub underfoot?"

"Nope." Shallow, uncaring, mercenary, and—

She snorted. "Between them and Genevieve, it's no wonder you don't like females."

Her statement slid like a blade between his ribs.

"My pa said your father adored our mother," Ben noted. "The new females probably didn't want you around reminding them—and him—of someone he really did love."

Ryder's brows pulled together. "You…might have a point."

Ben grinned at Emma. "Then the ugly cub grew up, turned studly, and now has females flocking to him. Even his sire's females were hanging all over him, and only because of his appearance. He hasn't changed otherwise."

"Asshole." If he punched his brother, chances were good that he'd wake the cub. Ben's summary was fucking accurate. When they were younger, it'd burned Ryder's ass that females wanted to mate for the sole reason that they liked the way he looked. As a cahir, Ben got the same treatment.

A muffled sound made him glance down.

Emma had her hand over her mouth to smother her laughter.

"What?" he growled.

"Oh, your face." She pointed at him. "Such utter disgust that some female might want you because you're gorgeous."

Well… His lips curved up as much of his bitterness receded. "Gorgeous, huh?"

She was so pretty when she turned pink. "Um. We should head back. I have to sing this evening," she muttered, releasing his hand.

"True enough." Ben rose, lifting Minette up with him. He reached back to yank Ryder to his feet.

Ryder gave Emma a hand and moved closer to run a finger down her flushed cheek. Her brown eyes were beautiful, big and wide and vulnerable.

Had she almost said she loved him? By the God, he wanted to hear that more than he wanted his next breath. But…he wouldn't push. This little bear was too easily spooked. Might flee rather than share.

And somehow, somewhen, he needed to let her know he'd already taken that leap.

Chapter Twenty-Five

"EMMA, DRAW ME a bear," Luke said. In the small building next to Ryder's workshop, the mischievous cub and his littermate sat on the floor with crayons encircling them. The other students had already been picked up by their mothers. An hour ago, Ryder had come for Minette and carried her across the backyard to the house. But Bonnie, the boys' mother, had called to say their pack meeting was running late.

"One bear, coming up." Emma traced out the outline of a bear. Before she'd finished, Luke's littermate demanded a wolf.

Wolves were trickier, but she managed. "There you go," Emma said and handed over the paper. "What color is the wolf going to be?"

"Purple," Tyler said after a glance at his brother's bear whose fur was the color of green lake algae.

"I look forward to seeing that," Emma told him gravely.

He nodded graciously and concentrated on coloring within the lines.

"Emma, I'm so sorry I'm late." Like a brisk breeze, Bonnie blew into the room. Her offspring jumped her, acting as if they hadn't seen her for months rather than hours.

After duly admiring the artwork, Bonnie sent them to gather their belongings.

"Did the meeting go all right?" Emma asked. "You look…tense."

The wolf's blonde hair was ruffled, and she carried the lingering scent of anger.

"Talk about a showdown." Bonnie blew a lock of hair out of her eyes. "Shay's been extremely patient with Chad and Patrick, but tonight, he stated the next time they get aggressive with a female, he'll either beat the hell out of them or drive them out of the territory altogether."

Wasn't Chad the wolf who'd deliberately squashed her fingers at the Gathering? Emma blinked. "Bree mentioned once that there was trouble left over from last year or something."

"Or something. Our last alphas and beta were belligerent and aggressive. Shay's different—controlled and patient. Unfortunately, some of the younger wolves see his restraint as weakness. They're sooo going to learn different." She picked up a stuffed mouse and tossed it to Luke to pack. "We also have a few young females who lack manners, but Bree's too soft-hearted to discipline them."

Bree was not only a sweetheart, but she'd also been raised human. What would it be like to change to such a different culture? She noticed Bonnie's worried expression. "Something else?"

"I'm afraid so. I stayed late so I could give you the scoop."

Uh-oh. Emma straightened. "Go on."

"Before we could deal with Candice and Ursula, a female came into the lodge. A really beautiful, skanky wolf who's moving to Cold Creek to be with her cub. She says the baby's father stole the child from her home—and that he's violent."

"Genevieve?" Emma whispered through numb lips.

"That's her." Bonnie squeezed her hand. "I'd hoped to say you needn't worry, but that bitch is good. She had the young males eating out of her hand like lap dogs. Candice and Ursula were fawning all over her."

"*She* was the one who was violent. Minette is just starting to get over being afraid all the time."

"Honey, I figured it was something like that." Bonnie shook her head. "Will you tell Ryder and Ben what's going on?"

"I will."

A few minutes later, Emma left her "preschool" building, crossed the yard, and went in their home's back door. In the kitchen, the fragrance of venison stew came from the crock-pot on the counter. She hadn't eaten, but her appetite had disappeared the minute Genevieve was mentioned.

She stopped to drink a glass of water and frowned at the refrigerator door where Minette's crayon drawings had been ordered into neat lines. Turning in a circle, she noted that the counters and sink were spotless, the floor clean enough to eat from, and even the stovetop scoured.

Interesting. Had they already heard about Genevieve? She knew she cleaned when she was upset—which had been most difficult to do in a cave—but which of the males reacted that way?

She followed the sounds of quiet talking to the great room.

Ryder sprawled on the sectional, reading one of his philosophy books. In front of the crackling fire, Ben and Minette were putting away the wooden cherries from a board game. Ben's hands were so big he kept dropping pieces. In the center of the room, Minette had built something that resembled Ben's house, complete with towers, from scrap lumber Ryder'd cut and painted for her.

Minette looked up and beamed, then dashed over with enthusiastic hugs and kisses. Emma's eyes stung with pleased tears—because that was how Bonnie's boys had acted toward her.

As the cubling trotted back to finish putting her game away,

Emma's face tightened. Genevieve's arrival might send the happy child back into a terrified waif.

Ryder set his book down and sat up. "What's wrong, Emma?" he asked in a quiet voice.

Still sitting, Ben studied her, and his brows drew together.

She gave a meaningful glance toward Minette. "We can talk later."

Ryder caught on immediately. His expression turned to concrete.

At the rise of tension, Minette quieted. Her thumb slid into her mouth.

Emma pulled in a slow breath. The child was overly sensitive to moods around her. Someday, the hard-won talent would serve her well, but it hurt to see a child so insecure.

"Look how late it's gotten," Emma said. "I think it's time a kitten had a bath, don't you?"

"Aye," Ryder agreed.

"Minette, since we're not going to wash your hair tonight, do you want me to braid it and pin it on top of your head?"

Her little face lit up.

"Why don't you run up to my room and pick out a scrunchie?"

As the cub dashed up the stairs, Emma sank down beside Ryder. "Genevieve attended the pack meeting and told them she's moving here. And that you're violent."

Ryder grunted as if he'd taken a fist to his stomach. But he put an arm around her and pulled her close enough to share his body heat. "Easy, bard. We'll work out whatever we need to work out."

Emma scowled. "Why can't people tell that she's lying? Her scent should show it, if nothing else."

"She wears human perfume," Ryder said.

Emma wrinkled her nose. "Ewwww." The cloying "fragrances" of the humans were nose-clogging torture. "Hmm. Can't we go to the Cosantir? Wouldn't he be able to make her tell the truth? And go away?"

Ben rose to his feet, his sheer size incredibly reassuring, and tucked the board game on a bookshelf. When Emma had arrived, the shelves held only a handful of Ben's history books, but games and toys had been appearing until no free space remained.

"Calum might help," Ben said. "But calling on him might be chancy. It's true that Cosantirs don't tolerate lying, but they're also very traditional. And, far as I know, cubs always stay with the dam."

"But she hurt Minette."

"Aye. And, since Calum has a good heart, he might take steps to ensure the cub's safety. That doesn't mean he'll pick a couple of males to raise a female cub. He might hand Minette back to Genevieve with someone ordered to supervise. Or require Genevieve to move into the wolf pack quarters."

"Oh." She certainly knew the dangers of a Cosantir's Judgment. Avoiding Calum might be a better idea. "You have a point."

Ben touched her hair as he walked past. "Like Ryder said. We'll manage."

Ryder looked up. "Where are you going? You cooked, so it's my night to clean."

"I need to do something. Scrubbing the fuck out of something will work."

Emma frowned. "The kitchen's clean already. Even that marker stain on the floor where Minette tried to draw a frog is gone."

"Can't be clean. Ryder always leaves a mess," Ben said and disappeared. The lights came on.

Emma and Ryder followed him, trailed by Minette who

clutched a bright pink scrunchie.

"Whoa, I didn't know kitchens could shine like this," Ryder said.

Ben grinned. "Never happened to me, but I've seen the Cosantir's kitchen this spotless. And Zeb and Shay's."

Emma tilted her head. "You hired Jody and her crew to clean here?"

Ben's laugh rumbled out before he pulled her against his body, kissing her lightly. Just his scent, his touch, the strength in his arms left her leaning against him, trying to remember the conversation.

Cleaning. Right.

"Nope." He'd turned her and pointed to the far wall. A small hole showed in the baseboard.

"That wasn't there before." Ryder picked up Minette, settling her on his hip.

"I think we've acquired a pair of brownies," Ben said. "We'll need to leave out cream and cookies for them."

Emma wrapped her arms around Ben and hugged him hard. In the old tales, which apparently were still true, the housecleaning brownies served families in exchange for goodies. But they only lived with families. *Happy* families.

Ryder's face held an unfamiliar expression, much like the wonder of a cub seeing the moon for the first time.

"Cookies and cream?" Pulling in a deep breath, Emma used one of Ben's favorite phrases, "I'll get right on that."

Chapter Twenty-Six

LATE THE NEXT afternoon, Ben walked into the grocery store and crossed to the dairy section to pick up a carton of cream.

Cookies had been on his list, as well, but the honey bear must have spent the morning baking. At lunch, she'd swung by the construction site and dropped off a sackful of cookies for him and the crew.

Seems Ryder told her how much Ben enjoyed peanut butter cookies.

He shook his head. She was always doing little things that said she'd been thinking of him, that she cared enough to discover his tastes. She did the same with Ryder. Was this what having a mother would have been like?

Who knew? Not him or Ryder. In fact, none of them, including Minette, had grown up with a mother's affection.

Emma's mother had certainly not taught her how to care for a family, but everything she did showed him and Ryder what they'd missed. And Minette drank in Emma's care and attention like a drought-starved plant. Must be instinct that showed Emma how to be a mother.

Neither he nor Ryder, nor Emma, either, had been blessed with mated parents to use for examples. But they were slowly moving into a real relationship. From friends to lovers.

He'd wanted her since the moment he saw her, but now…now that he liked her, loved her, and had mated her…the need was constant. He was worse than a testosterone-overloaded young male lusting after her from waking to sleeping. Ryder was in the same shape.

Apparently so was Emma. She'd been generously dividing her nights between them. And letting herself be lured into extras.

With a smile, he rubbed the itching scratches on his chest. Because Ryder'd been shaken to hear Genevieve was back, Emma spent the night with him. This morning, after Ryder had left, Ben had visited her bedroom to report Minette was still asleep and he was leaving.

Just out of the shower, the honey bear had been all soft and damp. The dawn light had set her hair aglow and burnished her heat-flushed skin with gold. Her eyes had still been sleepy when she saw him, but the scent in the room had quickly changed to interest.

That was all it took. Before she could move, he'd stripped off her towel and tossed her on the bed, starting them on the day's journey in the most old-fashioned of ways. Even without the full moon's influence, she…roused…to him easily. Hell, the female could be delightfully demanding.

And snuggly. Fuck, he hadn't been able to let her go and had ended up late to work.

His construction crew teased him all day about the lateness—and the bite marks she'd left on his neck.

Nevertheless, having her dividing her time between him and Ryder wasn't how he wanted their family—*fuck, he loved that word*—their *family* to operate. When she was more at ease, he and Ryder would enjoy her favors together as littermates should.

And he'd started using his fingers to prepare her for taking them both at the same time. Fuck, she'd been adorably shocked.

Giving an exasperated huff, he unobtrusively adjusted his sudden hard-on.

With the carton of cream in hand, he stepped up the cash register.

Old Albert Baty grinned at him. "Either the bard has started taking cream in her coffee, or you got yourselves some brownies."

Ben grinned. "Appeared yesterday. Never seen the kitchen so clean."

"The OtherFolk are something." As the door to the store opened, Baty glanced over. His mouth pulled down as if he'd bitten into days-old carrion.

Following his gaze, Ben saw Genevieve in the doorway. A glance at the wide storefront window told him she'd undoubtedly seen him from the sidewalk. *Fuck.*

"Ben." Her smile was sweet. Innocent.

He'd once watched an assassin bug tap lightly on a spider web. The spider thought it'd caught a fly. Hurried over. And died. What ambush had she planned for him? Ben nodded and turned away.

Moving far too close, she touched his arm. "I've come to ask you to return my child. I know you're not a thief like your brother."

"He's no thief," Ben growled. "Minette is his cub. I gave you my answer before—you'll get no money from us. And you won't get Minette."

She burst into tears. Her voice rose until the entire store could hear. "Please, please, cahir, make your brother give my little cub back. I love her so much. How could he steal her from me?"

Oh. Fuck. He was aware of the shoppers watching, enthralled by the scene. "You didn't take care of her," he said. "You hurt her, neglected her. I should—"

"Ryder was the one who hurt her—and me." She yanked at Ben's arm, sobbing loudly. Tears streamed down her face. "She doesn't even talk since he took her from me. She needs her mommy."

"By the God, Ryder would never hurt a female. No one would believe that." Ben jerked away.

She staggered back as if he'd hit her. "How can you be so cruel? No male, especially an abusive one like him, should care for a little child. I'll-I'll do something." She looked around the store. "I know the decent people here won't let this happen to a mother whose only crime is being poor."

"You lying—"

Before he could finish, Genevieve ran from the store, leaving stunned silence in her wake.

"Piece of work, that one," Baty rang up the cream and took the money Ben held out.

In the aisles, people were still staring at Ben.

"She was the one who hurt Minette. Starved her," he told them. His words weren't smooth and polished like Genevieve's, but were the clumsy fumblings of a grizzly.

As Ben left the store, he felt the heavy weight of the *audience's* disapproving regard. And heard the first whispers begin.

Chapter Twenty-Seven

EVER SINCE GENEVIEVE'S return from Farway two days ago, the tension in Cold Creek, and in Ben's little family, had increased.

On Friday at the construction site, the stench of animosity toward Ryder had grown until Ben was ready to go on a grizzly rampage.

All the crews knew Ryder. Liked him. Even when buried in his finicky custom woodworking, he'd stop and lend a hand to whoever needed one. The younger males appreciated having Ryder available to answer questions; the older ones liked having the extra help. Now, suddenly, half the crew wasn't talking to him; they were glaring at him.

Genevieve must have said something to influence them.

Ryder was never talkative, but as the morning went on, the cat had withdrawn. Finally, he'd simply packed his tools and left.

Ben growled under his breath. Over the past month, Ryder had changed, had been happy. With Emma's loving care, his contentment had radiated from him like rays from the sun. But when he'd left today, the cynical lines were back in his face. His defenses had slid into place.

By the God.

And yet every male on the crew was a good one; Ben didn't

hire assholes. A lot of the shifters really did believe Ryder'd done something wrong.

Ben set a nail in place and smacked it in so forcefully he dented the fucking wood beneath as well, which pissed him off. Good thing the spot would be covered by trim.

Sweat trickled down his face. The late morning air was starting to heat up. With an annoyed grunt, Ben stripped off his flannel shirt and continued working.

"Boss, got a visitor here for you." The call came from Kenner in the front room.

Now what? Wishing for a hellhound on which to vent his anger, Ben stomped outside.

Alec stood on the front lawn, hands in his jeans pockets, surveying the work being done. "Got a minute?"

"Sure." Ben detoured to the cooler on the tailgate of his truck, pulled out water, and tossed another bottle to the cahir. "You here in your official Sheriff role?"

Alec's jaw hardened. "I hope to hell not." He led the way to a big maple that shaded the front and was out of hearing from the crew.

Ben leaned against the trunk. "What?"

"Seems your brother took that little cub away from her mother without permission."

"For a damned good reason, yeah."

"Last night, in the diner, the mother announced Ryder has a history of violence, and she kicked him out because he was hurting her. Says when she saw him yesterday and asked for her child back, he punched her."

Ben straightened. "He never saw her yesterday."

"She showed her black eye off in the diner until Angie asked her to leave."

That's why the construction crew was staring holes in Ryder. Not knowing the female was a liar, they'd have taken her at face value. If they thought Ryder'd hurt a female, it was a wonder the entire shifter portion of the crew hadn't gone feral on his ass.

"By the God, she's lying. My brother would *never* hurt a female." His world took on a sharp-edged brightness with his rage. "Genevieve was the one who hurt Minette. That's why he took the cub."

Alec opened his water and drank slowly. "Genevieve hasn't come to me to make an accusation…yet."

The sheriff wasn't one to jump into action—not until he'd sniffed every scent and danger in the brush. Ben took a controlling breath and tried to think.

Would the female be stupid enough to go to Alec and accuse Ryder? Would she think she could lie to a cop? Or the Cosantir? Maybe. She was skilled—and wore perfume. "What's Calum have to say about this?" The Cosantir wasn't one to hide his head in the sand, not if there were problems. And these were fucking serious problems.

"He's out of town. Back on Tuesday." Alec scowled. "Ben, she tells a good story—and with that black eye, people are concerned about the cub. I've had people stopping me all day."

"You ever meet Genevieve?"

"I haven't, which seems a mite odd." Alec said. "Considering her accusations, I'd think she'd visit the sheriff or the Cosantir. Instead, she's inciting a witch hunt with your brother as the target."

"No shit." Ben scratched his shoulders against the tree trunk even though Emma would scold him for shredding the fabric. "Here are the facts, Alec. That mercenary shrew neglected Minette and smacked her around, too. When Genevieve saw our big house, she figured on getting herself some status and suggested she should live with Ryder and me. I said no way in hell and thought she'd left. But now she's back and doing a grieving mother act."

"By the God, that's an interesting scam," Alec muttered.

Did the sheriff believe him? "You think I'd let Ryder move in if he was some abusive asshole?"

Alec shrugged. "Family dynamics can be fucked. People, especially littermates, excuse a lot. Remember what Gerhardt let his brother do?"

"Aye." The previous alpha had allowed his brother to terrorize the wolf pack females. "However, both Ryder and I have the same instincts: females and cubs are protected. As a cahir, I wouldn't overlook abuse."

Alec half-smiled. "I saw you two pass the bard back and forth for some affection last week. She didn't look much traumatized."

Ben smiled. Emma never looked traumatized after spending a night with Ryder—just satisfied. He returned to the problem. "There's no way to prove Ryder didn't hurt Genevieve. But he didn't, so there can't be anyone—except her—saying he did."

"She hasn't mentioned any witnesses. However, the absence goes both ways, Ben. Have you got witnesses to her abusing the cub?"

"Not here." And, from what Ryder'd said about Farway, getting anyone to testify against Genevieve might be difficult. It sounded as if the townspeople were either convinced the female was wonderful or wouldn't oppose her for fear of her reprisals. "Dammit, Alec, Minette wouldn't be safe with Genevieve."

"I hear you. But, by human law, each parent has certain rights to a child. In fact, that mother could bring Ryder up on kidnapping charges." Concern darkened the sheriff's green gaze. "By Daonain tradition, males don't raise cubs when the mother is available. It's not unknown for males to be abusive, but a female hurting her cub is extremely rare."

In other words, there was a fucking good chance Genevieve would win.

IN CAT FORM, Ryder'd headed north through the forest at a fast lope, trying to burn off anger. And despair.

At the construction site, he'd heard the muttered comments. After leaving, he'd asked some questions at the diner and the grocery, and received the answers he'd been expecting. Genevieve had shown off a black eye and announced that he'd hit her. The reactions of the people he passed in town told him he was screwed.

He'd half expected Genevieve to use this tactic—she'd done it before—but to be maligned in Cold Creek hurt. What could he do though? Nothing—aside from making her accusations true and beating the hell out of her.

Fuck. He couldn't find it in him to be angry with the construction crew. He liked them, enjoyed working with them. It wasn't their fault that Genevieve was a master at manipulation. Hell, she'd conned him in the beginning.

However, the fact that the crew knew him and still had been taken in by Genevieve's lies pretty much proved he wouldn't be able to win against her.

He leaped over a winter-felled tree and landed on the mossy ground.

Fuck, he'd hoped to stay and build a family with Ben—and with Emma. He wanted to share her with Ben, to have her in their lives with all her shyness, her sweetness, her husky laughter, and the music that trailed after her like a new pup.

Forlorn hopes.

Over the forest canopy, a hawk circled, searching for an unwary rodent. As the sun disappeared behind one of the white puffy clouds, the temperature on the mountain plummeted.

Much like the atmosphere at the construction site today.

Hell, if it'd been just him, he'd fucking stay and fight Genevieve's lies. Fight for a life with Emma and Ben. But he couldn't risk it. He'd lose more than his reputation this time; he'd lose Minette. The kitten wouldn't survive undamaged at Genevieve's hands.

He heard a rustling in the underbrush—a rabbit or rodent. But, even though in cougar form, he had no appetite.

Although leaving Cold Creek would hurt like hell, he'd survive since he had Minette to live for. But what would this do to Ben? The stab of pain came so quick and sharp it felt as if a hunter had shot him, sent a bullet right through his ribs and into his heart.

Fuck, I'm sorry, Ben. Ryder'd pushed himself into the grizzly's life along with a cub to love, and now he was walking away. It didn't take any imagination to see the hole…the devastation…he'd leave behind.

And what about the little bear? He and Ben had been trying to win her favor. Hell, they'd been optimistic enough that lifemating bracelets lay waiting in Ben's nightstand. Now, they'd never be used.

She could be nurturing hopes of her own. By the God, she'd suffered enough in her life. To add to her pain was… Dammit, he knew life wasn't fair, but the thought of his actions hurting Emma was more than he could take.

The trail forked, and Ryder halted. His head hung as he stood there, undecided, as the wind whipped dead leaves and evergreen needles in circles, and a spattering of rain came through the fir canopy. He'd lost his path in so many ways.

And hurt so many people.

Finally, he lifted his head. Inhaled. Catching Owen's scent on the left fork, he followed the trail upward.

THREE HOURS LATER, Ryder finished wiring Owen's new solar panels and was feeling better. When Ryder had appeared, the cahir'd had studied him, and with a welcome lack of conversation, handed over some tools and put him to work.

The quiet had helped. Owen's peaceful log cabin was as isolated as the backwoods where Ryder and Ben had started their lives. Far more beautiful, though. The cahir's property was the middle of three small hanging valleys, which stair-stepped down into the main valley below. A waterfall cascaded from a notched cliff above Owen's valley and streamed into a small pool near his home.

Finishing the last wire, Ryder stretched and glanced across the room at the cahir. "How'd you get all the kitchen shit up here?"

Owen grinned. "On my back, usually. Anything I can't carry or disassemble—like the wood stove—requires a helicopter and that costs a whack. Then again, I don't have much overhead out here."

Only solar-powered electricity. No cable. No Internet. "How do you keep food cold?"

"Box in the water. The stream is glacier-fed. Gotta say, hauling beer was a pain until I learned to make my own."

"Yeah, I bet." Ryder set the tools back into Owen's case. "Why the solar panels if you hate technology?"

Sitting halfway up the stairs to the loft, Owen was working on the railing. A cropped tree formed the bottom post, and he was weaving the tree branches around the horizontal rails to create an intricate pattern. "Behind the house, the western ridge cuts off the sunlight early in the evening. And reading by lantern or candlelight sucks. I've been looking forward to real lights."

Ryder grinned. "Got it."

"Let's have a beer."

A few minutes later, Ryder sat on the porch in a chair carved from a huge stump and smoothed to a glossy finish. And the icy home-brewed beer was damned good. The shifter was pretty handy.

Had good taste in property, too. Surrounded by spring green grass, the clear blue pond emptied into a tiny stream, which plunged down to the next valley. White-topped mountains ringed the horizon. With a pleased sigh, Ryder put his legs up on the split log railing. "Beautiful location."

"Yeah." Owen took a sip of his beer and eyed Ryder. "Now that you had a chance to relax, you want to tell me what's chewing your tail?"

Hell.

A glance showed Owen waiting like a patient feline beside a gopher hole.

"Guess it's hardly a secret these days." With a bitter shrug, Ryder laid the story out for the cat in a few terse sentences, including the damage Genevieve had done to his rep in Farway.

Owen nodded as if unsurprised. "I saw the bad blood between you that night at the tavern. Got to wonder though—why didn't anyone speak up for you in that other town?"

"The people we hung with there were her friends." Ryder rolled the chilled bottle between his palms. "And like now, she had bruises. Someone'd obviously hurt her, and she said it was me. How the fuck do you prove a negative?"

"So, who did beat her up? Why didn't she point her finger at the real culprit?"

Ryder laughed cynically. "I doubt anyone hurt her without her permission. She was pissed at me, and when she's out for a buck—or vengeance—she's got no limits. She'd probably asked someone to mark her up."

"That's sick." Owen considered his beer and took a drink. "Don't know about Farway, but I doubt a Daonain would hurt a female around here."

"Why's that?"

"Last year, the Cosantir discovered an abusive shifter,

slapped a hand on his shoulder, and delivered him straight to the Mother. Hell of a deterrent, yeah?"

"No shit." Ryder'd heard a Cosantir could kill with a touch, but had never seen it. Then again, Calum held a lot of power. More than most Cosantirs. "Her attacker probably wasn't a shifter. I daresay she got a human male to bruise her up."

"A *human*?"

The shifter sounded so appalled that Ryder actually grinned...although he felt the same. Male Daonain occasionally mated human females, especially if they were desperate. But females didn't get desperate, not with males outnumbering them at least five to one. Humans didn't smell appealing, so for a female to fuck one was...twisted. In fact, discovering Genevieve'd fucked humans had been a major reason Ryder'd left their increasingly antagonistic relationship.

He glanced at Owen. "Using a human works. That's how she destroyed my reputation in Farway. No one believed me."

Owen grunted his understanding. "Clever move on her part. Although I'm surprised no one scented her lies."

Ryder grimaced. "She has a fondness for strong perfumes. Covers up lack of desire and lies."

"Damn, that's sneaky." Owen's brows drew together. "If the matter came before the Cosantir, he might not compel her to speak the truth—not the way he would a male. No matter that we're in the twenty-first century, the Daonain still have a whopping double standard. Bet she counts on that." He shook his head. "Don't let that female win."

"Owen, she already has."

"Fuck." The cat turned away, glowering. "Females. If they're not clingy sluts, they're manipulative liars. Can't think of one I'd trust to have at my back."

And Ben accused *Ryder* of being cynical. "Ah, that might be a little harsh. The bard is one to run the trails with."

"Sure she is." The tone and pitying look indicated the cahir thought Ryder was well on the way to toothless and senile. "You and Ben planning to claim her?"

The unexpected question speared him, fracturing his sternum, shattering his heart. "We...wanted to. I waited too long. Took me a while to get over what happened before, and how easily I'd been led by my dick. You know, after I'd lived with Genevieve for a while, I realized I didn't even like her."

"Yep. What I'm saying."

"Not all females are bad, cahir." Ryder shook his head. "Being with Emma is as comfortable as being with Ben. Having her around is...right. The more we're together, the better we all fit."

Owen shrugged and drank his beer. "But...you changed your mind about claiming the bard?"

"Yeah." Because fitting together wasn't going to help. Depression settled back on Ryder's shoulders. "I can't take the chance Genevieve will get her hands on Minette. When I get back, I'm packing up. The cub and I will go somewhere too far for Genevieve to find us."

"You'd run from a fight?"

"Can't fight a female." Ryder scowled. "I fucking hate this. The kitten was finally happy. Relaxing. I even heard her humming with Emma yesterday."

"Ben cares for the cub and for you," Owen said slowly. "Littermates belong together."

"I know." Leaving Ben again would destroy part of his heart. Leaving Emma? That'd wipe out the other half.

But a male protected the cubs first. Always.

Ryder studied the lean cahir. If Owen felt that strongly about brothers being together, where was his? Gawain lived in Pine Knoll, not here. And although Gawain'd been at the full moon, he'd disappeared soon after.

"You know, Ben, Alec, and I are a team. We've all saved

each other's asses in fights." Owen's gaze was on the mountain range. "But last time was… That hellhound had me down, was going for my throat. Ben was gushing blood and still threw himself on that fucking demon-dog. If Alec hadn't been right there to stab the creature…" He looked at Ryder. "I owe your brother."

Knowing Ben'd been so close to death dried Ryder's mouth, but… "He wouldn't see it like that."

"I know. Don't give a fuck how he sees it."

Ryder snorted. The cat was one opinionated shifter. He finished off the beer, leaving the dregs in the bottom, and rose. "I need to get moving." *Need to pack. Need to say goodbye. Need to rip our barely formed family apart again.*

"Right. Appreciate the help." Owen swirled the beer in his bottle. "Good luck fighting off the bitch from…from where again?"

"Farway. But I won't be fighting. Not anymore." After pulling off the clothes Owen had lent him, Ryder shifted, feeling the Mother's love ease his heart. As the wildness of his cat nature surged to the forefront, he sniffed the air, letting his worries drift away. Part of the glory of being an animal was the ability to live in the now. Worries about the future faded into the background.

With a leap, he cleared the porch railing and started down the trail to home. And Minette and Ben.

And Emma.

He hadn't realized how very much he'd hoped to lifemate her, to share her with his brother, to love her for a lifetime—not until the dreams were crumbling like leaves in the winter's first frost.

Nevertheless, for one last night, he could wrap himself in the warmth of being with his littermate and the female they loved.

Chapter Twenty-Eight

A S EMMA REACHED the last verse of the lullaby, she couldn't keep from nuzzling Minette's soft brown hair. Since Ryder was late returning from his trip to Owen's, Emma had put the cubling to bed.

Nothing was as heartwarming as a sleepy, trusting kitten. Minette's eyes were drooping, her breathing slowing, and small humming notes escaped her. The song must still be playing in her head.

Emma whispered the last few words and watched the little girl slide completely into sleep. Her cheeks and nose were pink from the sun, her hair glossy with health, her body now sturdy. She didn't flinch or watch Emma, Ben, or Ryder warily. Trust had been long in coming, and the gift was a prize Emma cherished more than she could express.

Minette still had far to travel before she would extend that trust to others, but Emma didn't doubt the time would come. However, with her vicious mother in town, the child's recovery might be delayed.

That nasty female needed a good lesson.

Be rude? With an effort, she pushed her anxiety aside. Yes, her mother had required politeness—if not silence—but every cub eventually grew up, and every season came to an end. It was time to shed her mother's control like last winter's fur.

She'd had enough of being a frightened bunny. Like all shifters, she had an inner predator.

Now that she knew what Genevieve looked like, their next meeting would be less one-sided. However, fighting with Minette's mother wouldn't help the cub. In fact, she hadn't thought of anything she could do to help Ryder and Minette defeat Genevieve.

Prayer seemed far too little. Nonetheless… "Mother of All, please watch over this cub and keep her safe."

She kissed Minette's rounded cheek. "Happy dreams, kitten." Emma started to rise, stopped…and eased her braid from the tiny fist. The cubling had been playing, teasing the end tuft over her chin.

As she left the room, she heard noise from across the hall. Had Ryder returned?

Emma stopped in the doorway. "Welcome back. I…" Her voice trailed off.

He was filling a suitcase on the bed. Every dresser drawer was open.

"You're leaving?" Her voice had emerged loud and shocked. She said more quietly, "Why?" The thought of him disappearing from her life rocked the floor beneath her. She curled her fingers around the doorframe.

His expression was grim, but his black eyes softened. "Minette and I can't—" At the sound of footsteps on the stairs, he winced. "The Griz has good ears."

Despite his size, Ben could move cahir-fast, and the thumps sounded as if he was taking the stairs three at a time. As he appeared in the door, his sharp gaze took in the signs of packing. His face tightened. "By Herne's horns and hooves, what do you think you're fucking doing?"

"You know what I'm doing, bro."

"You asked to live here. Said you'd stay." The anger didn't cover the pain in Ben's voice.

Emma felt tears sting her eyes. Both males hurt—and somehow that made her heart ache.

Ryder was leaving.

Emma's grip tightened on the doorframe until her fingers hurt. She firmed her voice. "Maybe Ben understands what's going on, but I don't. Why would you leave?"

Ryder opened another drawer. "From the reactions I got at the construction site and in town, everyone's convinced I'm violent. That I shouldn't have custody of Minette." His baritone was edged enough to cut flesh.

"People believe that?" Emma stared at him in disbelief. "They couldn't, not all of them. People know you, have worked with you. How could they possibly believe her?"

He stilled. "You don't have any doubt that she's lying?"

"Of course not. I know you. Even if I didn't, I could tell what kind of a person you are from how Minette trusts you."

Gratitude in his eyes, he cleared his throat. "Thank you, little bear."

"We can weather this, bro." Ben crossed his arms over his chest. "If we simply ignore the shrew and not give in to her demands, she'll move on to richer hunting grounds."

Emma nodded, hope rising in her heart.

Ryder shook his head. "That's what I'd planned. But she's too clever. I heard a couple of females saying I should be banished for stealing a cub and hurting the cub's mother."

"By the God!" Ben's fist slammed into the wall powerfully enough to rattle the windows. "I'll show her what hurt is."

Ryder gave him a wry smile. "You can't hit her, any more than I can."

"Hell." Ben's shoulders slumped. "True. No matter how well deserved."

They really were two of a kind. Tough—and protective. And this was going to break Ben's heart. Emma curled her fingers around his, and he held on.

"So, that's why." Ryder's eyes held the same grief as Ben's. "Minette and I need to be gone before people call on Calum to render a Cosantir's Judgment." His voice faltered. "I'm sorry, bro. I wouldn't leave you for anything less."

The same devastation shone in Ben's gaze before his jaw hardened to the granite of the mountains.

Ryder pulled in a slow breath, crossed the room, and took Emma's hand between both of his. "Little bear, I wanted...more...for us. For us all. But, can you find it in your heart to stay with Ben? He's going to need you."

Tears filled her eyes, turning his face blurry. He was leaving. Her heart already ached from the hole his absence would create. "Ryder," she whispered. "There has to be something we can do." Her fingers trembled in his warm hand.

"I can't risk it. No shifter can go against a Cosantir. Minette and I have to be away before he can speak."

"But—"

Ben set his hand over both of theirs. "He's right. He stole a cub from her mother. There's no telling how a Cosantir's Judgment might go." His eyes turned steely blue. "But littermates belong together. If you leave, I leave."

Ryder took a step back. "You can't do that. You have friends, a business, a home."

Emma stared at the males she loved. Both of them? Gone? *I only just found them.*

"I didn't realize how empty my life was until you and Minette and Emma arrived," Ben said simply, echoing her own feelings. "Let's move so far away the shrew won't find us until Minette is an old lady."

Ryder didn't seem able to speak, and Emma remembered

her first sight of him. She'd never have guessed then that his hard, cold face held a heart with so much warmth. How could she stand to lose him?

Ben put an arm around her and tugged on her braid. "Do me a favor and compose a nasty song about Genevieve."

She swallowed back her tears and forced a smile. "I will do that." She'd make a fine story. An evil, scheming mother. An innocent little cubling. Two intrepid males. Maybe even a nice female bear?

"Good." The corner of Ryder's mouth lifted slightly. "Fuck, I'll miss you, little bear." Leaning forward, he kissed her, unhappiness in his scent.

A song of mourning whispered in her mind.

He touched her cheek and stepped back. "Minette and I have to leave now, unfortunately. Do you want to think about this some more, bro? Meet us somewhere?"

"Nope. We stay together. I have business matters to hand off to others, but the Cosantir is out of town until Tuesday. Let's try to get out of here Saturday night." Ben rubbed his shoulder against the doorframe. "Sunday is dark of the moon. We don't want to be on the road then."

On the road when hellhounds were out? No way. Emma suppressed a shudder. She absolutely wanted to be in an impenetrable house on that night...and she needed to find a new place to live, didn't she?

"I'd consider it a personal favor if you'd stay here, Emma," Ben said as if reading her mind. "Until you find somewhere you'd rather be. The house would be lonely if we all leave at once."

She nodded, trying to imagine the house empty of male voices...and the patter of Minette's little feet. It was good, good that the others would be together and safe, but her heart kept crying at the loss.

"Saturday, then." Ryder's bed, covered in clothing and bags, received a rueful look. "Who wants to offer me a bed?"

"Mine is big enough for all of us." Ben pulled Emma against his solid body and anchored her to his side with a steely arm—and oh, she needed the comforting hold right then.

"But not until you take a shower, bro," Ben added. "You still have sawdust in your hair."

SAWDUST? SHOWER? RYDER turned. At Ben's nod toward Emma, he caught on. Two hunters. One adorable little prey.

By the God, how could they leave her behind? His heart already ached as if some creature had clawed it open.

He ran his hand through hair and nodded. "Yeah, I'm a mess. So are you, Griz." Picking up the bait, he ran with it despite the effort it took to keep his tone light. "And Emma looks as if she was mud wrestling with the cub. Is your shower big enough for three?"

"As a matter of fact, yeah. C'mere, li'l muddy." With a smooth move, Ben scooped Emma off her feet. When she gave an unbearlike squeak, he laughed, but Ryder could see the grief in his eyes.

"Let's go, bro." Ben led the way upstairs to his room and set Emma on her feet in his master bedroom.

Pausing to lock the door, Ryder watched as his brother pulled the bard's sweater up and off.

Her eyes widened. "Ben, this isn't… Ryder, we shouldn't…" When she anxiously looked at Ryder for help, he actually found a smile.

She was theirs—and they were going to share. To please their female as littermates should. No matter how far they'd travel from her, she belonged to them, and them to her. Perhaps someday, he and Ben could return and claim their mate.

For now… "Yes, little bear. We should." The rightness of

the moment filled Ryder, moving him forward. She was all pale, smooth skin covering luscious curves. He ran his finger down her arm. "I want to touch all of that silky skin."

"Aye. You have too many clothes on, sweet honey bear," Ben agreed and undid the back hooks of her bra.

Ryder slid the garment off and filled his palms with her full breasts.

Her pupils dilated.

Ben reached around to unzip her jeans and knelt to tug them down to her ankles. Since she was barefoot, Ryder gripped her waist and lifted her up so Ben could slide everything right off.

"By the God, you're beautiful, Emma," Ryder said. A confused flush lit her face and saddened him. She still didn't believe she was lovely. He'd only been working on her insecurity for a few days. And now, he wouldn't see her achieve complete confidence. Wouldn't be the one to help her become more secure.

"Yes, you are so very beautiful." Ben stood. Brushing Emma's hair to one side, he kissed the curve of her neck and put his arms around her so he could fondle her breasts. "Mmmhmm, I do love these."

Her laugh was husky with arousal and sadness. "You're male. Of course you do."

Stripping down, Ryder tossed his clothes in a heap on the floor. The cool air felt like a shock against his overheated skin.

She stared at his erect cock. "Um…I thought we were showering."

Fuck, she was sweet.

"Oh, darlin', you know we're going to do more than that." Ben turned her head far enough to ravage her mouth. "A lot more," he whispered. His eyes revealed his sadness, even as he smiled down at her before pushing her gently into Ryder's arms.

As Ben undressed, Ryder pulled Emma closer, storing up

memories of how her smooth skin felt against his. How her female form padded her muscles to make enchanting curves for his hard hands to caress. Her breasts flattened against his chest as he tightened his embrace, and her stomach and pelvis cradled his shaft in softness. His whole body tightened with desire as he bent and took her mouth.

He looked up. Ben had disappeared. The shower turned on.

All right then. He lifted Emma and cradled her close to his chest. As always, her expression held wonder, as if being carried made her feel special. If only he could stay, he'd carry her everywhere if that's what she needed to feel as beautiful as she really was.

The warmly hued Mediterranean master bath had granite tile flooring and brownish-gold marble countertops. Smoky glass surrounded a shower easily capable of holding three people. An equally massive soaking tub stood in front of the arching tower windows. "Obviously built by a comfort-loving bear."

"Damn straight." Ben lowered the overhead lights to a seductive dimness.

When Ben held open the door to the rectangular shower area, Ryder carried Emma in. Water fell in a steady stream from three overhead rainfall devices. Hand-held showers hung neatly on the left and right walls.

As Ryder set Emma on her feet, Ben entered the shower, closed the door—and pushed her under one of the downpours.

Her hair was drenched immediately. Rather than screaming, she laughed. "You're an evil bear."

"Aye," Ben agreed.

Ryder shook his head. Fuck, was anything finer than the way she enjoyed life? How could his love for her keep growing? He could swear the feeling had started the size of a pea and now felt more the size of a mountain—and the ache at the thought of losing her had grown to that size as well. If only they could stay.

Understanding in his gaze, Ben nodded to a container on the wall. "Shampoo."

"Right." While Ryder lathered Emma's long hair, Ben started washing the dirt from her body, making chiding noises when he found scrapes and scratches. "Gonna have to talk with those cubs, tell them to play a little less rough."

"DON'T YOU DARE," Emma managed to say, "or I'll wallop you." Her last words sounded strangled as the scent of the males' desire surrounded her, pulling her into a whirlpool of need. They both chuckled—and caressed her with firm, callused hands.

As Ryder's strong fingers massaged conditioner into her hair, her eyes closed with pleasure.

Ben stopped soaping her breasts to tease her nipples to hard points.

"Benjamin." Her attempt at a teacher's admonishment was ruined by the tremor in her voice. Her whole body seemed to shimmer with arousal. "You two were the ones who needed showers."

"You got a point, darlin'." He filled her right hand with soap gel. "Clean us up. Me… then Ryder." The utterly confident command sent a thrill of awareness through her.

Ben…and Ryder. Both of them. She wasn't sure if the trembling in her center was from anticipation or anxiety. After she'd spent the night with Ryder last week, Ben had warned her that he and Ryder would soon share her.

He'd even been preparing her so she could take them together. Now the time had come.

And he'd given her something to do, bless him. "Wash you?" She hadn't been very forward in their lovemaking, but the sensual set of his lips said he'd enjoy it if she touched him. A shiver of delight ran down her spine. She could enjoy him just as he did her.

She wanted to please them so badly her fingers trembled. Could she show how much she loved them with just her touch? "Hold still," she told Ben before glancing at Ryder.

Smiling slightly, the cat leaned against the marble wall, the water hitting his finely sculpted shoulders and chest. His eyes were dark with lust as he waited.

For her.

Oh Goddess, she was going to miss them so much.

Swallowing past the thickness in her throat, Emma flattened her left hand on Ben's broad chest, feeling the short, springy hair tickle her palm. Water streamed in rivulets between the muscular planes of his pectorals.

"Maybe some soap, pretty bard?"

She heard the rumble of his deep voice. Eventually the meaning registered. "Oh. Of course." Her right hand had the soap gel, didn't it? She sudsed his chest and had to remind herself to scrub. Slowly, she worked from his chest to his ridged abdomen. His whole body was a testament to power and strength. The reddened scar on his shoulder was only the first of the collection of past hurts, all showing how he'd fulfilled the God's trust in him and guarded the clan.

She ran her fingers down a taut muscle diagonally from his stomach to his hip, then traced the crease between his hip and thigh. And tried to swallow again.

Emerging from trimmed brown hair, his cock was massively erect and darkly engorged.

To tease him—and herself—she detoured to cup his full, heavy testicles, instead. When she fondled them, he growled in approval.

But his patience was limited. Within a minute, he moved her hand to his erection.

"Oh? You want this washed, too?" she asked, trying for innocence…and couldn't suppress her laughter.

He huffed, half in exasperation, half amused.

She closed her fingers. He was thick and hot in her grip with engorged veins swirling around the base. Irresistibly masculine. She gathered more soap and stroked up and down.

By the time she'd made sure his cock had reached previously unsurpassed levels of cleanliness, low growls accompanied his exhalations, and his eyes were alight with a menacing promise.

He gripped her wrists and pulled her hands from his groin. "Ryder's turn, honey bear, or I'll push you against the wall and take you right now."

His rasped threat sent heat pooling in her pelvis.

It wasn't easy to move away from Ben…but the minute her gaze met Ryder's, her feet took her right to him. Oh, he had such a magnificent face and body. A couple of inches shorter and not as broad as the bear, Ryder had the lethal, sleek muscles of a cougar-shifter.

His gaze held hers as she ran her hands over the dark, taut skin of his biceps, his hard, contoured chest, and his lean ribs.

Steam billowed up, wrapped around her, and turned the males to shadowy forms.

Exploring more from feel than sight, Emma stroked down Ryder's tight, flat belly to find his heavy erection. Ben's was thicker; Ryder's was longer. His male musk blended with the light pine fragrance of the soap and made her think of sex on a mountaintop.

Last night, Ben had shown her how much he enjoyed her lips on him. Would Ryder?

Unable to resist, she knelt and took him in her mouth. First, the velvety, spongy head and next, the silkier shaft with the skin so tight…

His groan mingled with the quiet *whooshing* of steam through the pipes and the sound of falling water from the rainfall showerhead.

Wanting only to please him, she used her hand and mouth, and heard his breathing change. Her other hand was on his thigh, and she was delighted beyond measure when she felt the uncontrolled quivering of his muscles. *I love you, Ryder.*

With a deep growl, Ryder lifted her easily to her feet. "You are too good at that, little bear." His kiss was slow and deep and lovely.

She glanced at Ben, but he shook his head to the unspoken offer and pointed toward the shower bench. "We have other plans for you, honey bear."

"Come here, my female." Ryder led her to one side of the shower and seated himself on the hip-high stone bench. The bench was wide enough he could lean back against the wall with his feet on the floor. His cock rose straight up in invitation. He patted his thighs and smiled slowly.

Her body broke out in goosebumps as she felt Ben move closer behind her. Two males. Anxiety dimmed her arousal. They were so big.

"Li'l bear," Ben murmured as he caressed her shoulders with his strong hands. "You've taken my fingers back there before, but, yes, I'll be larger."

She gulped at the thought of just how large he really was.

"We'll stop if you don't like this," he continued. "You never have to do anything you don't want to do."

Both males inside her. At her shiver, his hands tightened.

"I want...want to try." She looked over her shoulder, up into his observant blue eyes, seeing both the hunger and the self-restraint. She'd never met anyone more disciplined. He'd take care of her, as would Ryder.

How could she not share herself—all of herself—on their last night together? This was right. The way it should be. "Yes."

"*Cariad*, you are amazing." He smiled, grasped her waist, and helped her straddle Ryder's hips with her knees on the bench.

Cariad. Darling. Her eyes blurred with tears for a second. How would she survive when they were gone? She looked down into Ryder's hard face and saw the misery in his dark eyes.

He was hurting, too. *Oh, Ryder.*

His lean hands closed on her bottom, and she felt the head of his cock press against her entrance.

When she hesitated, his lips quirked. "This part isn't new to you, little bear." Firmly, he guided her down. His cock slid between her slick, wet folds and in, stretching her, filling her completely, and leaving a dark hunger in its wake.

Oh, she loved the way he felt inside.

His hands tightened on her hips. His eyes were now half-lidded. "Fuck, yes."

All along her nerve endings, she felt the hum of desire. Her clit throbbed a pulsing demand that she move. She lifted, almost all the way off his shaft, and started to lower, but his grip on her bottom stopped her. "Stay right there, Emma."

"But—"

He curled a hand around her nape and pulled her down for a kiss.

As Ryder's lips moved over hers, she felt Ben move closer behind her. "Hold on, darlin'. Let's open you up a bit." His lubricated fingers slid between her buttocks. A single digit pressed against her anus. Before she could tighten against him, he steadily pushed past the rings of muscle and inside.

He'd done that before, yet every time the foreign sensation was a surprise. Instinctively, she tried to straighten—and Ryder's hand held her in place, keeping her mouth against his. Keeping her bent and accessible to his littermate's touch.

Her head spun. New nerves awakened as Ben's penetrating finger slid in and out, pumping slowly and steadily.

She made a helpless sound, and Ryder squeezed her nape.

"Look at me."

With an effort, she lifted her head and stared into his mid-night-black eyes. He studied her, then smiled. "She's good. Keep going, bro."

A protest broke from her a second before he kissed her again, his tongue invading her mouth in the same way that Ben's finger—now two fingers—took possession of her most private area.

The ease with which they moved and positioned her told her they'd done this before—many, many times; that particular thought was unappealing. Did they even know who they were mating? Was she just another body? Would they forget her once they were gone? She stilled, bowing her head.

And the males instantly stopped.

"Emma?" Ben leaned over her, his muscular chest against her back. "What's wrong, darlin'? We can stop if you're not happy."

Ryder cupped her cheek with one hand, his gaze worried. "Tell us what's in your head."

"I just"—her uncertainty evaporated under the concentrated pressure of their attention—"just felt insecure for a moment. I mean…emotionally or something." Now she felt as scatter-brained as a pixie. "Let's just go on."

Rather than moving, Ryder caressed her cheek, his chiseled face softening. "Insecure, huh? Little bear, do you have any idea how much you mean to me? To us?"

Her breathing stilled for a long moment. The desire in his eyes had hidden the love that was there as well.

Love.

Oh. The world went hazy as her eyes filled with tears. "I…didn't know."

"Well, now you do." Ryder ran his thumb over her lower lip. "We don't have to take you at the same time, though."

"I…" His thumb was slightly rough, yet warm against her lip. His cock was barely inside her. Ben's hands were still on her hips, so big and powerful.

And her desire surged back to life with an added zing from knowing she'd mate with two males who…who cared for her.

Who she loved with all her heart.

With a wiggle of her hips, she smiled down at Ryder. "I want you both. Now. Together." *Want to keep you, to be with you.*

"As you wish, little bear." Ryder grinned.

"Darlin'." Ben kissed her cheek, so very gently, and straightened.

Ryder shifted her slightly and reached down between them. His fingers stroked her clit, sliding through her wetness, and the exquisite sensation sizzled right to her depths. Every other thought fled before the onrush of need.

She tried to move forward, to get more friction there. Or to lower herself onto his erection. Her pussy was hollow, craving to be filled. "More."

Ryder had a hand on her left hip. Ben on her right. They didn't let her move.

"Brace yourself, li'l bear." The head of Ben's shaft pressed against her. Her entire backside tried to jerk away without success within their unyielding restraint.

Ryder's cock was just inside her vagina as he waited.

The pressure against her anus increased as the head of Ben's shaft gained entry. As he moved in and out, advancing slowly, she started to shake.

He applied additional cool lubricant, and started again. He was, indeed, bigger than his two fingers. Everything back there was stretching. Burning. "Oh, please."

It felt good. It hurt. No, it felt *good*. The sound of her ragged breathing echoed off the glass walls, and Ben stopped.

"Look at me, my little bear." Ryder lifted her head with confident hands. His gaze searched her face, and he smiled. "Yep, still okay. Keep going, bro."

The sound of Ben's rumbled agreement broke over her before he gripped her securely. He slid all the way in, impaling her completely, and possessing her in a way that stole her will. Stole *everything*. Oh, Goddess, no mating had ever felt like this. A tremor shook her whole body.

As Ryder ran his finger around her clit, her fingernails dug into his shoulder, and his touch grew firmer. Pleasure seized her, tightening her around Ben's cock. With just the tip of Ryder's shaft at the entrance of her pussy, she felt empty. Yet the thought of him and Ben both being inside her was... Oh, that would be too much.

Ryder reached up to one of the handheld hoses and flicked it on.

Ben's low chuckle echoed off the walls. "I might have known you'd find a toy. Let me tilt her back, so you can play, cat."

"You're on."

Play? What did he mean *play*? Water was beading on her body, heat engulfing her from inside and out.

Ben cupped her left breast and straightened her up, leaning slightly back. The movement drove him deeper, and she wiggled, gasping. He curved his other hand over her right hip and buttock in a strong grip.

Ryder set the hose on his stomach, directing the jetting stream of water away from his face—and directly onto her clit.

"Ahhh!" She jumped, but was immobilized by Ben's implacable hands and the huge shaft penetrating her. "Stay still, darlin'." His laugh resounded through the shower.

Couldn't move. Could only take what they wanted to do to her. As the molten feeling deep in her core grew, her bones melted...right along with her willpower.

Ryder played with the shower controls until soft jets of water struck her vulnerable clit in a merciless *sh-sh-sh-sh*.

Under the intense pleasure, her clit was tightening. The unstoppable sensation gained in intensity, growing and growing, like nothing she'd ever felt before.

And then the tension hit a peak, fast and fierce, and the climax slammed into her, through her. Her back arched as her insides spasmed against the thick penetration in her backside, rebounding with added waves of sensation. Her body shuddered—and the hands on her held her ruthlessly as she came and came and came.

When she opened her eyes, she stared into Ryder's intent gaze and realized she was panting and whining.

"Easy now, darlin'." Ben helped her lean forward.

With hands splayed, she braced herself on Ryder's chest, feeling as if her world was crumbling around her. More than the climax, their concern for her shook her deep inside. *Don't leave me. Please.*

When Ryder caressed her cheek with a gentle hand, tears filled her eyes.

"Aw, now, don't do that, little bear," he said. "Ben..." The worried look in his eyes was wonderfully sweet.

She blinked quickly and managed to smile. Bless the master bard for teaching her how to control her voice. "I'm fine. Really."

The worry in his gaze didn't lighten, but he managed a slight smile. "You are so gorgeous when you come. Need a repeat of that."

As her eyes widened, he looked over her shoulder at his brother.

"We'll get right on that. You ready now, darlin'?" Ben gave her all of one second's warning before he slowly pressed her down onto Ryder's cock.

"Uhhhh. Oh, oh, oh." Suddenly she was impossibly full. Her pussy spasmed around Ryder's hard shaft; her back hole contracted around Ben's. She squirmed helplessly as the unstoppable pressure grew, coalesced, and exploded, sending blasts of pulsating pleasure throughout her body. "Ooooh, Goddess..." Her fingernails dug furrows into Ryder's chest.

Ben's cheek was scratchy against hers. "Fuck, sweetheart, I... *Fuck*." A low, sexy growl escaped him. "All right, darlin', we're going to take you hard now, so hang on."

Hard? Worry trickled in, but she was too satisfied to tense up. Instead, she leaned her weight on her arms and curled her fingers over Ryder's shoulders.

Carefully, Ben withdrew his cock from her almost completely. His hands on her hips tightened as he lifted her up and off Ryder's shaft, and a second later, he thrust back in.

"Oh..." Sensations blasted through her. The disconcertingly wonderful fullness in her back hole conflicted with the emptiness of her pussy. The rush of hungry need seared her nerve endings and hazed her mind.

Ben slid out, paused, and slammed her down onto Ryder's shaft, filling her pussy. Before she could moan, he'd lifted her off and plunged into her from behind.

Empty. Full. As the two cocks pistoned in and out, her fingers dug into Ryder's shoulders at the exquisite dance of pleasure. The air filled with the sound of pleading whimpers...from her.

"Ah, perhaps a little more stimulation would be good." Ryder adjusted something and then a pulsing stream of water struck her exposed clit every time Ben lifted her up.

A shaking started deep in her core as her whole lower half turned into one burgeoning sensation, and everything within her tightened. Tightened.

Without ceasing, without mercy, she was raised up off Ryder's cock so Ben could thrust into her even as the stinging force of the water would zing across her clit. Then, as Ben withdrew, he'd lower her hips to impale her on Ryder's shaft.

Over and over and over.

Too much.

Every muscle in her body tensed; her breathing stopped. Nothing existed except Ben's big hands on her hips, the sliding out of Ryder's long cock, the penetration of Ben's thick shaft into the other hole…and then the jet of water striking her over-sensitized clit.

Pleasure flooded her in a massive current of sensation, shooting through the rapids, shaking her helplessly in its grip as her cries echoed off the walls.

Slowly, the spasms eased. She realized her males were waiting, unmoving. Letting her recover. Her eyelids were heavy, but she opened her eyes.

Ryder's intense gaze was on her, satisfaction in his expression. "So fucking gorgeous," he murmured.

"Aye, she is." Ben lifted her again, starting the cycle, but this time, she could watch. Could see Ryder's jaw tense. Feel his muscles tighten under her hands. And then he lifted his hips to drive himself deeper as he growled his release.

Ben's hands tightened on her hips as he followed, holding her in place as he rumbled in pleasure.

The searing heat of their seed filled her and sent her over again with a helpless whimper. As her arms gave out, she went limp, dropping onto Ryder's chest, gasping for air.

Ryder stroked her hair. "Shh, shh, shh."

Ben leaned forward, his cheek against hers. "Easy, darlin'," he growled under his breath. The two held her between them as she shook, their hands as gentle now as they'd been firm before.

Cared for. Cherished. Everything she'd longed for. By the Mother, she loved them.

Eventually, Ben withdrew, cleaned himself and her, and lifted her up and off of Ryder. He steadied her with an arm around her waist, which was good, since her legs were trembling like aspen leaves in a pitiless wind.

"Thank you, Emma." Ryder stepped in front of her and kissed her deeply. And then he turned her to his littermate.

Ben's kiss was firm. Demanding. Dominating. And then he took her chin and lifted her face. In the steam of the shower, she saw his eyes, blue as the sky, level and controlled and tender. "Seems like we should have said this at the start rather than now, but…we love you, darlin'."

Her eyes stung with tears. The words—words she'd waited all her life to hear.

As if to emphasize the meaning, Ryder wrapped his arms around her from behind and rubbed his water-softened beard against her cheek. He whispered the words again. "We love you, little bear."

As a sob escaped her, Ben cradled her face against his broad chest. "Shh. You're not supposed to cry when you hear you're loved." He chuckled. "We love you, Emma."

Oh, I love you. Love you, love you. The words were there, on her lips, waiting. Not emerging. Trapped and caged in her own insecurities.

She had a feeling they already knew, though.

"Fuck, we're going to miss her," Ryder said under his breath to Ben.

Ben's answer was almost a sigh. "Aye."

How could she live without them? Then, with a startling blaze of understanding, she knew she could give them the actions of love, if not the words. "I'm coming with you."

Wait.

Oh Goddess, what had she said? What if they laughed and—

Under her cheek, Ben's muscles tensed. "You'll come... You'd leave Cold Creek? Come with us?"

She could hear the surging desire in his voice, and her heart leaped in response.

"What? No." Ryder shoved his brother without releasing her. "She has a life here. We can't ask her—"

"You want me? Really?" Like wind-whipped leaves, her hopes spiraled up into the air.

"Yes, honey bear." Ben's answer came from deep in his chest, emerging in the lowest of bass notes. "Very, very much."

Her eyes filled with tears at his unshakable certainty She pushed away from Ben far enough to turn and look at Ryder. "You want me? With you?"

"Emma." The hope on his face was raw and absolute. "Fuck, yes."

Abandon everything—her new friends, her work as a bard, this welcoming town—and go who knew where. The decision was huge. Momentous. And required no thought at all. They wanted her. Loved her. *Her.*

"You'll come with us? Be with us?" Ryder's voice was as rough as tree bark. "Stay with us?"

"Yes. Yes, yes, yes."

Ben snorted a laugh. "My bard, you got quite a way with words."

"Words are overrated." Heart overflowing, she wrapped her arms around them both so she could cover their faces with her kisses. *My grizzly, my cat. Mine, mine, mine.*

Chapter Twenty-Nine

Cold Creek, North Cascades Territory – dark of the moon

WISHING HE COULD change to grizzly and rip something apart with his teeth and claws, Ben stood with Amanda Golden in front of his house on Sunday morning.

The blonde realtor frowned. "I know how much work you've put into this place. Are you sure you want to sell it?"

Not fucking at all. Just the thought was a stab right through his heart. But it'd be a crime to leave the house to fall to ruin again. Houses had their own kind of souls, and the old Victorian had been happy when he'd started restoring it. He'd felt its pleasure when Minette trotted up and down the stairs, when Emma burst into laughter, when they sang together in the great room.

The old place had waited a decade to have a family again, and its disappointment at their move would be as heartrending as his own. "I'm afraid so, Amanda. Can you have some comparisons and a listing agreement prepared by tomorrow?"

She stared at him. "I… Well, that's fast. Make that tomorrow afternoon and you're on."

Monday afternoon? Uneasy, he rubbed the back of his neck. It'd be better if he and his family left right this moment.

But he couldn't. Looked like there'd be one *more* fucking

delay. Their plan to leave today had already been revised after Owen had texted that he'd be gone tonight. Damn the cat for choosing to leave Cold Creek on a dark of the moon night. Without Owen, Alec would need Ben. A single cahir couldn't survive a hellhound, and both teams were needed to cover the town.

The delay had pissed him off, but he, Ryder, and Emma revised their schedule to leave at sunrise on Monday. Now they'd have to wait until the afternoon. *Fine.* One minute after signing Amanda's papers, they'd hit the road and be well out of the North Cascades Territory before Calum returned on Tuesday.

The knowledge he'd be able to take his family—all of his family—heartened him. He and Ryder would have the time they'd need to convince the little bear to accept them as life-mates. She was already willing to leave the life she'd just started to stay with them. So fucking brave and loyal... By the God, he loved her.

"Ben?" Amanda prompted.

"Right. I agree."

"Then I'll see you tomorrow at three," Amanda said. "Actually, I'll be at the barbecue this afternoon for a while, so I might see you."

"Barbecue." He frowned. "Hell, I'd forgotten." Zeb and Shay put on a barbecue at the Wildwood Lodge every couple of weeks during the summer. And everyone would expect to see Ben and his people there. Right. "Yeah, we'll be there. See you then."

He'd patrol tonight. Sign papers tomorrow. Leave.

Once they were out of the territory, he'd call and let Zeb and Shay know they'd be down a cahir. To prevent any preemptive moves by Genevieve, they'd decided to keep the move quiet. Speaking of which... "I'd rather people not know I'm selling until the house goes on the market. You good with that?"

The realtor stiffened. "Of course. I consider everything confidential until given permission to share."

"Great. Thank you."

As the realtor got in her car and drove away, Ben turned and looked at his home. Small white buds were poking up in the flowerbed Emma had worked on. A light was on over the garage where Ryder was working in his office.

All too soon, everything would be dark again, and weeds would smother the tiny struggling plants. The house's loneliness chilled his skin. *I'm sorry.*

WITH BEN ON her left, Ryder and Minette on her right, Emma walked across the graveled parking area in front of the Wildwood Lodge. The signs of summer were everywhere—the leaves a deeper green, the high cheep of baby birds, tree fairies putting on weight. Planter boxes on the lodge railing displayed budding flowers.

The world was celebrating the fertile season—and Emma was in love.

Ben and Ryder loved her. *Loved. Her.* They'd said so, and neither was a puppy to be infatuated and blurt out something he didn't mean.

She saw again Ben's level, careful eyes. *"We love you, darlin'".* Ryder's dark velvet voice murmured in her memory, *"We love you, little bear."* A shiver of delight and sheer wonder ran through her. She'd never dared to dream they'd actually love her back.

Please, please, please, let everything come out right.

"Emma?" Ryder ran his hand up her arm. "You all right?"

"I'm fine." *Focus, bear.* She glanced at the parking area, only two-third's full. "I thought there would be more people here."

"Looks are deceiving. The tavern is just down that path." Ben pointed at a trail that started in the forested area on the far side of the parking area. "People without cubs park at the Wild Hunt and walk."

Ben led them around to the back of the lodge and under a purple clematis-covered arbor. As Ben paid for their admission at a reception table, Emma looked around.

One end of a wide patio boasted a massive grill, food-laden tables, and drink-and-ice-filled tubs. Townspeople were milling around, seated at the tables, and playing volleyball and other games on the lawn. A small playground swarmed with cubs, and their squeals of glee rang out into the clear afternoon air.

Her mother had hosted formal dinner affairs. This relaxed Sunday barbecue looked like far more fun.

Ben pulled her against his side. "I think you probably know most of the guests here."

Ryder shifted Minette to his other arm and took Emma's hand. Bracketed by her two males, she felt wonderfully claimed, giving her a stable home from which to venture forth.

"I think you're right," she said.

In the center of the patio, Alec sat at a table across from the tough old werecat who owned BOOKS.

Angie stood near the barbecue talking with an older human male. It was interesting to see both Daonain and humans at a party. In Pine Knoll, shifters avoided the humans.

The ruthless-looking cahir named Zeb was turning steaks on the grill.

"Ben, you made it." Shay, the other owner of the lodge walked out of the house with a box filled with beer and soda. The sandy-haired male was almost as wide-shouldered and tall as Ben. He grinned at Minette. "Hey, little one, you want an orange pop?"

Minette edged behind her father, but nodded.

The cahir knelt...and was still taller than the cubling. "I'm Shay. Your daddy Ben and I hunt together."

A shiver ran over Emma's skin. The statement sounded so innocent. Minette wouldn't know they hunted hellhounds.

Shay pulled a can of soda off the plastic ring, opened it, and handed it over, moving as slowly as he would with a wild animal. Bree had a good male.

Releasing Ryder's hand, Minette held the can with both hands to take a sip. She gave Shay a shy smile.

"Thought you'd like it." When he stood, he was joined by Bree, who curved an arm around his waist.

"Breanne, have you met my brother, Ryder?" Ben asked.

The way Ryder's fingers tensed on Emma's said the construction crew's animosity had made him wary. He'd have skipped this event if he and Ben hadn't wanted to present a normal appearance.

Bree smiled and held out her hand. "I've been wanting to thank you for the work you've done on the pack houses."

Ryder relaxed. "It was a pleasure."

"Emma, you're here. Ryder, Ben, it's good to see you." In a purple T-shirt and jeans, Vicki strolled over.

"Vicki, you're looking well." Ben paused and took a discreet sniff. "Very well."

Emma inhaled and caught a hint of something she couldn't evaluate before the breeze shifted away. No one else seemed to notice. Then again, the grizzly had an incredibly acute sense of smell, even as a human.

"I'm so glad you all came." Bree turned to Emma. "Especially you, Ms. Bard. Is there any chance we can get you to sing for us?" She hesitated. "Uh. Am I allowed to ask a bard to sing?"

Breanne was human-raised, Emma reminded herself. In fact, from the grief she'd shown when she spoke of her past, her tale was undoubtedly worthy of a song.

Only...I won't be here. I'll never hear Breanne's story. Pain slashed down, deep enough to hit bone. Pulling in a breath, she forced a smile. "You can do a bard no higher honor than wanting a song."

"Wonderful. Actually…" Breanne bit her lip and looked up at her mate.

"Let me ask her, *mo leannán*." Shay took Emma's hand with the gentleness exhibited by extremely large males. "We wanted to ask if you could sing for an hour at all of our summer barbecues. If you agree, Calum will let you move your Sunday performances here."

Emma hesitated. She wouldn't be in Cold Creek to sing, not after tomorrow. The pain in her heart ached like a pulled muscle. Soon she'd be without friends, without her work as a bard, without the cubs she'd taught. But, Ben and Ryder and Minette were worth it.

Shay was waiting for an answer.

What could she tell him? "If…" She faltered. Lying to these friends was…hard.

Vicki's perceptive glance went from her, to Ben whose face had tightened, to Ryder, and finally to Minette.

"I'm—" She thought of nothing she could say. "I need to, um, think."

"Of course." Although his gaze had grown disconcertingly sharp, Shay gave her a half-smile. "We'll discuss it later. How's that?"

Emma gave a relieved breath. "Thank you. And I'll be happy to sing tonight."

"Good enough."

Vicki was frowning.

Oh, Mother's grace, I messed up. Perhaps a quick retreat was indicated. Emma turned to Breanne. "I see some females I haven't met yet, and I'd love introductions."

"Of course."

THE AFTERNOON PASSED into evening marked by lively conversations. Ben would miss these parties. And his friends. And the community. The soft sigh of the sheltering forest seemed to echo his feelings.

He'd miss Breanne's cooking, too. There'd been enough food that even he was satisfied, although he'd prudently halted a couple of hours ago. Last week, a hellhound had been scented near the south of town, and with Owen gone, Ben's patrol would be short a cahir. With only him and Alec, if a fight happened, he'd need all the speed he could muster.

Leaning back, he stretched his legs under the table. Quiet had descended along with the setting sun and cooler tempera-ture. Most of the guests had departed. Tables arranged in a petal-like cluster, the cahirs and their families occupied the center of the patio.

Seated at one table, Zeb, Shay, and Breanne took turns mak-ing the rounds to replenish their guests' drinks and food.

Vicki and Alec sat between old Joe Thorson and Wells, the human who'd been Vicki's boss when she was a spy.

On Ben's right was Emma, then Ryder with Minette in his lap. She was sucking her thumb and sleepily rubbing the end of Emma's braid over her cheek.

Alec was studying the cub…and had been all evening, Ben realized.

Alec's green gaze met Ben's before the sheriff turned and said to Zeb, "It's good to have the summer barbeques going again. And I noticed the new playground equipment you added over the winter."

Zeb acknowledged the comment with a grunt of dismissal.

Ben grinned. The tough cahir wouldn't admit he had a soft spot for cubs, but he was the one who'd decided to add a playground to the lodge. And he'd built it from scratch. Minette loved the swings, slides, and monkey bars contraption.

After studying the playground, the human Wells har-rumphed and remarked to Vicki, "Guess those kids you're going to have will appreciate the fun."

Vicki's mouth dropped open. The retired Marine looked as if she'd been tossed unarmed into a firefight. "You… How can you tell? I haven't said a word."

"I'm a spy, Morgan; it's what we do." His thin lips curved up. "And you're rather obviously changing shape."

"Obviously?" Her gaze met Alec's, and her swallow was audible. "You knew, too. Didn't you?"

He shot Wells an irritated frown. "This wasn't the traditional announcement that Calum had in mind."

"You *both* knew." Vicki scowled at her mate. "How?"

Ben suppressed a smile. Having been human until recently, the werecat occasionally displayed amusing gaps in her Daonain education.

Running a finger down her cheek, Alec said, "A female's scent changes as her body does."

She growled. "Fucking scent-sniffing, snoopy cats. I'm going to find hot pepper lotion and burn you out for a week."

Over the laughter rounding the table, Ben heard her ask Alec, "Are you and Calum okay with this? Happy?"

Alec picked her up and set her on his lap so he could kiss her. When she emerged from his embrace, Alec looked equally content.

Ben leaned toward his own female and put his arm behind her back. *Mine.* He met Ryder's gaze. Even better. *Ours.*

Snuggling his mate against his shoulder, Alec said quietly, "Calum and I are still surprised at how quickly you got pregnant. Are you unhappy?"

She rubbed her cheek against his. "I'm in shock…but happy. Since Jamie's broken me in, maybe I'll be an okay mother."

"You're an awesome mom," Calum's daughter said. "Especially since you'll let me go to Hector's party next week."

"No." The word came from both Vicki and Alec.

"Jeez." The girl scowled. "Well, I'm happy anyway. I'm going to be a wonderful big sister. I hope I get at least four new siblings."

Vicki turned pale, setting off more laughter.

From the glint in Jamie's eyes, she'd known how Vicki would react. Tricky little female. She must drive her fathers crazy.

At that age, Minette might well have him and Ryder chasing their tails. But she, too, would be an excellent older sister. As a vision of Emma, ripe with his and Ryder's babies, filled his brain, he pulled her closer.

The strong current of joy pulled him into dreams of the future. He and Ryder would share her and create a family filled with laughter, bickering, and love.

He felt a touch on his chest and looked down into sunlit amber eyes. "Are you all right?" she whispered.

Damn, he loved her. "Oh, yeah." He ran his knuckles over the sweet curve of her cheek.

"A shame you'll be on the wagon for the next few months. This is excellent beer," Wells said to Vicki before lifting his glass. "To the Sergeant."

Vicki shot him a steaming look, but Ben noticed she had iced tea in front of her, rather than alcohol.

A chorus of voices joined in the toast: "To the Sergeant."

Thorson grinned. "You piss her off enough, Wells, and one of her cubs will be named after me and none will have your name."

When Wells' face blanked, Ben smothered a laugh. As a werecat, Thorson had a talent for gutting his opponents, whether with words or claws.

"*Cubs with an 's'?* Oh, fucking A, I'm not ready for *multiples*," Vicki moaned and laid her head on the table. "Someone shoot me. *Now.*"

Laughing, Alec pulled her up and hugged her. "You're not alone. You have all of us. Family, Vixen."

"Okay. Yeah. This is true." Vicki pressed her forehead against his shoulder.

A longing sigh came from the li'l bear pressed against Ben's side. He saw his brother had heard it as well.

Ryder curled his hand around Emma's.

"If you're finished with the mushy shit," Zeb said, "can we get a few songs out of the bard before sunset when we have to patrol?"

Emma sat up straight and beamed at him. "Of course."

Choosing to stay between him and Ryder, Emma launched into a song she'd taught them last week. As Ben hummed in harmony with Ryder, he watched and enjoyed his little female. As always, she had her audience in the palm of her hand. They loved her, both as a bard and as a person. Did she realize how quickly she'd become accepted in the close-knit community?

Damn, but he hated that she'd be leaving the first real home she'd ever had. Hated that for him and Ryder, as well.

Emma sang until she noticed the darkening sky and smoothly ended her performance. At the enthusiastic applause, she smiled—and only Ben noticed her bounce of delight. "Thank you all."

Rising, Ben pulled her to her feet. "We need to get going. I want to see you home and locked up tight for the night."

Zeb, who was stacking dishes, turned and glared at Shay. "You forgot to ask them, didn't you?"

His partner winced. "I did. Yeah."

Ben paused. "Ask what?"

"Ah," Shay said. "Our mate hates being alone in the lodge

on the dark of the moon. We'd planned to ask your family to stay the night."

Ben glanced at Ryder. He and Emma had figured on packing this evening. "Up to you, bro."

Ryder studied Breanne. "It bothers you to be here alone?"

Breanne flushed, but nodded. "Even someone sleeping upstairs is better than an empty lodge. But I understand if you prefer to be in your own home."

"Having hellhounds around would make anyone feel insecure." Ryder tugged on Emma's braid. "I'm fine with staying here if you are, little bear."

Ben smothered a smile. To strangers, Ryder often appeared as cold as a chiseled statue. Friends and family soon learned his façade covered a tender heart.

Emma said to Breanne, "I know how you feel." The way her hand tightened around Ben's let him know she'd worry over his safety, as well. "Company is better. We'd love to be your guests."

"Thank you both. We'll feel better if our mate isn't afraid." A corner of Zeb's mouth turned up, and Ben knew that was his equivalent of a happy puppy's tail wag. "Bree can show her gratitude by feeding you breakfast in the morning. You'll never have had better."

"Damn, you're getting fucking diplomatic, *a mhac*," Shay said.

Zeb growled. "I'm not your son, dumbass." He glanced at Ben. "You and Alec get started. Shay and I are going to drive to those outlying houses where we found spoor. If nothing pops, we'll return here to drop off the truck and take up our usual patrol pattern."

GOODBYES WERE SAID, and the lodge emptied. Ben and Alec left on patrol. Shay and Zeb drove away. Emma, Ryder, and

Minette remained with Bree.

Thank goodness they had work to do, Emma thought. Her nerves were screeching like an out of tune fiddle.

They'd barely finished the cleanup of the patio before the sun disappeared. After Ryder did his own version of the inside patrol—checking the ironwork on all the windows and the locks on the heavy oak doors, he pulled her close and gave her a light kiss. "Want some time with your friend? I can go play pool in the back."

Emma gave him a grateful look. He was a wonder of a male to know she longed for more time with her friend. It was difficult to discover the joys of having friends and lose them. Not telling Bree about their departure was even harder.

Picking up Minette, Emma glanced at the stairs leading to the bedrooms. It was the cubling's bedtime. But from the way the little fingers closed on her shirt, someone was reacting to the adults' anxiety. Minette wouldn't be comfortable alone in a strange room.

She carried the child into the sitting area and settled with her on the couch. Bree was already building up the fire in the river-rock fireplace.

Open to guests, the lodge's game room, library, and conversational areas had hardwood floors, colorfully braided rugs, leather couches and chairs, and fireplaces. The décor was rustic enough that antlers mounted on the wall would have been typical...except no Daonain would anger the forest god in that way. Herne often wore antlers, and pissing him off made for a markedly shortened life.

Bree set one more log on the flames and said to the resident salamander, "There you go, buddy. You should stay nice and toasty."

An impertinent swish of a glowing tail was her only answer.

Emma looked down to see if Minette noticed, but the child's

eyes were drooping. She'd had a busy day of playing, after all. "Lie down beside me, kitten."

With a soundless sigh, the cub curled up on the couch, her head in Emma's lap. Emma tucked the colorful quilt from the back of the couch around the child. Within a few breaths, Minette dropped into a sound sleep.

"I wish I could fall asleep that fast." Bree rose and filled their glasses from an unfinished bottle of wine.

"She doesn't always." Emma took a sip. "She often has nightmares scary enough to send her running into Ryder's room." *And my room.* Knowing the child trusted her to frighten away monsters gave Emma a world of satisfaction. "Her mother must have been dreadful."

"How sad." Bree's mouth turned down. "The Daonain usually care for their children far better than humans do."

"There's always the exception." Look at her own mother. Eyes on the fire, Emma scowled. But a sweet cubling like Minette should have been treated as a precious gift.

"Well, she seems to have found herself a wonderful mother on her own." Bree smiled and nodded at Emma's lap. While sucking a thumb, the cub was clutching Emma's flannel shirt to ensure her pillow didn't move away.

The unexpected compliment made Emma's eyes puddle with tears. "Thank you."

"You were gone all afternoon!" An angry male's voice came from outside. "Where have you been?"

"My activities are none of your business," a female said loudly. The voice was familiar. "You went to the barbecue. It's not as if you had nothing to do."

Emma frowned. She'd met the female somewhere.

The male snapped, "You can't just—"

"Oh, honestly." Bree jumped to her feet. After checking the peephole, she opened the door and called to the couple in the parking area. "Please go inside, people. It's not safe and you're too loud."

"It's a free world. Don't tell us what to do," the female retorted.

Thinking to provide support, Emma slid out from under Minette and joined Bree in the doorway. The wind carried the scent of the shifters standing near the porch—a young male and a beautiful redhead.

Oh no. Genevieve.

Emma took a hasty step back. Too late.

Genevieve's eyes thinned to slits, and her face flushed a furious purple-red. "You!"

The shout roused Minette who ran across the room to wrap her arms around Emma's leg.

"You have my cub!" Genevieve charged up across the porch toward the door.

Emma picked up Minette and backed away as the female attempted to push past Bree.

"No," Bree said decisively. When Genevieve persisted, Bree grabbed her arm, whirled her in a 360-degree circle, and sent her staggering back onto the porch.

To Emma's relief, Ryder appeared. "Who screamed?"

"Genevie—" Emma's answer was interrupted by more yelling.

"That's my baby. You can't keep me from her."

Bree stood in the doorway, blocking the entrance from Genevieve and her unhappy male.

Past Bree's shoulders, Emma saw a pickup driving through the parking area. It was still moving when Zeb jumped out. He strode across the porch, shouldering past Genevieve to ask Bree, "What the fuck is going on?"

"We have a situation," Bree said, scowling at Genevieve.

Genevieve turned her gaze on Zeb, and her voice dropped

to a sickening sweetness. "Oh, I'm so glad you're here. That giant female has my cub,"

Minette started trembling.

"Easy, sweetheart," Emma whispered.

"You're safe, kitten." Ryder kissed the top of the cubling's head and strode out the door, closing it behind him.

Whatever Zeb had said to Genevieve hadn't calmed the female. She yelled. "She's mine and I'm taking her back."

As the yells of fury continued, Ryder's voice could be heard. "Genevieve, this isn't the—"

Emma tuned them all out. She had her own battle to fight—comforting a trembling cubling. Heart aching, Emma snuggled her closer. "Shhh, sweetheart. Let's go upstairs where it's quieter." The little girl tried to burrow closer as Emma carried her up to the second floor. Bree hadn't said which room they'd stay in, so Emma picked the one in the back.

She settled on the bed and pulled the child close. The noise of the verbal battle was still audible. "Have you heard the story of when a flower fairy decided she wanted to leave her garden and live in the forest instead?"

Sucking her thumb, Minette shook her head.

Outside, Genevieve shrieked and something slammed.

Minette flinched.

By the Mother, Genevieve had strong lungs. Why didn't the males gag her? Fretting inside, Emma told the fairy story and sang one of Minette's favorite songs.

Eventually there was silence downstairs, but the little girl kept shaking. Emma felt appallingly helpless. What could she do to make it better? "Do you want your daddy?"

Minette nodded.

"I'll get him." And maybe bring up some cubling comfort food, too. Rising, she picked up the fluffy afghan on the foot of the bed and tucked it around the cub.

Curled up like a pill bug, Minette pulled a pillow closer as if creating a defensive wall before she closed her eyes.

"Okay then." She planted a kiss on top of the cub's head. If that so-called mother came within arm's reach, Emma would slap her into the next territory.

She met Zeb coming in the front door, his dark face terrifyingly angry. He slammed the door behind him violently enough to shake the house and stalked into the kitchen.

She followed to find Ryder, Shay, and Breanne.

Ryder spotted her in the doorway and held out an arm. "How's Minette?"

Emma curled into his embrace, needing his strength. "She's been shivering like she was left in the snow. She wants her daddy."

"I'll go right up."

"Is the female gone?" Emma asked.

Zeb answered. "I…took her to the cabin she's sharing with two males. Told them if she didn't behave, they'd be cabinless. With a hellhound in the area. They said they'd keep her in the cabin."

"I appreciate the intervention." Ryder rubbed his face. "Fuck, I can't believe how stupid I was about her back then."

Shay slapped his shoulder. "Stupid, yes. But you got a good cub."

Emma nodded. "There is that. You two created someone special."

"Yeah." The bitterness in Ryder's face eased. He nodded to the cahirs. "Excuse me—and good luck on your patrol."

As Ryder trotted out of the kitchen, Emma turned to Bree. "Any chance I could have a cup of hot chocolate for Minette and a picture book?"

"Absolutely." Bree rummaged through the cupboards and pulled out an instant mix packet.

Shay took it from her hand. "I'll make this, *mo chridhe*. You find a book for the lass."

"Thank you." Bree kissed her mate and motioned Emma to follow. "Let's go see what would work for a little girl."

RYDER REACHED THE second floor hallway to see several doors, none open. Which room was Minette in? He didn't smell her feet on the carpet runner.

Rather than calling downstairs—the baby had heard too much shouting already—he opened the closest door. Empty. Then the next. Master bedroom. Another master bedroom. One with female fripperies. Probably Bree's. An empty guest room. Another empty guest room. The last room. Also empty.

By the God, where was she? "Minette?"

He scouted the rooms again. The last room had a rumpled quilt on the bed with Minette's scent. This was where she'd been.

The bathroom was empty. Worry tensed his gut, and he called louder, "Minette. Come on out."

And louder, "Minette!"

Fuck. Even though his nose reported she wasn't in other rooms, Ryder still checked to ensure no child hid under the bed or in the closets.

Running down the stairs, Ryder met Emma with a cup of hot chocolate in one hand and a book in the other. "She's not up there," he said.

"What?"

"Not. There." His words snapped out. "Help me find her."

Without another word, Emma followed him downstairs. She set everything on an end table. "Bree! We need to find Minette."

Bree came out of the kitchen, followed by her mates. Barefoot and shirtless, Shay was obviously preparing to patrol as a wolf. Thank fuck the brothers hadn't left yet.

"I can't find Minette upstairs," Ryder said.

"Not good," Zeb muttered. He headed toward the rear of the lodge.

Shay ran upstairs, Emma to the small reception and library area, Bree to the game room. Ryder checked the closets and under furniture.

"Nothing up here," Shay called down.

"Nothing here," Bree yelled.

A whine drew Ryder to the laundry-room exit where a darkly colored wolf paced in front of the door.

"Zeb, what's up?" Shay entered the room, followed by Emma and Bree.

The wolf sniffed the floor, the doorknob, and whined again.

Ryder froze. Minette's scent shouldn't be there.

"No pup would go out in the dark. This can't be, bro." Shay's voice stayed even despite the concern etched on his face.

The wolf pawed the door in an obvious demand.

Icy fear ran up Ryder's spine.

"No," Emma whispered.

"Minette might," Ryder told Shay. "If people shout, she runs outside and hides. At Genevieve's, I found her cowering in a well-worn hollow under a tree."

"Herne's hairy balls." Shay started spitting orders, "*A bhràthair*, start the search. Ryder and I'll be right behind as soon as we shift. A howl says you found her. Two says call out all the assistance we can get."

The yip said Zeb got it. When Shay opened the door, the wolf leaped out.

His cub, outside. On dark of the moon. A cold, fear sweat dampened Ryder's clothes. He stripped off his shirt.

Shay gripped Bree's arm. "*A ghrá*, Calum isn't home, so Joe Thorson's at the tavern in charge of problems. Call and let him know what's up. He can redirect Alec and Ben."

Good. Call everyone in. But Emma was unbuttoning her shirt. Ryder shook his head. "No, little bear. We need you and Bree here, in case Minette returns."

Her mouth turned stubborn. His brave female.

"No argument. You *will* stay inside." He took her hands. "Remember, one howl means we've got her. If you hear two howls…"

"Two means we call Joe Thorson to say there's a hellhound near here." Although her eyes held fear, her legs were braced, her stance ready. She was amazing.

"Thank you, little bear." Ryder quickly brushed her lips with his. By the God, he loved this female.

Shay shifted to wolf.

A second later, Ryder dropped onto his paws and flexed his claws against the hardwood floor. *Ready.*

"Herne protect you," Emma whispered as she pulled open the door and let them out into the moonless, black night.

Kitten, where are you?

"MINETTE, WHEREVER YOU are, come back," Emma whispered to the empty room.

Rattling noises came from the kitchen. Bree was preparing something hot for the men—and Minette—when they returned. She said it was her way of working off her worry.

Emma paced through the lodge and stopped at each window and door to listen for sounds outside. But little silent Minette couldn't even cry out for help.

Tears blurred her vision. Genevieve's shouting and screaming. Had the slamming door driven the already frightened cub out into the night? It was getting cold out there. Dark.

Damn Genevieve anyway. Emma's hands fisted. If she ever saw the female again, she'd hit her. *Hard.* Knock her fangs out, leave her a toothless wolf.

She leaned her head against the back door to listen and heard an owl hoot and the gurgling creek at the forest's edge.

The fire was dying in the living area. Emma stopped to build it up. Minette would be chilled when she got back. The extra log wakened the salamander into doing a slow slither through the coals.

In the library, Emma listened at the windows, straightened the magazines on a table, picked up a jigsaw puzzle piece from the floor, and bookmarked a murder mystery book left face-down on a chair. Minette would adore this room, especially the bookshelf filled with picture books and children's board games.

Noises still came from the kitchen.

Emma started another circuit. Leaning her head against the front door, she heard…something. Not the Douglas firs sighing in the wind. There it was. A high, thin sound.

Only the men's warnings kept her from flinging the door open. She peered out the tiny viewing pane. Nothing was visible in the glow of the porch light. Beyond lay only blackness.

What had she heard? A cubling's cry? Or a screech owl, or a cat?

"Do it again, sweetheart. Did you yell?" Emma pressed her ear harder against the door. The rising wind made the lodge's hanging sign creak. Tree branches groaned in complaint. An owl hooted again.

Emma straightened. *Tell Bree.* Her friend could stand by the door while Emma went outside to check.

Before she'd gotten two steps toward the kitchen, she heard a high, thin scream. A child's sound of fright.

Emma broke fingernails undoing the bolt. She flung open the door. "Minette!"

No response.

She stepped out onto the porch and pulled the door shut

behind her.

"Minette, where are you?" The front parking area was empty. The narrow gravel road leading to the lodge was empty. Small log cabins extended in wings to the right and left of the lodge, but nothing moved. She squinted, trying to see into the darkness on the other side of the parking area. Somewhere over there was the path to the Wild Hunt tavern.

The wind caught her shirt, flapping it against her skin as she started down the porch steps.

There. Something moved.

Just past the glow of the porch light, a small figure stood unmoving on the path to the tavern.

Couldn't she see Emma? "Kitten…" Emma's voice trailed off as she realized the child was frozen, eyes wide with terror. She was staring off to the right.

The door of the third cabin to the south banged open. Followed by two males, Genevieve dashed out. "Where is she?" She spotted the girl and started across the drive.

Emma's stomach flip-flopped as the wind brought her the distinctive stench of rotting carrion and citrus.

"I smell a… Fuck, there's a hellhound around," one male shouted.

As if summoned, a nightmarish creature charged out of the darkness—straight for Genevieve.

One male yanked the female back.

The other male sprang in front. The hellhound didn't slow, and the male's fist bounced off the armored creature. Massive jaws snapped onto the male's arm, and he shouted in pain. And fell.

As the hellhound savaged its screaming victim, Emma raced across the gravel lot and snatched Minette up. Trembling, the cub clung to Emma.

The other male started toward the battle, but Genevieve

shrieked, "You have to protect me!" Grabbing his shirt, she dragged him into their cabin. The door slammed shut behind them.

No!

Emma's pulse roared in her ears. The male and Genevieve had left her and Minette outside. Alone. With that *thing*. Emma tried to breathe through the fear clogging her throat. *Oh, Mother Goddess, what could she do?*

All the cabins would be locked. She needed to get them to the lodge. Could they make it?

The creature stood in front of the row of cabins—not directly in front of the lodge. But there was no cover in the road or parking area. The minute she and Minette stepped onto the graveled area, the creature would see them.

Emma knew too well how fast the hellhound could move. It'd intercept them before they even reached the porch, let alone got the door open. The lodge was out.

Behind them was the trail to the tavern. Run to Joe Thorson?

But the gusty wind was already blowing their scent toward the hellhound. Once finished with the male, it would smell them. Probably hear them. They wouldn't make it to the tavern. Not before the creature caught them.

A whimper bottled up her throat. The wind swirled, carrying the scent of blood and death. A tiny sound escaped Emma. *Run. Just run.* She could smell her own fear. Courage was for those who hadn't faced a hellhound before. *Run.*

Minette trembled in her arms. It would attack the cub first.

No. Never. Emma's mouth compressed into a determined line. No hellhound would touch her cubling.

She whispered almost inaudibly into the tiny ear, "I want you to run toward that light. To the tavern." She pointed at the light flickering through the trees. She set the child on her feet.

"I'm counting on you, Minette. Run fast and get help."

Keeping an eye on the hellhound, she gave the girl a push.

After a second of resistance, the girl fled—her light footsteps still too loud in the still night.

The hellhound lifted its head from the now lifeless body. One red eye blazed viciously; the other was covered in white scar tissue. It'd lost an eye in the past.

Oh, Mother, help me. This was the very hellhound that'd almost killed her. That'd hurt her and left her crippled. Fear welled up until she was drowning in it. Choking.

It hadn't seen her. Yet.

Every instinct demanded for her to run, to take the only possible escape down the path behind her.

Minette was on that path.

The shark-like head moved to the left and right as it surveyed the area, the closed cabin doors, the lodge, the graveled lot. The one-eyed gaze settled on Emma.

Despite her heart slamming against her ribs, terror froze the blood in her veins. Her body cringed at the memory of razor-sharp teeth ripping into her leg, of her bones snapping like kindling, of…agony.

The strength seemed to drain from her bones, muscles and sinews.

Trawsfur. She should shift into bear shape, be faster, stronger. *No.* No time to undress. Her clothes would tangle and trap her.

Eye fixed on her, the hellhound sniffed the air. It stiffened and then snarled, revealing savagely pointed teeth.

It knew her.

Run. Run, run, run. Every cell in her body was screaming, a cauldron of noise.

But she still heard the pattering footsteps and rustle from Minette on the path. The gusts of wind held the scent of the terrified cubling. Such easy prey. The monster wouldn't be able to resist.

Then give it an easier kill.

On a sucked-in breath, Emma lunged into a desperate sprint directly away from the path to the tavern. *Here I am. Panicking game.* She darted toward the lodge, keeping her gaze only on the target.

A snarl from the right made Emma run faster. Blindly. Genuine, mindless panic flooded her. She couldn't outrun it. It'd get her. Kill her. Her skin shrank in anticipation of the pain.

The scraping sound of the paws on the gravel increased as the creature narrowed the distance. Just before it reached her, she veered sharply left.

Much heavier, it overran her position before circling back toward her.

She dodged again, almost too late. Its spiked armor plates snagged at her clothes.

Each breath, each step felt like her last. Regret grayed her sight. *Ben. Ryder. I love you.* What might have been...

The beast hit her from behind, knocking her onto her face. Gasping for breath, she rolled onto her back and kicked frantically.

It lunged for her vulnerable stomach. Her foot knocked the huge jaw away.

The hellhound twisted back, snapping, catching her thigh. Savage teeth bit down through her jeans and deep into her flesh.

Pain. Sharp, horrible, inescapable. Screaming, she shoved and kicked and then, fighting off her terror, she poked her finger toward its unscarred eye.

Instinctively, the hellhound released her, turning its head to avoid losing its remaining eye. Growling hideously, it darted at her so fast she could only grab its throat as it went for hers. Gore dripped from its mouth onto her shirt as she struggled to hold it back.

Her arms shook uncontrollably, weakening against its massive weight.

From the corner of her eyes, she saw a dark shape. It streaked across the lot. With a chilling scream, the cougar landed on the creature's hindquarters. As the feline's claws scraped uselessly over the bony armor, the hellhound whipped around.

A COUGAR'S SCREAM split the night air. Ben recognized the sound. *Ryder!*

Swiveling his ears to mark the direction, he charged through the forest, pushing his limits. Branches slapped against his heavy fur and stung his muzzle.

Alec was in human form and racing after him.

They had far too much distance to travel, dammit.

After Shay and Zeb had lost Minette's trail in the creek behind the lodge, the two had headed upstream. Taking the other direction, Ben and Alec had followed Ryder's scent downstream. Then screaming—a child, a man, a female—from the lodge had sent him and Alec running back.

Dread filled Ben as he galloped around the back of the lodge toward the front. He tore into the graveled parking area and spotted the hellhound.

A cougar faced it. Alone.

Snarling, Ryder was pacing back and forth, slashing feline-quick at the hellhound's single eye. On the ground behind him, Emma tried to drag herself away from the battle.

With a last burst of speed, Ben bulldozed the creature, knocking it away from Ryder. The scent of Emma's fear added to Ben's fury as he spun and bit the hellhound's hind leg. Bearing down, he ground his fangs into the crevasses between the armor plates and got the foul taste of demon blood.

Roaring with pain, the hellhound snaked its head around.

Fuck. Ben jumped away. A fiery burn over his ribs said the demon-dog had nailed him.

Something flashed past him, the scent was Shay's. The wolf's snarl was deep and ugly. As the hellhound lunged at the alpha, a darker wolf attacked from the other side.

Alec ran into the lot, skidding to a stop on the gravel. He had a knife in one hand, his pistol in the other.

As Zeb and Shay darted away from the hellhound, Alec yelled, "Stay back," and Ben realized other shifters had appeared from the cabins.

"All-in," Alec barked—the cahir code for a full-out attack.

Ben lumbered into a run, and the hellhound turned to face him. If it went for Ben's throat, it'd win.

Before Ben could hit, Ryder sprang from behind the hellhound and landed on the creature's head in a frenzy of claws and teeth and shrieks.

When the monster turned in defense, Ryder sprang off and darted away.

Perfect. Ben rammed into demon-dog's shoulder so violently the pointed plates slashed through his fur and skin and deep into his muscle.

Knocked off its feet, the hellhound landed on its side and scrambled to stand. The wolves attacked from the rear, tearing and worrying at its legs to keep it from rising.

As Ben gathered himself to attack again, Alec ran forward, dodged a snapping jaw, and slammed his pick-thin dagger straight into the creature's one good eye.

The shriek it gave curdled Ben's blood. Air shimmered around the creature, leaving behind a naked human. A dead one.

Sides heaving, Ben let his head drop as he tried to regain his breath. The stench of the creature still clung, returning every time the wind shifted direction. Instinctively, Ben shook his fur—which only made every scrape and bite hurt like hellfire. *Fuck.* Growling at the pain, he headed for his family.

He passed the lodge porch. Hair blowing in the wind, Breanne stood on the bottom step, pistol in one hand. Near her, Zeb and Shay shifted to human and stood.

Farther down, in front of the south cabins, a body lay in a lake of blood, mangled into something unrecognizable. Ben's heart skipped a beat—but the size was too big to be Minette. And was a male. Phone to his ear, Alec was already heading toward the body.

Ben padded quickly toward the center of the gravel lot.

Transfurred to human, Ryder knelt beside Emma. The yellow porch light turned blood a streaky brown—and it covered Emma's clothes. Ryder's skin.

So fucking much blood.

Why wasn't Emma moving? *By the God, no.*

Ben broke into a run and paused only to shift in the last moment before reaching them.

Emma...

His heart hammered far worse than during the fight with the hellhound. And then...then he saw her push Ryder's hand away as she tried to sit up. Relief buckled Ben's knees. Lacking any grace, he half-fell beside his brother and their mate—because she damned well was. *Thank the Mother.*

"Who's bleeding?" he growled out.

Ryder gave a half-laugh. "Who isn't?"

"Yeah, well." He could feel the warmth of blood pouring down his left arm from the punctures all over his shoulder. "Breanne, get your first aid kit." Even shouting hurt.

"Will do." She disappeared into the lodge.

"Good plan." Pain deepened Ryder's baritone to a low rumble.

"Bro," Ben said, unable to keep from touching Ryder's

shoulder to check for warmth. *Alive.* He curled his other hand around Emma's nape. *Alive.* "Where's Minette?"

"I told her to run. We must find her." Emma grabbed his arm to try to pull up. "I'll show you. *Now.*"

Ben pulled her hands free and held her still. "Darlin', just tell me where."

"I sent her down the trail to the tavern, and I ran this…"

Her voice faded under his stare. She'd made herself into bait. He pulled in a breath. How easily she could have been killed.

"Ben, we need to find her!" Emma shook his hands. "What if there are more of those things?"

"Unlikely." Hellhounds avoided each other. But other animals roamed the woods. The mite needed to be found immediately. "I'm going,"

"We'll go, cahir," said a renter from one of the cabins. His brother stood beside him. After a second, Ben recognized them as cousins of Kenner from the construction crew. At Ben's nod, they took off running toward the tavern. Their words drifted in their wake, "Did you see? The cat took on a hellhound—and he's not even a cahir."

More shifters headed over to help Shay and Zeb and Alec.

"They'll find her." Ben squeezed Emma's fingers. "We need to get you and Ryder patched up until the healer gets here."

"Donal will be here in another minute." The Cosantir's distinctive deep voice cut through the commotion, bringing a moment of silence.

Ben stiffened. Calum must have returned early. *Oh, hell.*

"Daddy!"

Ben turned so fast, his head spun.

"Minette?" Ryder whispered.

In the center of the parking area, Calum had the cub in his arms. She wiggled frantically until he set her down.

The cub hit Ryder in a half-tackle, and he gave a pained grunt. Crying, kissing, burrowing into him, she was purely hysterical. And alive.

"Daddy, Daddy, Daddy."

By the God, her tiny voice was the finest sound in the world. She lunged at Ben and climbed him like a tree to hug him with her tiny arms. Fuck, it hurt, but he wouldn't have complained for the world. The relief of feeling her squirm, smelling her little girl scent was a warm rush, easing tight muscles. He heard himself huffing with pleasure.

She released him to throw herself on Emma. "Emma."

"It's all right, kitten. You're safe," Emma whispered, half strangled by Minette's arms around her neck. "We're all safe." The bard was scraped, bleeding, and had narrowly escaped death, yet it was obvious her only thought was to comfort the cub.

He noticed Ryder had a hand on Minette—and so did Ben. Minette wasn't the only one who needed physical reassurance.

"Here you go, Ben." Breanne set a first aid kit down along with a couple of blankets. Before he had it open, the healer arrived.

"By the God, I hate hellhounds." The healer squatted beside Ryder, his silver gaze flashing over each of them in turn. "What's the damage this time?"

"Emma's leg," Ryder said. "My arm. Ben?"

"Bite on the ribs, shoulder punctures—and my right arm's not moving right. Nothing urgent." Blood was trickling rather than gushing down his arm and side. With his acknowledgment of the wounds, fresh pain hammered him as if he was on the receiving end of a pneumatic nail gun. "Start with Emma."

"No, you first," she said instantly.

Donal snorted at Emma's protest and turned her leg to examine the wound. "Sorry, bard. Unless someone's dying, I treat the females first. Otherwise, I'd waste time arguing with the males. Looks to me as if you're all equally mangled."

DESPITE THE GHASTLY pain in her leg, Emma choked back a laugh. Donal couldn't be much older than Ben and Ryder. He shouldn't be so cynical. "All right."

Donal eyed Minette. "I need the cub off your lap."

"Of course." Shaking uncontrollably, Emma tried to release the cubling, but her arms wouldn't relax their hold. *Mine.* "I c-can't."

"Know how you feel, darlin', but it's only for a bit." Firmly, Ben disentangled Emma's arms and lifted Minette up. "C'mere, kitten. Emma has an owie for the healer to fix. I'll hold you till they're done."

With a sob, Minette turned and wrapped her arms around Ben's neck.

"By the God, you scared me, cub." Pulling her close, he kissed her head.

Emma's eyes filled. The male had a heart as big as his body and courage to match. She'd been sure Ryder was about to die, but Ben hadn't even hesitated, just charged right into the hellhound. Just as Ryder had done to save *her.*

"Now, let's see what we've got." With a surprising strength, Donal tore her jeans from the hem to above her knee.

Ow, ow, ow. The slight jarring sent agony through her, and she tried to jerk her leg away only to realize Ryder had an unyielding hold on her thigh.

"Easy, my little bear," Ryder murmured. His right arm tightened around her shoulders; his left hand held her leg steady. "Hang onto me while he works, yeah?"

"It'll hurt when I wash off the gravel, Emma." Donal pulled a bottle of water from his bag. "Then it's all downhill."

More pain. Why was the apprehension worse now that the

fighting was done? She wasn't sure she could take it. Her eyes filled with tears; her breath hitched in her throat.

"Shhh." Ryder tucked her head against his chest.

The water struck her wound and the pain flared into sheer agony. She clenched her teeth. Screaming would scare Minette.

Slowly, far too slowly, the scarlet-edged burning eased to a sharp throbbing, and she pulled in a breath.

"All cleaned up, girl. Now, let me make it all better." Donal placed his hands on each side of the wound and bent his head.

The Mother-blessed warmth of his power touched her, melding the tissues, and the pain drained away.

With a faint smile, he lifted his hands. "See? Much more effective if I see you right away." Pink, unbroken skin covered the area where the gaping flesh had been.

She swallowed to clear her throat and whispered, "Thank you, Donal."

A lean hand grasped hers, and she was pulled to her feet and steadied by...Calum. He studied her for a second. "Better. Go sit there, please." He gestured to the porch stairs where Breanne sat. Three other shifters stood nearby—probably renters from the cabins.

"But—" She didn't want to leave Ben and Ryder. Calum's stern expression stopped her protest. "Yes, Cosantir."

"Come here, cub." As he took Minette from Ben, the cub didn't say a word. "Benjamin, sit down before you fall."

Ben looked as if he'd argue, then painfully lowered himself to sit beside Ryder.

With Breanne's help, Emma settled onto the steps, and to her surprise, Calum placed Minette in her lap.

With a pleased sigh, Emma wrapped her arms around the cub. When Minette leaned into her, sucking her thumb and holding Emma's braid, the world felt as if the Goddess had taken a broom to the disorder.

His face grim, Calum studied the cubling and Breanne, Ben and Ryder. "Explain what happened. Start with why I found the cub running across my parking lot."

Emma rested her cheek against Minette's. Thank the Mother the Cosantir had been there for Minette—even if he looked as if he was in an unhappy mood now.

Despite the healer working on his arm, Ryder tried to turn around. "It was—"

"Let the bard talk," Donal snapped. "Busy here." He turned Ryder's arm to catch the light. Exposed muscles and white tendons glinted as blood streamed down the smooth skin.

Emma flinched. When Minette stirred, she turned to keep the child from seeing.

Growling under his breath, Ryder sat back.

To keep Ryder from losing his temper, Emma said hurriedly, "Ryder, Minette, and I were spending the night at the lodge. Minette was half-asleep with me on the couch. She didn't want to be alone upstairs."

Calum's lips curved in a reassuring smile. "Jamie was the same at that age. I understand."

"We heard shouting in the parking area." Emma hesitated. Did she want to talk about Genevieve? To the Cosantir?

She'd paused too long.

Breanne stepped in. "A female—a pushy wolf who'd showed up at our last pack meeting—was yelling at a male who'd rented a cabin. I told them to quiet down, but she saw Emma and Minette and had herself a hissy fit."

A hissy fit? Emma blinked. Interesting phrase—must be human. How would the term fit into a tune?

"Emma took Minette upstairs, and... Breanne continued with the events up to when she came out of the kitchen. "And I found Emma was gone."

"Yeah, how did that happen?" Ryder growled. "I told you to

stay inside."

"I heard Minette scream. Of course I went out." Emma tightened her arms around the child, reassured by her heavy, warm weight, by the tiny noises of a thumb being sucked. "And I'd do it again."

Ryder's harsh expression softened. "I'm sorry. The thought of losing either one of you is…"

Losing me? He put her in the same category as his beloved daughter? Tears filled Emma's eyes as she smiled at him.

"Pretty good save for a male," the healer said under his breath. He rose and moved to Ben.

"Continue, please," Calum prodded.

She met his dark gaze. "The female ran out of the cabin, because…" The reason wasn't important, right? How much had Calum heard about Genevieve and her accusations? "The hellhound charged her, but a male jumped in front of her." Emma shuddered, knowing she'd never forget the savage way the creature ripped into the male. The shifter's cries of agony. She swallowed. "The hellhound killed him. The female and the other male ran back into the cabin."

Leaving us alone. Her own child.

Expressionless, the Cosantir followed her gaze to the silent, dark cabin. "Go on."

"I-I didn't know what to do. So I sent Minette toward the tavern."

"And you ran toward the fucking hellhound—as bait. You think we didn't figure that out?" Ben's voice rose into a roar as he started to rise.

The healer yanked him back down. "Sit. Down."

"Fuck!"

Donal chuckled. "Easy, Griz. You're pissed at your crazy-brave female, not at me."

"Sorry." With a grumbling noise, Ben turned to Emma.

"Sorry, darlin'. I got a problem with you being in danger."

He cared. She knew he did, knew he'd risk his life for—oh, any Daonain—but his uncontrolled anger said he really did love her. Her lips trembled as she smiled at him so brightly that he blinked.

"Finish, please." Calum recalled her to her task.

"Right," she said. "Um… The hellhound charged me. Ryder came out of nowhere and attacked, saving me. Ben slammed into the creature, and then everyone attacked, and Alec killed it."

"Your account will do for now." Calum studied her. "Now tell me why the renter had a"—his lips twitched—"hissy fit. And why the female ran out of the cabin."

He knew. He did. He was going to force her to tell everything. She sighed. Evasions were one thing, but she couldn't lie to the Cosantir. "She's Minette's mother—a horrible, abusive mother who's telling lies everywhere."

"Thank you, Emma." Calum's gaze rested on Minette. "Alec, please call a meeting of the Daonain for tonight at the tavern."

Emma's breath caught. A meeting. Would he hand Minette over to her evil mother? Her gaze met Ryder's, then Ben's. Could they run?

When the Cosantir turned, the power of the God shimmered about him, muted by the glow of the porch light. "Benjamin, you are ordered to bring the cub, your littermate, and the bard to the meeting. All of them, cahir. Am I clear?"

"Yes, Cosantir," Ben replied in a tight voice.

And that was that. No Daonain would go against a Cosantir's direct orders.

A surge of rage shook her. Calum wasn't supposed to be here. Why had he come back early? Only she knew. She'd messed up when Shay asked her about performing this summer. Vicki had undoubtedly told Alec…who'd called his littermate.

Emma curled around Minette and kissed the top of her head. She and her males would bring Minette to the meeting. But even if she had to defy the God Himself, she wouldn't let Genevieve have this precious cubling.

"Done here." Donal handed Ben one of the blankets and rose. "I want you all to eat something, drink at least three glasses of water—no alcohol—and go to bed for the day." His brows drew together and he added, "The healing will make you sleepy. Do not try to do *anything* requiring concentration or alertness. Am I heard?"

He knew. Emma felt her muscles sag, felt the weariness pulling at her body and mind. He was warning them that they'd risk Minette's life if they tried to drive today.

"You are heard, healer. Thank you for your care." The wind whipped at the blanket as Ben pulled it around him. "Cosantir, will you need me?"

"No, cahir." Calum tilted his head. "Shamus and Zebulon and Alec will finish the rest of the patrol tonight. Can you get your family home?"

Family. The look on Ben's face matched what was in Emma's heart. "Yes, Cosantir. I'll take my family home."

Chapter Thirty

THEY'D TAKEN TURNS showering, so someone could stay with Minette in the kitchen. Now clean and aching in every muscle, Ryder had Minette on his lap. His emotions hammered at him, impossible to control.

There was delight as his cub chattered about her night, her words flowing as if she'd stored them up to use all at once.

There was rage as she told him about being scared and how dark the trail to the tavern had been. He felt as if he had a noose around his neck at the thought of losing his little kitten.

He'd thought love was an on-off emotion, not one that expanded to fill the universe.

Sensing she'd lost his attention, Minette twisted in his arms, took his face between her tiny hands, and frowned at him. "Daddy, d'ink you mi'k."

"Right, kitten." The kitchen was brightening as the morning sun streamed in the windows. He caught Ben's glance. What the fuck were they supposed to do now?

Ben's face was pale. The deepened lines bracketing his mouth showed the strain of the night, of being hurt, of the healing that had drawn on both the patient and the healer's reserves.

"We're clean and hydrated as the healer ordered. Let's get

our li'l females to bed." He put his arm around Emma, lifting her off the chair.

"You're the only two people in the world who call me little," The light in Emma's amber eyes said she didn't mind at all.

"Keep telling you, bard, to males like us, you're the perfect size," Ryder said.

Ben shot him a grin.

"Pretty Emma," Minette chimed in.

"Aren't you just the ego-stoking group?" Emma leaned forward to kiss Minette's cheek as Ryder rose.

His cub was already falling asleep by the time he made it up the fucking, unending stairs. At the top, he waited for Ben and Emma. Neither was moving any faster.

Emma glanced at Ryder and Minette. "If you're not planning to sleep next to her, do you mind if I do?"

Before he could answer, Ben tilted his head. "My bed's big enough for three and a half."

"Aye," Ryder said, no thinking needed.

Emma's mouth dropped open. "But—"

"It's a big bed, darlin'," Ben said. "We've been in it before, aye?"

"Well, true, but—"

Ryder studied her. She didn't look unhappy at the thought as much as surprised, and he'd bet a breakfast bunny her mother'd never shared her bed with a cub. But with their animal heritage, most shifters reverted to needing tactile contact during stress…like cubs piling in a heap on their mother.

Emma's shivering hadn't stopped despite a hot shower. She needed them. He admitted the rest—they needed her just as much. "We'll even let you sleep between us. No nightmares will get past us."

She looked shocked he'd join Ben in ganging up on her. Then, with a soft accepting sigh, she showed her courage. "I want that. I want you both and Minette with me, so I can make sure you're still alive each time I wake up."

"Yes. Exactly."

When they were all piled in the bed, males, female, and cub, Ryder gave a long, low, contented sigh. Minette was against his chest. Emma's cinnamon scent drifted to him. He could hear his brother's slow breathing.

Alive and together.

As a gentle afternoon rain began, Ben woke and lay still, taking stock. The weariness was better. The aches in his shoulder, arm, and sides—gone. Thanks to the God's gifts, cahirs had more resilience than most shifters.

He also hadn't slept so deeply in years. Didn't take a genius to know why. On his side, he faced the center of the bed, curled around a soft, lush body. Emma's round ass was pressed against his groin, her back was against his chest, and he had his arm over her and Minette. Ryder was in the same position, facing the cub, his arm over both females.

For long, contented minutes, Ben soaked in the joy of having his female and cub in his arms. Of having his brother beside him to love and protect their small family. This was how it should be.

Last night had been...bad. If he lost his family now, he doubted he'd survive. His mouth tightened as he recalled his terror at hearing Minette was missing, seeing Emma on the ground, and Ryder fighting the hellhound.

His littermate had risked his life to save Emma, and afterward, charged in to help Ben. Emma would've sacrificed herself to save the cub. Could a male have any more worthy partners in life? Fuck, they made him proud.

He loved them. His littermate. Emma. Minette.

That needed to be shown. Made fact. If the Cosantir thought to take the cub, he'd face them all.

But a united front was merely a side benefit, he admitted. The step they'd take now was what his heart, not logic, demanded.

Emma's breathing was slow and even, the flush of health in her cheeks. She'd recovered. His brother's color had returned. Minette looked like any happy, sleeping cub. From the little twitches, she'd awaken soon.

Sliding out of bed, Ben headed for the phone to call Angie.

Fifteen minutes later, Angie showed up, her van filled with her grandchildren. A bouncing, talkative Minette was delighted to join them.

After waving the cub off, Ben trotted back up the stairs to find Emma and Ryder were awake.

"Who was at the door?" Emma's voice was husky with sleep as she stood beside the bed.

"Angie and her grandchildren. They took Minette to join them for an afternoon of frosting cookies." He shook his head. "She said something about the cookies having the shapes of shifters and OtherFolk."

"Oh, I saw the cut-outs. The dwarf one was really cute. All beard and nose," Emma said.

Ben winced, hoping Gramlor never saw the cookies. The dwarf wasn't known for his sense of humor.

"I can imagine it now. Purple pixies and green salamanders with stripes." Ryder grinned, and then lifted his eyebrows at Ben, asking silently why he'd sent the cub away.

"Almost dying last night made me think." Why couldn't his tongue be smoother? More persuasive? "I saw how easily I could have lost you two. How much I love you both." He stepped closer to Emma, crowding her slightly to run a finger down her cheek. "Seeing you in danger sets my blood to boiling. I have a need to…feel…for myself that you're alive."

He knew his scent was changing, conveying his desire.

Emma's mouth formed an "O." But as Ben's finger trailed down to the hollow of her neck, her scent took on the fragrance of arousal.

Ben glanced at Ryder, then at the bedside table.

Ryder hesitated before nodding. No further explanations were needed. This was what they wanted. What they'd planned to do all along. As always, since meeting as adults, he and Ben were running the trail, shoulder-to-shoulder, as littermates should.

Ben pulled Emma into his arms and kissed her, slowly and deeply, savoring the way her mouth softened, how she melted into him, how her arms came around his neck. *Cinnamon and spice, and everything nice.* Yes, this was the right time to make her theirs.

A drawer opened and closed.

He lifted his head and turned her to face Ryder. As Ryder's arms came around her, Ben took one bracelet from his littermate's outstretched hand.

Despite the anxiety welling within him, he smiled as Ryder took his time kissing Emma. When his littermate stepped back, their female was flushed, and her arousal scented the air. Nothing in the world could smell as sweet.

Now…if she agreed, they could celebrate properly.

She reached for them and frowned when they didn't move. "What's wrong?"

Ben glanced at Ryder and knelt.

Ryder's shoulder was against his as he did the same.

Ben cleared his throat. "We love you, Emma. And you love us, don't you?"

Her hands covered her mouth. "I still haven't said it, have I? But…it's so hard." Yet even as her lips trembled, her eyes grew determined. Straightening her shoulders, their female gave them all that was her. "Yes. I love you both."

She pulled in another breath. "I love you, Ben. I love you, Ryder."

"She makes it sound as if her claws are being pulled out." Although Ryder grinned, his voice rasped with emotion.

"Let's see what she sounds like when she says yes to something else," Ben said. He lifted his hand, the lifemating bracelet on his bear-sized palm. The silvery, moon-shaped discs ranged from the thinnest crescent to a full circle. "Emma Cavanaugh, we love you. We want you as our lifemate, to carry in our hearts and souls throughout this life and into the next."

Tears filled her eyes.

Ryder lifted his hand, his lifemating bracelet on his callused palm. "You'll be our center, the heart of our family. We'll laugh with you in times of joy, hold you during the sad times, and guard you from danger." He grinned. "And teach you to cook." Trust the cat to add something extra.

Even as her tears spilled over and down her cheeks, she gave a hiccupped laugh.

"We'll sing with you, make love to you, and..." Ben pulled in a slow breath. "And gift you with our cubs."

Her eyes went solemn—she knew, she *knew* what offspring meant to him. Her smile appeared, turning her beauty into something shining. She held her arm out. "Yes. I say *yes*."

Ours.

With careful fingers, Ben slid a bracelet on her left wrist.

Ryder's eyes were moist as he did the same.

By the God, nothing in the world looked as beautiful as their bracelets on her arm. When Ryder rubbed a shoulder against his, Ben's throat thickened. *Family.* They had a family.

Eventually, their female noticed the two other bracelets on the nightstand. The discs were larger. Magicked by a blademage to make them "elastic" during a *trawsfur*, these gleaming silver wires were much thicker. "Those are mine for you, aren't they?"

When Ben nodded, she picked them up.

"Whatever happens tonight, we'll be together." Her soft golden-brown eyes were filled with love. "This is right."

She put one on Ryder's wrist, one on Ben's, and marked them as her own. With a lilt in her clear voice, she added, "For as long as life shall last and long beyond, I'll be your lifemate."

THAT NIGHT, RYDER parked the SUV in the Wild Hunt parking lot. As the others got out, Ryder walked around the vehicle. Despite the full day of rest, weariness pulled at his bones and muscles, making him feel as if he was wading through waist-high wet snow.

Emma clasped his hand. "It'll work out."

"Sure it will." Fuck, he was a liar.

"Ready?" Ben plucked Minette out of the backseat and handed her over as if he knew how much Ryder needed her in his arms.

"Hang on, kitten." He jiggled his cub and pretended to drop her, just to hear her laugh. To *hear* her laugh. She had an infectious little-girl giggle, and all three adults grinned.

Worry filled Emma's eyes.

Oh, he understood the aching dread of never hearing the cub after today. Ryder squeezed her hand. When his loved ones had been safely cuddling in one bed earlier, he'd felt as if the Lord of the Hunt had granted him his heart's desire. But, the closer they came to the tavern, the more his emotions shredded.

He could lose Minette—because of a vindictive, lazy, greedy female.

Stay calm. Don't give up. But wasn't this depressingly familiar…right to the glares from Genevieve, a male, and a covey of females who entered the tavern.

The trip across the parking lot was made in silence.

The tavern door had a large CLOSED sign, and two males stood outside to ensure no humans entered. Since the Wild Hunt occasionally closed for special events of the human's social clubs, no one thought twice when Calum closed it for the quite imaginary *Celtic Mystics Club*. Calum told curious humans the group was private and exclusive, something like the medieval Templars. Thus odd shifter happenings—like Zeb and Shay kneeling before the Cosantir on Main Street—could be explained away as initiation rites.

While the guards and Ben exchanged greetings, Ryder looked around. Despite the short notice, the room was filled. Daonain from around the territory lined the walls and sat at tables and on bar stools. Calum stood behind the bar. Alec, Zeb, Vicki, and Angie sat at one end.

Near the pool tables, shifters from the two construction crews along with their relatives had commandeered tables.

The wolf pack occupied a cluster of tables with Bree and Shay at the center. Genevieve and her covey of buddies had joined them.

"There she is. There's my baby!" Genevieve jumped to her feet.

Sudden silence shrouded the room.

Minette buried her face in Ryder's neck.

He tightened his arm around her. "Easy, kitten. I have you."

Emma drew closer. "We're here, sweetie. It'll be all right."

With her thumb in her mouth, Minette grabbed Emma's shirt, keeping her close.

"The Cosantir's at the bar." Ben nodded toward Calum.

"Aye. Let's get this over with," Ryder said grimly.

"Ryder." Bonnie approached from the side. "Brady and Van have our cubs in the kitchen. Calum asked my males to guard your cub with our own."

Let his kitten go somewhere else? He noticed Genevieve approaching, undoubtedly planning on an earsplitting confrontation. Minette didn't need to hear her mother yelling. The kitchen would be a safer place; no one would get past Bonnie's big mates.

"Thank you, Bonnie." He kissed Minette's cheek. "I'll come and get you when the adult talk is over. If you've been good, we'll have a root beer."

The cub hesitated, but nodded. Silent again.

"Come, young catlet." After taking her gently from Ryder, Bonnie carried her away. "Tyler wanted popcorn. Do you want to help us make some?"

"I hate letting her out of my sight, but this is better," Ben said, voicing Ryder's thoughts as Genevieve arrived with the male beside her.

"Minette is my child, you abusive thief," she yelled. "The Cosantir and the shifters in this territory won't let you keep my cub. No male should steal a child—especially someone who likes to hit females and cubs."

"I've never hit a female or cub in my life." His voice came out strong, but he already knew no one would believe him.

"Oh, right." The female named Candice rose from the wolves' tables. "I saw Genevieve's bruises. All over her body."

Another female chimed in, "By the Mother, look at her face and arms."

Obligingly, Genevieve tilted her face to let the lamps highlight the purple bruising on her jaw and cheekbone. To show off the rest of the damage, she'd worn a low-cut, sleeveless shirt.

Even knowing what a shrew she was, the marks on her body made him sick. That was…just wrong. "I don't know who hurt you, Genevieve, but you know it wasn't me."

"No one else would want to hurt her," Candice yelled. "You

hit her."

Yeah, this was going just as it had before.

"He wouldn't." Tullia, the wolf whose house they'd remodeled rose from the wolf pack's tables. He couldn't believe the elderly recluse had left her home. "I've seen Ryder with the cub. He's an excellent sire."

"Yeah, the cub adores her daddy." To Ryder's surprise, the yell came from the construction crew. More shouts from them followed...

"He's a great father. He'd sure as hell never hurt the pup."

"By the God, he almost panicked the day she fell down and cried."

"Helped kill a hellhound to save his cub, for fuck's sake."

Face flaming at being opposed, Candice put her hands on her hips and faced the crew's table. "Ryder is worse than any hellhound."

"Like you know him at all? You ever even spoken to him?" Kenner, the drywall finisher, crossed his arms over his beefy chest and lifted his chin at Shay. "Control your mouthy wolf, alpha. That's *our* cat."

Our cat. The construction crew had claimed him. The sensation filling Ryder was...indescribable.

Rather than take offense, Shay glanced at his mate. "Sorry, *a leannán.* I think this one is yours."

Bree scowled at him. Then she stood, leaned her hands on the table, and stared at Candice. A menacing growl rolled through the room.

Candice turned pale and sat abruptly. When Bree continued to growl, she went all the way down to her knees. With a satisfied nod, Bree resumed her seat.

"This isn't right." The young male standing next to Genevieve planted his feet. "Cubs don't go to sires if a mother is around. Ever."

As others in the room nodded, Ryder tensed. He couldn't let Genevieve win. Minette wouldn't survive the neglect, let alone the abuse.

As if he felt Ryder's despair, Ben squeezed his shoulder. His voice boomed through the room as it often did on a construction site. "Most females take care of their cubs, but Genevieve doesn't. She's a damaged female who'd rather fuck than care for her baby." He lifted his chin at Genevieve. "You're damned good at manipulating males, but the Cosantir and the shifters in this territory are smarter than you think."

Ryder pulled in a breath. *Don't give up before the fight is over, cat.* His inhalation brought him Emma's angry scent. She stood so close her arm brushed his.

"How could you say such a thing to me?" Genevieve burst into tears and pointed to Ryder. "He—he's such a terrible person that he was driven out of Farway. Everyone there knows how vicious he is, so out of control. He can't be trus—"

"Actually, female, the town was delighted he rescued his cub." Owen's deep voice filled the room as he entered the tavern.

"What?" Genevieve puffed up.

Using a loud voice, Owen said to Ryder. "Everyone in Farway knows you dumped this female before leaving. After you, she took up with a wolf pair, but they kicked her out of their house for fucking every tail in town."

The crudeness triggered gasps from the older females in the room. Ryder almost joined them.

The corner of Owen's mouth tilted up. "The wolves wanted to keep Minette, but the shrew wouldn't let them, since the wolf pack provides money to unmated females with cubs. Yeah, so when Ryder took Minette, the Farway alpha cut off her funds."

Ryder exchanged a look with Ben. No wonder she was fighting to reclaim a cub she didn't love.

"You liar," Genevieve screamed.

As she went into another yelling fit, Ryder turned to Owen. "You went to Farway?"

Owen nudged him with his shoulder—a cat's equivalent of a slap on the shoulder. "Thought I might get answers you couldn't."

Ryder felt a strange tightness in his chest and managed a low, "Thanks."

Owen shrugged. "I owed Ben—and hey, even cats can have friends."

"Don't listen to that male. Ryder is violent. Look what he did to me yesterday." Genevieve pulled down her shirt to show an ugly red welt along her shoulder blade.

EMMA'S ANGER GREW and grew at the lies coming out of the female's mouth.

"Yesterday? But...when?" The male who'd hidden in Genevieve's cabin last night blinked in confusion. "The only time you weren't with me was yesterday afternoon when I went to the barbecue. That guy"—he motioned to Ryder—"he was at the barbecue the whole time."

Emma leaned closer to Ryder, holding her breath in hope.

"He wasn't," Genevieve stated.

"Yeah, he was," the male said, looking confused. "He was with the bard the entire time." The male's gaze took in the lifemating bands on Emma and Ryder's wrists. "His lifemate."

"Lifemate? He lifemated that"—Genevieve's voice rose to a piercing screech—"that huge thing calling itself female? He wouldn't have anything to do with her." Her lips curled back off her teeth. "He's mine." She lunged at Emma.

Huffing in annoyance, Emma smacked her alongside the head—hard.

Genevieve staggered backward, flapping her arms like a startled goose. With a loud wail, she landed on her ass.

Oh, Goddess, what did I do? Trying to feel remorse, Emma found only satisfaction in her heart.

Ben's roar of laughter was almost drowned out by the cheers of his construction crew and an amazing number of clapping and laughing shifters.

Ryder slung an arm over her shoulders. "My female, you have no idea how much I enjoyed seeing you take her on."

"I hadn't anticipated *you* doing a smackdown." The sheriff sauntered past Emma, patted her arm in a disconcerting approval, and went down on his haunches next to Genevieve. "Not many shifters are stupid enough to take on a bear."

"She-she hit me!" Genevieve started crying again.

"Mmmhmm. Seems someone else did, too." Alec turned the female's face to the light and scrutinized her bruises. "You wear rings, Ryder?" he asked in an easy voice.

"What?" Ryder frowned. "No. They get caught on shit— good way for a carpenter to lose a finger. I don't even own any."

"Figured." Alec pointed to two purple marks in the center of each bruise, which resembled the dark center of a flower. "I've seen injuries like this before. We've got a human in town who gets off on punching his girlfriends. He wears two oversized rings to increase the damage."

"A human hit her?" Angie's voice added to the comments from the rest of the room…

"Seriously?"

"She got beat up by a human?"

"Why'd she say Ryder did it?"

Outraged noises filled the room.

"Not a bad punch, bear." From nowhere, Vicki appeared next to Emma. *Sneaky cat.* "It lacked style, but was surprisingly effective."

Well. Emma blinked. The Cosantir's mate wasn't critical of

Emma's lack of control, only her…technique?

"Um. Thank you." She leaned down and whispered a confession. "It felt good, too."

Vicki actually laughed. "You have the makings of a Marine."

"Herne forfend. Do *not* encourage her, Vixen," Alec muttered, joining them. "I better take control of this before it deteriorates further."

Emma frowned. Wasn't running a meeting the Cosantir's job? But Calum still stood behind the bar, hands resting on the top, simply watching.

Vicki leaned in. "Calum is letting Alec run with this so everything will get brought into the open. Once the Cosantir invokes the God, there's not much talking. Judgment is swift."

Judgment. The word sent a chill through Emma. She sent up her own invocation to the Mother of All. *Please, don't take Minette from us.*

Two females helped Genevieve to her feet. It appeared as if her covey had decreased. Emma spotted her other two followers kneeling beside Candice at Bree's feet. Shoulders were hunched, heads bowed. Any movement netted a growl from a pack member.

"Genevieve, come here, please." Alec said, voice level.

Gaze averted from Emma, Genevieve walked over.

"Shifters." Alec's raised voice quieted the room. "By Daonain tradition, a cub is placed with her mother, especially since litters often have more than one father. We must remember, however, that tradition is not law."

The noise rose.

He waited until he could be heard again. "This female here has been proven to be untruthful and she has lied about another shifter." His nose wrinkled. "Does she wear human perfume to conceal the scent of her lies?"

Whispers ran around the room.

"I know all the mothers here would understand." Genevieve clasped her hands over her breasts, and tears brimmed in her eyes. "He'll steal my baby from me. Please don't let him take my cub."

The female was dodging the whole issue of her lies. And the mothers in the room looked concerned. Emma wanted to hit her again.

"We should ask which of these two parents is most capable of caring for the cub," Alec said calmly.

The room grew silent again.

"When did Minette leave your care, Genevieve?" Alec asked.

She named the date and straightened her shoulders. "I've been searching for her ever since." Her face crumpled. "I'm so sorry for creating a scene. I-I just want my baby. I want her safe from him."

When frowns appeared, Emma felt Ryder stiffen. Shifters protected females and cubs. Tears were appallingly effective.

"Ryder and Minette arrived in Cold Creek a week after that date. Am I right?" Alec asked Ben.

"Right," Ben said.

"Did you see any signs of abuse?" Alec asked.

Ben tried to recall his first sight of the cub. "She was several pounds lighter than now and—"

"He's Ryder's littermate. Of course he's going to lie for his brother!" Genevieve shouted. She turned to the people in the bar. "Please, just tell him to give me my baby."

Alec frowned. "Cahirs in the North Cascades Territory don't lie. But let's call an impartial witness. Is the healer here?"

Donal moved forward. "Aye, Alec."

"Did you see Minette when she first arrived?"

"I did. She was very underweight. She also had healing bruises on her face and hands and back. I'd say most of them were far older than a week. She was also unable to speak and terrified of her shadow."

"Her condition improved while she was living with her sire?"

"No question about it." Donal's silver eyes iced when he looked at Genevieve. "If you feel this one needs to be starved a bit to show her what hunger feels like, I'd be delighted to do so."

The mood of the crowd swung back. The healer was respected—and everyone knew tactfulness wasn't part of his personality.

"She's my little baby, and I didn't have any money for food. You can't blame me for being broke." Genevieve turned to Alec, her beautiful face appealing. "I need to stay with her. You wouldn't keep her from her mother, would you?"

Emma heard Ryder's growl before Ben stated, "You're not getting anywhere near her."

"You don't have anything to say about it," Genevieve said. She turned to Alec, laid her hand on his chest, and rubbed her breasts on his arm. "The Cosantir makes those decisions."

Alec chuckled and stepped away. "Wasting your time, wolf. Wrong prey."

"Genevieve is right, however. I believe all the facts have been aired." The interruption came in a deep, clipped voice as Calum moved out from behind the bar. His dark face was as remote as Emma had ever seen it.

Scowling, Genevieve turned her venom on the intruder. "What's it to you, you—" Her voice strangled in her throat when she met Calum's gaze. A blind person could see the power crackling off him, and she must have just realized Alec wasn't the guardian of the territory.

Emma had a feeling the female wouldn't attempt the breast-rubbing technique with this obviously pissed off Cosantir.

"Donal stated the child was underfed while in your care." Calum's gaze ran over Genevieve. "It seems you didn't stint your own portions or attire." He turned to Shay. "Does the wolf pack fund single mothers?"

Shay smiled slightly. "The pack provides cub-sitting so mothers can work. In addition, Angie gives free meals to cubs and mothers for dishwasher services at the diner."

Genevieve's mask slipped for a second to show her fury. Then she said smoothly, "Oh, but my home is in Deschutes Territory. I can give little Minette a far better life there where we both have friends."

"And where you can receive money for possessing a cub." The Cosantir turned to Ben. "You were seen talking with Amanda Golden—the realtor. Are you putting your house on the market? Did you and Ryder plan to leave everything, take the cub, and run?"

Gasps sounded around the room along with loud protests from the construction crew.

Emma noted the past tense. Because there would be no running now, would there?

Ben's lips compressed at the incriminating question. But a cahir didn't lie to the avatar of his god. "Aye."

Calum's glance landed on her. "Emma? You're respected here as our bard. As a teacher. Did you intend to go with them?"

"Yes." She showed her wrist and smiled at the lifemating bands. "I go with my mates—and our cub."

"Felicitations, bard." Alec's pleased grin earned a reproving look from his brother.

"Well, honestly." Genevieve crossed her arms over her chest, pushing her breasts up. "I don't see what the big deal is. They were afraid and planning to steal my child."

Joe Thorson put a foot up on a chair. "I see the point you're making, Cosantir. Ryder, his brother, and lifemate want the cub enough to give up the life they've made here."

"Leaving isn't the only sacrifice they were willing to make,"

Zeb said in his harsh voice. He gave Genevieve a dark look. "That so-called mother fled into her cabin, leaving her child outside with a hellhound."

Genevieve glared at Zeb.

The uproar in the tavern increased. For all he looked like he'd terrify demons, Zeb was held in awe and respected by the community.

"She sure did." Shay rose to sit on his table. He pointed at Emma. "The bard almost lost her life saving the cub from the hellhound. Ryder attacked the hellhound to keep it from ripping her apart."

Emma realized the entire tone of the tavern had shifted. Sympathy for Genevieve had faded to nearly nothing.

"But...but, I was afraid." Genevieve held her hands out to the crowd. "You would have been also."

Calum said something to Alec before turning to answer Genevieve. "Everyone is afraid of a hellhound. The question is who were you trying to save—yourself or a cub?"

The male standing beside Genevieve dropped his gaze and moved away from her.

Calum crossed his arms over his chest. "I think it's clear where the cub is better cared for and better loved."

A hum of agreement ran around the room.

Calum continued, "However, the bond between a mother and child can't be ignored."

Genevieve nodded vehemently. "Yes. See?"

"So. Has anyone ever seen a well-loved child willing to be parted from her mother?"

As Calum's keen gaze swept the crowd, Ryder saw the shifters shaking their heads. No one volunteered an exception.

"Excellent. We shall allow Minette a choice in her future." The Cosantir motioned to where Alec was crossing the tavern with Minette in his arms.

Calum plucked Minette from his brother, set her on her feet, and went to one knee in front of her. His hand cupped her little chin. "Cub, should I send you to live with your mother?"

He paused.

Minette's forehead crinkled with worry. Thumb going into her mouth, the cub looked at Genevieve.

Genevieve held out her hand. "Come here, baby. I love you, and I'll take care of you."

Bitterness rose in Emma in a foul cloud of darkness. Why would Calum do this? Minette couldn't stand against her mother influence.

But Minette was shaking her head. She backed away until she could hide behind Ryder's legs like a terrified puppy.

Genevieve stepped forward.

Emma felt her hand close in a fist—and she stepped in front of Ryder at the same time Ben did.

Genevieve stopped dead.

Calum spoke. "Ryder, ask Minette if she wants to live with you."

Ryder knelt to face his cub. He had to clear his throat twice before he could speak. "Kitten, do you want to stay with me?"

"Daddy." Without any hesitation, she burrowed into his arms.

As he lifted her, she wrapped her legs around his waist, clinging tighter than a burr. His eyes were wet before he closed them and rested his cheek on the top of the cub's head.

Emma heard his whispered, "Thank you, Mother of All," before he took his place between Emma and Ben.

The entire tavern filled with cheers.

IT WAS OVER. *By the God, the cub was safe.* Ben's eyes burned as if he'd peeled a sinkful of onions.

"Nice job, Cosantir," Alec said to his brother, then motioned toward Minette. "But I hope it's all right if the greedy cub demands more than one parent."

The cub wanted Genevieve, too? Dismayed, Ben looked at Minette.

Not Genevieve.

The cub had her fingers wrapped securely around Emma's braid—and her other hand was fisted on Ben's shirtsleeve. The kitten was claiming all three of them as her own.

Laughing in relief, Ben put his hand over hers. So little. So beloved.

"Indeed, I do believe her wishes are quite clear. Herne agrees as does the Mother." The Cosantir turned to Genevieve. His eyes darkened to the deepest of blacks with the presence of the God. "The bond between you is broken."

Ben saw Minette jolt.

Genevieve staggered back, and her hand pressed her chest at the cleaving of the mother-child bond. "You can't..."

"You abused one of the Mother's precious cubs." The Cosantir's expression turned to granite. "Last night, your greedy, vindictive actions caused the death of one of *my* shifters. If you are within my territory by morning—or ever again—I will find you and send you back to the Mother."

Genevieve's face went white at the promise of death. Her mouth opened and closed, and she fled the tavern, abandoning her male companion without a backward look.

The Cosantir's gaze took in the male who now stood alone. "Jeffrey, you came to the rescue of your female, Genevieve, but abandoned another female and child to the hellhound."

"I did." The shifter bowed his head. "I...I let her push me into the cabin. I wanted to come back out, but she shifted to wolf and stopped me." The lad pulled up a sleeve to show oozing marks from a bite. So he had tried.

The Cosantir waited silently for...Ben didn't know what.

And then he did when Jeffrey pulled in a breath and turned to face Emma. "A wiser male wouldn't have listened to Genevieve. Wouldn't have been pushed around—or cowed by a bite. I'm sorry, bard."

"I understand," she said softly.

Ben felt her shiver. Donal had healed her body, but…Ben could only imagine what she'd felt when left out in the dark and cold with a cub, left to face a hellhound. His mate had a soft heart. Ben did not.

"You have summed it up well, Jeffrey." Calum's face softened slightly. "I will not banish you, but you will leave this territory. After three winters, you may return and we'll discover if you have acquired some wisdom. The Mother has given you gifts. Endeavor to prove worthy of them."

The stiffness drained from the young male, and his eyes gleamed with sudden tears. "Thank you, Cosantir. I—I will return at the appointed time and show you that your mercy is justified." Head bowed and without a glance at the front door through which Genevieve had disappeared, Jeffrey moved toward the back of the bar and the portal leading into the wilderness.

As he left, Ben discovered his heart held sympathy after all. Jeffrey wasn't the first male Genevieve had almost destroyed. Thank the God that Ryder had learned and was back where he belonged.

Next to Ben, Ryder whispered to the cub, "I love you, kitten, forever and ever."

With her arms around his neck, she planted a kiss on his cheek.

So fucking little. But not alone any longer. It was time to make the changes clear.

"May I hold the cub?" he asked his littermate.

"Our cub," Ryder corrected, even before knowing what was

on Ben's mind. He passed her over, kissing the top of her head as he did.

Gripping Minette around the waist, Ben lifted her over his head.

To his delight, she showed no fear, but beamed down at him.

"This is the cub of my littermate." His voice boomed through the room. He turned so all the shifters had a chance to see her. "I say she is my cub as well. Her heart and body and soul are mine and my mates' to guard as long as life shall last." He lowered her to kiss her forehead.

Her little hands patted his face before she planted a kiss on his big nose.

He laughed and shouted, "Have I witnesses?"

The room shook with the voices of his clan. "Witnessed."

The Cosantir smiled slightly. "Let it be so."

Joy surged through Ben, and he couldn't keep it from his face. As he held Minette in one arm, he gave Ryder a bear's smack on the shoulder. "We share, bro. Aye?"

Emma's cheeks were wet with tears as Ryder gathered her in one arm and pulled her between them—the place their lifemate belonged. "Aye, brother. By the God, aye."

Chapter Thirty-One

North Cascades Territory; first quarter moon
Human "Memorial Day"

THE SUN WAS retreating into the west, turning the tips of the tall conifers a lovely glowing green and sparkling off the clear mountain lake. Seated in the middle of her friends, Emma looked around the clearing.

A game of keep-away was going on between the wolf pack and some first- and second-year shifters. Calum's daughter Jamie, a sleek panther, had teamed with three young wolves and one black bear. With better teamwork and coordination, the older pack members were running the paws off the youngsters.

"And Alec told me—" Vicki broke off, her gaze on her stepdaughter. "Go, Jamie!"

Jamie had leapt up a tree trunk and now rebounded straight into a cluster of wolves. With a swift paw, she batted the oversized rubber ball right out from between Zeb's fangs and into the air.

Her bear teammate fumbled before catching it in his jaws. With a burst of speed, he scurried toward the first-years' goal, protected by the young wolves on his team.

When the bear reached the goal, winning the point, he shifted. The rest of the youngsters followed suit, and their loud cheering echoed through the mountains. Jamie did a victory boogie around the wolves.

"I can't believe she stole the ball from Zeb. She'll be gloating for days." Vicki handed out drinks, grinning proudly.

As Jamie gave another piercing whoop of victory, a pinecone smacked into her head. Pixies in the quiet mountain areas didn't take well to noise. With a grumble, Jamie shifted back to animal, and the game resumed.

"That's one feisty little tree fairy." Bonnie motioned to the scowling sprite swinging on a low limb, chittering insults at the pack.

"Aren't they adorable?" Breanne smiled. "The one in the spruce near our patio acts as if she hates the parties, but when Shay tried to convince me to start the season late, she bombarded him with twigs."

"I can't believe how many OtherFolk have moved close to the lodge," Jody said. She did cleaning there, so she'd have noticed the increase.

"What kinds?" Vicki asked, turning away from the game.

Emma smiled. She'd noticed Vicki and Bree—previously human—were fascinated by the OtherFolk.

"Each cabin now has at least one tree fairy nearby," Jody said. "Salamanders are in all but the least used woodstoves and fireplaces. There are even a few undines teasing minnows in the creek."

"There's also a gnome under the footbridge embankment," Bree said. "Even though the kitchen's a mess after the Sunday barbecues, there are more brownies. They seem to think cleaning is fun. But I don't how why the rest of the OtherFolk have increased."

With every breath, Emma could feel the zinging energy around the lake. "Of course the OtherFolk love the lodge. You not only have people on vacation, but you have parties where people eat and talk, and laugh and play. Look at all that energy." She motioned toward Minette and her cubmates.

Ryder was in cat form. Minette was shouting commands to her troop of small friends as they played Pounce on the Panther. When enough little bodies piled on him, Ryder obediently collapsed. One little boy was giggling so hard he rolled right off the heap.

Laughing, Bree opened her hand in acknowledgement. "I never thought about how the guests would affect the Other-Folk."

"Bards are taught to sense the energy in a room." Emma took a sip of her drink. "Ben told me hellhounds feed on negative emotions. If true, the OtherFolk, like sprites and brownies, probably get a boost from happy emotions. And, Bree, even your smallest parties generate so much joy the air tingles."

Vicki nodded. "Calum says laughter and song are the human race's gift to the gods."

"As are babies." Emma grinned at the brunette. "Speaking of which, shouldn't you be showing by now?"

"What a disgusting word. *Showing*." Vicki scowled, and yet one hand tenderly covered the invisible baby bump. "The thought of turning into the Goodyear blimp doesn't make me happy."

"Maybe you won't be that big." Bree frowned. "How many are you having? Did you get a sonogram?"

"No sonograms. Shifters only use healers. Donal says he might know the numbers and sexes, but he won't tell." Vicki glowered. "The bastard is unbribable. I tried."

"Daonain are crazy," Bree muttered. Her exasperated expression was identical to Vicki's.

"You two are Daonain now, in case you forgot." When Vicki and Bree turned their scowls on Emma, she grinned. "I've never met humans turned shifter before, but it's certainly fun to view our world through your eyes."

Bree nudged her shoulder hard enough to knock Emma sideways, despite her greater size. "And now you know how much fun we've had with you, Miss Shyness, as you get your ass integrated into the"—she waved her hands—"greater whole."

Emma opened her mouth. Closed it. She knew they'd understood her trepidation and worries, but apparently, they viewed her tentative steps with the same affectionate amusement as she watched their human missteps. That was…lovely.

Vicki noticed and pointed a finger at her. "Do not start with any teary-eyed stuff. This is a party."

"Yes, uh…"—What had the human spy called her?—"Sergeant. As you wish."

EVENTIDE. THE FINEST hour of the day, and even better when celebrated with family and friends. Ben took a slow breath of the moist lakeside air. The last rays of sunlight glinted off the glacier-tipped peaks, and the first hint of coolness had appeared. Across the lake, a deer stopped to drink, ears tipped toward the commotion.

As he discussed remodeling Alec and Calum's over-the-tavern apartments, he could hear Emma laughing with her female crew. Her happiness warmed him, inside and out.

And Ryder… He didn't often see his taciturn brother play. Then again, staying in cat form meant he didn't have to talk…and all cats loved games of pounce.

Just then, Minette pulled herself out of the heap of children, put her hands on her hips, and scowled. It was an exact copy of Emma this morning when Ben had stolen some of her newly baked cookies.

"Mama!"

Minette's yell silenced the lake clearing.

Undoubtedly recognizing the cub's voice, Emma turned, eyes wide. Her drink tipped sideways, spilling onto the grass until Angie righted it.

The bard's voice, which normally could fill an entire room, emerged shaky. "Y-yes, my kitten?"

"Tyler got Luke for his bodder. And Jamie is getting bodders and sisters from her mama's stomach. I want bodders, too."

The expression on Emma's face was…indescribable, and the look she gave Ben then Ryder, held equal amounts of love and joy and helplessness.

Ben grinned at his littermate.

The panther's purr filled the air—Ryder agreed with his daughter.

After clearing his own throat, Ben answered his cub in the only way possible. "Don't worry, darlin'. We'll get right on that."

Daonain Glossary

The Daonain use a conglomeration of handed-down languages from the British Isles. Some of the older villages still speak the Gaelic (Scots) or Irish Gaelic. Many of the more common (and mangled) shifter terms have descended from Welsh.

Errors and simplification of spelling and pronunciation can be attributed to being passed down through generations…or the author messing up. Below are a few of the more common words and terms used by the shifters.

a bhràthair: brother

a chuisle mo chridhe: pulse of my heart

a leannán: sweetheart, darling

a mhac: son

brawd: brother

cahir: warrior

cariad: lover, darling, sweetheart

cosantir: guardian or protector

dùin do bhuel: shut up

mo bhràthair: my brother

mo charaid: my friend

mo chridhe: my heart

mo leannán: my darling / my lover

tha gaol agam ort: I love you

trawsfur: transform or shift

Want to be notified of the next release?

Sent only on that day, Cherise's newsletters contain freebies, excerpts, and articles.

Sign up at:

www.CheriseSinclair.com/NewsletterForm

Have you tried the Mountain Masters & Dark Haven series?

Master of the Mountain

Mountain Masters & Dark Haven: Book 1

Available everywhere

Get Master of the Mountain Now!

I loved it! Every word, every page, every moment until the end! So that is my review in a nutshell........ OK I can do better than that, but seriously a melt your panties right off, intriguing love story that forces you to turn the pages until the wee hours of the night just to get to the end! How about that!

~ Book Junkie

Rebecca thinks she is overweight and boring. Logan disagrees.

When Rebecca's lover talks her into a mountain lodge vacation with his swing club, she soon learns she's not cut out for playing musical beds. But with her boyfriend "entertaining" in their cabin, she has nowhere to sleep. Logan, the lodge owner, finds her freezing on the porch. After hauling her inside, he warms her in his own bed, and there the experienced Dominant discovers that Rebecca might not be a swinger...but she is definitely a submissive.

Rebecca believes that no one can love her plump, scarred body. Logan disagrees. He loves her curves, and under his skilled hands, Rebecca loses not only her inhibitions, but also her heart.

Logan knows they have no future. Damaged from the war, he considers himself too dangerous to be in any relationship. Once the weekend is over, he'll have to send the city-girl subbie back to her own world. But will driving her away protect Rebecca or scar them both?

Excerpt from
Master of the Mountain

THE SUN WAS high overhead and unseasonably hot by the time the trail descended, leaving the pines behind. He led the group across a grass- and wildflower-filled meadow to the tiny mountain lake, clear and blue and damned cold. Granite slabs poked up through the wildflowers, glimmering in the sun. With yells of delight, people dropped their backpacks and stripped.

Logan enjoyed the show of bare asses and breasts as the swingers splashed into the water like a herd of lemmings, screaming at the cold. As he leaned on a boulder, he noticed one person still completely dressed with wide eyes and open mouth. The city girl. Considering she and Matt bunked together, Rebecca couldn't be a virgin, but from her reaction, she was pretty innocent when it came to kink.

"C'mon, babe," her boyfriend yelled, already buck naked in the lake. "The water's great." Not waiting for her response, he waded out deeper, heading for a blonde who looked as if she had substituted bouncy breasts for cheerleading pom-poms.

Rebecca glanced from the water to the trail, back to the water, where Matt wrestled with Ashley, and back to the trail again.

Logan could see the exact moment she decided to leave. He walked over to block her way.

"Excuse me," she said politely.

"No."

Red surged into her cheeks, and her eyes narrowed as she glared at him. Red-gold hair. Freckles. Big bones. Looked like she had Irish ancestry and the temper to go with it. Stepping sideways to block her again, Logan tucked his thumbs into his front pockets and waited for the explosion.

"Listen, Mr. Hunt—"

"It's Logan," he interrupted and tried not to grin as her mouth compressed.

"Whatever. I'm going back to my cabin. Please move your… Please move."

"Sorry, sugar, but no one hikes alone. That's one safety rule I take seriously." He glanced at the swingers. "I can't leave them, and you can't walk alone, so you're stuck here."

Her eyes closed, and he saw the iron control she exerted over her emotions.

The Dom in him wondered how quickly he could break through that control to the woman underneath. Tie her up, tease her a bit, and watch her struggle not to give in to her need and… Hell, talk about inappropriate thoughts.

He pulled in a breath to cool off. No use. It was blistering hot, and not just from his visions of steamy sex. Nothing like global warming in the mountains. He frowned when he noted her damp face and the sweat soaking her long-sleeved, heavy shirt. Not good. The woman needed to get her temperature down.

At the far end of the meadow, the forest would provide shade. He could send her there to sit and cool off, but she'd be out of sight, and from the obstinate set of that pretty, pink mouth, she'd head right back down the trail in spite of his orders.

Shoulders straight, chin up, feet planted. Definitely a rebellious one, the type that brought his dominant nature to the fore. He'd love to give her an order and have her disobey, so he could enjoy the hell out of paddling that soft ass. But she wasn't his to discipline, more's the pity, since a woman like this was wasted on that pretty boy.

And he'd gotten sidetracked.

With a sigh, he returned to the problem at hand. She needed to stay here where he could keep an eye on her, and she needed to cool off.

"Even if you don't strip down completely, at least take some clothes off and wade in the water," he said. "You're getting overheated."

"Thank you, but I'm fine," she said stiffly.

"No, you're not." When he stepped closer, he felt the warmth radiating off her body. Being from San Francisco, she wouldn't be accustomed to the dryness or the heat. "Either strip down, little rebel, or I'll toss you in with your clothes on."

Her mouth dropped open.

He wouldn't, would he? Rebecca stared up at the implacable, cold eyes, seeing the man's utter self-confidence. Definitely not bluffing.

Well, he could be as stern as he wanted. Damned if she'd take her clothing off and display her chunky, scarred legs. She shook her head, backing away. If she needed to, she'd run.

Faster than she could blink, he grabbed her arm.

She tugged and got nowhere. "Listen, you can't—"

With one hand, he unbuttoned her heavy shirt, not at all hindered by her efforts to shove his hand away. After a minute, her shirt flapped open, revealing her bra and her pudgy stomach. "Damn you!"

She glanced at the lake, hoping for Matt to rescue her, and froze. He was kissing the oh-so-perky Ashley, and not just a peck on the lips but a full clinch and deep-throating tongues. Rebecca stared as shock swept through her, followed by a wave of humiliation. He... As her breath hitched, she tore her gaze away, blinking against the welling tears. Why had she ever come here?

"Oh, sugar, don't do that now." Logan pulled her up against his chest, ignoring her weak protest. His arms held her against chest muscles hard as the granite outcroppings, and he turned so she couldn't see the lake. Silently, he stroked a hand down her back while she tried to pull herself together.

Matthew and Ashley would have sex. Soon. Somehow she hadn't quite understood the whole concept of swinging and what her gut-level reaction would be. But she could take it now that she realized...what would happen. After drawing in a shaky breath, she firmed her lips. Fine.

And if Logan insisted she strip to bra and panties, that was fine too. So what if these people saw her giant thighs and ugly scars. She'd never see any of them again. Ever.

For a second, she let herself enjoy the surprising comfort of Logan's arms. Then she pushed away.

He let her take a step back and then grasped her upper arms, keeping her in place as he studied her face.

She flushed and looked away. God, how embarrassing. She had melted down in front of a total stranger, showing him exactly how insecure she was. But he'd been nice, and she owed him. "Thank you for...uh...the shoulder."

With a finger, he turned her face back to him. "I like holding you, Rebecca. Come to me anytime you need a shoulder." A crease appeared in his cheek. He ran his finger across the skin at the top of her lacy bra, his finger slightly rough, sending unexpected tingles through her. "You think I can talk you out of this too?"

Get Master of the Mountain Now!

Also from Cherise Sinclair

About Cherise Sinclair

A *New York Times* and *USA Today* Bestselling Author, Cherise is renowned for writing heart-wrenching romances with devastating alpha males, laugh-out-loud dialogue, and absolutely sizzling sex.

I met my dearheart when vacationing in the Caribbean. Now I won't say it was love at first sight. Actually since he stood over me, enjoying the view down my swimsuit top, I might have been a tad peeved—as well as attracted. But although we were together less than two days and lived on opposite sides of the country, love can't be corralled by time or space.

We've now been married for many, many years. (And he still looks down my swimsuit tops.)

Nowadays, I live in the west with this obnoxious, beloved husband, a puppy with way too much energy, and a cat who rules us with a fuzzy, iron paw. I'm a gardener, and I love nurturing small plants until they're big and healthy and productive...and ripping defenseless weeds out by the roots when I'm angry. I enjoy thunderstorms, collecting eggs from the chickens, and visiting the local brewery for the darkest, maltiest beer on tap. My favorite way to spend an evening is curled up on a couch next to the master of my heart, watching the fire, reading, and...well...if you're reading my books, you obviously know what else happens in front of fires.

~ *Cherise*

Connect with Cherise in the following places:

Website:
CheriseSinclair.com
Facebook:
www.facebook.com/CheriseSinclairAuthor
Facebook Discussion Group:
CheriseSinclair.com/Facebook-Discussion-Group

20973707R00249

Printed in Great Britain
by Amazon